PRAISE FOR THE GI

One of the most enjoyable crime novels I have read. Loved this book and am looking forward to reading the rest of the series. Crime novel par excellence!

Penmar

Came across Peter Ritchie by accident and a great surprise it was. The fourth in the Macallan series and a real page turner on the underbelly of Edinburgh with crime families to rival the Corleones. Funny at times but equally frantic.

Patrick Browne

Fans of crime fiction will delight in Peter Ritchie's Grace Macallan series. His writing is a breath of fresh air in the Scottish crime genre. His writing skills are phenomenal and vast, providing a visceral hypnotism that will suck you right in and keep you there, unable to put the book down. His wealth of experience as a police officer shines on every page. This man knows what he is talking about… he has lived it.

SarahKate

First crime novel that I've read – edge of the seat stuff and couldn't put it down. Gripping from the start! The writing was so descriptive that I felt the women's fear at the hands of the human traffickers. The main character, Grace Macallan, in charge of the operation, shows grit and determination to solve the case, but there are many twists and turns along the way.

E.S.

This book is an awesome read. I couldn't put it down once I started reading it, kept me up many a time and I would defo recommend this book to family and friends.

Grace

The plot is impossible to summarise. It's incredibly complex but due to the author's storytelling abilities, you never feel lost. Instead, you become completely immersed in the characters' machinations, bracing yourself for the next hit. I can think of only a handful who have any redeeming qualities. As for the rest, their scheming ad subterfuge would reduce Machiavelli to tears.

If noir and hard-boiled fiction had a conjugal visit, this would be the result. Following Hadden and Grainger is like watching two speeding trains heading straight at each other… you fear what will happen but you can't look away. If you're a fan of cosies and / or HEA, move along. Nothing to see here. But for those who love the dark, gritty stuff of authors such as Ken Bruen, Malcolm Mackay or Stuart Neville's *Ghosts of Belfast*, you just found your next great read.

Sandy Sandilands

The scenes set in Barlinnie prison are some of Ritchie's most powerful pieces of writing. He manages to set the scene perfectly, convey the harshness of the atmosphere and the bleakness of the situations facing his characters without being overly dramatic or taking away from the seriousness of it all. But for me, what really steals the show is the characterisation. Being able to see another side to an already complex character really fascinated me. Ritchie's writing has this wonderful way of making a reader not only feel the emotions of the personas at play, but to feel as though they are there in the moment, and I applaud him for this impressive feat.

Kate

WHERE ANGELS REST

ALSO BY THE AUTHOR

Detective Grace Macallan thrillers

Cause of Death

Evidence of Death

Shores of Death

Where No Shadows Fall

Our Little Secrets

Maxine's Story

WHERE ANGELS REST

PETER RITCHIE

First published in the UK in 2021
by PR Publishing

ISBN 978 1 9162291 1 2

Typesetting and cover design by Laura Kincaid,
Ten Thousand | Editing + Book Design
www.tenthousand.co.uk

Printed and bound by Amazon

'The dead cannot cry out for justice. It is the duty of the living to do so for them.'

— Lois McMaster Bujold

'Do not be dismayed to learn there is a bit of the devil in you. There is a bit of the devil in us all.'

— Arthur Byron Cover

PROLOGUE

Detective Chief Inspector Danny Oliver looked at the clock beside his bed and groaned. It was still the early hours and, as always, the booze had dropped him into sleep without any effort and then just as easily woken him in the middle of the night. He'd been at a king-size piss-up with some colleagues in The Hague and was already suffering the hangover from hell. Like a true Scot, he'd tried everything on the booze menu – beer first, wine with the meal and then spirits. He'd never been able to do the sensible thing and have just one or two, but it had been a hoot. Everyone seemed to have overindulged, and the bonus was he hadn't punched or insulted anyone; could remember everything in fact, so he didn't have to suffer a day of self-loathing and worrying what embarrassments lay hidden in the blank pages of his memory. He reassured himself that at least he could have the next week booze free with no social events on the calendar and stick to the day job as a UK liaison officer in Europol.

Oliver had been seconded to the British office in Europol three years earlier. His job had been coordinating operations against international organised crime groups and meant cooperating with the other European officers based in the same building. He'd enjoyed good years in Holland, but his time was running in and he was due to return to Police Scotland, where he'd been promised a posting in one of the major investigation teams – or MITs as they were better known. They had more than enough to cope with in these troubled times, so if he landed a job there, he'd have a chance to get his hands dirty again. He'd been pretty well office-bound at Europol, dealing with the intelligence side of operations, and he missed the banter and the raw thrill of the front end when operations were running well.

He'd been staring at the ceiling, wondering if sleep would come again and let him escape from whatever was punching the inside of his head and draining the saliva from his parched mouth, when the phone ringing dragged him back into the real world. He looked at the bedside clock and saw it was almost 2 a.m. In the Netherlands, that was still early for socialising; the bars and restaurants would be going full tilt.

Oliver rubbed at his gritty eyes and muttered, 'God,' but knew the Almighty wasn't taking calls for hangovers that night. It had to be work because he was on call for any out-of-hours requests from the other liaison officers. He knew he shouldn't go on the piss when he was duty officer, but he lived alone so there was no partner to show him a yellow card when it was necessary.

It was Jan Peters, the on-call officer for the Dutch team. He was an experienced intelligence officer and possessed one of the calmest dispositions Oliver had ever worked with in almost twenty years in the job.

'Sorry to bother you, my friend, but this is rather urgent.' Peters describing the issue this way meant something had gone near nuclear and Oliver was wide awake now because sure as God made little green apples, he would need to be. He completely forgot the hangover and focused – like the career detective he was, some inflamed grey matter never got in the way of the job. He'd had too much practice for that.

Peters' voice was as calm as if he was discussing the latest score from his beloved Ajax football team.

'We've been running a job on a gang of human traffickers. Bad people, Daniel.' Peters always used his first name. 'The problem is they plan to kill someone in Amsterdam tonight who they think – quite rightly – is informing on them. He's an important agent for us but we can't get in touch with him; all we know is he's in the centrum somewhere, but that could be any one of a hundred bars or the red-light district, where he spends half his life. He has a tendency to drink too much, which might explain why we can't get him.'

Oliver said, 'Okay,' because he knew the punchline hadn't arrived yet.

'The thing is, Daniel, this team have brought in contract killers to do the job. We have the gang who hired them monitored through an intercepted phone and are picking up conversations so we know the contractors are on their way to kill our agent. We're working all out trying to get a fix on his location but nothing yet. We don't know if we can get to him before they do. It's a bad situation, Daniel.'

Oliver managed a grin because the Dutchman was a master of understatement, and the situation was clearly in the file marked *Possible Clusterfuck*!

Oliver said, 'Okay,' again and waited because nothing the Dutchman had said so far concerned the British office, but of course Peters hadn't called in the middle of the night because he was lonely. Oliver fumbled for the cigarette packet next to his bed then remembered he'd stopped smoking four weeks and two days earlier. Peters got to the point.

'These guy are speaking English, and maybe it's lucky you're on call because they have a similar accent to you. Listen – I'm going to run a clip for you.'

Oliver winced as he always did when the Europeans mentioned phone intercepts. The Brits, as with so many other issues, never discussed phone intercepts and almost pretended they didn't exist. The Europeans – and almost everyone else in the world – thought they were crazy and were quite happy to discuss and share information openly. Everyone knew phone taps went on so why pretend they didn't exist?

Oliver swung his legs out of the bed, stared at his toes and realised his nails needed some serious clipping as he listened to the series of clicks that indicated the recording was being set up for him. He exhaled quietly through his teeth and felt his pulse bump as the voices crackled over the line. The one who was giving the orders was Dutch. The man answering – well it was like being home. The hard tone of Central Scotland whacked his ear.

'No bother, pal. We find him, job done then it's a stand down, right?'

There was something else in the voice that Oliver couldn't quite place but it would come to him. He needed coffee and headed for the kitchen as Peters spoke again.

'I think from listening to the other conversations that these men are military – or rather ex-military. It's clear they've been trained to a high level.'

That was it, Oliver realised, what he'd heard in the voice – the clipped edges on the words, the reference to a 'stand down'. Sounded like military to him too.

'This guy's a Scot, Jan, but off the top of my head we don't have intel on any team working in this part of the world, though that means nothing. I'll phone the London desk right now and see if we have anything.'

'I think this will be over soon, Daniel. Either we'll get there first or our informant might have more than a headache to deal with.'

Oliver got the London desk officer working within ten minutes and he was still talking to her when his house phone went off again.

'Bit chaotic, Daniel.' It was Peters again and he remained unfazed. 'Our people have located the informant – he was in a quiet little bar in Amsterdam – and when we finally got hold of him, the contractors were almost on top of him. He managed to climb out of the back window of the bar when two gunmen came in with their weapons drawn. All hell broke out because everyone thought it was a terrorist attack and people were stampeding so they missed our man by a hair's breadth. We have him in safe custody, but the contractors are gone and the phones we were listening to have all gone dead. I need to go but thanks for your help, Daniel, and see you at the office tomorrow.

Oliver called the London desk back, told them what had happened and said he'd call again when he had more information. Then he sat on the edge of his bed, sipping coffee, shook his head at the near miss and decided he wasn't going to sleep again that night.

In the end, no one knew who the contractors were and the intel dried up. All the intelligence systems could throw up was a team of Scots nutters who'd migrated from Paisley to Essex, but they were mainly counterfeit goods men, although they'd carried out a couple of killings for extra pocket money. They definitely weren't military and would have failed qualification for the armed services anyway as they were just plain radio rental.

The Dutch ploughed on with their investigation, but apart from saving their asset, they got nowhere. The British drew a blank too, but like the thousands of other intelligence contributions coming in every day to the UK systems, it was stored securely in case the contractors showed their hand again. There was too much going through the systems though, with thousands of problems demanding immediate attention every day.

1

Six Months Later

Grace Macallan was working late in her office in Leith when the DI from the Source Handling Office called her. A covert human intelligence source had phoned in to say that a notorious wee ned called Frankie Ross was visiting his sister in Newbattle and was there as they spoke. Macallan perked up and shoved aside the paperwork that always bored her to death, especially in the evening turn. Everyone and their auntie had been trying to get their hands on Ross for months – there was a string of warrants out for his arrest for tie-up jobs all over the country. The reason he'd become public enemy number one was that the majority of the victims were elderly. It was a wonder that none of them had died.

'I want to see this one get a result.' Macallan looked up and spoke to her DCI, Danny Oliver, who'd walked into the office cradling two steaming mugs of tea. He'd only been with Macallan a few months after returning from his posting in Europol. So far, she was impressed with him, and he seemed to be in his element after working in the intelligence world for so long. He was a front-end detective by nature and loved nothing better than being out on the ground.

The previous DCI, Lesley Thompson, who'd been with her for years, had moved to a job in Glasgow to be near her fiancé. Macallan missed her but was happy Thompson's life had turned out so well after she'd nearly been killed in a bomb blast near police HQ.

'Grab whoever's clearing up paperwork in the main office and get as much support as the uniforms will give us.'

Oliver had already about-turned and headed back into the general office as she started pulling on her jacket. He would let the cups stick to the desk where he'd abandoned them.

'While you're at it, Danny, try and get a dog handler if Police Scotland have any left!' she called after him.

No way is he getting out of this one, she thought, thanking the gods for an excuse to leave the hated paperwork behind.

The reason she wanted so many troops was that Ross was something of a legend for his ability to escape arrest. He was like an Olympic gymnast when he needed to be, climbed like a monkey and had slipped through their fingers on a number of occasions. The last time, he'd managed to get onto the roof of a building and left the uniforms scratching their arses, wondering where he'd gone. The local press had loved it, delighting in Police Scotland's inability to catch their man. The force didn't need any more negative publicity so Macallan was determined to get the bastard in a nice cold cell.

'I dealt with the Ross family years ago, before Europol,' Oliver confided to her on the drive over. 'Frankie might be bad, but the rest of them are something else,'

Oliver was quite reserved for a detective, so Macallan paid attention when he spoke. If he said the family were *something else* that probably meant the operation was unlikely to be straightforward. It didn't faze her at all; if anything, the news that the family were bams was good for her – her drug of choice, in fact. When a lot of cops had too many years in, they grew weary of the same old shite and the abuse that just wore away their youth. Macallan, however, was one of the rare ones who knew it drained her but still needed it again and again, as if it proved she was alive.

She pressed the accelerator as she replied. 'The info is that he's with his sisters at a party in Bogwood Road. Are they worse than the brothers? I'm guessing if they're all there, it'll probably kick off big time?'

'Guaranteed,' was all Oliver said.

'Mind you, the intel is they're at Betty's flat and it's the second level of a tenement so I don't see how he could get out onto the roof and it's too high to jump without a parachute.'

Macallan had heard some of the stories about the Ross family – or Mayfield ISIS as they were known by the locals, including the uniform cops who covered the area.

'Well we seem to have plenty of troops on the way to cover it, and if there's only one way in and out then the ball's in our court. Describe the front and back to me.' Macallan wanted a picture in her mind before she arrived at the locus.

As Oliver was briefing her, they received another message from the Source Handling Unit that the CHIS had called again – Frankie was still in his sister's flat and the party was in full swing. In other words, they were all pissed!

'Great, be there in ten,' was all Macallan said till they arrived at the RV point.

The local sergeant, who was waiting for her to arrive, stepped towards Macallan's car, nodding in acknowledgement at the arrival of a senior rank.

Macallan felt her back rebel as she got out of the car. Pain at the base of her spine was becoming a regular issue and

Jack kept nagging her about physio. She shivered in the cold December air, the freezing rain adding to her discomfort, and pulled on her gloves, watching her breath steam into the air and wishing she was wrapped up with Jack and the children. It didn't sound like it would be a straightforward operation from everything she now knew about the Ross family.

'Sergeant Duncan, ma'am. I'm supervising the area tonight. Just let me know what you need and you have it. This crowd give us nothing but bother so good to get a shot at them.'

Macallan nodded and studied the young woman with the three stripes. Duncan looked to be in her early thirties and wasn't the biggest cop she'd ever seen; indeed, she was almost boyish looking. *How times have changed,* she thought. When she'd joined the RUC, someone the size and shape of Duncan would have been laughed out of the recruiting office.

Oliver had met Duncan before and, upon learning she would be supervising the scene on the drive over, had told Macallan that she was known affectionately by the troops as the 'Mighty Atom'. What she lacked in size, she made up for in enthusiasm for the job plus a black belt in judo. She was also an all-round sportswoman who'd represented her school, county and the police in a variety of competitions and had done years in the military police before joining Police Scotland. The word was that she was destined for the top of the greasy pole or would probably die in the attempt.

'Good to meet you, Maggie.' Oliver had told Macallan her first name.

The recognition clearly pleased the local cop; she gave Macallan a warm smile before getting down to business.

'We've got every pair of hands we can muster, and the dog handler will be here in a few minutes. To tell the truth, Frankie boy caused us a few redders the last time when he did his best Spider-Man impression and legged it over the roofs.'

A message crackled over the air and Duncan turned away from Macallan, dropping back into her marked car as she acknowledged the call and gave out some instructions, deploying uniforms who were still arriving. She looked satisfied, and Macallan was impressed with her laid-back manner. It wasn't an act she was putting on for the benefit of a senior rank; Macallan could see that from the reaction of the other uniforms. It all added up to someone in control of her situation. Macallan nodded and looked at Oliver, who raised his eyebrows and turned the edges of his lips down with a nod, which all said *I agree*.

'I think we need to get this moving, Maggie; the locals will be banging the bin lids with all this activity.'

'Banging the bin lids? Haven't heard that one for a long time, ma'am.'

Macallan liked her response. Most junior officers would have just left it there, pretending they knew what she'd meant.

'Sorry, I don't often lapse into Belfast talk. It's from the Troubles. If the army or Peelers arrived in force, the women used to start banging whatever they could get a hold of – usually the bin lid – to warn the bad boys and put off the security forces. It was before my time but the saying hung around.'

Duncan nodded and smiled. 'I did some time over there in the army as things were calming down but heard the stories about the bad days.'

She looked like she wanted to hear more from Macallan, but it was time to act and she snapped back to business. 'The dog handlers are in place at the back of the flats and the block's surrounded by a wooden fence with a gate that seems to be locked. We have confirmation of the warrants so we're good whenever you want us to go.'

'I'm coming with you; I want to see this one.' Macallan looked round at Oliver. 'You stay with the car, Danny, and coordinate our team. We'll let the uniform guys do the hard work and then assist in any way they want if there's a need for further searches or enquiries.'

She paused and looked at Duncan. 'That okay, Maggie? We're not stealing any thunder here – just want to assist and see this boy away. I know they'll be screaming for your guys to get back to their beat as soon as it's done.'

'Just surprised you're going in, ma'am.'

Duncan clearly regretted the words as soon as they left her mouth – it wasn't for her to question someone like Macallan.

'Tell the truth, I miss the sharp end, Maggie. I know it's not what the rank does normally, but I just like it, know what I mean?' Macallan smiled. 'Right, let's go and spoil the party.'

2

The problem for the police piling into the tenement stairway was that the target's door would be reinforced; it had been kicked in before both by other neds and Police Scotland – or its predecessor, Lothian and Borders Police.

Frankie Ross's family were every bit as active as he was – just in different lines of crime. Macallan was sure there was no way out for Frankie boy, and the police didn't need some siege situation waiting for the villains to come out with their hands up, so they decided to throw the dice. The CHIS has said it was a giant piss-up so she thought it was worth a gamble.

One of Macallan's team who looked like a jakey even when he was scrubbed up was sent to the door, lugging a carry-out bag filled with all the juice cans – full and empty – they could muster from the various police cars at the job. He knocked at the door as Macallan and the team waited on the stairs a few feet from him. There was no response, the noise of the music coming from inside the flat painful even at a distance.

A couple of other doors opened as the rest of the police team moved up the stairs and the citizens who all hated and feared the Ross clan nodded encouragement. One old lady put her head round the door, did a thumbs-up and smiled, revealing only gums, her falsers no doubt steeping in a glass somewhere.

'Ye no got guns, son?' she said to one of the passing cops. 'Shoot the fuckin' lot o' them.' The old woman was clearly on the side of law and order.

The uniform, who'd clearly encountered the Ross family before, gave her a furtive thumbs-up, and Macallan suppressed a smile.

The detective knocked on Betty Ross's door again – or more accurately hammered it so he might be heard above the noise inside.

As the police team began to despair, there was a response from inside.

'Whae's that?' It was a female voice.

The detective threw the dice. 'It's me.'

There was a spyhole in the door so the cop tried to look as demented and pissed as he could so the eyeball that was no doubt examining him would see him as a friendly coupon. Even so, no one could quite believe it when the locks were undone.

'Aye, right.'

That's all it took – the woman behind the door had fallen for it probably because it looked like more bevvy was arriving at the party. Sometimes it was that easy, but just sometimes.

Macallan heard one of the uniforms whisper, 'For fuck's sake. You believe it?'

As soon as the door opened, the detective did what needed to be done and threw himself forward like a rugby player so at least the breach was in place. The team behind him, including Macallan, piled in as all hell broke loose.

The female hooligan who'd answered the door was a fully pished second cousin of Frankie Ross – mostly regarded in the family as a junkie eejit, but she *was* family so he'd invited her to the party because she could source nuclear-quality coke for the doo. Frankie and his siblings would never have answered the door without checking first, but Sod's law had intervened on the side of the police.

Frankie and his sisters had the instincts of sewer rats, so even with the quantity of bevvy and powder they'd consumed, the commotion at the door turned them on to fight mode – it was almost second nature, given the practice they'd had in life so far.

The most violent of the Ross family wasn't Frankie himself but his elder sister Betty – a woman even her family agreed was severely cracked and, for all intents and purposes, the head honcho. She knew immediately what had happened and screamed as if fire had been applied to her arse.

'It's the fuckin' pigs!' came out almost as a scream, and she ran towards the struggle at the door because Betty Ross never avoided a skirmish.

The first detective was in but blocking the paths of the other invaders and defenders because the eejit cousin – who now realised she'd fucked up – was on the detective's back as if he was giving her a cuddieback, and he was spinning round and round, trying to dislodge her. Maggie Duncan was behind him and took control by gripping the spinning detective and dragging him and his jockey onto the stairs so she could head for the living room with Macallan and the team pushing behind them.

Betty came through the door into the hall like a charging bull, crashing into Duncan, who fell backward. But rather than losing control, she pushed one foot into Betty's stomach as she grabbed the collar of her blouse and carried out a controlled backward roll, throwing the enraged woman through the air so she landed behind her, right in front of Macallan. Duncan was back on her feet in one continuous move then surged into the living room, where the rest of the partygoers had decided to let Betty take the strain – they offered less resistance, having realised the party was over.

Duncan looked round the room then did a double-take when she saw Frankie Ross perched on the window ledge with a beer can in his hand, smiling as if it was all one big fuck-off joke. What she couldn't see behind her was that Betty Ross was back on her feet – not quite as quickly as Duncan but as speedily you might expect of someone with fighting instincts hammered into her DNA.

Macallan and one of the uniforms had pulled her up to her feet, but Betty wasn't finished. The uniform was fumbling nervously with his set of handcuffs; he was still in the first weeks of his probation, which showed in his hands, which were trembling from the adrenalin of the most violent confrontation he'd seen in his short career. Betty glowered at him through inflamed eyes, then at Macallan, who was trying to help the boy but whose presence only seemed to add to his discomfort. Macallan wanted to take over the job of cuffing the prisoner but knew he needed to do it or take a kick in the confidence organ.

Betty became tired of the delay, growled, 'Fuck it,' and whacked the unprepared probationer on the forehead. Macallan saw it coming too late but at least managed to drive the heel of her hand into the side of Betty's jaw. It took most of the weight out of the attack so the probationer was only stunned – though more at the blow to his pride than his face. Betty groaned when Macallan hit her and sank to her knees. The shot was a beauty, and her resistance was over.

'Get the cuffs on her, for God's sake.' Macallan already had her back to the probationer and was in the living room behind Duncan.

'What the...?' was all she got out when she saw Frankie Ross on the windowsill, taking a last slug out of his beer can before waving bye-bye and disappearing over the edge. The uniforms piled in behind her and controlled the rest of the partygoers. Macallan and Duncan pushed their heads out of the window and saw Ross on his hands and knees, clearly hurt and trying to crawl to the gate in the fence that surrounded the rear of the flats.

'Jesus… nooo.' Macallan watched what was happening but knew it was too late to stop what was about to happen to the soft parts of Ross's anatomy.

Police dog Lance appeared over the fence like a guided missile and knew exactly what his job was. Ross looked round and made a sound that was a mixture of a groan and a prayer in a vain effort to save himself from the slavering jaws that were heading straight for him.

By the time Macallan, the dog handler and the uniforms could intervene, the fugitive had been the subject of a good chewing and looked like the victim of a serious car crash.

'Christ almighty. Did we need this level of hassle?'

Duncan had said exactly what Macallan was thinking. It wasn't the point though; an injured prisoner meant hassle none of them needed.

Ross was hurt but took it like a soldier. Once he'd been seen by the duty doctor, it was decided he'd need to get an X-ray on his damaged ankles, but in the meantime, he was being kept safely locked away in a cell. Macallan managed to get a word with him and, to her surprise, it was all very civil.

'You're away for a long stretch on this one, Frankie. You know that, don't you?' She wanted to see the reaction of a man who'd caused so much suffering – not that she expected much in the way of remorse. He was one of those neds who just saw it as what he did and never lost a minute's sleep for his victims' ordeals.

'Well, Ah'll just take ma chances as normal, hen.' He didn't know Macallan from Adam but seemed pleased that someone so senior in rank wanted to chat and looked her up and down with lustful eyes.

'It's no' like I'm admittin' anythin'. I mean, I'm innocent as fuck.' He grinned as if it was all a game.

'Well don't book your summer holidays just yet.' She turned to go then stopped as she remembered there were always other options.

'If you can help us with anything else, Frankie, well, we could help you back. There were a couple of these jobs where you or whoever did it was with someone else. Just saying.'

'Aye, right, well I really hope ye get the bastards that done the jobs, Inspector. It's ridiculous what these criminals are gettin' away wi' these days.' He grinned again as Macallan left the cell.

When the door closed, Ross shut his eyes, the grin disappearing as fast as he'd manufactured it. He said, 'Fuck,' very quietly a couple of times because he knew he was facing ten in the pokey and it frightened the shit out of him. Acting the hard man to the bizzies was required, but he was in his late thirties so he would morph from a still-young man to an old waste of space if he lost the next decade. He wouldn't be fit for running across roofs at that time of life, and it looked like his ankles were in a bad way, so he was just going to end up another old ex-con telling war stories in the pub where no one could really be arsed to listen or, worse still, would buy a round for the privilege of his company. He was well aware that in his trade, there was no ex like an old ex-con.

Macallan headed back to her office, pleased with the night's work. Things were going well, and this was another result in the bag, though she quickly reminded herself that as soon as you let yourself think it was all going swimmingly then sure as shit something would come along and ruin your delusion. At the end of the day, Ross was a result, but on the great scale of things, he was nobody, and out there in the dark, more dangerous predators were still at work.

3

The two beat officers almost synchronised the words 'What the fuck?' when they saw what was happening. They were driving along Bogwood Road in the Mayfield area and the shift was nearly finished. They'd agreed to meet some of the team for a few beers after a shit few days where everything possible seemed to have dropped in their laps. The week had started with the arrest of Frankie Ross and had never let up.

'Am I seeing this, Pete?' Maggie Duncan said to the cop who was driving the marked car. He slowed down to take it in.

'Seein' it, sarge, but no sure I'm believin' it. Ta-ta tae the beers the night.' His frown barely concealed the fact that he was hacked off at getting caught up in something so close to the end of a shift when there was a piss-up waiting. He slowed the car down about a hundred yards from the drama. To their left and ahead, they could see an unusual grass mound in front of the tenement buildings. It was a favourite spot with the local jakeys, who loved to sit there on a summer's day, enjoying their cans of choice.

What was taking place was a kind of Scottish Alamo scene. On top of the mound, a big man was the centre of attention, pished, mental or a combination of both, though if he was out of his skull, he seemed to be remarkably able, and he had to be as he was surrounded on all sides by attackers. He was swinging a carry-out bag round his head, and in the short time the cops had been watching, he'd bowled a couple of local neds on their arses.

'Don't know who that is, Pete, but he's doin' a crackin' job there. Leave him long enough he'll rattle most of our local customers.' Duncan grinned, though she knew they would have to intervene in the chaos. They would need backup though.

The Police Scotland car cruised slowly alongside the kerb. Duncan rolled down the passenger window as the car idled and they picked up the sounds of the conflict.

'Come ahead then, ya fuckin' bams! Is that your best shot?'

The man on the hill stopped for a moment to roar the challenge as the attackers had backed off and looked confused, obviously wondering how one guy had managed to survive their best efforts to knock fuck out of him. He laughed loudly as he pulled a can from the bag, snapped it open and slugged half of it before letting out a long, satisfied sigh, as if he was having the time of his life. He necked the rest, then squashed the can and threw it towards one of his attackers in a gesture of complete contempt. That was when Duncan and her partner noticed there were already two casualties, lying to the side of the battleground.

'Absolute quality battlin', sarge, absolute quality, but I think we'll have a problem stoppin' this one.' The driver seemed content to let the battle run its course without his participation.

'You're right, Pete. I'll call up some cavalry an' we can watch it for a bit. God knows who this guy is but he's definitely the business.' Duncan decided that letting the warriors tire themselves a bit was sensible. It was good street craft handed down by every tutor constable to their probationers.

They watched in admiration as the attackers found new courage and coordinated their battle plan then rushed the big man again – but with a bit more strategy. He went down fighting then disappeared under a mound of arms and legs all trying to deliver the winning blow, but the big man just kept on going under the squirming heap.

'Right, Pete, think it's time to intervene before there's a murder.' She said it light-heartedly, uttering the word 'murder' with a Taggart flourish. 'They should all be a bit knackered now, and unless I'm mistaken, that's a couple of blue lights coming to the party.'

They stepped out of the car, adjusted their equipment and uniforms, drew their batons then weighed in for all they were worth. It was the best part of the job, cracking a few heads on a Friday night.

The tussle was a classic – a story the neds, cops and local witnesses would talk about for a long time – full of noise from the local residents and spectators, threats for future revenge plus an assortment of injuries, though none were too serious. The arrival of the reinforcing bizzies meant that a few weapons were tossed into gardens as the fighters were overwhelmed by the forces of law and order. A few combatants tried to escape a lie-down in the cells – they scattered and legged it, or limped off into the darkness as best they could. This pleased the dog handlers no end, and the hounds of hell were unleashed on the escaping warriors, keen to get a bite of some prime leg of ned.

Back at the station, Duncan dealt with the big man who'd been playing the part of Davy Crockett when they'd arrived on the scene. He was impressive close up in a worn and slightly scarred way, but they hadn't seen him around before. His accent was West Central Scotland but clipped, and Duncan recognised the effect immediately, thanks to her years in the military police. The tattoo on the Popeye forearm of the man told its own story. He was an ex-para, no doubt about it.

'Right, big man, let's get you sorted. Maybe let the doc see you first. Few cuts an' stuff there. Mind you, the gang you were battlin' are in a worse state than you, pal. Ex-army?'

The prisoner said nothing.

'Just so you know, I did eight years as a red cap.'

'If you want me to be impressed then sorry. No can do. So you were one of the monkeys, eh? We were always told MP stood for military pussy. Is that right then?' He seemed pleased with his answer but disappointed when the dig made no impression at all on Duncan.

'You cherry berries just love yourselves, eh? Never mind. I've heard all the one-liners before. That's *before* as in before I stuck them in the pokey. So, what's the story tonight, soldier?'

'Those fuckin' bams tried to steal my carry-out. Just defendin' myself, that was all. An' that's all I'm saying... right?' He spat a wad of bloody spit about three inches from Duncan's left shoe. She wasn't that easily put off and stared at it for a moment.

'Impressive little speech, pal, but the business still needs to get done or we'll be here all weekend. Know what I mean? So you can piss about, though we'll still get what we need from your prints and the army, or you can tell us now and maybe get bail. Sure you don't want to lie in a cell all weekend. I mean, it's a great forecast tomorrow, an' sure you'd rather be workin' in your garden', eh? Now, name, please, and date of birth?'

He threw the ball back at her with some serious eye contact, as if he was measuring her before his next move. She'd seen it all before though and had wiped the floor with a few solider boys in her time. This one was genuine material.

But in this world – where they were now – she was holding the best cards and gave him the eyes right back.

The prisoner saw he was probably wasting his time trying to intimidate her and looked straight ahead again, folding his arms.

'Name's Sam Taylor, and I want my brief right now.' He gave them the name of his lawyer, which raised Duncan's eyebrows for a moment. The big man had asked for Sandy Tait, one of the top briefs in the country and notoriously anti-police.

'You have to be kidding me, pal.' Duncan's partner came in. 'That particular gentleman, and I use the word gentleman sarcastically, doesn't give up playing with himself for some ex-squaddie in a street battle. He's premier league; just does the big boys.'

'Call him!' The big man rattled off a phone number; it was done with too much confidence and made the uniforms feel slightly rattled. He'd moved them onto the back foot. Duncan nodded to her partner to stay with the prisoner while she made the call.

Less than an hour later, Sandy Tait had arrived and the uniforms had accepted that there was more to this guy than a Davy Crockett impressionist. The trouble was there was nothing on record, and the brief had told him to say nothing apart from a short statement that he'd been attacked and had merely defended himself. The cops realised they'd lost any control they'd thought they might have had and struggled to get anyone interested.

They called the CID but they couldn't really explain to the suits what it was that was bothering them about the man they'd arrested.

'So, he's no record, and apart from meltin' a few local neds, he's pals wi' a top lawyer. Big fuckin' deal. He probably sells Sandy Tait his coke, so don't call us, etc., etc.' The CID were up to their eyes and something not feeling quite right to a couple of uniforms didn't float their boat. The phone went dead in Duncan's hand – she was getting nowhere.

After another couple of wasted hours, her harassed inspector told her to get rid of the prisoner and he was bailed. They watched Sam Taylor step into Tait's Merc, and he gave them a little nod as the car pulled away.

At the same time, the inspector called them and spoiled the rest of their night. 'Ye'll have to stay on so get your arse into gear. There's a chip-pan fire that's set some jakey alight and the place is going mental.'

They jumped into their car and got on with the job – they'd done all they could, but Taylor had bothered Duncan. *Why does a smart-arsed brief like Tait come out for you, Sam*? she thought. A Friday night battle didn't rate that kind of attention, and she wondered what their relationship was.

There was no time to worry about it now though – within half an hour they were dealing with a drunk who'd set his kitchen on fire after putting on the chip pan and forgetting about it, distracted by the telly – at least until he saw the flames coming from what was going to be his supper.

4

Grace Macallan drew her fingers through her hair in frustration. It was a bit longer than normal because Jack had convinced her to let it grow a bit. She'd always hated the fuss that long hair caused, particularly in the morning, but despite her initial resistance, she liked the new style, although she tended not to admit it. She wondered if it was another sign of ageing. A need to throw off the habits of a lifetime and change the plain old image that had always served her so well. There was more to worry about than this though.

Staring out of the office window, she sipped some water in her effort to wean herself off coffee and shook her head at the typical crazy mix of weather in Scotland. They were supposed to be having a dry spell yet the rain patted the window as the sun shone out between the clouds, and it was freezing.

'Only in Scotland,' she muttered.

It should have been a headline job, solid information from Europol in The Hague. A team of their analysts had been researching a number of contract killers operating throughout Europe. A Finnish ex-soldier had become a top target, and the Helsinki authorities had pulled out all the stops to cooperate.

Mikael Kangas had never been in any trouble apart from a couple of bar-room brawls when he'd been part of the Jaeger Brigade. Special forces training in northern Finland needed occasional relief so as long it was other soldiers involved in the fights, there was no problem. The arctic warriors were a precious commodity and wouldn't be binned without good reason.

Kangas had left the army and realised, like so many special force soldiers, that in a war-torn world, there were endless opportunities to get rich. All you had to do was make sure you weren't taken by the enemy. Mercenaries were never loved by the other side, wherever they fought. Kangas had fallen into personal protection for rich Arabs, then ran into a couple of Russians who'd made him an offer he couldn't refuse. It was ironic that Russia had been the ever-present threat when he'd trained in Lapland and now he'd agreed to work for the bastards.

As far as Kangas was concerned, he'd never trust a Russian; in fact, he hated them, but in the private contracting world, he accepted that all that mattered was the pay cheque. The first job they'd offered was to take out a Dutch people trafficker, who seemed to deserve a bullet by all accounts. This kind of job was almost too easy for someone with his special skills, and unless a cop walked past him as he pulled the trigger, there would be nothing to connect him to the target. Another couple of jobs for the Russians and it turned into semi-permanent work that topped up his personal protection earnings nicely.

The Russians would contract him out to other employers when they didn't need him, the money gave him all he needed in life and he was still young man with no ties – life was good as far as he was concerned. Kangas invested wisely and had fairly simple needs, apart from the most expensive hookers when he felt the need, though he never visited the same one twice. He was careful but knew that no one was completely invisible in this modern, technology-driven world.

The Europol analytical team had come up with his name after a Russian source had been turned by the FBI and, during days of interrogation, had mentioned a Finnish contractor working mainly in Europe. Weeks later, the snippet had been passed to Europol and entered into the system, one small scrap among the endless bits of intelligence waiting process or investigation.

Although Kangas was careful, he'd made mistakes in his first couple of kills – he'd travelled to Amsterdam and then Paris for the second one on his own passport. The FBI source had mentioned that the unnamed contractor had been a specialist in Arctic warfare in the Finnish Army and had been a trainer before he'd left the service. When the Europol project started, it had taken weeks to refine, but eventually a determined Belgian analyst had sewn the fragments together then dived into the electronic sea of information and come up with Kangas as a possible fit. The Finns had been only too happy to support the investigation and Kangas had become a top priority, under constant electronic surveillance when he was in his homeland. He'd rented an expensive flat in Helsinki, which was probably a mistake, as it was too close to the authorities who knew him best.

Then the covert team watching Kangas had caught a thin piece of intelligence from a Russian source's phone traffic – that Kangas had been hired to kill someone in Scotland – but the problem was that he always received instructions via some form of hard copy rather than electronically. It was another indication that criminal organisations were going back to old methods of communication rather than electronic trails which the intelligence community seemed to be able to pick up anywhere anytime. The ancient Indian and Middle Eastern hawala system was a perfect example of how, despite electronic wizardry and the best efforts of the advanced authorities, a system based on honour and word of mouth had rendered investigations into money laundering in particular almost impotent.

The battle between the sides was like racehorses whose noses were always just behind or just in front of the competition. As far as the Finns could tell, whatever document Kangas received would be destroyed, transferred into code or simply held in his head. The professionals were trained to memorise information and knew exactly what law enforcement would look for and, more vitally, what they could use as evidence. It was always the way; nothing was ever straightforward at this level and answers didn't fall off shelves. You got a start if you were lucky, then it was up to the detectives, the analysts, the surveillance teams and all the other resources needed to track a target. All they knew was that whoever was to be killed lived in Scotland, along with the date and time Kangas was flying to the Scottish capital.

5

Macallan chaired the meeting in Leith, listening to the Finnish officers who'd arrived that same morning. They had two days before Kangas was due to fly in. As they made their presentation, what became clear was that they would need everything to go right on this one and there were bear traps everywhere. Another problem was that they didn't know how Kangas was sourcing a weapon. He was capable of killing with his hands, a knife or a gun, but the intelligence for this job was inconclusive. It seemed unlikely he'd try to smuggle a gun through security checks – that was much too risky for a pro – and the Finns had said he tended to pick up his weapon of choice from an agent of the employer.

'So, we only know he's going to be here and can't be sure he'll be in possession of a weapon.' Macallan looked round the table for someone to produce a rabbit out of a hat, but that didn't happen. It seemed they would have to make their own luck.

Macallan looked across the table at Danny Oliver. He'd turned out to be a star, and all in all she had a team made in heaven, but this was going to be a tough operation because so many things could go wrong. If they knew who the target was, it would be easy because an identified threat to life had to be disclosed to the potential victim. It was a get-out-of-jail-free card in case someone ended up with a hole in their skull.

Macallan was getting ready to close things down and take the Finns for lunch, tired of focusing on the increasing problems and pitfalls she could see with the op, but her new comrades had saved the best for last.

'One last thing, and you'll be happy with this one, Superintendent Macallan.' The Finnish detective spoke perfect English. 'Kangas has what he thinks is a clean phone secreted in his luggage. But we intercepted the phone in transit and bugged it with proper authority in our country.'

Macallan lifted her head; she felt like the man from the lottery had just called with big news. 'Yes,' was all she said and she blinked, a little rush of adrenalin fluttering through her.

'So, presuming this phone is for his contact here then we can feed it live to you or through whatever system is appropriate for your legal authorities. One of my colleagues here is an expert on these matters and will liaise with whoever your equivalent is after the meeting.' The Finnish detective sat back and watched as the mood in the room changed completely.

'Right, my friend. I'm going to buy you guys a really nice lunch,' Macallan said with a rare smile. Maybe, just maybe, there was a God.

She gave the surveillance job to Oliver and they put together the best team they could muster to track Kangas. From then on, it would turn into a little black comedy – a tale that would enter the section marked *legend* in police circles.

6

The surveillance squad picked up Kangas easily enough at Edinburgh Airport. He performed some pretty smart anti-surveillance moves, but the team had been briefed to prepare for that and gave him enough room to complete his manoeuvres. The unit had double the normal resources because this was no routine follow, and if things went wrong, Police Scotland would have more bad press it just didn't need.

Kangas stepped out of the airport doors, scanned the area in front of him and connected what was in his vision to the maps of the area he'd studied. He knew if there was surveillance, they were somewhere around him but probably not in his field of vision. It was unlikely but an ever-present risk – most likely a long-distance view of him that could be either human or electronic. He was playing it safe; chances were there was nothing, but he was a professional, and anti-surveillance had to be done so he could relax a bit then concentrate on the job.

He studied his surroundings again. There was nothing obvious, though if there was a team, they'd probably know his background and that he'd be looking. He lifted his head and scanned the sky for drones or helicopters – nothing, but again he wasn't surprised as drones and airports didn't mix. He spent the first couple of hours trying to draw out any possible watchers. Although he hadn't been told as such, he also knew that his employer would have a third eye on him to look for the same problem.

He hadn't hired a car or booked any accommodation – there was too much of a risk they could be bugged or, in the case of the vehicle, tracked. He'd do everything fresh, unplanned and all with cash payments. He carried only a suitcase with enough to do him for a week – that was more than enough time to complete the job. Staying any longer would mean too many hours spent watching a target on his own and carried too many risks.

Eventually he headed back into the terminal then started to do a walkabout, drinking a couple of coffees, flicking through books in the newsagents and talking to strangers as if they'd met before. This would throw any potential watchers, who would have to decide whether they might be contacts and thus deploy resources, which would also then give the third eye opportunities to ID the opposition.

Oliver had expected all of Kangas's tactics so they were relying on the CCTV system to cover him in the terminal. Macallan watched the activity from a link in their office but remained in contact with Oliver, who was out on the ground leading the surveillance operation.

'This man is good, Danny. All the right fieldcraft, and I guess there's a third eye somewhere, but it doesn't sound like the team are picking it up if there is,' Macallan said, chewing her forefinger.

'We've a great team out here, boss, and we're fine. We won't be drawn into a trap by him. He knows what he's doing alright, but then so do we.'

Macallan nodded; Oliver had proved himself over and over again and she knew he was revelling in being back in operational work.

'I know, Danny. I just hate sitting in the office when it's all happening. Nothing beats being out there.'

Coffee! The word went off in her head and she decided to give in to the craving. She'd failed again to get off caffeine, but it was the wrong time for abstinence – there would be little rest coming in the next few days and coffee would prove to be an essential friend.

7

Kangas seemed satisfied that his back was clean and headed out, squeezing himself onto a tram alongside an excited gaggle of tourists. He'd researched hotels in Edinburgh, so he would simply walk into one of them and take a chance that there was availability. No one could get ahead of him that way because he had no idea himself where he was going to end up.

One of the tourists behind Kangas was a surveillance officer who'd managed to get a perfect position watching the Finn's back and alerted the team that they were settled. He never spoke a word, responding to the questions coming through his earpiece via a click system – indicating yes or no with one or two clicks of the button plunger in his pocket.

Kangas barely moved a muscle, didn't look at his phone and focused on his training. Give nothing away. But he didn't know about the bugged phone.

He headed into the centre of town and got off the tram at Princes Street. The surveillance officer stayed onboard, handing over to a team of footmen deployed among the hordes of tourists.

He stared up at the castle and hoped he could see a bit of the city before he left. Scotland was a country he'd wanted to visit for years, although he'd taken part in a training exercise in Sutherland during his army days.

The first three places he visited were full, but he struck it lucky with one of the best hotels in the West End – they'd had a couple of cancellations just before he walked through the door. He used his assumed name and settled into one of the best rooms in the house.

A wave of tiredness hit him so he unpacked quickly, showered and drank a pot of coffee as he lay on top of the bed. He wanted to gather his thoughts – plan, plan and plan again. When everything was in order and spiked by the caffeine hit, he took out the clean phone, inserted the SIM card he'd concealed and dialled the number he'd memorised. It rang four times before the call was answered.

'I've arrived. No problems. Did your friends see anything unusual at the airport?' He didn't know the man at the other end of the phone and didn't need to. That wasn't the arrangement, and the less face-to-face activity, the better for everyone.

'Nothing. You're clean.'

'What now?'

Kangas listened to the reply and although his English was good, he had to strain, as there was an accent. There would be a number sent via text within minutes, which he should call immediately. The conversation ended without goodbyes.

Kangas put his head back on the pillow and waited. Two minutes later, the number lit up the screen. He called it and made the arrangements.

8

Danny Oliver was pleased with the job so far and the hotel Kangas had booked into gave them good cover for the job. One of the team had gone in behind him and had managed to get the room number. Oliver called it in to Macallan.

'How's it going, Danny?'

'All good, boss, and we have a wee lucky. I know the head of security here and he's a top guy. Mark Dunbar – gold class DS in his day, moved through here after he retired.'

'Mark – yes of course. He helped me out on the Slab McMartin case. Top guy. Didn't know he was here or I would have looked him up.' Macallan was pleased with the news – Dunbar was someone she rated highly and genuinely liked as a person.

'Know it's a sensitive case but he'd be an asset on this one, boss.'

'That's on me, Danny, but I agree. Having access to the hotel systems might pull us out of a hole at some point.' She saw one of her team signalling that there was a call for her. It was the Finnish liaison officer.

'Get back to you, Danny.'

Macallan walked through to the office designated to the Finns, which had secure links back to Helsinki. The Finnish liaison officer, Edvin Halko, was stooped over his notes and looked up when she entered.

'Edvin – you have something for us?' She smiled at the tall thin intelligence officer, who so far had seemed completely unflappable.

'I've had a message from my colleagues in Helsinki. Kangas has received a call and then made one himself. He has had instructions from a male. Apparently, he was to make a call at some point and order something. We couldn't understand what at the time but it sounds like an escort agency. We have the number for you. So, a women will arrive at the hotel later tonight around eight. The transcript is on its way.'

It helped Macallan make up her mind about involving Mark Dunbar. She thanked Halko and called Oliver.

'Danny, call Mark and ask him if he could come here ASAP. When you've done that, get that number and see what we can dig up. Whatever this is, it's important. What do you think?'

'Well, they could be delivering further instructions by word of mouth or a package so impossible to know. Can we get technical kit in the room? Whatever it's about, they're bringing something more to the party than nice underwear.'

'I'll see what's possible with technical and get back to you once I've seen Mark. Tell him it's urgent.'

9

When Dunbar heard it was Macallan and it was urgent, he was in his car within the hour. He walked into her office grinning and she saw that, as always, he was immaculate. He was typical of most ex-detectives in that he'd never really left the job, at least in spirit. Macallan could only tell him so much, but he was no fool and knew the job was serious.

'You can have access to anything you want, Grace. We have a state-of-the-art CCTV system. If you want access to the room when he's out then we can arrange that if you have the proper authorities, but I'll take that as read. Just say the word.'

They agreed that a couple of her team could occupy the adjoining room, which was part of the day's cancellations, and that would allow a technical attack on the room Kangas was using. With a short phone call, Dunbar organised a link to the CCTV system so that Macallan's team could monitor in real time.

'We know an escort is going to arrive around eight. We might miss her outside depending on how she arrives, but we need photos.' She pushed coffee across the table as she spoke.

'That's not a problem, and we know a lot of them anyway so can usually spot them a mile off. We should get her on CCTV, and I'll confirm they've arrived.'

Dunbar knew through long experience that this operation was live so they needed to be on the job and not chewing the fat about old times. He wished he was still part of it, but life moved on, so he didn't hang about. Macallan had promised drinks when the job was finished and that was good enough for him.

The top-end escort, who looked more like a fashion model than a sex worker, arrived right on time. The intelligence team were already building a file on the escort service and had discovered there were markers that the agency had come up in relation to British and foreign criminals in the past, though there was nothing concrete.

The woman was in his room less than ten minutes. The team in the next room had already set up a technical probe and they were recording. It sounded like the woman – probably Eastern European – had just sat and talked for a short time. There seemed to be nothing from Kangas apart from his greeting when she'd arrived. Their best guess was that he was in the small lounge area on his own and the woman was in the bedroom having a drink. Oliver relayed back to Macallan what they had, which wasn't much.

'There's nothing going on and definitely not sex. There was almost no conversation so we don't know if something has been delivered. The woman had a shoulder bag but who knows?'

'Okay. Too much of a risk to lift her now so we wait and see.'

10

The next day Kangas went out and it became clear he was looking for a motorbike. He ended up buying a good class but second-hand set of wheels. He then caused the surveillance team a real problem by driving out of the city; they lost him when he seemed to break the land-speed record after a couple of insane manoeuvres that would have exposed the team if they'd tried to follow him. This was always a risk, and although they had two bikes on the surveillance operation, they couldn't risk screaming up his arse and alerting him. They had the registered number of the bike and had ANPR in reserve.

When Macallan got the news there had been a complete loss, she started to sweat blood. She considered calling Assistant Chief Constable Elaine Tenant but knew that it would send panic through the executive, and they could force her to make a bad call. Tenant was her friend but ran everything by the book and that might not suit the circumstances. She had no doubt they would order a general lookout and it would end up with some uniform patrol stopping him. They'd likely find nothing incriminating on him and that would be the job compromised. *Fine but what happens next? Will some other killer come later to do the job*? she thought. They might get no warning the next time.

She was sure Kangas would have to recce the job first. She chewed her finger and fretted as she waited, knowing this could be a job that killed her off as well as the target, whoever that was. The nerves in her stomach jangled. *Is this it*? she thought.

She wondered, as she had so many times, whether there would be some cosmic payback for what she'd done to Dominic Grainger. She hadn't been able to put him in prison, so she'd exposed him as an informant to Loyalists in Belfast, and he'd later been found with his brains outside his skull. She'd given in to her instincts, and although it had felt right at the time, it still haunted her, and for years she'd agonised over the possibility that all she'd fought for in her career had gone up in smoke as soon as Grainger's executioner had pulled the trigger. Lately, those thoughts had grown worse – torturous even – but what could she do? There was no way she could offload that burden on anyone.

She wanted to call Jack, just to hear his voice, but couldn't quite bring herself to pick up the phone. Instead, she reached once more for the coffee and resumed waiting, trying hard to turn her restless mind to other thoughts.

As Macallan stewed over her own integrity, her team took up their positions back at the hotel, waited and prayed that Kangas didn't kill someone when they had no eyes on him. Two hours later, he turned up on foot back at the hotel; the team let out a collective sigh, their blood pressure instantly lowering. Oliver knew Macallan would be waiting and worrying so he called right away.

'Jesus, thanks, Danny. I was imagining the worst.'

'Think we all were, boss, but back in the game and just need to find the bike now.'

11

The next morning, the surveillance team had a break when they monitored Kangas picking up the bike he'd stowed less than a mile from the hotel. The bigger break was that he had it in a garage in a quiet off-street lane in the West End.

'How the hell did he manage that?' Oliver asked. He'd called Macallan when they had a stop – Kangas had gone into a coffee shop for some breakfast.

'God knows but looks like someone has arranged this beforehand,' Macallan said. 'Seems likely he'll use a firearm for the job, so where is it? Could be in the garage. If we knew it was on him then we might need to consider taking him out. Couldn't let him run if we knew he was armed. By the way, a firearms team are on standby and ready if and when you need them. They're now monitoring the surveillance and will stay close enough but not interfere. The team leader will be in touch with you after this call and you can coordinate directly.'

She was interrupted by Oliver. 'That's the target on the move, boss. Speak later.' He rang off and Macallan bit her lip, wishing again that she was on the ground with her team rather than sitting worrying about her caffeine intake.

As the day wore on, the surveillance operation had a break as Kangas headed outside the city and took up a position where he was clearly watching a travellers' site from a safe distance. There was no way of working out who he was after so there was no possibility that they could issue a threat to life. It might not have been a major development, but it was progress and that was all they could ask. He didn't hang about too long; it looked like he was just reconnoitring the area.

Oliver called Macallan and gave her an update.

'There's one thing, Danny,' she said, relieved. 'He won't march in to the site or those boys will spot him a mile away and bury him. So far so good.'

12

That same night, when Kangas was settled back into his hotel, a covert entry team opened the garage and beaconed the motorbike. Fortunately, the garage was in a secluded spot and almost empty. A team were placed round the area to cover the men and women making the entry in case of any approaching problems.

Pam Fitzgerald and a team from the MIT searched the garage and found a Makarov pistol concealed beneath the floor. Macallan had already arranged for technicians to be available if a weapon was found during the job. In normal circumstances they would have arrested the suspect and charged him with possession of the weapon, which would get him serious time, but if they took Kangas in, it was unlikely he'd talk, so they still wouldn't know who the target was. Then a replacement would likely be sent to Scotland, perhaps under their radar, and they would end up with an unsolvable murder on their hands.

'Get the gun to the technicians and let them do the job. The target is in bed and sleeping as far as we can tell.'

Withing two hours, the gun was back exactly as it had been found. The only difference was that it wouldn't fire when the time came – Kangas wouldn't know till he pulled the trigger. For Macallan that was another worry put aside.

13

The following day, they monitored Kangas going to a secluded area about a mile from the travellers' site. He left the bike and made his way on foot over some high ground overlooking the area, then sat there for hours using a set of binos to constantly scan the site.

Oliver called Macallan again. 'Nothing to report. He's taking his time. Thorough boy, but I guess that's his training. There's no way he's going in there to try and do the business in the site itself. He might be special forces, but these boys are no mugs. My guess is he's watching for a particular vehicle carrying whoever his target is and will then track them and do the job well away from the site.'

Macallan knew the team had relaxed slightly now the gun was disabled, but they still had a hard job to do trailing Kangas and trying to identify his target.

'My guess is he has information on where his target goes on particular days. He's just making sure of his ground. We just need to hold the nerve. It can't go much longer, Danny. Big problem is the exec might get cold feet and just tell us to lift him and do him for the gun.'

*

Later in the evening, it looked like Kangas was back in his room and everything seemed to be quiet. Oliver handed over the night turn to another team and headed to Leith for the briefing with Macallan.

When he arrived at her office, Macallan tapped the desk with her pen.

'Okay, we're well in the game, and at some point, we'll maybe have to take him rather than waiting and watching him actually try to shoot someone. It's a tricky one. I briefed the ACC and they're definitely getting edgy. Still, let's call it a night and hope he sleeps soundly so you can go and get some serious Zs.'

14

The following day was almost routine and a rerun of the previous one, with Kangas parked on the high ground and recceing the camp again.

The Finns called Macallan to tell her that Kangas had made a call to what they believed was a Russian, and that whatever the job was, he was aiming to do it the next day. They knew his target would be leaving the camp and going to a meeting in Edinburgh.

It was from then on that a dark comedy took control. What Macallan and her team didn't know was that Kangas had underestimated the travelling community in Scotland. They'd spotted him themselves but hadn't worked out what he was up to, or who he was interested in. It was enough that he was a hostile, and they did not fuck about with perceived threats. They were on his tail as well and had tracked him back to the hotel without the police being aware of it.

The same evening, Kangas decided to take a break and explore the area around the Royal Mile – he had to take the chance now because if everything went according to plan, he'd be on the plane back to Helsinki the next day.

It was just as darkness was coming down that he headed down Johnston Terrace, under the looming presence of the castle. It was quiet enough at the best of times in contrast to the nearby Royal Mile, with its never-ending streams of tourists. As he was on foot, the surveillance team gave him plenty of room, letting him run out of sight. They knew he'd arrive near Castle Terrace, alongside the walls and rock supporting the ancient fortress. But in that ten minutes he was out of sight, fate played against both him and the police team.

Almost at the same time, both Macallan in her office and Danny Oliver in his car noticed that the beacon on Kangas's bike had been activated and it was now on the move.

'What the fuck?' Oliver sat bolt upright and stuffed the half-eaten sandwich back in his rucksack. The bike wasn't covered as they'd thought it was safe enough to leave it tucked up in the garage given that Kangas was the target. They had no evidence or intelligence that he had an associate. Oliver called Macallan.

'Are you seeing this?' He was trying to make sense of what was happening and what instructions were needed for the team.

'I see it, Danny. This wasn't in the script but that's not unusual with surveillance jobs. Look, it's heading your way so you just need to wait, but be prepared to split the team if it's an associate. I'll organise the backup team to be with you ASAP so sit tight till we see what this means.'

'I'll get a footman to make ground down from the castle to see what he's doing. It's a risk of spooking him but we better cover it.'

It was the right call and Macallan agreed, tension squeezing her gut. There was always some problem that hadn't been covered and this was it.

She started to call the backup team to deploy as the footman headed down from the castle to try to get an eyeball back on Kangas. At the same time, Oliver was relaying to the team to be on the lookout for the bike. They should presume it was an unknown associate.

But they were wrong; it definitely wasn't an associate.

15

It was just about then that a vanload of nail-hard travellers pulled up beside Kangas. For all his training, he was thrown. His first instinct was that they were undercover cops, so he took the decision that, as the gun was stashed safely and all he had on him was a false passport, he might be able to brass it out. That was a mistake: the travellers were there to beat the shit out of him and that's exactly what they did. It was quick, very efficient, and when they were finished, they really surprised him by pulling his bike out of the back of one of the vans and dumping it near his slumped body. Thirty seconds later it was nicely alight.

The surveillance team were waiting to re-establish the eyeball on Kangas when the balloon went up with a call from the footman.

'There's something alight halfway down Johnston Terrace!'

The surveillance team could hear that the footman was now running.

Alarm bells were going off in Oliver's head. 'Get there now and investigate,' he called out. It was the only order he could think of as he tried to work out what might have happened and what his options were.

Another message came in. 'There's a van just passed us at speed heading away from the Terrace. Saw it going in and thought it was heading up to the Royal Mile. We've got a number.'

Oliver swore a couple of times and tried to make sense of it. He was the furthest away from the team, in Lothian Road, but put the foot down. He was almost there when he picked up the next call.

'The target is a hospital job and the bike is nicely toasted. We've checked the number of the van and it belongs to the travellers.'

'So we've no chance there then but put out a lookout request.' Oliver sounded weary; he was glad Macallan would have to make the next decision. He called her with the news, but she had been listening to the radio traffic and picked up on the communications already.

'Well by the sound of it, the contract job's off for now, and at least he'll not kill anyone on our patch for the time being.' She tried sound positive as her mind worked to unravel the options, knowing Oliver would be gutted and feel responsible. Shit happened on surveillance operations though – she'd been there often enough herself.

'Right, first and most importantly, we have him for the firearm, and with the supporting evidence, he's going away for a long time so we have a result. Be positive: we have him and no one's been shot. The problem is that we still don't know who the target is, and his employers might send someone else another day, but there's nothing we can do about it at the moment so let's make a good case watertight. We'll have to front him up but sounds like he's badly injured so that'll have to wait. Still, we've done what we can, and we can follow up the intelligence we have so far. Get a hold of the escort and see what happened when they came to his room.'

Macallan and her team struggled to take the investigation much further. Kangas refused to speak, and when he recovered, Sandy Tait turned up to represent him, making sure the Finn never opened his mouth.

'My client is the victim of a terrible attack and should not be treated like an accused.' Tait did his usual theatrical act to the custody officers, who wished they could strangle him but just had to grin and bear it.

The arrival of Tait was a surprise to Macallan and her team. They didn't miss the fact that he'd turned up to defend a contract killer. This seemed to be a new low for the man reputed to be organised crime's go-to lawyer.

The van used by the travellers had been dumped off Lothian Road so they must have had a backup vehicle waiting – no surprises there.

When he was on remand, Kangas cursed his luck and moaned to his cellmate.

'This fucking place is full of crazy people and the weather is shit. Those gypsies are bastards.'

The cellmate just nodded and wished he could get a Scottish co-pilot – preferably one who knew something about football.

The Russians were pissed off that he'd failed and intended on taxing him when he got out for any expenses incurred, though any unpleasant fallout would mean a complete severing of their relationship and probably his head. There was always the possibility a job could go wrong but one was the limit as far as Russian organised crime was concerned.

The rule book for contract killers tended to work best for the employers, and Kangas knew the Russians kept to their promises or threats.

16

Pam Fitzgerald was one of Macallan's most trusted, multi-skilled and dedicated officers; she'd been with her on some of her toughest cases and had never let her down. Her job was to try and find the escort who'd called on Kangas at the hotel. Her employer was a sauna owner, pimp and general creep called Benny Green – more often known by his moniker *The Thumb*. This was a result of having lost the top half of his left thumb over a debt when he was still in his teens, well before he built up his reputation as a villain. That was long in the past and in the days when he didn't have an arse in his pants. He'd always been ambitious though and had climbed up the criminal ranks through sheer force of will. At various times, he'd been involved in money lending, drugs trafficking, money laundering, and when he'd reached the top, he'd done them all at once then invested in his favourite commodity – women.

The money had rolled in and he'd bought more and more women through his contacts in London, where he'd worked as a minder in his younger days. He wanted to be a star, playing in the big league, and his success gave his ego all the stimulation it needed.

When Fitzgerald asked to see him, he lapped it up and intended to enjoy it but tell her fuck all. The occasional hassle from the law was part and parcel of his business, but they'd never laid a glove on him so far, and he loved nothing better than treating the law like idiots. He suggested his posh office in the New Town; he enjoyed sitting behind the expensive oak desk he thought proved he was so much better off than whoever was on the other side.

'I'm really sorry, Miss... ' He pretended to forget her name, but Fitzgerald just stared at him, not playing his game, so he carried on. 'The girl you asked about left us rather suddenly. You never know with these women – here one day and gone the next. I treat them like daughters but sometimes they just let you down.' He put on his best pained face with a hint of *I'm taking the piss* mixed into the non-verbals.

Fitzgerald was normally the calmest of souls, but she wanted to lean across the desk and draw her nails down his face. She kept it together because the last thing she wanted was to give him the satisfaction of seeing her lose it, plus she knew he was probably recording them.

'Did she take anything to the punter that night? Or did you give her anything to take to him?'

Green did his pained face again. 'I'm sorry but I don't like the term punter – they are customers and often important people who make things happen in this world. The answer to your question is: I take little to do with organising the business itself. You must understand, I run many businesses and this is just one of them. I've checked: the customer asked for a beautiful woman as an escort for the evening and that's what we provided. She was contacted by phone and attended. That's all I know.'

'So when did you last see her or when were your colleagues last in touch with her?'

Green smiled and examined his nails – or at least nine of them.

'Strangely enough, she seems to have taken off after that job. It happens, and we never saw a penny of what she was paid by the customer. It breaks my heart.'

'Names? Or any details of the girl?' Fitzgerald knew if Green gave her any information it would be false anyway, but she'd play along.'

'I'll see what I can do and get one of my staff to bring it to you. I always like to help the police where I can. Thank God you girls are there to look after us.' He scratched his groin under the desk and imagined the detective in one of his fantasies.

'Thanks, Mr Green. You've been very helpful. I've no doubt we'll meet again.' She stood up as Green offered her the hand he'd been using on his balls. She smiled, and it was all teeth. 'Naw, you're okay – I forgot my hand sanitiser!'

Then she turned and headed for the door, breathing a sigh of relief, and promised herself if she got evidence against him, she'd be there to watch his ugly face when she put the cuffs on him.

17

Fitzgerald reported back to Macallan and Oliver at a debrief in the Leith office. Macallan gripped the pencil in her hand just a bit too tight when the young detective described Green – she knew the type straightaway. They got rid of one of these creatures and some other leech crawled out of the slime to take over – it was never-ending. A bloodsucker who drained the life out of victims just so he could pretend he was important.

'Apparently the intelligence team have known about this man for a while. There's a number of markers against him so let's get an investigation started on Mr Green. We might not rope him into the Kangas case, but let's see what else there is.' Macallan said it quietly, but everyone in the room knew she meant business. Human traffickers always touched the red button with her.

'You take the lead once you get clear,' she said to Fitzgerald, who smiled.

'I've no problem with that one, ma'am – I'll enjoy getting the goods on that particular gentleman. You know the type; you need a shower after being in the same room as him.'

'With you on that one, Pam.' Macallan nodded before the room emptied, leaving her alone with Oliver.

'Listen, Danny, Edvin's going to give us a closed-door briefing on what they have on Kangas from their various sources.' She picked up the phone and called Halko to come through to her office. He'd become popular with the team. Initially coming across as serious and work driven, he'd soon been recognised as a man with a wonderfully dry sense of humour and, like a true Finn, an enormous capacity for vodka.

Macallan hung the *Do not disturb* sign on the door as ACC Elaine Tenant arrived, then Halko kicked off the meeting. They ran through the preliminaries and by the time they were halfway through their first coffee, things seemed routine. Halko was precise and wanted to make sure he gave a good account of what his authorities had been doing to support the Scots.

'So, what we have is more or less what you have seen in the intelligence we passed to you, albeit sanitised by your officers in Europol before transmission to you.'

He was referring to the protocol issues between the Finnish and UK systems. Even though Macallan knew much of the intelligence was coming through technical and highly covert sources, it had to be sanitised before coming to the UK to eradicate any chance of the source being identified.

What Halko produced next was unexpected and probably stepped outside the protocols, but no one in the room objected.

'You know there was an initial call between an unknown male and Kangas. This male seems to have been an important link in this criminal operation. We hear him only the once, but he seems to carry authority. We decided to bring this to the table because we know you Brits have many regional accents, and determining where exactly this person is from may help us identify them. You've seen the transcript of the conversation but here is the voice. Our listeners struggled at first and thought it was Scottish, but having spent time here, I don't think so.'

He flicked the switch on his equipment and waited. Tension crackled through the room as they waited for the recording of that first call Kangas had made from the hotel to play.

'Call the number I'm going to text you. You were given instructions previously on what to do. Order one and they'll deliver the package – take it from there. You're on your own now. I'll let your employer know it's been done, and if there's a problem with the law, you'll be given the man to get in touch with. That will be provided with the package.'

Tenant was looking at the floor as the recording started then gradually pulled her head back, stiffening when she saw Macallan's face. Her friend looked like she'd seen a ghost, and in a way she had.

Macallan had needed the first sentence to sink in, but now that it had, it was as if that ghost had materialised and his hands were on her throat, squeezing the life from her. Her face paled and she stood up to relieve the surge of adrenalin wiring through her veins.

'What is it, Grace?' Tenant stood as well and told Halko to stop the machine.

'It's alright. Honestly, just give me a moment.' Macallan tried to convince herself she was wrong, but it was him… she knew it.

Halko sat back, realising that they'd entered a new road on the investigation. He'd thought it would be a dead end, but Macallan had learned something yet to be revealed.

'Play the recording again, Edvin… please.' She leaned over the table and poured more coffee.

Halko flicked the *on* switch again and all eyes fell on Macallan.

She imagined his face the last time she'd met him, imagined him saying the words. The lilting Northumberland tones were still there. Slightly altered, but it was him – no doubt about it. She'd always wondered if he might be dead. *How could he have gone off the radar all this time if he wasn't?* she wondered. It was strange because she'd wanted him to live despite all his sins – all that killing. That was one of her flaws – a form of selfishness. She wanted him to come back so she could take him down herself, and it had tortured her since. Pete Handyside, the man who'd once ruled the criminal world of north-east England – who'd slipped through her fingers in Perthshire when she'd been so close to catching him. A man who gave the order to kill without flinching; who had so much blood on his hands they were dripping with it. One of his many victims had been an undercover PSNI officer she'd known personally; it still hurt.

'It's Pete Handyside. I can't believe it – I was sure the bastard had to be dead.'

'You sure, Grace?' Tenant asked, but she already knew the answer from Macallan's face.

'It's him, Elaine. Don't know how we prove that, but it's him alright… Jesus.' She gathered herself; she knew she had to lead. So she sat up and looked round the room.

'Edvin, this is an important development. If I'm right, this man was one of our targets in the past, and although we dismantled his organisation, he escaped. We lost him completely. We'll supply you with a full brief on him and the original case.' She sighed deeply, letting her pulse slow. Her mouth was a straight line as she considered what might be coming. *I'm going to meet you again and this time I'll finish it,* she thought.

'Thank you, Grace, and we'll support in any way we can if we can take this forward.'

Macallan turned to Oliver. 'Danny, can you find a recording of Handyside's voice so we can get an analysis. I know we have some radio interviews. He had lots of business and property interests and often played the good-guy local entrepreneur in Newcastle.'

'Leave that with me and I'll get right on it,' Oliver said. He didn't know Handyside himself but had heard the story of how he'd disappeared off the radar after all of his team, plus a bent detective, had been taken out.

'What do you need, Grace?' Tenant wasn't a detective, had never pretended to be and never wanted to be one, but she trusted Macallan and knew this wasn't a problem they could stick in the *pending* tray.

'At the moment I need to think. This changes everything. So many questions – why he's back and of course where the hell is he?'

'I can maybe help here.' Halko was reluctant to interrupt but knew he had another lead. 'We have one other piece that may help you. We're able to say this man you refer to was in Dublin when he made the call. We were able to do this through cooperation with our security services. That's all, but maybe it's a start.'

'Dublin.' Macallan said it quietly and let it sink in. 'He's not far from us then. He couldn't stay away – the bastard just couldn't stay away.' She managed a smile – unusual for such a serious woman. 'Right, let's get to work. We'll have a full briefing this afternoon once I get this all through my head. Let's get the best intelligence team we can put together.'

She looked towards Tenant. 'Can I pick my team?'

'Of course – get what you need and I'll do the arguing if there's a problem. I'll come to the briefing, but I'll leave you to it for now.' She stood up and thanked Halko then left the office.

'As I said, let's get to work, guys.'

Macallan looked out of her window as her colleagues left the room. *Pete Handyside. You've come back,* she thought *I wonder how often you think about me*?

He was one of the demons who haunted her.

I wonder what you look like now? Can't be the same – too distinctive; too much a one-off! I'll find you this time and end this.

She shivered as she realised that she wanted to speak to him, be close to him again and look into his eyes when she delivered him to a court. There was an attraction between them that made her uncomfortable.

She shook her head and stared at her reflection in the dirt-stained glass. *Where did those lines come from? Who is that woman*?

She turned away, almost frightened by the image of herself.

18

1 Week Later

Nancy Gilhooley walked through the empty streets of Leith, heading for her home in Newhaven. The heavens were angry, and rain turning to sleet burned her face. After a spell of beautiful clear weather, Scotland had returned to form and it was now more like November with freezing artic winds.

As she blinked into the squall, she shivered. What light there was seemed to exist only in shades of grey, and there were deep, impenetrable shadows in the doorways and places hidden from the street lights. This was the second day of the storm. The lashing winds hadn't given the citizens a moment's peace, and the dark rivers of water that surged alongside the kerbs made the whole world seem threatening.

She pulled the strings of her hood tighter, enclosing her head but leaving her face to endure the night, and buried her left hand into the pocket of her jacket, but even this normally warm haven was wet so it did nothing to heat her numbed fingers. Gripping the handle on the briefcase even tighter, she was tempted to throw it in the first bin she came to, but it wouldn't have made any difference to the can of worms that was now wide open – the bastards were already crawling all over her life.

It was late and there was hardly a soul around, only the occasional car splashing by in a cloud of filthy spray before it was gone forever. She walked as fast as she could, trying to keep some heat in her body, but there was another reason for her effort.

Gilhooley was afraid, close to panic, but she wasn't quite sure why at that particular moment. She'd been frightened for days, but it was as if the night was hiding some new threat. She knew it was likely just an accumulation of stress plus self-doubt; she was on a path she wished she'd never chosen – completely out of her depth. Now there seemed to be threats in every sound, every shadow, every passing stranger, and she cursed herself for not being able to walk away from the story.

She was a great reporter, still young and with so much promise. There were another million stories out there she could have followed and still been able to sleep at night. Now her life was a horror tale – the demons were out there somewhere, watching her. When she'd picked this story though, she'd felt like an actress in an action thriller – *All the President's Men* maybe – and dreamed of the awards she'd win, the ceremonies where she'd pretend she wasn't worthy. Now she was cold, anxious and somewhere out there were forces that wanted to do her harm. Real harm – the kind that makes you die choking in your own blood as bowels and bladder open through sheer terror.

She wiped the back of her hand under her streaming nose. The thought of her flat, the place she'd put so much into since stretching her budget to the limit to buy it, warmed her a little. It was her small piece of heaven, close to the old harbour that had witnessed so much over the centuries, and she picked up her pace, keen to be safe within its walls as soon as possible.

19

Newhaven had been redeveloped, but the skeleton of the original place was still there in the narrow streets and lanes. Gilhooley passed the old square where generations of fisherman and sailors had crammed into a couple of days what they'd missed after weeks at sea.

They were fading memories, the families who'd inhabited that little land round the old fish market long gone now. It had been a place full of characters: wild fishermen, whalers, fisherwomen with backs like iron, all crowding into the Market Buffet, where fine dining hadn't been invented and wasn't needed. If what you wanted wasn't gargantuan bread rolls filled with artery-busting fried food and mugs of man tea then, as Rae the legendary owner would tell you, 'You're in the wrong place, pal!'

The new inhabitants who saw the port as a fashionable place to live came from everywhere but Newhaven. The old families, men and women with traces of Dutch, Nordic as well as good Scots blood in their veins, were no more than ghosts, like the fleet of local boats, the endless shoals of herring and beds of scallops that used to fill the Firth of Forth like wheat. All that was left of that race were those ghosts watching a young, frightened woman trying to reach the safety of home.

She almost broke into a run as she passed the old fish market building, splashing through the rain-soaked pavements, her panic growing – though every time she stopped to look round there was nothing there, human or spectral. If she could have known the truth, she would have turned and bolted in the opposite direction because the gun that was primed to pump bullets into her skull was already in place and ready.

Only yards from her door, hidden in a dark corner, Sam Taylor was waiting to end her life. He crouched patiently, the rain hardly bothering him; in fact, he almost welcomed the cover it gave, as only a professional could. The noise of the wind and rain was everything he could've hoped for – it would make his target look down instead of up. She would never see him coming.

Gilhooley had nowhere else to go; she wanted to be home and almost sprinted the last few yards towards her door and the man waiting for her. The ultimate sins always carried risk and there was no perfect crime, even though many were never solved.

Taylor's problem was that he was human, and not the man he'd been at the peak of his powers. The horrors he'd seen had robbed him of a functioning soul, compassion and feeling left on the killing grounds he'd inhabited since his youth, while drink and increasing lines of powder had destroyed the precision sharpness he'd once had. And although the army had taught him how to deal with ops that didn't go to plan; that the top guys made their own luck, he just had too many miles on the clock now.

As Gilhooley covered the last few steps to the door that would have taken her to the safety of her flat, he rose out of the shadows just a few seconds too soon.

Her nerves were stretched so tight that the moment she saw the death spectre rise from the shadows like an extension of the darkness, she screamed. Taylor cursed as he raised the gun and fired off two shots, double tapping her at the breastbone. Even as she was dropping, he took three steps closer and put two into her grey matter to make sure the job was done.

He stood for a moment and stared at the body, watching the dark swirling patterns of the blood in the water running past his feet, then glanced up. His blood pressure rose as he waited, feeling the seconds start to drag. Nothing was stirring, so he crouched, picked up her briefcase and stuffed it into his rucksack. *Job done – time to get to fuck,* he thought.

Then lights started to go on, and he watched a couple of citizens come to their windows and peer out into the night. The woman's dying scream had alerted witnesses – his timing was off so a small fuck-up, and he knew it. Ten years earlier she would have died with barely a sound beyond the *whup-whup* from the effect of the suppressor, which the storm would have swallowed. He should have had time to walk away and meld into the night, but now the clock was running too fast. Half of the victim's body was illuminated by the street light; any one of those witnesses might have seen her and be dialling the law, so he had to make tracks.

He had to stay in shadow; knew not to run. *Keep cool,* he thought. Dragging her body out of the light risked a possible transfer of evidence or DNA so he left her alone. That was the training, and it nearly always worked; men like him knew the cost of falling apart with a gun in your hand and a dead body lying on the pavement.

Adrenalin still surged through his body like a sexual high. It was always the same after a kill. The rush after taking a life had no equal, and he felt full of energy. The rain eased suddenly, but the cold sea winds chilled the exposed skin of his face. The streets were still quiet and he was only a couple of minutes' walk from the motorbike that would take him away from the scene and the risk of being spotted by anyone else.

Unfortunately, that was where the whole episode went wrong. As he knew all too well, shit really does happen sometimes.

20

Four slightly pissed low-level villains had left a mate's house at the heart of Newhaven and took a shortcut to get to another flat where even more bevvy and some charlie waited for them. One of them stopped for a slash as the other three walked on. They headed towards old Newhaven Main Street, unaware that a professional killer was heading towards them. They came round the corner close together, too pissed to talk, and the moaning north-east wind covered the sound of their footsteps. That's when they ran straight into Taylor.

The tallest of the three men was a steroid boy, a pile of muscle, and when he turned the corner, he collided with Taylor, who almost landed on his back dropping the rucksack that had been slung over one shoulder. Fit as he was, he wasn't prepared to run into a man mountain, and as soon as it happened, he knew he'd just made his second mistake of the night – he'd been walking too fast himself, dwelling too much on his first error and the likelihood that his team leader was a bastard of the first order who'd probably already noticed that he might not be match fit anymore.

He'd intended that no one would ever know who'd killed Gilhooley, especially not his team leader, who'd had no part in sanctioning the op. He knew if the man realised the extent of his drink and dope habit then he'd be finished. He must have heard he'd been lifted after the battle in Bogwood Road; Sandy Tait would have had to tell him. That was one black mark already, and although he could get away with a yellow card, the Gilhooley job could compromise him and thus threaten the rest of the team. That was a capital offence in his game, and the men that would come to kill him would be relentless, younger and know every trick he did.

'What the fuck?' Man Mountain saw an opportunity for a bit of a laugh. After all, Taylor was a full head shorter and certainly no pumped-up steroid junkie.

'Watch where ye're gaun, ya fuckin' bawbag.'

His two pals saw the game starting and grinned in anticipation of a little bloodletting. Three against one was no contest – or at least that's what they thought.

Taylor kept his eyes fixed on the three men, deciding who was likely to move first. It had to be Man Mountain. He knew the type – he thought size was all it took and should have had *twat* tattooed on his large forehead.

'Sorry, boys, I'm not looking for any trouble. I'll be on my way. Okay?' He picked up the rucksack slowly but kept eyes fixed on the three men. He'd just turned slightly to the right to walk round them when Man Mountain put his hand on the killer's chest.

'Where the fuck dae ye think ye're gaun, sunshine? I'm no finished wi' you.'

His two pals moved left and right, cutting off Taylor's options; he was almost surrounded. He knew the first blow was coming in a matter of seconds and there were no good options left. It was a fuck-up, one of those things that no amount of planning could foresee, and whatever happened next was going to be remembered, even if it was just by the three men threatening him.

He couldn't kill them – that would create too much evidence, and things could go wrong fighting on the pavements. He might get two and lose one – there'd be evidence everywhere and there was too much heat already on its way.

Through the lane to his left, he saw a couple of blue lights flash by on Pier Place – no doubt on their way to where Gilhooley had taken her last breath. Time was running out – Man Mountain's hand was still resting squarely on his chest. So Taylor grabbed his thumb, twisted it back against the joint and felt it snap. The surprise of his action gave him a brief moment to act against the other two men.

He'd dropped the rucksack again so his right hand was free, and he pushed hard with the heel of his hand against the chest of the man to his right, throwing him off balance for a second – which was all he needed. He dipped his knees slightly then drove his left elbow into the man's top lip and up into the soft cartilage. The force of the blow broke the two small nasal bones, and blood gushed from the pulp. The man gasped in pain and dropped to his knees.

Taylor swung round to face the third man, but milliseconds count in hand-to-hand combat, and though he'd done everything right in the face of such odds, he had no way of knowing that there was a fourth man in the group. He came out of the lane as Taylor turned to face the third man.

Taylor was waiting because the man had hesitated and was getting ready to leg it when he saw the little flicker in his opponent's eyes as he looked over Taylor's shoulder. He made to turn, but it was too late, and Taylor wheezed out in pain as the blow hit him hard in the left kidney. The fourth man was ex-army himself and knew how to hurt.

Taylor went down as the two men weighed in and started to give him a good old-fashioned Scottish kicking, complete with the usual war chants.

'Kick his fuckin' heid in, Tam!'

They did it good style. Taylor was hurt and tried to crawl away, aware that there was now more than one set of police two tones somewhere in the area.

The sound attracted the attention of the men kicking him, and they stopped for a moment. Man Mountain, who was cradling his damaged hand, loomed over Taylor, his face contorted with pain.

'I'm gonnae fuckin' waste this bastard. Get his hands.'

Taylor had crawled a short distance, turned on his back and pulled out the gun. He didn't want to, but he had no choice.

'Now fuck off, or I swear to God, I'll do you all.'

He pulled himself up onto one hand, trying to control the pain in his back.

The villains had seen enough to know the guy was serious business and probably had the balls to do exactly what he said.

The noise of the two tones and word that there was a battle in Main Street was bringing people to their windows, so Taylor had no option but to back away. He saw two uniforms appear in the west end of the street and begin heading towards the ruckus. The rucksack was now behind his attackers, as was the baseball cap he'd been wearing, but there was no time to retrieve them – he turned then half jogged towards the motorbike before the whole job went completely belly up.

The uniforms and some additional cavalry arrived, arrested Man Mountain and his gang, and picked up the rucksack.

'That's the bastard there ye should be liftin.' Man Mountain pointed with his good hand, but all they heard was the sound of a motorbike somewhere in the distance. The police weren't that interested in a street fight when there was a murder victim at the other end of Newhaven. They hadn't tied the two events together and that gave Taylor all the time he needed to create distance from the job.

21

Taylor cursed as he made his way through the city but there was nothing he could do about what had happened. The rucksack was a major problem – or at least what was in it. It was the reporter's papers. He hadn't read them, but there was the possibility they could reveal the darkest of secrets – secrets that could raise the dead to accuse their executioners.

The man who basically owned and ran the team was an unknown to him. He had no idea who he was or where he was but guessed it would be London. His old troop sergeant Billy Dolan led the team on the ground when they were working together, but the man above him stayed well behind a firewall, and that was okay as far as he was concerned – firewalls were good practice in this game. The boss would always be safer than the poor fucking expendables who worked at the coalface.

None of that made any difference because what had happened in Newhaven was a serious failure on his part, and for Taylor, failure was becoming a habit. What was in that rucksack was potentially so explosive he'd have to go dark till things quietened down.

'Fuck it,' he muttered every few minutes, as if it would make any difference. He'd head to London for a few days to assess the damage, cursing again at mistake number three – not carrying the rucksack on his back but draping it over one shoulder like a tourist. Three mistakes was amateur level. He was looking at time if the bizzies managed to put it all together and, worst still, a red card if the boss decided to take more than his bonus.

He'd have to find some rathole to lie in till he decided what to do next, stay dark for a while then undertake another series of journeys to make sure there were no eyes on his back. He wondered if Dolan or whoever was above him would forgive this one, but it seemed unlikely. Sandy Tait would have reported the drunken brawl in Mayfield, and he was sure the lawyer would have been making his own enquires since to see if Taylor had become a risk.

He was due a meet with Dolan for a catch-up in London anyway. It was a regular thing so Dolan could make sure the troops were all behaving themselves and match fit. He'd known Dolan since the South Armagh days during the Troubles, and although they didn't like each other, they were good soldiers and that meant respect. So maybe there was a chance he could talk his way out of this one – chalk it all up to bad luck.

The only problem was that Dolan had noticed the hangover he'd had at their last meeting, and all those other little signals that showed he'd forgotten what discipline meant. It wasn't the first time either, and Dolan had tried more than once to get him clean, but as soon as he was on his own again, there was just too much time to think – too many horrors spinning on the carousel in his head – and he was soon choking for a drink. That was his problem – binging. He used to be able to control it; could stay dry for weeks into a job, but now he was acting like a useless jakey. No, Dolan would decide he was too big a risk. He really was on his own.

The other problem was there would be DNA all over the rucksack and the men he'd fought in Newhaven, and his DNA had been taken after his arrest at Mayfield, so it would take a monumental failure by the police not to ID him eventually. Dolan or his boss would pick that one up at some point and that would be it. Once the organisation knew he was a serious threat to them, he would have nothing left – nothing.

Taylor ran the bike to an old quarry about a mile from Mayfield, torched it then jogged back to his flat. He wasn't worried about the law for the moment so he was confident he had time to clear the flat and do whatever came next.

22

Sam Taylor's mind spun as he tried to work out the consequences of what had happened in Newhaven. He'd already accepted the law would find his DNA – he knew enough about the subject to take that as a given – so he needed to focus on getting rid of the other evidence, like the laptop and a few other items.

He still had the gun but also picked up a couple of hunting knifes. The knife was Taylor's preferred weapon, and in the service, he'd had the reputation as the best in the business with a blade. He had spare ammo too, and although he didn't like the idea of travelling long distances with a firearm, he might well need the gun at some point. He couldn't approach anyone else for weapons as it could set off alarms, and trust was a rare commodity in his game. He'd been seen by the fuckwits he'd battled in Newhaven so no doubt a description would be all over the news at some point, but these things took time and he had kit that would allow him to make some initial changes to his appearance – just enough to get him away from the city.

He thought again about his own team and employers, but no matter how he looked at the situation with Gilhooley, he was fucked. The whole idea of the unsanctioned hit on the reporter was to clean up the story without them ever finding out about it; instead, the opposite was now likely.

He felt old and damaged, and his hip flask was empty by the time he cleared the flat and put on his cap and glasses. That was as much as he could manage for the time being, but it would do. His grooming routine was almost non-existent – his hair hung over his ears and neck, and his beard was thick. Taking it off would transform him, but he'd leave it till London, where he would have time to think. London was a place he could get lost for a bit and work out what he could do.

The killing would be headline news here but would die off quickly south of the border as world events and the growing horrors of the coronavirus overwhelmed every news bulletin.

A few hours later, Taylor sat on the early train feeling exhausted with all that had happened, knowing he could count any friends on just a couple of the fingers of one hand. There had been only limited news on Gilhooley's killing so far; the police were remaining tight-lipped and hadn't mentioned a suspect, but that couldn't last long. His options were few and limited. *Very fucking limited*, he thought as he stared at the paper and the headlines that didn't lift his mood.

Brexit had moved to the next stage and was on hold, but other threats were approaching and the world seemed to be moving from crisis to crisis. All this as Boris promised golden horizons as he tried to evoke memories of Churchill in full flight.

He skimmed over the lines on the second page that declared the coronavirus was now stampeding over the Far East and into Europe and grunted, shaking his head. The world seemed to reflect his own life – probably fucked.

23

Grace Macallan had arrived in the office well before anyone else and even the cleaners were still at work. She stared out of the grimy office windows, but there was no panoramic view to ponder, just the other side of the street. The awful weather continued, which didn't help her mood. Her mind was somewhere else as she chewed the side of her forefinger, an uncontrollable habit that betrayed the fact she was worried and all that had seemed to be right in her life was under strain. Up until now, getting back to running an MIT had been a boost; it was always where she'd felt most comfortable, the months had flown by and her team were as good as any she'd had in the past.

It had always been her nature to be reserved, and in later life, this manifested in a way that made it even more difficult for her to share and unload her problems. The Troubles in Northern Ireland, her departure from the PSNI and her catalogue of dealings with the darkest sides of the human soul had damaged her over and over again. She'd been able to survive in the past, but the cumulative experience had drained her, and the demons she thought she'd driven off were now coming back. What worried her most was that she almost welcomed it. It was as if she wanted to be there, choking on the stench of the corruption that most people only read about.

She wondered if the real world was actually where she came from. People regarded her as a pillar of integrity, but they didn't know what she'd done to Dominic Grainger. It had torn her sense of justice, but she couldn't watch him walk away so had given in to the dark side. As a detective, she knew fine that worrying about guilty men walking free came with the territory. If you couldn't stand it then you shouldn't be doing the job – that's what every young detective was told, and she'd seen plenty of guilty men and women go free in her time, but she'd always avoided letting her anger lead her.

In Grainger's case though, she'd committed a serious crime, and she was still struggling to come to terms with the secret she'd have to carry to her grave. Although Grainger was a vicious criminal who'd deserved the bullets that had ended his life, the decision to send him to his death should not have been hers, and that haunted her.

Part of it was that she knew she couldn't share it with Jack; it would have broken the way he'd always perceived her – damaged but defined by her integrity, and this knowledge made her worry that their relationship might be a sham like so much else in life.

She was in her dream job now, heading up the MIT, and it had notched up a number of high-profile cases, with the recent dating-site-murders case the icing on the cake. The problem was that the moods that had calmed as she'd built her life with Jack were slithering back and had started to hurt like a physical illness.

She'd tried to shrug it off, but over the years the moods had lengthened and deepened. Jack knew her so well and had tried to talk to her numerous times, but she'd avoided facing it until the previous night – when everything had finally come to a head and she'd realised it was affecting their relationship.

As she reflected on it now, she realised Jack's words hadn't come as any surprise.

'Jesus, Grace, you're suffering from depression. You're the detective – can't you see it yourself? For God's sake, do something about it. The kids see it and that can't go on. You're a wonderful mother, but you're permanently melancholic now, and they need to see that smile again. I know it's a rare commodity, but you could do it before.'

He'd put his arms around her as she'd squeezed her eyes shut, wishing she could confess the great sin she'd committed but not sure he could live with it. *He doesn't deserve that anyway*, she'd thought.

'Promise me you'll see someone, Grace?' he'd asked, holding her tighter.

She'd realised then that his patience wasn't endless and that she had to take action, or the worst of all scenarios could actually happen: she could lose him. There were already times when there seemed to be an increasing distance between them – when she was preoccupied with the job and he was left trying to write and be both father and mother to the children. He was only human, but it was more than just wear and tear on the relationship – the fact that he seemed to invest more in the family than she did.

She'd often wondered if she was exacting some form of subconscious revenge on Jack for leaving her at her darkest moment in Belfast. What she didn't realise at the time was that he had been having exactly the same thoughts. Whatever was happening to them was painful, and it was slow burning, which made it even more insidious.

She'd felt a moment of anger at his words – like an alcoholic confronted with the truth – then it had subsided as she'd stared at the man who knew her better than anyone else. He'd lanced the abscess, and a well of suppressed emotion had poured out of the dark corners of her being, where they'd been buried, festering and poisoning her soul. She'd almost collapsed, sobbing like a child as Jack had pulled her to him, one great arm round her waist, the other cradling the back of her head like a newborn.

'It's fine, Grace, promise,' he'd said. 'It's all fine, and strange as it seems, I'm glad you're crying. You need to face this.'

In that moment she'd felt their connection again; that there was hope.

'You need help, Grace. I'm not the shrink here, but for God's sake admit what's going on in your head and I'll stand by you.'

She'd looked up at him, realising that she'd stopped seeing his handsome face, the good things he offered, because of the permanent feeling that she was never quite good enough.

She hadn't moved for an age, the tears only subsiding slowly till Jack had pulled her chin up and kissed the end of her nose. It was a gesture she loved – something that he used to do a lot.

'Jack, I'm sorry.'

He'd told her to stop being sorry and promise to do something about it and she'd agreed, but it wouldn't be through the force. The notion of a caring, sharing organisation was still, to some extent, a façade, and a high-profile detective getting help for a mental-health problem would still attract all sorts of negative responses. Not to her face, but the critics would whisper behind her, and the first time something went wrong on a sensitive case, she'd be gently moved into the office marked paper clips. Sometimes she almost wished she was a Catholic so she could go to confession and unload her burden there.

Now, in her office, she took a deep breath and called the shrink who'd been recommended to her, her heart thumping the whole time. Yet it turned out to be easier than she'd thought. There was no one on the other end of the phone laughing at her weakness, just the voice of another woman taking notes and setting up an appointment.

Macallan put the phone down when it was done and wondered what a shrink would make of what was in her head. Could she disclose? Could she just give part of it up? It was for Jack *and* her. Marriages go wrong and Jack might have sinned for walking away from her after the Belfast incident but... *I've paid him back with interest since,* she thought.

24

The knock at the door drew Macallan away from her thoughts. Danny Oliver pushed his head round the door and walked in carrying two brews. The smell of fresh coffee was like medicine. He'd picked up the vibes that she was troubled, but he also knew that Macallan wasn't one for sharing. In the investigation world, nine times out of ten it was a domestic problem, but he couldn't believe that was the case with Macallan and Jack, who seemed to have it all.

'Thought you'd like some of this dark nectar, made by my own hands in a proper cafetiere?' he said, trying to lighten the mood hanging over Macallan like a cloud, despite her attempts to hide it. They'd become close over the months he'd worked with her and knew she'd likely resent any intrusion into her personal life so played it safe.

'Thanks, Danny. I'll need it no matter what.'

Macallan tried to get her head into gear. She was the boss – there were problems and requests piling into the MIT every day and she knew better than anyone that if she wasn't on top of her game, the whole show would fall off a cliff. She decided she'd call her old friend Mick Harkins later, though she knew it would probably cost her a painful morning after.

'What you got for me, Danny?' It was their daily get-together before the MIT team – or at least those who weren't involved in a job and out already – was briefed in the morning.

'Everything seems to be under control and the report for the dating-site-killer job is nearly done. Glad to see that one away. Have to admit I never thought we were going to solve it – that man was the coolest, and one of the smartest I've seen.'

Macallan nodded. Although the team would get gold stars for the investigation, the killer had almost got away with it.

He'd been near forensic in the way he'd stalked women on internet dating sites, befriended them and killed them; had done almost everything right, but on his second date with his first victim, he'd come home and, about to undress, had noticed a few long blonde hairs on the sleeve of his jacket. Before he could take a more well-thought-out approach, he'd heard his wife coming up the stairs and so had just flicked them behind a dresser. With a bit of luck, he would have survived this little error, but to be fair, he hadn't decided to kill anyone at that point.

The hairs had been missed on the first police search, but when they thought there was nowhere else to go, Macallan had ordered a second one, and that was when the hairs had turned up, crashing his previous denials that he'd ever met the first victim. There was a degree of luck, but she'd taken it, and although the trial had been touch and go, the jury had seen him for what he was.

'Anything else apart from the routine, Danny?'

'The ACC wants to see you pronto. Sounds like something kicking off for us. There's the murder down in Newhaven last night, so maybe they want us in on that. There's a team already been there through the night so would be a nice one to get our hands on.' Oliver looked pleased, already full of the energy that seemed to buzz round the MIT as soon as a job looked like it was about to move.

'Give me a couple of minutes, Danny – need to make a call, and can we do the Benny Green briefing with Pam after I see the ACC?' He nodded and headed out.

Macallan ran her fingers through her hair. She had already heard that the Newhaven killing looked professional, so that was good and bad. Professional probably meant difficult to solve, but on the plus side, it would take the detectives well away from the routine. Still, a tiny alarm bell went off in her head. These jobs didn't turn up too often, and the Kangas case was still part of the job against Benny Green. *They can't be connected, can they*? she asked herself.

Macallan was impatient to see where they were with the intelligence development and the amorphous image that was Pete Handyside, who seemed to be living permanently in the back of her mind now. Oliver was leading on it, and Macallan struggled to resist interfering. Case development took time, and they had other work on the go. She needed to make a good case to go live on Green, but all she had was the taped recording that she was sure was Handyside, though she couldn't prove it. She had to make sure this wasn't more about her own issues and demons than what the force needed to prioritise.

She put the thoughts aside, lifted the phone and called Mick Harkins.

'Any chance we can get together for a drink, Mick?'

'Of course. I thought you'd forgotten the man who taught you all you know. Usual place?' The gravel in his voice eased her and she smiled.

They made an arrangement to meet and she explained that she had to go to a meeting.

'Meetings – the thing I miss least in the job, Grace.'

When Macallan put the phone down, she felt the weight lifting. So much of her problem was her reluctance to share, and the thought of unloading on Harkins gave her a brief sense of relief.

25

ACC Elaine Tenant had only been in her post for a few months and was still getting used to the rarefied atmosphere at executive level. For most of her career, this rank was all she'd wanted so she'd led a fairly solitary personal life that lacked warmth, apart from the occasional contact with her cat. She'd been Macallan's line manager for a while, and although it had been a difficult relationship to start with, they had both come to see something in the other person, and most importantly there was respect for what they were both trying to achieve in different ways. More importantly – and much to her surprise – a man had walked into her life. She'd almost no experience of the species on a personal level, but he had gradually coaxed the woman from the shell and life had turned around nicely.

Sometimes she could hardly believe it. It was too late for them to have their own children, but they were happy, and his two grown-ups kids and their offspring were enough. The promotion she'd once thought was all that mattered now seemed less important, but she did the job and had already made up her mind to retire at the same time as her partner, who only had a couple of years to go.

She thumbed her way through a discussion document about complaints from residents in the Drylaw area – as always, it wasn't about major crime or Mr Bigs but petty offences and anti-social behaviour. She sighed, wishing it would go away, and was pleased when Macallan provided a distraction by knocking at the door.

'For God's sake come in, Grace.' She lifted her head when Macallan stepped in. 'You've saved my life – or at least saved me from starting to reply to a document I don't really care about.' Her smile was warm, something she'd only learned through her relationship and finally having to share or compromise rather than control everything she did.

Macallan nodded in response. She was by nature a dour individual, but when she did manage the occasional smile, her face changed, and like all humans, the other spirit that inhabited her soul looked out on the world.

'How are you this morning, ma'am?' Macallan knew what the reply would be.

'Grace, how many times do I have to say it to a friend. First names when we're on our own… please!'

They hadn't seen each other since the Kangas briefing and the warmth of the reception seemed to ease Macallan's mood, though the tight smile told Tenant what she'd suspected for a while – her friend was struggling. Macallan rarely shared her feelings though, even with the few people who were really close to her, but Tenant thought her friend at least deserved to see she cared.

'You look tired, Grace. You okay?' Tenant regretted the weakness of the line as soon as she'd said it and noted the flicker in Macallan's eyes – she'd seen exactly where the ACC was going with the question.

'Fine, Elaine, just been really busy. There's never enough hours, more operations than the service can handle, and God knows we're still getting hammered from the press. The latest headlines about the force aren't going to help.'

Macallan had kicked the ball back at Tenant, deftly avoiding the prompt to speak about her personal life.

'Like a hole in the head… anyway, you know if I can help in any way, I will.'

She paused and Macallan smiled, this time with some warmth.

'You'll know about the shooting down in Newhaven last night. Strange one. We have four low-life bandits who actually came face to face with who we think was the killer, but make of it what you will.' Tenant paused and checked a note on her desk. 'I want you to take this one, Grace. I know you've enough on your plate, but there's complications here. The victim was a reporter – a good one by all accounts – and looked at as something of a rising star. A lot of her reporting was on political corruption and crime stories.'

'I read a lot of her stuff,' Macallan said, nodding. 'Good reporting, and the girl didn't mind getting her hands dirty. Apparently, she's a protégée of Jacquie Bell.'

Macallan left it there; her friendship with Bell was a sensitive subject as the force had always taken a negative view on 'off-the-record' relationships with journalists. It was a genuine friendship though – both women cared about each other, and on one occasion, early in Macallan's career in Scotland, she'd actually slept with the reporter – something she'd never been able to explain or sought to repeat. They used and supported each other professionally when it suited and kept the relationship as quiet as possible. People knew there was a friendship – Bell had done a feature of Macallan's history and career and had turned her into a high-profile figure in law enforcement – but not to the level anyone could use it against the detective.

'That's a handy start because Jacquie might be vital to building up a picture of what she was working on,' Tenant said. 'Anyway, the press will give us more grief over one of their own. If it's someone or an organisation trying to close down a story then we'll get pressure to resolve it. Freedom of the press and all that.' Tenant lifted a file from her desk and walked round to Macallan who was on her feet.

'Unusual here, but I saw enough intimidation of reporters in Northern Ireland. I have to take my hat off to some of those guys – they take hellish risks all on their own.' But dead reporters gave the impression that the police were impotent, and if they remained unsolved, the damage to the force was always substantial.

'This is all we have at the moment but you know better than I do how do this, so over to you.' Tenant handed her the file; Macallan took the folder without looking at it and turned to head for the door.

'Remember, Grace, keep me in the loop, and for God's sake, if you need anything please ask.' She put her hand on Macallan's shoulder and saw her friend's lips stiffen, as ever trying to stifle something.

'Of course, Elaine. It's appreciated.'

'What about the Kangas case? Or is it the Handyside case? Can you handle all you have?'

'Well we have a briefing this afternoon with the intelligence development team. Danny's been working on it, and we have our senior analyst Felicity Young involved now so should get a fuller picture soon. Do you want to sit in?'

'Why not? It takes me away from the pile of complaints I'm dealing with for a while.'

'I'll oversee the case, but Danny Oliver will do the Newhaven one day to day, and depending on how this afternoon goes, Pam Fitzgerald will take on Benny Green or whatever the hell this is.'

'What about Kangas himself?'

Macallan shook her head. 'Saying nothing so far and unlikely he will. Too much to lose and he can just sit it out here until he's released. He's been remanded and likely to be kept when he comes up again. We've got prints on the gun, DNA and so on, so we're sound for a conviction there at least. The Finnish team will monitor him again whenever he's back in Helsinki, and Europol are running a job on the contract killing so it won't fall off a cliff.'

Macallan walked out of the ACC's office and closed her eyes for a moment, trying to steady herself. She'd been handed a hard one and all she could do was keep coming back to Jack and what he meant to her. There was so much to worry about and the children were still so young.

She headed to the office and whatever the case might bring, excitement and doubts all battling for primacy in her mind. She felt like a drink; in fact she wanted to get drunk – that lovely delirium where, at least for a few hours, the real world all went away. Thank God she'd arranged to meet Harkins.

26

Macallan stepped out of the car with Danny Oliver and nodded to the uniform supervising entry to and from the crime locus in Newhaven. The police were treating it as two crime scenes – the site of the killing, including Gilhooley's home, and the area where the suspected killer had gone toe to toe with the local desperadoes.

The weather was foul. There was hardly any wind, but the air was raw and damp, and a grey mist hung low over the coast, where all colour seemed to have been transformed into no more than a mixture of greys. It didn't help Macallan's mood, and she hadn't said a word to Oliver on the journey over. He was uncomfortable with the silence, but he'd learned over the previous months that it had nothing to do with him and not to take it personally.

He remembered what his predecessor Lesley Thompson had told him: 'She's complicated, Danny, but you'll work it out eventually. Trust me, there's no one better to have on your side. If she's having problems, there's no way she'll discuss them. It's just the way she is, so trust her.'

A local DS, Jimmy Gordon, was waiting on their arrival. He'd been involved since the early hours and looked like he'd been dragged through a hedge sideways. Macallan knew him well, and he'd been attached to the MIT during the dating-site murders. Gordon was one of the best, although DS was as far as he'd ever go – or wanted to go, as he'd so often claimed. Normally, his appearance was immaculate, but the long night on the damp Newhaven streets had taken its toll.

Macallan often thought that a night with the dead seemed to pass something on to the men and women who tried to make sense of the first impressions of the ultimate crime. *They always seem dark under the eyes; pale, as if they've discovered an awful truth*, she thought. Every time she attended a locus, she thought of the old line: *Where do I live? With the ghosts – that's where we all end.*

Macallan liked Gordon – he was a bit stiff but dedicated to his bones. Although he might have been lacking in imagination, something the best detectives seemed to possess in spades, he made up for it in drive. He was almost the opposite of her friend Mick Harkins.

'Jesus, Jimmy, you look like you've been in a square go and lost… badly,' she said, and smiled for the first time in hours. Gordon tended not to do banter, but his serious yet sincere way of doing things always appealed to her.

Gordon liked Macallan right back, mainly because he was the kind of person who never had the complete confidence to make the really big calls. He liked a boss who could do that and would jump off a cliff for the ones he trusted. He thought Macallan looked weary too, but it had been too long a night to care who looked like what.

'What have we got – or rather not got – so far, Jimmy?' Macallan knew that most of the support systems would already have been working for hours, the scientific and legal processes kicking in like a machine – the days of a grim-faced detective trampling through the locus, flicking fag ash over the evidence were long gone. Macallan was already suited up, as was everyone else there; all she needed was to view the scene then make sure that all the necessary resources were in place.

'What about the intel side? Anything kicked off or do you need me to get that going?' she asked.

'They're on the case and have been working the deceased's mobile already, but the woman was a journalist so we can't dive right into her phone history.'

Macallan closed her eyes for a moment. The first pain in the arse had cropped up. Journalists had a form of protection against certain investigative methods and she guessed they'd have to go for a sheriff's warrant to get that line of investigation moving. Any delay in the first 'golden hours', as they were known, could cause serious problems further down the line. In the modern era, phone history was vital to the SIO in order to open up early lines of investigation.

'They're working on the warrant as we speak and should have that sorted as soon as we can get a hold of a sheriff to actually sign it. You know they won't be rushed, boss.'

'Too well, Jimmy.' Macallan smiled at the irreverence, but it was true. A Scottish sheriff would not be rushed – it didn't matter who it was. In the world they occupied, they were gods, and the mere death of a journalist would do nothing to disturb the natural order of things.

'Anyway, good work and that one is a priority.' Macallan was making notes as she went – the next pain in the arse was to transfer the decisions she made at the locus into the administration system so there could be no doubt who caught the flak if it all went wrong. The system demanded it.

'I want you to stay on the investigation, Jimmy, so get some sleep and see you later in the day. I'll square it with your boss.' Macallan was already thinking that she might need to add to the team she had and knew they were on the edge of a problem with the limited resources available.

Gordon looked pleased though, and that was enough for her.

Nancy Gilhooley's body was still in situ – the forensic teams would not move the victim till they were sure they had everything they needed, so that no evidence was destroyed by disturbing the deceased too early. This one was straightforward though, so they were almost ready to take Gilhooley's body to the mortuary, which was a relief for Macallan, who wanted to get things moving on the investigation rather than hanging about the locus.

She looked at the girl's body as they prepared to lift her and bit her lip at the waste of another young life. It didn't matter how often she watched the dead, it was the same reaction; the same question every time – why? So many times Macallan wished she had religion, just a simple belief that all would be well; that the big man in the sky had a plan that the simple punter just couldn't comprehend. But there was a story; they had the ending, and all they had to do was find the rest of the pages and discover why it had been so important to take this young woman's most precious gift. They would find some of it, maybe not all, but then whatever the rest of this drama was would hopefully come into the light. That was her job: find out why this young talented woman had died on a cold Edinburgh street.

What had she done to draw someone to her and take her young life?

Double tap then head shots, thought Macallan. It smelled like a pro. Most murders were solvable, committed by someone close to the victim – often a pissed-off partner who'd had enough and couldn't get their way. This was different, very different, and if it was a pro, it was already in the *might not get solved* bracket. She was ready though and she'd dealt with the pros; she knew they made mistakes – maybe few, but they were still human. They also had luck work against them at times, and it sounded like that was the case here, given the killer had ended up in a fight so close to the body.

She walked further up the taped-off street, Oliver alongside her. It suddenly dawned on her that she'd hardly said one word to him since they'd left the station. It was as if she'd walked out of a dark room hidden in her mind. *Jesus, what must this guy think? I'm treating him like he doesn't matter,* she thought and turned to him.

'What do you think, Danny?' She managed a smile and it did the trick – Oliver visibly relaxed at that small dose of warmth.

'I think we're in for some sleepless nights, headaches and another few years off our lifespan.'

'Too right. At this rate, I must already be dead and this is my punishment in eternity. Walking through endless crime scenes.'

It was an attempt at levity, but there was more in the banter than Macallan had intended, and she realised she was losing the ability to suppress her demons – her pain was beginning to leak like a wound that just wouldn't heal. She squeezed her eyes for a second and forced her thoughts back to the job.

The story they had was that whoever had ended Gilhooley's life had made a mistake – although one he couldn't have accounted for. He'd knocked the lights out of three heavyweight locals and that took class – it had just been bad luck for him that a fourth with army training in his background had appeared behind him. But doing those three by himself told them he had to be similarly trained.

Macallan saw the outline of the man – he was a shadow like Handyside, but he was there in her mind. He'd been forced to knuckle the three hoods and that should mean DNA, potentially from several sources, plus the rucksack.

Apparently, there were notes in the rucksack, but the lab wanted to examine the bag first so they would have to wait to work out the significance of what was in it. It sounded like that was what the killer had been after and could be a huge lead if that was the case. The killer might well be a pro, but the rucksack's loss would put the job in the bracket of major failure.

It was strange how things worked out, Macallan mused. Two professional killers turn up in Scotland and end up having their plans taken apart through a bit of good old-fashioned Caledonian Street violence. The thought made the edges of her mouth stretch into a tight little smile.

Their killer was no ghost – she could almost see him, and more importantly, she knew he would know that. Had he been clumsy or just plain unlucky? she wondered. There was nothing much to see where the fight had taken place, but they needed to have the picture in their minds. Briefing and maps were fine, but nothing beat seeing it for yourself.

'I'll come back later when it's dark, boss,' Oliver said. 'I want to see it at the same time it happened. Helps to see what light there is, the shadows.'

It was at that point that he remembered who he was speaking to and his cheeks reddened. 'You know what I mean.' He decided to stop digging.

'Good, Danny, just what I'd do myself. It's two different worlds, isn't it, the light and the dark? Never know what you might find in those shadows. Great minds, Danny, great minds. Let's head back to the factory, or do you want to stay here? You'll be taking the day-to-day strain on this, but I'm the SIO, so for God's sake keep me in the loop. If you need me or are struggling, call me day or night. I'm there.'

Oliver felt easier, like he was finally getting it with Macallan – when she said something, it mattered. Every word carried weight. Some officers just talked rehearsed shite or more often the acceptable lines that offended no one and created no ripples. He realised if he was struggling, he didn't need to pretend he was the man – there was somewhere to go and seek counsel.

'I'm going to hang on here for a while,' he told her.

'Good, Danny.'

She headed back to the car. She was feeling better – her mind was back on the job and there was a killer to run down. She was a detective, and that's what they did.

27

'So what do we know about the deceased?' Macallan looked across the desk in Leith Police Station. Jimmy Gordon and Danny Oliver had joined her, along with senior analyst Felicity Young, who'd been seconded to the team at Macallan's request because she'd worked on so many of her hardest cases and they seemed to have an almost telepathic understanding of what was required. Young lived with Macallan's friend Mick Harkins, and although they were an odd couple, it seemed to work.

Macallan had that thing going on in her head again – she sometimes imagined it as a worm gnawing away at the back of her mind when there was something out of sync. She trusted her instincts. The way modern detectives were trained, there was no room for *the nose, the gut feeling,* the way some people were able to sense something where pure logic hadn't taken them. As far as Macallan was concerned, sometimes, just sometimes, human instincts outperformed systems. *It's Pete Handyside, I know it,* she thought but kept that off the script for the meeting. She knew it had to be proved, or they had to be as certain as they could be that he was involved somewhere.

When he'd disappeared, there had been nothing to indicate what had happened to him. He must have had a well-planned exit strategy before Macallan tore down his organisation, and though she'd tried everything to pick up a scent, it was as if he'd never existed.

Gordon swigged from a tin of Coke and rubbed the back of his neck. He was tired out but knew he needed to fully brief the team taking over before he headed off for a few hours' sleep. He should have gone off in the morning but he was the kind of man who kept taking one more call or completing one more bit of paperwork that he felt just had to be done. Some people called it dedication; his ex-wife had called it grounds for divorce.

'Still sketchy at the moment. We found documents in the rucksack that have given us a start but not much else till you follow up with her work and family. That's still being examined for forensics at the lab.'

He flipped open his notebook and, as always, struggled to read his own writing.

'She's lived on her own at the address for a couple of years. We don't know about relationships, but there's not much in the house to indicate that as far as we can see, and no signs that someone else spent time there, but who knows? That seems to be confirmed by door to door with the neighbours. A couple hinted that she was gay because when there was a caller or she went out with someone, it was always a woman. She seemed physically close to one in particular who seemed to have spent the odd night at the flat, according to one very nosey neighbour.'

He looked up at Macallan to see if she wanted to ask anything. She just said, 'Okay,' so he continued.

'From open-source research, she was a journalist – and a good one by all accounts. Concentrates on the juicy stuff and won a couple of awards, even though she's still young in the game. I've typed up a summary of the notes before I go.'

'I thought you were going to get some sleep this morning, Jimmy?' Macallan knew it was the pot calling the kettle black and she wasn't being serious. Everyone in the room knew she was a serial offender. He just smiled, shrugged and carried on after swigging again from his Coke.

'As you know, there seems to be only one suspect at the moment. What we know so far is a pretty good physical description, if we can rely on the pissed-up neds. To be fair, the fourth one who put the suspect on the deck was more or less sober and seems reliable. So, our man is average height, good build, unruly dark hair combed hard back off his forehead. A couple of them describe a heavy-duty scar high up on the right side of his forehead. Obviously fit, and altogether it looks like our man is well trained.' He looked again at Macallan, who nodded.

She remained silent for a moment to let the images settle in her mind.

'You're right, Jimmy, sounds like we'd want to consider ex-military, specialised police officer or a real pro gangster. Of course, let's not shoot off in the wrong direction – we don't presume. It's quite possible a civvy could have the same skill set by other means. We keep all possibilities on the table and let's work the usual ones first. Despite the possibility that she was gay, it could still be the ex-boyfriend, a stalker or someone she'd investigated as a journalist.'

Macallan watched them take in her direction. Her worry on every investigation was following what seemed like obvious leads. They were often wrong, and chasing them had crashed major investigations in the past.

'Carry on, Jimmy.'

Gordon checked his notes again; he knew Macallan didn't thank people for missing details in briefings.

'One thing we're sure about though is the accent was West Scotland, but something about it struck ned number four, who's ex-military himself. You know that clipped accent our boys and girls seem to pick up in the services? Well this witness was sure that's how the killer spoke. Anyhow, we'll be really unlucky if we don't get DNA or some good forensic off the rucksack, the baseball cap and the neds' clothing.

'What about the weapon?'

'The ex-army ned seemed to know his stuff. He thinks it looked like a Russian Makarov, but we'd have to be wary of that one in the half light. Possible though, and not that rare.'

Macallan came in again – the mention of the weapon had set off the worm in the back of her head.

'Make sure we check ned four's army record to see how much we can trust his judgement. I know this weapon; it was used a lot in Northern Ireland by the paramilitaries, and you might remember the IRA commander Jock Davidson was killed a few years ago – that was a Makarov. It's been used in Dublin gangland killings as well.' *So maybe another connection to Dublin*? she thought. *Would make sense*. 'So those weapons are widely available, simple to use, reliable, and a pro would use one.'

As Macallan spoke, a memory flashed through her mind like a line of still frames. It was the aftermath of an army ambush on two terrorists who'd thought they were just planting a bomb then going home to their firesides. Macallan had provided the information from one of her sources, but the slaps on her back had done nothing to erase the memory of the terrorists' shattered bodies. One of them had tried to draw his weapon as the troops opened up. It had been a Makarov. She pinched the bridge of her nose, worried how tired she was already – the investigation had barely started. *What's new*? she thought.

'Anything from CCTV, Jimmy?'

'Nothing so far. The team were right on it, but apart from a grainy possible sighting, no joy. They'll keep at it, but I wouldn't hold my breath on that one. If he's a pro, the bike will be toast somewhere or other.'

Macallan nodded. 'Okay, I'll take what you've typed up and start calling everyone who needs to be called, plus the ones who just want to feel important.' She sighed and half-smiled. 'Some people think this stuff is glamorous – if only they knew.'

Gordon smiled in reply.

'Right, Jimmy, if there's nothing pressing, you get a few Zs and see you later in the day. You're officially on the team.'

Gordon wasn't going to argue – the thought of his bed was like a magnet. He was knackered and the job had a way to go, so he was going to take his rest when he could grab it.

As Gordon left the room, Macallan's phone buzzed – it was a text from Jacquie Bell, who wanted her to call ASAP about the murder.

'If you guys want to grab a brew, I've a call to make.'

They all nodded and headed out of her office.

When Macallan was on her own, she called Bell. She considered the woman one of her closest friends, although she hadn't seen her for a couple of months. That wasn't unusual though, given their careers, which seemed to swallow them both whole at times.

'How's my favourite detective?' As always, there was an irreverent edge to Bell, no matter what the occasion or how serious it was.

'Honestly, I'm up to the eyes, Jacquie. We're involved in the Kangas case, and that's led to other things. Now Nancy's murder. This is going to be a hard one. I was going to get in touch about Nancy, but what can I do for you?'

There was a pause on the line, and when Bell did speak there was something new in her voice that Macallan hadn't heard before. The irreverence had gone.

'Look, Nancy and I worked together; it involved some serious stuff and I think the killing was connected.'

What happened next threw Macallan completely – Bell broke down, sobbing like a child.

'Jacquie, what is it? Tell me – I'm your friend. Do you want to meet or come here?' She waited and finally heard her Bell gather herself together.

'Maybe better if I come to you. I'm sorry, Grace.'

Macallan sat back in her chair. In all the time she'd known the journalist, she'd never known her like this. It didn't seem possible for a woman who'd reported on politicians and criminals, giving her bosses nothing but headaches for the risks she ran.

'Listen, Jacquie, I've got a few things to do but I'll probably be free in about an hour. So get yourself here as soon as and we'll talk. Do you want someone to come and get you? It's no problem.'

'No, it's okay. Sorry, what the fuck am I like? Jesus, I must be getting old.' She sniffed loudly. 'I'll jump in a taxi and see you there. Do you have anything to drink?'

'Yes, rank coffee or rank tea – take your pick. See you soon.'

Macallan put the phone down and stared out of the window. This case was poisonous – she knew it in her bones. The pieces didn't form a picture yet and they didn't need to. Her instincts told her all she needed to know.

28

While Macallan thought on what was to come, Sam Taylor was arriving in London. He'd contacted no one, and kept the clean phone switched off so far. He had to make a decision whether or not he'd call Dolan – he'd gone back and forth on it so much his head was fucked, so for now it would have to wait.

Taylor got off the train at King's Cross. He felt as if his body stank with stale sweat, and it did, like everyone else who'd had to suffer the train's overheated carriages, but what was new? Overwarm or freezing cold – that was the lot of the regular commuter. Sweat was nothing to a soldier, but it was the added stress of the past hours that had made things worse.

He headed for a shit area close by where he'd stayed in the past, when he was still in the army. It had been an off-the-books job where the team had been tasked with quietly taking out an INLA cell in London. It was one of those specially selected for them – no trial and no mercy, with a death sentence guaranteed for the accused. There was no presumption of innocence. The government had wanted to send a clear message that it was time to come to the negotiating table and had decided selective kills could be written off in the press as organised crime warfare, so no one would care. As long as the terrorists who were determined to continue the fight got the message, that was the big picture – or so they'd been told.

He booked into the shittiest B & B in the area, which was no more than ten minutes' walk from the station. With a bit of luck, he could stay off the radar till he'd worked out what his position was. He knew he wasn't thinking straight and needed to work out a plan; monitor the press for what was being reported about Gilhooley's murder. They were bound to find DNA and confirm it was his, so eventually they would go public and name him. Then there would be a small window before his employers found out and he ended up with a target on his back. That's when it would be make-your-mind-up time.

His first stop was an off-licence, where he bought a bottle of cheap whisky and a dozen cans of the brew. Taylor knew he was in a bad place, with no backup and no plan B, so for now, getting pished in his room seemed as good a course of action as any.

29

Taylor woke at four in the morning, his head pounding from the mixture of tobacco, cheap booze and the stinking air of a room where the windows wouldn't open. His problems downloaded once more into his overheated brain, and sweat broke out all over his body.

He stumbled to the bathroom and swayed above the bowl he managed to miss by a mile, but who gave a fuck? The floor was filthy anyway and it would dry.

When he was done, he stared at the wreck in the mirror and said, 'Fuck it,' before drinking two glasses of water. He wished he had some toothpaste to help with the foul taste in his mouth.

Taylor lay back on the bed and decided he'd clean up later. He managed to fall asleep again for a while, but the terrors that haunted him were never far away.

In his dreams, he was walking through complete darkness, no stars or lights able to break into the black world he inhabited. All he could feel was his breathing, but he knew the team were nearby.

In his head, the name spun on a carousel – Conlan Regan. The name repeated again and again, and he knew the terrorist was somewhere in front of him in the darkness. He heard Billy Dolan's voice on the radio, shouting for help. He'd been discovered in his hide by the PIRA commander.

The rest of the unit appeared by his side; they looked as if they were illuminated from the inside. That's when he saw Dolan materialize in the darkness, blood pouring from his ear as he stabbed a man on the ground. His arm drove the knife into the man's body over and over again. Together, they pulled Dolan off the pulp that had once been human.

'Why the fuck are we killing him, Billy?' Taylor's voice seemed to play at half speed as Dolan looked round, his face a skull pushed forward, so close now that he could feel the other man's breath.

'Big picture, Sam. Always the big picture. By the way, you really fucked up this time, son.'

Taylor sat bolt upright, heaving in stale air and realised it was morning. 'Fuck's sake,' was all he said as the dream faded, giving way to sensations of thirst and discomfort. He was soaked, and he cursed again when he realised he'd pissed the bed.

30

As Taylor struggled with his hangover and the demons in his head, Pete Handyside walked out of his front door and scanned the street in the half light of morning. His senses were always on point in the early hours, and he made sure there were no watchers – no one with a loaded gun carrying the bullet that would take him out. There shouldn't be – he'd been ultra-careful. He wasn't even Pete Handyside now; Joe Stafford was who he'd morphed into – or at least that's what it said on his passport.

He'd created a completely new legend for himself and his family so any checks would throw up an almost perfect cover. Only the most sophisticated investigation could trace him back to the man still wanted for crimes that would put him away for the rest of his life. He'd gone on the run three years earlier, his ace up the sleeve that he'd planned for the day in advance. Everything had been in place, and they'd disappeared like dust in a storm. After six months living on the beautiful Croatian coastal town of Split, he'd realised he was safe and rebuilt a new criminal enterprise from scratch.

A year later, they'd moved again to Hampton and settled in a beautiful riverside house on the upper Thames.

He'd opened an office near Lambeth Bridge and built a legal and highly illegal business side by side. He'd thought about staying safe in retirement but knew that crime was what made him and what he was good at. More than that, it made him feel alive in a way that nothing else could, and he'd accepted that his drug of choice was risk. It was the only thing apart from his family that made him want to go on living.

He'd also accepted that Macallan had come within a hair's breadth of taking him down in his old life and so it followed that some other detective could do it too. But it was what it was, and he'd decided that he'd cross that particular bridge if and when he came to it. Only his wife knew the truth, and even then only part of it – she'd decided years earlier that the man she lived with and the man the authorities had called the number-one gangster in the north-east of England were different people. She'd rarely asked a question and that was how it would stay.

He started to run steadily, enjoying the quietness on the streets, the time to be by himself – to think alone. He pounded the road and ran the day's business through his head.

Sam Taylor seemed to have fallen off the radar, and that was on top of the story from Sandy Tait that he'd been in a street brawl near Edinburgh, pissed out of his mind. Dolan had been trying to trace him but without success.

Apart from Dolan, Handyside had never met the rest of the team in order to keep a partial firewall in place. Whatever was happening with Taylor was a concern but not a crisis, although in his business, missing contract killers could mean problems. *But what*? he wondered.

He'd already spoken to Sandy Tait, who'd confirmed that Taylor had lost discipline. The Mayfield fight might have been funny on its own, but the back story to it wasn't what he wanted to hear. The rest of the team were hard, disciplined men who kept match fit – but the difference was they had women and kids in their lives. That was important.

The only ace he had was that the 'clean' phone Taylor had been supplied with on his last job had a tracking bug installed. Handyside had deployed them on all the contractors' phones he supplied to Dolan as insurance – just in case something like this problem with Taylor came up. There was the risk that Taylor might ditch it of course, but no one had worked out so far that the phones allowed Handyside to find them – or that they could also help indicate whether anyone had turned rogue or met with the law. The mics could be turned on for conversation. It wasn't always top quality if the phone was in a bag or pocket, but it all helped.

He knew all he could do was monitor the situation as the days went on, but there was no need to press the panic button yet. His other problem was slightly more pressing – the Russians were pissed off about the failure with Kangas, although all he'd arranged was the weapon and the option to use Sandy Tait.

That was how the business worked – on most occasions, Handyside would control and organise the whole contract, but because of his connections in the UK, he often provided partial support to a job organised by other contacts. In the Kangas case, it was the Russians. He'd been in bed with them since his time in Croatia, and they had a lucrative relationship that included various criminal enterprises. It had worked well so far, but he knew they were the most hard-nosed bastards on God's earth and didn't exactly celebrate failure. Which meant the other guy paid or lost out. The collapse of the Kangas job wasn't down to him, but they were looking for a scapegoat. They'd wanted to send a message that the target couldn't fuck them about. They'd consigned a fortune in counterfeit goods to him and he'd ripped them off.

The last phone call from Moscow had said it all. *'It's unacceptable, Joseph. We should have known better than to employ someone from Finland. These peasants always fuck up at some time.'*

The historic and deep-rooted hatred between the two countries came up every time Finland was mentioned, but Handyside didn't want to get anywhere near the middle of it, or the geopolitics of the region.

He'd realised he'd probably become too involved with the Russians. It was ideal when he'd first got back into the business, and they'd been profitable clients, but he'd set up some good business lines in other places now and wanted to loosen his ties to them. There was no panic. This was his job – to steer his way through problems that would have most men on their knees crying for their mothers. The Russians only had themselves to blame; Handyside had fulfilled his part of the job with Kangas.

As for Kangas himself, he'd remained silent so there was no need to worry on that front. Sandy Tait had told him that the Finn had remained tight-lipped when he was interviewed. The gun the detectives had recovered had yielded DNA so he was unlikely to be bailed, and Tait was sure he was looking at some serious time inside, so that was probably okay. He'd called Benny Green and told him that he should be safe enough but to be on guard with the law, who might pick up a connection to him. Green was another contact who'd actually been put in touch with Handyside through the Russians. They had a long connection with the Edinburgh businessman through his trade in sex workers.

After about twenty minutes, Handyside started to sprint, wanting to feel his legs burn – to push himself to the edge as always. It was a bit harder than it used to be. He was twenty pounds heavier than he'd been in his Newcastle days, though weightlifting meant it was nearly all additional muscle. His hair was dappled grey, and that alongside his beard and contact lenses did enough so anyone who knew him would have to look closely to recognise the man he'd once been.

Back at home, when he stripped to shower, his wife came out of the bedroom and kissed him. She was enjoying their settled life in this beautiful area in the London suburbs. She loved the life they now had although she always had to be on her guard and worked hard to maintain her own new identity. The likelihood of a third chance was doubtful if things went wrong again.

'How was your run?'

It was one of the little questions that they could live without but was part of the fabric of a loving relationship. She'd known exactly what he was from the start, and they hardly ever touched on the subject, both wanting to keep family and the business separate. The man she knew was kind and loving, the perfect father, but she saw his strength. She didn't want to know the other man.

'Good one, lass, but I feel the extra weight when I'm running.'

'I like the extra muscle. Always thought you were too thin anyway.' She kissed him again. 'Handsome lad – want some eggs?'

She headed for the kitchen, knowing the answer would be, 'You know me, pet.'

31

Macallan was joined by Elaine Tenant before meeting with the rest of the team. She'd decided to disclose the call from Jacquie Bell, who in all probability would turn out to be a witness. She'd speak to her first, but after that it would have to be on the record, and someone would have to sit for hours taking a statement. It was the tortuous, dull part of the job never seen on TV dramas, but the truth was that the vast majority of time on murder investigations was spent sitting in quiet rooms writing – for hours, sometimes even days – to take down what people knew.

'Let's wait to see what she has to say first before we tell anyone else. I've never heard Jacquie like that, so it must be serious. She's coming in right after this so I'll brief you when I've seen her and we can decide what it means.'

Tenant nodded. 'That makes sense. Where are we with the notes found in the rucksack?'

'The lab is finished with the examination and it's on its way here. Apparently, there's an A4 notebook half full of some kind of information. Whether it's all on the same subject or various stories she was looking at, we don't know yet. As soon as it arrives, Felicity is going to get to work on it.'

'This case has *interesting* written all over it,' Tenant said. 'Right, for now, where are we with the Kangas case – or is it Benny Green or Pete Handyside?'

Tenant was trying to introduce some levity, but it didn't quite work – Macallan's eyes told her that.

The detective stood up, called in the rest of the team and they did the prelims first before settling down for the main event.

'Danny, your shout, so what have we got?' Macallan nodded to Oliver.

'Well, we've worked away on it, though Felicity and a couple of researchers have done the lion's share of work. I'll hand you over to her after my bit. As you know already, Kangas was saying nothing, and I mean nothing. He got Sandy Tait on his case and that's interesting on its own. Number one on the policeman's hate list, and we know that Tait has sources inside the job. He'll probably get some information on what's going on so we need to keep it tight. Tait must have been recommended by someone who knew what they were doing. According to the guys who dealt with him, Kangas asked for Tait by name so he'd obviously been instructed beforehand what to do if the job went belly up. Anyway, Tait isn't going to tell us how that happened, is he?

'After Kangas had his wounds patched up, he appeared at court and has been remanded so unlikely he'll get out with the seriousness of the charges. He's still saying nothing and I can't see that changing. So might be a dead end. I'm going to have a discreet look at what we know about Tait, and before anyone says it, of course we'll be careful and within the law. We know that our friends in the legal profession would be screaming for blood if we dared to break the rules on their privileges.'

'Quite right, Danny. We don't back off because someone is a lawyer – or anything else for that matter. As long as we're working within the rules then no problem.'

Macallan wanted Oliver to know she was supporting him but cursed Tait repeatedly in her mind.

He nodded and carried on. 'We've looked at Benny Green's operation, and the legal side of the business is much bigger than we thought, never mind the illegal. Intelligence markers on him have cropped up over a number of years from various sources. Europol have flagged him a couple of times where his number appeared in call traffic in investigations by the police in Amsterdam and the BKA in Germany. They were working on targets involved in human trafficking, mainly Eastern European women, so that would make sense given Green's involvement in the escort business and prostitution.

'His number or numbers associated with his businesses have also appeared in a couple of DEA cases in the States, but that's not hugely significant, and to be honest, he's been talked about in the east of Scotland for years as a big player and yet nothing much has been done about it apart from talk in the canteens. Think he's been in the *too hard to catch* bracket, and he seems to sit just below the radar – he's clever and been smart in devoting so much to the legal side of his operations. That's what the good ones do. So if he's dirty and we have such a dearth of intelligence, it either means we're completely wrong about him or he runs a very tight ship. If that's the case then he has to be a ruthless bastard. It's the only way he could manage.

'Anyway, a lot to be done before we have a hypothesis or firm conclusions. Felicity's now working on him as well, so we'll see how that goes over the next few days.'

He waited for any comment then carried on.

'Now lastly, we've had the voice patterns of the man speaking to Kangas compared with the radio interviews with Pete Handyside a few years ago. It's not conclusive but it's very likely the same person.'

'How sure are we, Danny?' Macallan tried to sound calm; she didn't want them to see how tense she was.

'Best guess is ninety per cent,' he said, checking his notes.

'Okay,' Macallan replied. 'So nothing proved, but we have a start with Dublin and the weapon. Let's work the intelligence and evidence. If Handyside is involved, it'll take us to him with a bit of luck and a lot of hard work. Is that it for now?'

Oliver agreed and handed over to Young, who just confirmed that she'd started on the phone analysis on a couple of numbers they had for Benny Green.

'Of course, if he's as careful as he sounds then he may well use clean phones for illegal transactions. I do wonder about two separate contract killers turning up here though. It may just be coincidence, but Sandy Tait representing both men? I just wonder if that's a coincidence too far.'

Macallan agreed. 'I'm wondering about this as well, Felicity, but we don't want to be led down the wrong path. Let's see what we can prove or make reasonable assumptions about.

'So, we have the same lawyer and probably the same kind of gun. Kangas is a highly trained individual, and I know there may be no connection, but Europol is running its project on European contractors, which is handy.

'I'll liaise with the British office in Europol to see if there's anything of interest there,' Oliver said quickly, keen for an excuse to chew the fat with his old office.

'You can help Felicity make contact there. You're not that long away from the place.' Macallan smiled. 'Don't think you're getting a jolly back there though. You've had your share of Holland.'

Oliver smiled back, remembering all the good times he'd had over there – and that was when he remembered one very particular night six months prior.

'Look, this might be nothing, but there was an incident in Amsterdam not long before I came back. We might be adding up the wrong numbers, but just to come in on Felicity's point…' And Oliver recounted the story of the Scottish contractors and their attempt to take out the Dutch agent – leaving out the state he'd been in when he'd picked up the phone.

Young scribbled as he spoke, and the small group of officers began to bond into a focused team. The game had started and they all felt it. Young asked Oliver a couple of follow-up questions and he reassured her that it was all on the Europol system and they could obtain the intelligence log from the London end.

'To be honest, we finished up with a dead end and could find nothing on our intelligence systems in the UK. But you never know.'

'Okay, thanks, Danny. Might be nothing, but as always we follow the evidence. Now, the next thing is Dublin. We need to make contact with them so just leave that to me. If they want a meet, I'll invite them here or we'll go across and enjoy a Guinness or two. They have more than enough problems there with gang wars; the Garda have some serious characters to deal with.'

Macallan closed her notebook. 'Right, boys and girls, we have a lot to do and it's all in bits at the moment, but you know how it goes. The picture will fill in if we do it right. Elaine, can I speak to you for a minute before you go?'

32

The team left Macallan's office, and when they were on their own, Tenant grinned.

'I'm glad I was never a detective, Grace. What a task you have there, but you have a great team round you. What else can I do for you?'

Macallan hesitated before she spoke, hoping Tenant would understand what she wanted to do.

'Listen, Elaine, we'll do the murder briefing this afternoon, and this might sound a bit off the wall, but if Handyside is involved, we have to think outside the box. I know what makes him tick. He's brilliant in his own way.'

'You sound like you might admire him. I don't get that.' It wasn't a criticism; she just didn't understand.

Macallan carried on. 'He has few weaknesses, but he does have an ego and he's the ultimate control freak. He has to be in some kind of business because I just don't think he can leave the game behind. For men like him, it's about more than money. I think I'm unfinished business with him, and even though we could call it a draw after last time, he'll see it as a challenge if he knows I'm on his case and that would be a mistake on his part, a distraction. We have this press conference on the murder later today so what about also mentioning the Kangas case at the same time – keep it a bit vague but sexy and say that we're following important lines of investigation both here and abroad. We're handling both cases so no reason I can't do it. Put me in front of the cameras and hopefully he'll see it. I want him to know I'm the opposition again. I haven't come up with what I'll say, but I want to send a message that I know it's him.'

'Won't that spook him and send him underground again?' Tenant asked.

'I'll say it again – he's never been away from the game and will keep himself informed. It's just that we haven't been able to see him. If he's involved in this kind of business, it can't have happened overnight.'

'Does this put you in any danger? I wouldn't be happy about that, Grace – you've been through enough already.' She paused. 'And so has Jack.'

Macallan's mouth tightened at Tenant straying onto private property.

'With the greatest respect, this isn't about my private life. You asked me how you could help and I've just told you.' Macallan couldn't hide it any longer – the strain on her private life and the job had spilled over.

But as soon as the words were out, it felt like the pressure had come off, and she pulled back.

'I'm sorry, Elaine. Not having a go at you.'

'Listen, we're friends. I've known you for a long time now and you keep the Grace Macallan we all see pretty well locked down, but I see it. I'm no detective but no fool either. What's up? For once in your life, let me help you beyond allocating resources. You're a human being, and my God you're going to have to face it one day. That day's not far off for both of us.'

Somehow, agreeing there was an elephant in the room made Macallan relax a little and she explained that she was worried she'd been neglecting Jack. She didn't mention the confrontation they'd had, or any of her other problems.

For a moment she looked beaten, and Tenant worried that she'd given a mammoth task to the wrong detective. She'd hate to admit it, but she'd done it before.

'Do you still love him, Grace?'

'Of course.'

'Does he still love you?'

'I think so.'

'Right, well tell him that. Before this investigation heats up, sit down and tell him that. Sort it, instead of trying to bring down every criminal in Scotland. Make a plan, for God's sake, so when this is finished dump the kids somewhere – on us if you like – and get a few days away with your man. You know wine, whispered intimacies and all that kind of stuff.'

They both looked at each other and laughed at the same time.

'Elaine Tenant, never mind me, but how you've changed,' Macallan said, grinning.

'Do we have a deal?' Tenant prompted.

Macallan nodded in agreement but still seemed troubled.

'You can have your press conference and send whatever love message it is to Handyside if it is him.'

Tenant got up to leave the room.

'Elaine.'

Tenant saw the look that said please.

'I'm listening, Grace.'

'Look, obviously you've noticed I'm struggling a bit, but just between us, I'm doing something about it. It's hard for someone like me to share, but I trust you.'

'And I trust you. You know that. Just remember you're worth saving.' She grinned, leaned forward and gripped Macallan's hand for a moment.

It surprised both of them – their friendship had never involved touching. This small gesture drew them closer, confirming trust in a world that both of them had found difficult to believe in for different reasons. They'd both escaped their old lives for something better, and Tenant didn't want to see Macallan go back there. She was also fond of Jack and the children, so there was more than the detective in front of her to consider.

'I've been struggling for ages, though maybe nothing new there I suppose. Anyway, I've arranged to see a shrink but outside the job. I just want to unload this stuff, so I'll give it a try. But I'm scared, because I realise I might lose everything if I don't do this. Jack just wants us to be happy, and we were, but I've slipped into the old shell, as if I'm not trusting him. It's the way I am. Jack's all for it – he gave me the push actually – so I already feel a bit better. What do you think?'

'I think you've done the right thing, and we'll keep it within these four walls. Promise me this though: when we get this one wrapped up, you have that time away with Jack. We'll take the kids and spoil them to bits. They love the dogs. Are you okay for this case though?'

'Of course. It's what stirs me – you know that. And I want it. This is something I've been carrying for too long – I just need to rearrange my life and get it all out of my head. You know I never really got Belfast out of my system. Dampened it down for a while, but it was just locked away.'

Macallan looked away for a moment, feeling guilty. She knew she was leaving out the greatest sin of all – Dominic Grainger.

'It's a different job now, Grace – we can admit when there's a problem. If it's any conciliation, I had years of treatment for depression. How do you like that?' Tenant said it easily, but the revelation surprised Macallan again. She stared at her friend.

'Jesus, Elaine, I never would have guessed.'

'See, that's typical of you detectives – you think we who serve the queen in uniform have easy lives.'

She stood and Macallan followed her lead. They hesitated then put their arms round each other, and Macallan felt the weight drop from her shoulders. The disclosure had been so much easier than she'd imagined.

'Right, I've got letters to write to politicians and the public that will make no difference to anything, but such is the lot of an executive officer. Now go catch your killers, Superintendent.'

33

Jacquie Bell walked in the door of Macallan's office enjoying the moment after so long apart. The bond between them was as strong as ever, and despite Bell's breakdown on the phone, she seemed more like herself now. As usual she asked if Macallan had any booze, though she already knew the answer. It was just part of the ritual.

'Well you can keep that shite you pretend is tea or coffee. Is it something in the police to prove how tough you are, drinking that sludge?'

'It's public services, Jacquie; it's broke, with no money even for the simple things in life.'

They sat down and studied each other, looking for the small changes that always take place whenever too much time passes between meetings. They could see the years on each other, but they were both in good shape physically, and Bell still looked like a Hollywood star despite a lifestyle that should have had her going heavy on the make-up every morning.

'So, what's up, Jacquie? Tell me about Nancy.'

'Nancy and I were friends…' Bell hesitated and wished she could smoke. She sat back, sighed and ran her fingers through her thick dark hair. 'I know Nancy had a regular girlfriend, but I'll come to that. I really liked her – a lot, and as you know, I don't like people easily.'

Bell heaved another sigh. Macallan could see the strain on her friend and tried to comfort her.

'Okay, Jacquie, but obviously we'll need to take a statement eventually.'

This was the first time the initial minutes of a meeting with her friend hadn't consisted purely of banter – mostly at Macallan's expense – and it was making her tense. Bell was the eternal optimist who always thought things would all work out in the end – and do so the way she wanted. People, and some hard ones at that, turned to putty in her presence, and men in particular didn't stand a chance. Her looks and personality saw to that, which was ironic given that she was gay, although she kept that quiet for business reasons.

'I was trying to give her a push up, and she was a terrific young reporter. Thing is, she was working on a story involving a team of ex-soldiers who'd been used for illegal killings during the Troubles, then in the Middle East. Three of the team were Scots so it was a big one for us and relevant with the part the West, and particularly Glasgow, played for the Loyalists during the Troubles. Nancy first got wind of the story through the relationship she was involved in, but I'll come back to that. She took the lead, but our boss wanted me to support her as it was a bit above her pay grade or experience. It was all hers though. My name wasn't on the story; I wanted her to get her head into it so I'd just help pull the strings. I was working on another story anyway so it suited both of us. The plan was that when I'd put my story to bed, I'd step in and work with Nancy when we were getting into the hard stuff.'

Bell took a pack of tissues out of her bag and dried her eyes. 'I fucked up, Grace. Thought she was going to get her name in lights. Strange, because I've never let myself get too attached to colleagues, but she was special. I should never have let her get in so deep. She didn't have the experience of this shit. I do.'

'Hang on, Jacquie.' Macallan pulled open her drawer and produced a bottle of her favourite Speyside. She was sure Bell would take the piss out of her somewhere down the line for lying about having it, but her friend obviously needed something to take the edge off. She had a glass that looked like it needed a wash but poured regardless.

'Just the one glass?' Bell asked.

'Nothing for me.'

Bell took the glass, slugged down half its contents and thanked Macallan before carrying on.

'The story kicked off over a year ago. Nancy had a source who works in intelligence gathering in the army. More than a source. They were an item – became involved almost from the moment they met. Before you ask, I never met the source and don't even know her name. All I know is that they met at a security conference. Obviously, an army intelligence officer sleeping with a reporter might not go down well in the military, and Nancy said this woman was a bit fragile about it coming out. Anyway, she told Nancy a story about a team who'd operated in Northern Ireland at the end of the Troubles who were tasked with taking out leading paramilitaries who weren't playing ball with the peace process.

'There's always been stories about this,' Macallan replied. 'I heard things during my time in the Branch, and undoubtedly it happened. Don't want to trivialise it, but it's not new – there are all sorts of issues still going on over the water with army killings, or murders depending what side you sit on.'

'This was a bit more than that, Grace. I know what you're saying, and to be honest that was my first reaction, but the point was that this source said that they carried on in the Middle East till they were basically shown the door – when the army began to worry it might all come out. It was obvious there'd be all sorts of enquiries into the Troubles and the army thought they were just too dirty, so they were all encouraged, for want of a better word, to leave the service at the same time. After that, intelligence had picked up indicators that this team had moved on to contract killings. Working internationally. In the original team of five, three were Scots, so quite rightly Nancy's nose was twitching, although she was worried that it would just be too complicated getting a story together.'

Bell swallowed the rest of the whisky; it must've been helping because she seemed calmer now. 'She asked my advice and we put it to our boss. I was surprised because he didn't tell her to fuck off and stick to something with a bit less potential for fallout. I was up to my eyes in the ex-First Minister's travails and a police death in custody so all I could do was advise. I know the boss was a big fan of Nancy though and thought she was up to it with me pointing her in the right directions.'

Macallan interrupted. 'Listen, Jacquie, before you go any further, I can't keep this off the record. You do know that – you have to make a statement.'

'That's okay, Grace; I get that.'

She carried on. 'The army contact was a good source to kick it off and she provided the names of a few PIRA and INLA dissidents who'd been killed or gone missing where no one had admitted responsibility and intelligence had drawn a blank. From there, Nancy kept digging and started to ruffle some feathers. She managed to get the name of one of this team – a man – an ex-para who seemed to have been involved in this stuff. Nancy got in touch with him and it sounded like he was going through a bit of a breakdown. Drink, drugs, all the old stuff. The demons of the past, the guilt, but you know all about this.'

She paused and looked at Macallan, who felt that familiar tug in her chest. *The demons I know too well,* she thought and nodded.

'Well it turns out Nancy's charm and the guy's guilt problems worked out and he agreed to talk. Nancy asked me to go along to one of the meets. The plan was I'd not be named but just introduced as her boss. So we had a meeting with the guy in a neutral site – a café in Glasgow city centre. He was a bit of a mess, a broken man – hard to believe he'd been a bit of a Rambo in the past. He told us enough, and for all this guy was in the past, he was a frightened creature – tortured. He seemed riven with guilt and wanted to get it all off his chest. You know, he told us he was afraid for his soul.

'Anyway, the story is that he'd been part of the team in Northern Ireland and he could provide names, dates and all the rest of the shit they'd been involved in. We asked him about the contract killings after they'd left the army, and he said he'd gone for it at the start but withdrawn after the first couple because his "bottle had crashed" to use his own words. One had been a mother of two – he'd found out later she was part of a clean-up job and had committed no sin of her own. Collateral fucking damage to use his words again. So far so good.'

'Why didn't you come to me?' Macallan asked her friend, frustrated. 'I know about this stuff, understand it, and to be honest, you don't.' This was way outside Bell's comfort zone.

'I thought about it but decided we should flesh out the story. I'm a reporter – that can't change. Anyway, we thought we were heading for a Crime and Legal Affairs Journalism award. Delusional or what?' She managed a grim smile.

'Been there done that, Jacquie.' Macallan wanted to reassure her friend as disclosing seemed to be lifting the weight from her – she was slowly transforming back into herself.

'The thing is that the man – Tam Hunter is his name, by the way – disappeared last week, and I mean *disappeared*. He wasn't answering the phone, and Nancy tried his door a couple of times. The worry is that he'd mentioned to Nancy that one of his old team visited him from time and they would usually get seriously pissed up. So I don't know if he's run off at the mouth to this other guy. He referred to him as Sam and apparently he's quite the hard nut.'

'Do you want a break, Jacquie? We can have a coffee if you like.'

'No, it's fine. I feel better now we're speaking. A problem shared and all that.

'We – or rather Nancy – had gathered a lot of information and Tam Hunter would have really taken us inside what the story actually was. I was all for carrying on, and Nancy started to contact what family he had – which wasn't much – but they didn't care and had no idea where he was. His friends were just pissheads he would meet in the local boozers, so they were a waste of time.

'I was up to my eyes with the other stories and hadn't seen Nancy for a few days. All I know is that she tried to call me the night she died, but I was out on a story and never got a hold of her. I did text her – told her I was involved and that I'd get back to her for a meet at the weekend.'

She sat back relieved. 'That's it all, Grace. I just feel responsible, like I let her down.' She looked at the floor as if she was waiting for judgement.

'What can I say?' Macallan replied. 'We all get it wrong and no one more than me. Look, she was carrying notes and the kill seemed highly professional, so it may be the way to go for us. Let's see – the documents are being examined right now.' She lifted the phone and asked Felicity Young to bring them to her office.

'That's her stuff,' Bell confirmed when Young placed them on the desk. Each page was in a separate cellophane cover.

'I need to get one of the team to take a statement from you, Jacquie, and it could take a couple of days. During that process, we can show you the documents to see if you can throw any light on what we're looking at.'

She left Bell in her office, called Oliver and Fitzgerald and gave them the job to get on to Glasgow right away and arrange a team to go to Hunter's house with them.

'I want this done now. The chances are that something has happened to this man so we need to find out where he is as soon as possible.'

She made the arrangements with Bell to get her statement under way and examine the documents properly.

They both felt better – the revelations had cleared the air, and Macallan now had a solid lead. A hard one to resolve, and if it was what it seemed then Macallan was taking on a different foe this time. This was no case of a bitter lover, a ruthless psychopath or corrupt police. Whoever these men were, they would be skilled in the dark arts. *But then*, Macallan thought, *so am I*. She'd trained in the same school and had fought in the murky world of counterterrorism.

She suddenly felt exhilarated, a rush of energy that was like a drug hit – she was in the game and this one would take her to the edge; the place where she came alive. Few wanted to inhabit that space, but she did, and she knew the men she was looking for were exactly the same – only they worked with no rules.

34

As Macallan worked on the way ahead for the job, Pam Fitzgerald drove through to Glasgow with Danny Oliver in the passenger seat. It turned out that the duty DCI in Glasgow was Lesley Thompson, Oliver's predecessor in the Edinburgh MIT. He was pleased as he knew she'd been close to Macallan ever since the Fettes bombing that had almost taken their lives.

He was quiet for a while as he turned over the mass of problems they were facing. It was a big test for him, and although Macallan was in overall charge, his role as DCI was crucial in making things work. Macallan couldn't do it all, so he had to make it happen on the ground. Much as she loved to get out with the troops when she could, she had to keep the whole ship working in tandem.

The HOLMES system and its administration team, the analysts, an intel unit and operational detectives were working non-stop, and although they'd been working full-on since he'd returned from Europol, this case was different. He was a confident detective, but he was thankful Macallan was at the helm because there was so much potential for it to go wrong, and he knew her experience would be worth its weight when the wheels started to wobble.

When they arrived in Ruchazie, Lesley Thompson greeted them warmly.

'This sounds like the case from hell, Danny. Trust Grace to draw this one – she's like a magnet for the tough ones. Still, let's get on with it and see if we can find our man. Our team are going round the neighbours as we speak, but no one's seen or heard from him for days – seems he kept to himself. We did get a decent description from one of the neighbours who saw a man leaving Hunter's flat the other day though. Can't be certain what day it was, but the guy sounded like a reasonable witness and gave a good description. The bad news is the flat below reported a dodgy smell to one of our team, so be prepared. We've brought plenty of protective suits if the worst comes to the worst.'

When they arrived at the tenement flat, the whole place seemed to signal despair. The front garden was strewn with rubbish, and they'd already attracted an audience of locals, hoping for something to break the monotony of their everyday lives.

They tested the door then Thompson tried a number of shouts through the letter box before drawing herself back, her face puckered up.

'Jesus, it's ripe in there. I think we have a problem. We've a warrant but I think preservation of life and all that gives us the right to force entry anyway.'

She turned to the heavyweights behind her. 'Right, boys,' she said, waving to the two search team officers, who stepped towards the door with their metal ram. It went first time, and they recoiled when the air from inside wafted past them.

Thompson held them all back. 'First, we suit up before we go in there – we treat this as a possible crime scene.

Once inside, there wasn't much doubt about what had happened. Tam Hunter hadn't helped by leaving the heating on, and with the relatively mild spell of weather they'd been having on this side of the country, the place was moving with insects. He'd collapsed on his right side, and the gaping wound at his neck had bled into the old cloth sofa – now black thanks to the stain of his life blood.

'Right, let's get a doctor here pronto to pronounce life extinct, but I don't think he's going to have much trouble with that one.'

Thompson immediately issued orders to seal the locus and preserve whatever evidence was there. It was a murder scene and the priority was not to disturb anything till the technical officers had done their job.

'Looks like you'll be working with us, Lesley,' Oliver said. 'Has to be linked to the Gilhooley murder in Edinburgh. Don't like to presume but it seems a reasonable assumption.'

'It'll be good to work with Grace again, at least,' she replied. 'I'll need to get briefed up on your evidence through there.'

'Can I have a look at this description of the man seen leaving his flat, Lesley? I'll need to give Grace a call and she'll ask for this.'

Macallan would have all the right questions, so Oliver wanted to make sure he had the right answers.

35

Taylor had sobered up but still felt like shit. The temptation to continue his drinkathon was strong, but he had limited funds, so sooner or later he'd have to face the future. After that, if he was flashed the red card, he could just drink himself to death or put a bullet through his brain and be done with it.

He stared in the grimy mirror again and thought, *Who the fuck is that*? Where had the soldier gone? His old life had burned the evidence of itself into the lines carved in his face. He never used to think about the past; he'd always been able to lock the memories away in the same place he had his abusive childhood, stuffing them away as if they'd never happened.

Taylor's problem was that the vault was full and what was inside was escaping. He was a fuck-up, and the future wasn't a place he wanted to dwell on.

His friends – or what might pass for friends – were just other pissheads, so they were no help, and the only person he'd kept in touch with from the old days had been Tam Hunter – and that was only because he'd been as messed up as Taylor. He thought again about how this whole mess had started just a week earlier; now Hunter was gone, and he'd be haunted by it till his grave.

Once every few weeks, he'd go visit Hunter, who was the only one of his squad he'd ever been close to. Both were single men, and both had never liked crowds.

Taylor cursed him again and gripped the edge of the sink, remembering how off his head the man had been.

'I can't do it now, Sam,' he'd said. 'Head's fucked up an' God will judge me.'

Taylor had thought it was just the drink till Hunter had blurted out the truth about his meetings with Gilhooley. Taylor had wanted to kill him there and then, and once Hunter had told him he'd given her Taylor's name, he'd realised he had no other choice.

'You're just like me, Sam. You're better than these bastards we worked for. This is how we clear the slate.' Hunter had been so drunk he'd struggled to stay coherent, tears streaming down his face.

Taylor had played along till he had all the details he needed and knew just who this reporter was.

'Gimme your glass, mate, an' I'll get a refill,' he'd said, taking himself into the kitchen so he had a moment to clear his head. The shock of Hunter's revelation had cut through the effects of the booze, but he needed a minute to think.

When he checked back, he'd seen Hunter was almost asleep on the sofa, so he'd drawn the combat knife he always carried on him, walked quietly behind the sofa and sliced open the throat of the man he'd been through so much with His free hand had sat over Hunter's mouth till his body stilled.

Eventually he'd eased his grip and let the body sag like a broken ventriloquist's doll. Then he'd gone through to the bathroom to clean up.

Now, Taylor looked away from the mirror and the memory of the man he'd killed. He felt numb with what he'd done and trapped in a situation that might have no way out.

He shook his head, trying to clear it, and went over it all again to be sure he'd been careful. Ideally, he would have torched the flat because his DNA had to be everywhere, but that might've set the whole building up and killed people who had no part in all this – kids even. And he knew he'd prefer to just shove the gun in his mouth rather than live with those kinds of ghosts.

36

When he was cleaned up, Taylor left the B & B and walked to a half-decent café he knew near King's Cross station, where he enjoyed a full fat meal that calmed his acidic stomach. When he was done, he headed back to his room, showered and slept again till midday. When he woke the second time, he felt a bit more human, and his head had cleared. He headed out, walked for an hour to get the blood flowing, then went to a Turkish barber he remembered from the past.

'A shave, pal, and when you're at it, shave the head as well, nice and short. Want a new look for the girlfriend.'

'You'll be a new man, sir. Sit back and relax.'

The barber was friendly and clearly loved his trade, but Taylor didn't want to talk and showed it.

The shave was fabulous, the hot towels felt wonderful and he wished he could just lie there forever.

'Would you like a head massage?' The barber was matter-of-fact about the offer. In the past, Taylor would have told him to fuck off and stick to the original task, but he surprised himself by saying, 'Why not?'

The Turk knew exactly what he was doing – it was like sex through his head, and Taylor wondered why he hadn't done it before. When it was done, the chair was pushed upright and when he looked in the mirror, he wondered who the new guy staring back at him was.

'You look good, sir. Like a younger man. Your lady will love the change.'

The barber obviously took pride in his work, and Taylor thought it must be wonderful if all you needed to worry about was a customer's reaction to a haircut.

'Good job.' He gave the barber a decent tip and told him he'd see him again, which was highly unlikely.

Taylor felt clear-headed again, although his mouth was dry. He resisted the temptation to head for a boozer and ruin it all, and walked to Lewis Cubitt Park, where he bought some water and coffee before finding a quiet spot where he could work out his next move.

Although it was cool, the sun had come out and the grass was dry, so he sat below a tree that gave him a good view of the area around him. Everything seemed in order, so he sipped the coffee and water and worked out how he needed to play things.

He had no idea what was happening in Edinburgh; he hadn't been online and had no idea what the latest reports were. There wasn't a lot in the English press beyond a few lines that said the victim had been a reporter, so no details that would help him. He relaxed for a while and then decided he needed to get online.

He also had to call Dolan at some point so he could figure out the lay of the land. Best to get it over with now he felt stronger.

He finished the bland excuse for a coffee, pulled the phone out of his pocket, switched it on and called the one number it held. It rang four times before Dolan answered.

Dolan didn't know anything about Gilhooley so far but was concerned about Taylor, who had missed checking in twice. And then there was that story from Sandy Tait about his arrest after the fight. There was little room for forgiveness in their game, but he would play it easy till he decided whether there was a problem.

'You okay?' He didn't use any identifier and kept the tone friendly.

'Yes.' It was clear to Taylor that Dolan didn't know anything about what had happened in Edinburgh so far, and that helped calm his stress levels.

'Where are you? We could have a job coming up so might need to get you at short notice.'

'I'm still north of the border, just taking it easy. Could do with another job.' The last bit was a lie, but he said it for effect.

'Okay.' But just then Dolan received a text from Handyside on another phone, saying that Taylor was in London. Dolan wondered how he knew that but let it go for the time being.

'Obviously not in the wilds though with the background noise.' Dolan played along. He was sure now that Taylor was becoming a liability but didn't know what they should do about it.

Taylor cursed internally. But Scotland had its cities so he kept it cool. 'In the city and enjoying the sun.'

'Right. You okay for money?' Dolan asked, trying to draw him out, but Taylor said he was fine for the time being, which was another lie.

'Roger that.'

Taylor switched the phone off again and headed for an internet café to see what was happening in Edinburgh. He couldn't make up his mind about Dolan. It was hard – all he knew was that the man was ice and not to be fucked with.

When Dolan put the phone down, he thought for a moment and called Handyside – the man he knew as Joe Stafford.

'We need to have a meet. The boy has called in but I have a bad feeling about him.'

'Suits me. I'll come to Dublin?'

The voice on the other end of the phone was hard to pin down – it had a number of influences – but there was no mistaking the Northumberland tones. They contrasted deeply with Dolan's Highland lilt, which was still discernible despite the years way from his homeland.

'Usual place.'

'Usual place. Roger that.'

'Be there at green five.'

Green five was part of their code system, which meant in this case the meet would be at a fixed time in Glasnevin Cemetery.

Handyside would fly from London to Dublin but that wasn't information he'd share with Dolan. No one had any idea where he lived, and he wanted it to stay that way, preferring to travel to meet Dolan, who lived in Malahide, not far from the Irish capital.

37

As the two men agreed to their meeting, Taylor was sitting in an internet café, but there was nothing new from the murder investigation in Edinburgh. Although there was mention of the fact that the body of a man had been discovered in a Glasgow flat and the police were treating it as suspicious. One of the detectives – Superintendent Grace Macallan – was going to make a statement to the press later in the afternoon. There was nothing yet about the documents, but he knew the police had to have them and that remained the problem.

He sat back when he saw another headline about the Glasgow victim. The police had mounted a full-scale murder investigation now, so it was just a matter of when Dolan and his boss joined the dots and worked out that Taylor was involved. They wouldn't know why, but if they found out the truth, he was as good as dead.

It was what he would do if he was the boss. They would try to cut off any association to the organisation because there was just too much at stake, and too many serious people could be damaged.

He still had some money in the bank, and besides the flat in Mayfield, he'd also invested in a mobile home on the outskirts of Edinburgh. He'd bought it when he was flush, and had thought about selling several times, even though he'd procured it for exactly this eventuality. He thanked his god that he'd kept it and not pissed it against the wall when he'd been short, which had been his original plan.

Hide in plain sight was the answer. Most criminals would make space between themselves and a crime locus, but the mobile home and his change of appearance could work for the time being, till the fog round the situation cleared a bit. It might not be the best idea he'd ever had, but he had a real desire to get back home, despite having just arrived in London.

The thought of staying any longer in the shithole B & B suddenly overwhelmed him. It would never have bothered him in the past, but this wasn't the past and he felt alone – more alone than he'd ever been.

38

Glasnevin Cemetery covered over 120 acres of Dublin's north side, housing the remains of 1.5 million souls in wondrous parkland. As well as containing many of the stars of Irish history – including the martyrs from the Easter Rising – it also hid thousands of unnamed victims of the Great Famine and various cholera epidemics. It was a gorgeous and almost haunting Victorian site, full of complex and sometimes grand monuments, graves and towers.

It was also home to the Angels Plot, a corner of the cemetery where around fifty thousand infants were buried – mostly premature and stillborn babes, plus some who'd died shortly after birth. Melancholic angels stare down at the ground that covered them, an air of sadness hanging over everything like a cloud. It always left Handyside slightly uneasy, but the fact that others seemed to feel the same made it an excellent meeting spot – people didn't tend to linger too long.

He entered the cemetery through the main gates and skirted past the busload of American tourists eager to see one of the most popular sites in Dublin. For all the sins he'd committed, Handyside was always fascinated by the way the Irish had compressed so much history, so much pain and sorrow, into this one place. Perhaps they needed to display the intensity of their history's tragedy so both the children they'd lost and those responsible would never be forgotten. The great tourist attractions in Dublin – the General Post Office in O'Connell Street, Kilmainham Gaol and Glasnevin – almost dared the populous and visitors to ignore what had happened, and why the country's population had never recovered from the exodus of its people.

Handyside always arrived fifteen minutes early so he could check his back and take in some of the millions of words carved into the stone forest in the acres of parkland. He stopped at the grave of Michael Collins and watched an American couple lay some flowers at the site. They stood, took a selfie and then he noticed tears trickling down the woman's face. He wondered at this level of sentiment and realised there was no one he cared for like that beyond his wife and children.

His family history meant nothing to him, and an abusive father had broken any affinity he might have had for his forebears. He had no fear of death, and even accepted that in many ways he could be regarded as deviant – not sexually, but in that few experiences stirred his emotions enough to make him feel the least bit human. Winning and taking decisions that led to success was what he lived for. If it involved life or death, that only heightened the experience.

To have lasted the way he had and to have avoided capture when Macallan had come so close was proof that, in his hard game, he was premier league. It required constant discipline, and he despised gangsters who abused their bodies, strutting the stage like coked-up rock stars, then wondered why the law eventually took them down. He thought that was probably why he liked working with his team – they were all ex-military, drawn from the toughest units, and they knew better than anyone that order came from discipline.

So what the fuck happened to Sam Taylor? he thought. If there was a problem with the man then why had they missed it? Or worse still, did the team know and Dolan just hadn't mentioned it?

Handyside only allowed himself the occasional release from his own form of discipline. He smoked, but limited himself, and it was the same with alcohol. These were pleasures to be enjoyed but they couldn't become habits.

He was lost in thought and realised he was still staring at the spot where the Americans had taken their selfies, but they'd gone. He blinked, looked at his watch and headed slowly towards the meeting with Dolan.

The old Angels Plot corner was quiet, but he soon saw the ex-soldier walking slowly from the direction of the Botanic Gardens. Not for the first time he thought that for all Dolan had done, he looked nothing special – but that was often the way with the hard ones.

Dolan was average height – in fact, average almost everything, with a face you could forget easily unless you looked closely. Then you might notice the chunk missing at the top of his left ear from when an Armagh farmer, Conlan Regan – who was also a commander of the local PIRA unit and a hard bastard – had discovered him in a hide on the perimeter of his farm. The discovery had been almost accidental but ended up in a hand-to-hand fight.

The paramilitary had managed to tear the top of Dolan's ear off before the soldier had stabbed him to death. When the rest of the unit had reached him, they'd done what they'd thought they had to and disposed of the body. There were no orders on paper, and as far as the report and press had it, the farmer had simply disappeared. The speculation was that a Loyalist team had somehow managed to get into the bandit country that was South Armagh and take him out; Republican voices said that was impossible, but the lack of a body meant the problem had gone away with time.

'You okay, Billy?'

'Good, Joe. It's the wife's birthday so I have to look for a fucking present or she'll give me gyp.' Dolan grinned. He was one of those characters who remained normal because of his partner; he swore she was what kept him alive and grounded. It was another reason Handyside liked him – he believed in family, and they were similar in so many ways.

'Know that one. Has to be done to keep the peace.' Handyside nodded back towards the Botanics and they walked slowly in that direction.

'As I told you, Sam's been in touch, but I'm concerned. You know he was lifted recently for a street battle. We let that go as he said nothing to the police, but I wonder if there's a problem. Sam was a true warrior, Joe. As good as they come, but he's always been a real loner, and we used to wonder because he never bothered about women. Tam Hunter was the only one you could say was close to a mate, though it was more that they both liked a drink and thought women were just something you paid for occasionally. He just seemed to live for the next job.'

Dolan took out his smokes and lit one up, shaking his head as he did so. 'We worked for years in Ulster and there was no one I'd rather have had at my back when there was a problem – and believe me, we had problems. Saying that, he's hard to love so the men didn't like him, but they respected him.'

He offered the packet to Handyside, who declined, then carried on.

'We hardly see each other now apart from when there's a job, but I noticed on that job in Holland that he looked a bit rough at times so it could be he's into the dope or booze. It happens to a lot of the loners in our game. They can't adapt to ageing. That's all I know, but he doesn't get in touch very often and it makes me wonder.'

Handyside thought for a moment before speaking. 'Sandy Tait in Edinburgh has heard from his sources inside

Police Scotland that there's going to be a press conference, and there's mention of contract killers. I'm going to plug into it here. I made some arrangements in Edinburgh for a third party recently. The job went wrong but nothing to do with us. Anyway, let's not get ahead of ourselves. I have some other business here, so leave it for now, Billy, and I'll get back to you.'

Dolan turned to him. 'Before I forget, how did you know he was in London? He told me he was north of the border.'

'I'll get back to you on that too, but not right now.'

They shook hands and separated.

As Dolan continued walking towards the Botanic Gardens, he thought as he always did how little he knew about the man he'd just met. They got on well and they made money together, but he knew almost nothing about the guy beyond his name. He had no idea where he worked and lived. Their meets were always in Dublin, but if he lived here, chances were they would have run into each other in the city. He accepted that it just meant the man was a pro and keeping his background dark, which was good practice, so he left it at that.

39

A couple of hours later, Handyside stared at the screen and waited. Sandy Tait had called him again with news from his police sources that they were going to mention the Kangas case during the press conference.

He'd stayed in Dublin, booking in to a hotel in the city centre where he'd stayed before that he knew to have several escape routes, in case he ever needed them. In his game, there was never a moment he could avoid taking precautions because as sure as the Pope is a Catholic, that would be the one time someone would come for him.

Handyside's mind drifted for a moment as he wondered what the reaction would be if he ever had to give the order to take out Taylor. It might never come to that, and he would never rush to such a judgement, but if he had to give the order, he'd do it. There were options, and he knew other contractors – or the Russians could connect him with people who could do the job.

The Russians had warned him that Europol were running a project on contractors so there had to be care in communications. The technical ability of law enforcement to listen in on illegal business was changing the very nature of their trade, and Handyside now had his own technical people, who were necessary attributes to stay ahead of the game. At one time, all you needed was corrupt officials and the balls to kill when necessary – now you needed to have cyber warriors on your team. Times were changing, and for a moment that thought made him feel old. He wondered what that meant – what happened when a man like him started to age, really age. Maybe like Taylor, the world he'd once dominated was being inhabited by young bulls who wanted to taste the glory and wouldn't hesitate to squeeze him out.

The sound of the Scottish reporter mentioning Edinburgh snapped him back to attention as he sipped a bitter black coffee – just the way he liked it. He stared at the laptop screen, studying the scene. There was some kind of podium emblazoned with the Police Scotland logo dominating the space, alongside two seats.

He turned the sound up and watched the camera angle move slightly to the right. When Elaine Tenant walked in, he stopped the cup halfway to his mouth and put it back on the desk. He sat back and breathed in deeply through his nose, his lips tightening as Grace Macallan walked in, pulled back her seat and looked straight at the camera. It was an unusual shot and seemed almost personal – an acknowledgement to someone beyond the hall.

He reached unconsciously for the packet of cigarettes on the desk. As Tenant took care of the introductions and the preliminaries, he flicked the lighter and inhaled deeply, enjoying the rush. He felt light-headed for a few moments as the nicotine worked its magic and wondered how people could be bothered with vaping. Sticking a machine in his face held no appeal. *This is how it should be done*, he thought and then sipped more coffee as Tenant handed over to Macallan as the senior officer in charge of the investigation.

He shook his head. Although he was an entirely logical man, this almost seemed like their fate – he and Macallan. *I should have known it would be her of all people.*

She looked a bit tired but good. Her hair was a tad longer but she still had that serious face that would no doubt give her premature lines. Handyside smiled grimly at the screen; a bitter but respected enemy had walked back into his life.

During the briefing, he forgot completely about the coffee and drew heavily on his cigarette. He wondered if it was his imagination, but he felt like Macallan was addressing him. She stared fixedly into the camera, and it was as if the audience of reporters had picked up the dramatic tone in her delivery; the room was almost silent.

'Nancy Gilhooley was a young, talented reporter in the prime of her life. Although we're keeping all options open, we have to consider that Nancy was killed because of the job she was doing. We have evidence to suggest she was involved in a very sensitive investigation that created a threat to her life.'

'Fuck it.' Handyside wasn't a man who swore very often; he believed it had more effect when used sparingly. But he needed this small release with the confirmation that Macallan was in his rear-view mirror. There should have been nothing to spook him yet, but her mere presence seemed to be a sign that something was dragging them together again.

He'd decided long ago that he would never run like a fugitive again, or drag his family into hiding half way round the world. His wife and children didn't deserve that. *Who would have guessed it, Grace*? he thought as she continued speaking.

'Significant evidence has been recovered from the locus and this evidence is being examined at the moment.' Macallan paused, looking down at her notes for a moment, and then stared down the camera again.

'I want to say to the individual who carried out this crime. To the man who attacked Nancy in Newhaven. We will find you;

we have evidence. Your best chance is to hand yourself in. You will receive fair treatment.' They were stock-in-trade lines but Macallan looked like she meant every word. *'We have a very detailed description of the man we are seeking in connection with this case.'*

She listed the main points of the description, including the vivid scar on the suspect's face.

'Finally, I would remind the public that this man may still be armed and should not be approached. If you have any information, please phone the numbers we will provide at the end of the conference… thank you.'

Macallan sat back and wondered if Handyside was watching somewhere. If he was, how would he react? He was such a hard man to read, intelligent and able to think outside the box. *What will he think if he sees me*? she wondered. *Will he be angry or does it make any difference? Am I flattering myself*?

Elaine Tenant took the stand again and offered the floor up to questions.

There were a couple of routine enquiries about what the police were doing locally, was there any evidence of the killer and Gilhooley knowing each other and about the fight with the four neds near the locus. All the reporters wanted to know who they were. Jacquie Bell waited for the moment she'd agreed with Macallan then stuck her hand up.

'We've heard that Nancy Gilhooley's killer was a professional and that a contract killer from another country was disrupted recently and arrested in Edinburgh. What can you tell us about that? And are they connected? Two contract killers in Edinburgh seems highly unusual.'

Handyside stubbed out his second cigarette, even though he'd only just fired it up, and started to tap the desk with the end of his pen. He felt like he was in the room with Macallan. She was doing it again with the eyes, and he waited for what he knew in his bones was bad news.

'I'm limited in what I can say other than a threat to life was disrupted recently. A Finnish national known to the authorities in his country was arrested and charged with documentation, road-traffic offences and possession of a firearm and ammunition. We are continuing investigations into this situation and will be pursuing other lines of enquiry to trace other people who may have been involved.' She paused. *'As far as the murder of Nancy Gilhooley is concerned, I would not want to comment at the moment.'*

Bell piped up once more. *'Can you confirm though that you are liaising with Europol and the Garda Síochána in Dublin?'*

Why did she mention Ireland? he wondered and then remembered that when he'd called Kangas, he'd been in Dublin. That was the only connection he could think of. *Is that possible? But how would they know it was a professional hit*?

It shouldn't have worried him, but it did. He wasn't a religious man, but sometimes it felt as if forces beyond the wit of man were pushing the players about in a game of chess where he was powerless to leave the game until there was a checkmate. He pondered the questions that had no answers for the time being, and knew he might be drawing conclusions based on next to no evidence.

Handyside swore again; things were getting serious. He knew exactly what Macallan was doing but couldn't work out how she knew he was involved.

Macallan responded to Bell exactly as they'd planned.

'Any enquiries are sensitive so I'm afraid I can't comment any further on this case other than to say again that I will pursue those involved and through international cooperation… our reach is long.'

Bell came in again. 'Are there connections between these two cases?' She had rehearsed the next words carefully.

'And the very last question: is there any truth that you're looking at connections to the murder of Mr Tam Hunter, who was found dead in his flat in Glasgow?'

Macallan had rehearsed her lines with as much care as Bell and she waited for the ripple of murmurs to subside as most of the reporters in the room wondered why the fuck Jacquie Bell was always ten steps ahead of the rest of the pack.

'We can rule nothing out at the moment and are following all lines of enquiry. That's all I can say right now.'

Tenant and Macallan picked up their papers and took no more questions because the job had been done.

In his flat in Malahide, Dolan squeezed his hands into fists at the mention of Tam Hunter and the description of the Edinburgh killer's scar. 'Fuck it,' he snarled. They did indeed have a problem. *What the fuck have you done, Sam*? he thought.

40

Handyside slammed the desk with his fist in an unusual display of emotion from a man who was almost permanently buttoned down. The foundations of his world were shaking, the tremors coming all the way from Scotland, and he squeezed his eyes closed, trying to clear his thoughts.

Macallan hadn't confirmed a thing, but the statement was all the evidence he needed that they had a serious problem. It was time to clean up, but he might already be too late. He'd never hesitated in his life when there was good business reason for someone to die and Taylor had just qualified. The fact a reporter had been taken out throbbed in his head. He could only guess what it meant, but whatever it was couldn't be good.

The Kangas job had just been shit luck, and he couldn't be blamed for it, but when they'd described the reporter's killer, the deal was done. He'd never met Taylor face to face but had a file with photographs of the man, and the mention of that scar had told him everything he needed to know. 'Jesus,' he murmured as he picked up the phone and called Dolan.

'Did you see the conference?'

'Sure did. Fuck-up. That scar is like a signature. It was Sam alright. What do you think?'

'What I think is why would Sam kill a reporter? A reporter – that smells, and it explains why he's staying low. You heard the description, Billy – no doubt? The scar confirms it, and then there's Tam Hunter dead. That can't all be coincidence. I think we might need to clean it up!'

There was a pause as Dolan absorbed his meaning.

'I get it. I fucking hate it, but I get it. If he's done this then he was way off-script. If it's a reporter, why did he need to kill her and what was it she knew that made him take action? Did it involve us?'

'If it's him, it's bad karma for us. The Finn was just one of those things – shit happens. But if Sam's done this on the same turf, it could put us in a difficult position. Sod's Law and the old problem of unforeseen consequences. If we need to do this, I can get an outside firm in. I understand what this means to you.'

There was a serious edge to Dolan's reply. 'We'll do it. Our mess so our job. Bringing in another firm just means more risk. How the fuck do we find him though if he goes dark?'

'Leave that with me. I have a way to do that. Speak to you later, but are you ready to go if I make the call?'

'I'll be ready and I'll take one of the team with me – the new boy.'

Handyside put the phone down, looked at the crushed cigarette and couldn't remember stubbing it out.

He poured another coffee. *Macallan knows I'm involved,* he thought – he just felt it in his bones. It was his worst nightmare. Could he outmanoeuvre her again? He knew well enough that she was good at what she did – very good – and if she knew he was involved, she'd cover every base to get him.

He looked at the picture of his wife and children that he took with him wherever he went and wondered if he would see his kids grow up.

41

Taylor had watched the conference at the same time as Handyside and decided he was fucked. The description of the suspect had put a great big target on his back. Now they were tying together the cases in Edinburgh *and* Glasgow.

He was fucked if he was caught by the police and even more fucked once his team worked it all out and got a hold of him. There was no doubt they would try to find him.

The gods had turned on him big style. At the end of the day, he'd tried to clean up Tam Hunter's mess, though he knew his employers wouldn't see it that way.

He decided to phone Dolan again and try to work out what he was thinking. It was time to run – the only decision was how fast and where. Hiding in plain sight still seemed like the best idea – heading back to Scotland and the mobile home.

His appearance had changed significantly now, and Taylor was experienced in camouflage. With glasses and his new clean-cut look, he was confident that he could at least avoid random identification by a nosey citizen. He couldn't make the scar disappear, but careful make-up and a cap would probably do for that.

He packed his small bag, went to the front desk and told the horrible bastard who ran the place that he was leaving.

'You're booked in for the week so I need full payment.' The guy was pure East End and that immediately set him on edge. He'd always had a thing about Cockneys – they just plain fucking annoyed him.

'I'm leaving now so I pay up to now. Let's not fuck about Del or Harry or Frankie or whatever the fuck your name is.'

Unfortunately for the Cockney, he took Taylor for a Jock wanker, wondering in his drink-addled brain how he'd arrived looking like a fucking beggar but was leaving like Clark Kent.

'Look, you tartan cunt. Pay up or I'll come round there and—'

It was on the word *and* that Taylor grabbed the guy's long greasy hair and slammed his face into the top of the counter, pulping his nose and displacing a couple of rotten teeth that needed extraction anyway.

The loser slid off the counter and dropped to the floor. Taylor felt better for the bit of violence, and doing the business to an East Ender was a total bonus. He'd committed a serious assault, so there was no point in going only halfway and he decided he might as well add robbery to the situation.

He lifted the hatch, stepped behind the counter and stared at the heap on the floor, who was moaning through the new gap in his top teeth. Taylor grinned – this was like medicine for him.

He opened the cash drawer, took out a fat bundle of notes then realised he'd hit the jackpot when he found twenty deals of coke all wrapped nicely and ready for the customers. He found another few ounces stashed below the counter. It was an unexpected answer to his short-term cash-flow problems and he grinned at the bounty from a fairly easy bit of violence. The place doubled as a drugs shop – booking in there had turned out to be a bit of luck that lifted his spirit.

'Jesus, you've been a busy wee boy, eh? Don't think you'll be reporting me to the cops.' He guessed he had a couple of grand in cash now, a lifesaver for the time being.

He stuffed the coke into his bag and made to leave just as some radge came in the door for their daily whack of powder. He had a second thought then turned and unzipped his flies. His bladder was nicely full and he played the stream all over the prostrate figure. 'There you are, pal – some nice Jock pish. Enjoy!

42

He headed for the station, feeling much lighter than the wreck who'd arrived at the B & B. When he got to King's Cross, he found he'd just missed the Edinburgh train, which meant he had about fifty minutes to wait, so he decided to make the call to Dolan now. There was too much identifiable background noise in the station so he walked a hundred yards away and switched the phone back on.

He decided he'd have to ditch the phone eventually and get a new number when he was back in Scotland. The phone rang four times again and Taylor took a deep breath when Dolan answered.

'Good to hear you. You okay?'

Dolan tried to make sense of the background noise. It was clear Taylor was somewhere in a city. He wanted to let Taylor speak before he made his judgement.

When he did, it was with a renewed air of confidence. Melting the Cockney had helped, but it was crystal clear now what his situation was and he saw no point fucking around. Even if Dolan hadn't seen it the conference, he would pick up on it all eventually – the police would have to release his name once they identified the DNA. Taylor was many things but as far as he was concerned, he was also a warrior, and the time for fear was past. He heaved in a breath and decided to go for it.

'Did you see the police conference in Edinburgh, Billy?'

Dolan was in tune with Taylor at least on exactly where they stood. There was no need for pretence once Taylor had posed the question. It would make no difference – they both knew what was coming. He paused for thought, and Taylor grabbed the moment to come in again.

'It's a fuck-up, isn't it, Billy? You're not going to give me a bonus so I think I'll go dark. Why not leave me to it? If I'm lifted, I'll say fuck all, so you're safe enough. Just don't come after me, right?'

'Why, Sam? Why the fuck did this happen?'

Dolan was staring at his laptop screen when a message came through with the words: 'He's somewhere near King's Cross.' *What the fuck*? Dolan wondered again how his boss knew this. There was only one explanation he could think of, but that was for later.

'You'd be okay coming in, Sam. We'll put you somewhere safe for the foreseeable. A bit of a holiday.' Dolan knew he was wasting his breath, but he had try.

'Aye right. I know exactly where you'll put me.' Taylor snorted the reply. 'Look, you owe me fuck all, and I owe you fuck all. I'm no fool and I've been in the business long enough to work out the options. I'll keep this phone for a few days more in case both of us have to rethink, depending on what the pigs are up to.'

He killed the call before Dolan had the chance to answer and headed back to the station with the phone switched on.

The text came in less than a minute later. 'The caller is in King's Cross.'

Dolan stared at the text and wondered where Taylor was headed. He guessed Scotland. If you were going dark, it was always better to go somewhere you felt comfortable;

somewhere you'd blend in. But where exactly? He'd said he'd keep the phone for a few days, which was a bonus, and if he did, they'd soon know more.

He picked up another phone and called Handyside.

'He's been on and said he's not coming in. Going dark.'

Handyside took his time answering but he knew now that the decision to take out the man who'd been Dolan's brother in arms was a no-brainer.

'You know we have to act on this, Billy. We're all in danger now.'

Dolan shook his head at the thought of what he had to do. They'd been in combat situations together, and although there was no love lost between them, it meant something that no civilian could understand.

'Okay, I'll be ready. Going to take Ronnie Baker. He's never worked with our man so it's just a job for him. They don't know much about each other. Won't give him the why, just the plan when we're ready to do the job. What about kit?'

'I have the contact in Edinburgh who'll provide the gear when you get there. He's safe.'

'Fair enough.' Dolan said it almost wearily then paused before getting out the idea that had been troubling him.

'One thing bothers me. How the fuck can you work out how a pro who decides to go dark can be found? It works okay in the movies but it's fucking difficult when the target knows what he's doing, and this man has almost fuck all close friends or family *and* travels with just what he can carry.'

'Your point?'

'Well, it has to be technical, and I know Sam has nothing he doesn't need. So it has to be the clean phones. Is that it, Joe? It doesn't bother me, but I'd rather know. I'm the team leader and no fucking idiot. Don't treat me like one and we'll stay sound.'

'It's only for insurance, and it proved to be the correct move in this case, but you're right to ask. I have technical people who do this for me. Are we okay?' Handyside knew it was pointless and counterproductive to lie to a man like Dolan. This was his life.

Dolan ignored the question because it was meaningless. 'I'll get in touch with Ronnie and we'll be ready as soon as you get the next indication.'

43

Maggie Duncan walked out of the station at Dalkeith and headed for Eskbank on foot, breathing in the damp early evening air. Milder weather had finally arrived in Scotland and it helped dispel the never-changing gloom of the world news.

She lived in walking distance of her work, which was a bonus for her, and she avoided driving whenever she could, preferring to experience the world at normal speed. She saw so much more that way; developed the sense of where she was and the way the world around her was shaped. Duncan loved to draw so enjoyed studying the most mundane features in her environment, wondering why they were where they were.

She was halfway along the wooded drive and completely lost in thought. The birds were giving it laldy, as if they were celebrating the end of the cold spell, certain that better times were ahead.

Duncan wasn't even listening to the music coming through her earphones She was trying to figure out whether she'd been right to say yes to the guy who'd asked her out. Her relationships so far never seemed to last more than a couple of dates, so she'd turned to online dating, despite the horror stories she'd heard from some of her friends.

She almost missed the movement in the bushes near her before her training kicked in. She'd turned her thoughts again to Macallan's press conference and wondered if she was right – was it Taylor? The description Macallan had put out, and the more detailed one being circulated round the force, seemed to fit. Murder squads were always snowed under when a description was put out but, in any case, she'd left a message and been told that someone would be back to her as soon as to discuss it.

The bushes rustled again, and she was startled when she heard what sounded like soft laughter and realised that something – or more likely someone – was mirroring her route along the path. Looking round carefully, she went into hyper-alert mode. It wasn't a dog, unless the canine had somehow managed to mimic a human laugh. Duncan didn't spook easily but instinct put her on guard. She hoped it was some numpty teenager having what they thought was a laugh.

That was when the man pushed through the bushes and carried out the performance he'd been waiting to stage for the last half hour. He was bollock naked and at full attention.

His name was Andy Hickman, a thirty-year-old nutter from Edinburgh's south side. His life was a catalogue of minor criminality and failure. Locally, he was known as 'Andy Nae Pals', which summed up his life perfectly. The original eight-stone weakling, he'd discovered a great release for his disappointment with life by flashing. He was good at it, and it gave him a great high when he saw the expressions on his victims' startled coupons – although there had been the one disappointment when a bold older woman had said, 'Thanks. Any chance o' comin' in the bushes wi' ye, son?'

He reckoned he was smarter than the police and always moved to a different part of town to carry out his work. This was his first trip out into the county though; he'd picked Dalkeith at random, and that's how he'd come to meet Duncan.

'Dae ye like chicken, hen? Well huv some o' this – it's fuckin' foul.' The bam thought he was a hoot and sniggered at his own joke. He obviously expected his victim to scream and leg it like the other women he'd flashed over the previous weeks. But this woman stood her ground, as if she was making her mind up about something, and he frowned. Deciding to turn the screw a bit, he grabbed the much-loved part of his body and made a monkey face for effect.

'Come on then, see if ye can handle this for me, hen.' He giggled again, but it didn't last because the woman dropped her bag on the ground, took off her sunglasses and calmly put them into her pocket. It looked like she was still considering just what do with him.

He ran out of steam. Her eye contact knocked him back and he was quickly – and obviously – losing his excited state. That's when he realised that his plan wasn't working and he'd probably picked the wrong victim.

As far as he could see, the woman had only a determined look in her eye; there was no fear or alarm, which was what got him off when he was back in his room, fantasising about his latest adventure.

'Looks like you've lost your mojo there, pal. Disappointing really. Can't for the life of me think why you want to show that wee thing off. I mean, it's not scary – more tragically funny.'

Hickman wondered where this was going. *Why the fuck is this daft burd no' bothered*?

'Ye're a fuckin' bam, hen, ye ken that?' The irony of his statement didn't register and his annoyance turned to utter confusion as Duncan started towards him.

'What the fuck?' he managed to splutter before she pulled out her warrant card and told him he was under arrest. That's when he started to leg it.

He might have been a skinny character, but he was quick off his feet and started pounding up the road forgetting that his clothes were all carefully hidden in the bushes. Duncan took off after him and cursed giving him the chance to get on his toes.

Fit as she was, Duncan was only an average jogger, and as she ran up to Eskbank Roundabout, she still hadn't managed to close the distance between them. However, she knew her fitness meant that she'd catch up eventually – or hopefully an upstanding member of the community would come into play.

Hickman was in a blind panic, and when he reached the roundabout, he turned right – without realising he was heading straight into Dalkeith town centre. His legs were starting to drag a bit, but the cop behind him was still there. He was trying to think of a new plan, but the bollock-naked bit was a big problem – how the fuck could he get on a bus with no clothes and no money?

Besides a couple of cars that passed with open-jawed drivers, the team of neds heading for the nearby supermarket to buy some cider were the first to really enjoy the chase. They were on the other side of the road and started clapping as if Hickman and Duncan were part of a charity run.

'Let the lassie catch ye, pal – she just wants a ride, for fuck's sake.' The neds all pissed themselves even though the joke wasn't that funny.

The number of pedestrians started to increase as they approached the town centre, and the reactions varied from the odd scream to belly laughs, but no one came to Duncan's assistance. Hickman started to tire badly, realising the gap was closing, and near the town centre he became completely confused – he had no idea where he was supposed to be heading. He couldn't come up with a plan B.

Aw for fuck's sake, he thought when he saw the police patrol car arrive on the scene, although he had no idea the officers were on their way to another job.

'Here, is that no' Maggie Duncan chasin' a bam wi' nae claes?' the driver said to his partner and they both grinned in unison. 'Well I suppose we better gie the sergeant a hand.'

The car passed Duncan and cruised alongside Hickman as the driver wound down his window.

'Look, pal. Sorry tae interrupt yer run an' aw that but I think ye forgot yer shorts. Come on an' we'll gie ye a wee lift.' The cops were enjoying themselves – this would make a cracker of a story for the next team booze-up.

'Aw for fuck's sake,' Hickman gasped and came to a complete halt, accepting where he'd be spending the night now. He bent over, put his hands on his knees and heaved in deep gulps of air. Duncan pulled up behind him and tried to avoid the sight of his on-display arse.

'Thanks, guys. This one flashed me down the road. No luck though, eh?'

'Aye, nae luck flashin' you, sarge.'

The two cops were out of the car now and enjoying every moment – as far as they were concerned, it was times like this that made policing the best job in the world. One of them pulled a blanket out of the boot and handed it to Hickman, who was upright now and cursing his luck.

The driver looked down at Hickman's tackle and grinned again. 'You sure he was flashin', sarge? Cannae see that the boy's got anythin' tae flash.'

At that, Hickman felt even more miserable and humiliated.

'Right, enough of the second-rate humour. I'm off duty so you two comedians will have the paperwork to take care of.' Although Duncan had done her best to sound serious, she knew there was serious banter waiting for her and couldn't hide her smile. They all got in the car and headed back to the station.

44

Once they'd finished with Hickman, Duncan headed back to her flat, showered and suddenly felt knackered after the day's events. She was due for a session at the gym but decided to give it a miss and stare at the box for a bit instead. She was almost asleep on the sofa when the phone rang, and she went straight to wide awake when she realised it was Macallan on the other end of the line.

'Noticed you phoned in, Maggie, and thought I'd call to see what you've got.'

'Sorry, ma'am, just surprised to get a call from an SIO on a job like this.'

'Suppose it is a bit odd but we just heard the story about the flasher and it raised a few smiles on the team. Heard it was you and thought I'd call you just to say well done… again. What have you got for us?'

Duncan explained her thoughts about Sam Taylor and what had happened when he was arrested. 'Might be nothing but thought I'd call in.'

'So, he's ex-military, and the Sandy Tait thing is interesting. What happened to him?'

'He pled guilty, and Tait seemed to work a great deal for him. Sold it as Taylor was the one being attacked by a gang and he was merely defending himself. To be fair, that's probably true. Anyway, it was accepted and he just got a small fine for a breach of the peace.'

'So we've got DNA from him. Excellent, and we should have plenty for comparison from the locus.' Macallan sounded positive even though Duncan knew there must be hundreds of suggestions piling into the HOLMES system.

'Ah well, you would have got to him anyway, ma'am. He was an interesting guy, ex-para, and could handle himself in a battle. I'm ex-military myself and know the type. Hard, hard bastard. Anyway, not much else I can provide.'

'Listen, we'll get a statement from you anyway, Maggie. What branch were you in?'

Duncan told her a bit about her time with the military police.

'One of the reasons I called was to see if you'd ever thought about trying the type of work we do?'

Duncan had caught Macallan's attention at Frankie Ross's arrest. There was something about the young sergeant, and her previous army service only added to Macallan's interest.

Duncan had to keep her voice level at the carrot being dangled – she'd cut a finger off to work for Macallan.

'Of course. It's what I've always hoped for, but the bosses want to keep me in uniform.'

'Leave it with me – someone will be in touch.'

Tired as she was, Duncan couldn't sleep – not because of the images of a bollock-naked Andy Hickman still fresh in her mind but from the thought that she might get a crack at major crime.

45

If Duncan had been surprised by Macallan's offer, she was astonished by the speed of subsequent events. She was at lunch the following day when her inspector came into the office and more or less bollocked her – as if she'd somehow betrayed the force.

'Never knew you were making moves to get into plain clothes. I saw you rising through the ranks, maybe the chief's office, admin, that kind of thing, but not major crime.'

'Sorry, Inspector, but I've never made an application.' Duncan's stomach began to rattle at the implication of his words.

'Well someone has pulled all the strings and you're off. I mean as of now. You've been seconded to the MIT with Superintendent Macallan. Call the incident room and get cleared up.'

He got up with no *goodbye and good luck*, and Duncan just sat there, trying not to look too overcome with joy, though she was actually thinking, *Ya beauty*!

By the afternoon, she'd said goodbye to her shift, arranged to attend the incident room the next day and that was it – her time in uniform was over. She spent the night overcome with spinning thoughts, pulling open her sparse wardrobe half a dozen times and wondering what she should wear.

It was 8 p.m. when her date called, wondering why she hadn't turned up when she'd initially seemed so keen. But for Duncan, everything had changed, so she gently broke the news that their relationship was over before it had even started. He took it well, and she left him with the white lie that they should keep in touch, though they both knew that probably wouldn't happen.

Duncan lay in bed, googling all she could about Macallan. She knew a lot about her already, but her CV was something else. What surprised her was that when she talked to Macallan, it was like she'd known her for ages. There was genuine warmth there, and that's what was always said about her – she could be dour but led from the front and always by example. Duncan had seen it first-hand at the Ross incident and was excited to learn from the woman herself.

Her career meant everything to her, and the chance to face a different order of villain was something she'd wanted since she'd taken the difficult decision to leave the army and join Police Scotland. She was an experienced military investigator, but this was a different order of things, and although she lacked the normal training that officers going through detective ranks would have, she knew she could make that up.

She put out the light and stared at the ceiling, guessing there would be no sleep that night, but she was wrong and fell over easier than normal. Things were working out well, and life was good.

46

Taylor stepped off the train at Edinburgh Waverley and immediately felt the difference in temperature. It was always the same – you boarded the train in London with only a shirt on and stepped off in the Scottish capital needing at least one extra layer, though it wasn't actually too bad for his native land.

He stretched his back then slung the rucksack over his shoulders. He had nothing but time for the foreseeable future and would have to go into a bit of a lockdown, being careful of where he could be seen and leaving no electronic clues behind.

He only had the phone supplied by Dolan, who he knew sourced kit from whoever was above him in the food chain, but maybe he didn't need it. *Who the fuck would I call anyway?* he thought as he saw two transport cops patrolling the concourse. He breathed a little easier when they completely ignored him.

He was still carrying the weapon. In normal circumstances, he would have ditched it rather than carry it among Joe Public, but it was all the protection he had, and there was always the chance he might need it.

The two cops walked off so he decided he'd grab a coffee in the station and people-watch for a bit.

He was going into a long period of hibernation so why not? He patted his pockets by habit, making sure everything was where it should be. Wallet and phone. When he pulled the phone out of his pocket, he realised he'd left in on. There was no need for that, and he'd leave contacting Dolan for the time being – maybe forever – so he switched it off.

The coffee was a relief after the overpriced shit he'd bought on the train so he ordered another one. As he sipped it, he studied two attractive women strolling across the concourse, both carrying briefcases, and wondered what they were laughing at. He felt flat for a moment and wondered why he felt nothing now for the opposite sex. Most of his old comrades were still like rabbits, but the years had killed the healthy appetite he'd had as a younger man. The horrors that lived with him had numbed those old desires.

He tried to shift his line of thinking and turned his thoughts to the mobile home. That had been one of the few good financial decisions he'd ever made – maybe the only one. Men in his game had to have a plan B – one that kept them safe if they had to fall off the radar. He'd bought it years before under an assumed name that would hold for routine checks. It was just outside the city border, but Edinburgh was an easy place to commute to and from, and he could be back in the centre within twenty minutes.

The fact that he'd kept it meant he could survive for a while, though eventually his cash would run out, even with the extra he could make from selling the coke. But he decided to put that out of his head for the time being. He needed to get there safely and switch off for a bit.

The coffee was almost finished and the effects of the alcohol binge had almost worn off completely. He felt okay – or at least as okay as he could be these days. He wished he could take another coffee but knew he'd be climbing the walls if he had any more caffeine. Sighing, he settled back in his chair, not quite ready to leave civilisation yet. A few more minutes wouldn't hurt.

People-watching was one of his few pleasures, and he drifted off absentmindedly, trying to guess what the figures who crisscrossed his view were thinking and what secrets they might be hiding. *We all have them*, he thought.

With all his training, Taylor should have seen the doped-up ned and his girlfriend eyeing the bag at his feet. The ned was in serious need of a hit, and in his state, all risks became worth the effort. The girlfriend kept shottie, with her back to Taylor, covering the ned between the two of them. He reckoned that Taylor was nicely distracted and preoccupied by a tidy bit of skirt with massive mams standing just outside the café.

He managed to get his grubby paw on the strap of the bag when Taylor felt the change in pressure on the outside of his right boot. As the bag started to move, the change bolted him back to the real world, and his subsequent reaction came from years of training and experience.

He looked down, saw the hand on his bag and started to assess the situation. The first thing he noticed was that the ned's hand and wrist were too thin to belong to someone who could be a real physical threat – so he drew up his boot and stamped down hard. The heavy rubber sole he always wore did enough to stop the ned, though the bag cushioned him from any real damage. It didn't stop him yelping with fright as much as pain, and he drew up, clutching his damaged hand.

Taylor took any threat as serious, and when he spun round, he immediately realised it was a junkie who'd tried to lift his stuff. He grabbed the boy by the throat but decided there was no real threat unless someone else had put him up to it.

The other customers had started to scatter, and the baristas were trying to decide what they should do – whether it was worth getting involved given the shit wages they earned.

'Did someone put you up to this? Tell me or I'll tear your ear off.' He grabbed the boy's right ear and applied enough pain to make the threat seem real.

'Fuckin' leave him, ya bastard. He wis daen' fuck all.' The girlfriend had decided to become involved, but Taylor could see she was wasted and no threat apart from making too much noise. He kept eye contact with the boy, whose own eyeballs were popping with fear and the realisation that he'd picked the wrong victim.

'Honest, mister,' he croaked as best he could with the vice still clamped round his throat. 'I'm a fuckin' junkie, right. Gimme a break please?'

Taylor decided it was what it was and accepted the plea was genuine.

'That'll do, sir. Leave it with us.'

Taylor turned to see the two uniforms appear in the café. He was thrown for a moment – the last thing he needed was the police.

Fortunately for him, the junkie and his girlfriend kicked off at the sight of the uniforms and demanded Taylor be lifted for assault. The uniforms ended up struggling with the two of them, and by the time they'd pacified the would-be robbers, Taylor was gone.

'What the fuck?' was all one of them got out, but without a complainer they had no case so they marched the junkie and his partner up to Market Street and told them to fuck off.

Taylor was already well along Princes Street. A line of sweat trickled down his back as he realised he'd nearly fucked up again by leaving the bag exposed. It was a truth that almost choked him. He'd lost his edge completely and that could cost him his life.

That's it – no more risks, he thought. It was time to get to the mobile home, close the door and switch on the telly.

Staying low and staying alive was the objective, though he wondered whether suicide would end up his only choice. He'd thought about it often enough in the past – knew exactly how he'd do it – and felt it would be preferable to ending up like the mess that had just tried to rob him.

It was too far to walk so he hailed a taxi and headed for lockdown.

47

As Taylor was sipping coffee in Edinburgh, Handyside received another message from the technician monitoring the bug in the ex-soldier's phone: 'In Waverley Station, Edinburgh, but off air now.'

Handyside realised his luck was holding… so far. He called Dolan.

'He's in Edinburgh but not settled yet. Might be an idea to head there now anyway – the sooner we get this done, the better. I'll phone my contact in Edinburgh to arrange the kit. You fine with that?'

'All good – we'll get going as soon as I get my stuff together. Ronnie is ready and waiting.'

Handyside started to think of all the angles – what needed to be covered? Was there anything he was missing? He called Tait, who he despised but was perfect for what he paid him for. As far as Handyside was concerned, Tait thought he was God's gift to the legal profession, but for all his ability, he didn't give a damn about the rule of law – it was all about him. He was still worth his weight north of the border though.

It was Benny Green who'd first put Handyside in touch with Tait. He'd always thought it was a strange turn of events because it was the Russians who'd put him in touch with Green, meaning they'd been responsible for his two most important contacts in Scotland. It always reminded him that the men from Moscow had a long and sometimes deadly reach.

He settled back in his chair, suddenly weary, and that worried him – he didn't normally do weary. That came when you'd lost your edge, which is probably what had happened to Taylor.

He went through to the kitchen where his wife was at the sink, washing vegetables – she always said the kitchen was the heart of the home and that she loved nothing better than preparing food for the family. He stepped quietly behind her, wrapped his arms around her and kissed her neck.

'You fine, Jeannie?'

'I'm good.' She turned, dried her hands and put her palms on his cheeks, but the smile she'd been wearing changed to a look of concern. 'What about you though? You're worried – I can see it. It's been good here and we've been happy. Promise me it's not going to go wrong again. I don't ask much from you, I don't question, but the children are growing up so how can we explain if we have to change names again?'

'We're fine, lass – it's just one of those business deals that needs a bit of work. I never thought it would happen but I think I'm getting old; it creeps up on you. Honestly, when I was young, I thought thirty was old. I never wanted to get to middle age – that's when the men who've ruled the roost get taken down by the young bulls.'

They kissed and held each other without another word. There was nothing else to say. Finally they let go, and Handyside told her he was off for a walk in the sunshine.

'Aye, you go ahead, lad – do you good.'

He pulled on his jacket and made sure he had his personal phone and the clean one, in case Taylor switched his own on again.

48

As she did so often, Macallan stood at her office window and thought through where they were. She knew with both the Kangas case and the reporter's murder, the issues would only mount, and with it the problems to be tackled. It was unusual because she had a gut feeling that they'd find the truth; there was something working in her subconscious that told her they would get there. Maybe not put people in court, but at least discover what it all meant. She believed that if they worked the evidence properly, and everyone was on their game, it would come. They had a better start than would normally have been the case in most contract jobs and that meant a lot.

The man who'd killed Nancy Gilhooley might have been a professional, but it had all gone wrong and he'd left DNA and witnesses who could tie him to Newhaven. If it was Taylor then they just needed to wait on confirmation from the lab. So, her task was to make her team believe they were getting there. Macallan had been on enough jobs where heads went down when there wasn't a quick result, and with it the discipline to see things through.

The knock at the door startled her, but when it opened, she smiled warmly at Duncan, who'd been told to report to her when she was settled in.

'Maggie, great to see you. How you feeling about it all?'

'Still catching my breath, ma'am. Chasing a flasher through Dalkeith one day and here today! Takes a bit of getting used to.'

Duncan was an experienced officer but she looked nervous and Macallan wanted to settle her down.

'Sit for a minute, Maggie. Only a minute though because I've got a couple of meetings shortly. Just to say, I want you to work with Jimmy Gordon for a couple of days. Know you're both sergeants but he'll give you a good idea of where we're at and what we're about. He's in the middle of taking a long statement from an important witness – Jacquie Bell. This statement and interview is vital, so get all you can from her. When you feel comfortable, we'll ease you in and then eventually give you more work than humanely possible. How does that sound?'

'Sounds good to me – I just want to get started. I'll do my best, ma'am, you can be assured on that one.'

Duncan looked serious and Macallan knew she was going to like her. It was like looking at herself a million years earlier.

'A couple of things, Maggie. Am I right in saying you underwent developed vetting in the army and can handle secret material?'

'Yes, of course, and I worked on all sorts of sensitive and covert investigations. I was in the SIB and was attached for a while to the FIB.'

'I've read your file but wanted to confirm. We'll get it reviewed and renewed so you can handle the sensitive material we have. What about surveillance training and operational experience of surveillance?'

Macallan locked eye contact with Duncan – this question clearly had some deeper meaning behind it.

‘All I can say, ma’am, is I’m trained but can’t discuss operational experience.’ Duncan shifted on her seat, but it was the answer Macallan had wanted.

‘You forgot to add “or I’ll have to kill you”,’ Macallan said with a grin. ‘It’s fine. Remember I worked on the dark side in Northern Ireland. That’s what I wanted to hear. Right, go find Jimmy and get on with your new career, Detective Sergeant!’

Duncan stood up and thanked Macallan. It felt like she’d just been told she’d passed an important exam. She headed back to the incident room hoping Jimmy Gordon was as good as she’d heard.

49

Macallan had a few minutes before the next briefing and called Jack. When she was looking at where things had been going wrong between them, she'd realised she'd almost stopped calling or texting from work.

'Hi, what's up, Detective?' The surprise in his voice at hearing from her confirmed her suspicions.

'Just calling to see how you are.' It was hard to say, despite how routine it had been for her in the past.

The pause before he replied was too long.

'Grace, what is it. Something wrong?' He sounded worried and that helped.

'No, I'm fine. Just wanted to say hello… I love you, Jack.' The small declaration surprised her and a tear bubbled up in the corner of her eye.

Again there was a long pause and she bit her lip at the silence.

'Good, I'm glad. You sure you're okay?'

'I'm good, Jack. This is a big job, but it's a great team and I'm finally learning to delegate. Listen, I was thinking, why don't I treat you – or I should say us – to a posh weekend away when this is done. Elaine said she'd take the kids and spoil them rotten.' She shut her eyes, waiting for a knock-back.

'Sounds good to me. We've too much at stake... Look, I love you. That's the easy bit, but we've stopped working at it. Anyway, enough discussion and more action. I'm in the middle of writing a dramatic scene so I'd better get back to the keyboard. I'm just glad you called – and it better be a posh weekend with all the trimmings. I'll buy special jammies for the occasion.'

A rush of pleasure washed over her. It had been too long since she'd felt that way.

'It's a date. I've got a killer to catch so better go.'

She put the phone down just as a knock sounded on the door. Macallan called for them to enter, and Danny Oliver and Felicity Young came in and took their seats. They both noticed that Macallan was flushed, and the almost permanent frown she'd worn for a while seemed to have disappeared.

'Okay, let's begin. What have we got, Danny? Let's start with Nancy Gilhooley.'

Before he was able to start, Tenant rushed in, apologising for her late arrival.

'Press are all over this now and picking up on the possibility of the contract killing. It seems they might have got to the men our suspect took on after the killing.'

Oliver went through what they knew already, reporting that door-to-door enquiries had thrown up a few witnesses who'd heard or seen things that added to the evidence they had, though there was nothing too significant. The forensic work was well advanced and with the information from Duncan, they were near certain that the DNA from the rucksack and cap would end up matching Sam Taylor. The notes inside had fingerprints identified as belonging to Nancy Gilhooley so which confirmed Jacquie Bell's statement that they were Gilhooley's work.

'The motorbike Taylor used to get away has been found burned out as we'd expect so I don't think that's going to take us far. There's no trace of the weapon, so we have to presume he's still armed. The search teams have done a big job over a wide area round the locus but they've found nothing else that helps us.' He looked to Macallan for questions.

'Anything else from the locus?'

'Only what I've told you, and it's all in the system, including the statements from the police who attended.

'The PM?'

'More or less as we'd expect. The gunshots killed her. The two to the chest were very close together – classic double tap – followed by the two to the head to make sure. Otherwise she was healthy and no medical history of serious illness.'

'The house?'

'Nothing really. Nancy seemed to live pretty simply. Her laptop has been recovered, and it's being analysed at the moment. Felicity is liaising. Nothing so far but again, the technical guys are on it. As you'd expect from a reporter, there are masses of emails and notes so it'll take a bit of time.'

'It would be strange if she wasn't putting her stuff on the laptop so hopefully it'll add to the evidence.' Macallan rubbed the side of her head. It was a complex case, and keeping hold of all the strands was crucial, but she had confidence in her team.

Young came in next; as always, she'd been scribbling notes since they'd started. She never stopped analysing, even in the middle of a meeting. Macallan often wondered how someone like this ultra-professional analyst and her friend Mick Harkins, who was a dinosaur from the past, could work, but they did. There was something quite reassuring about it – it meant anything was possible.

Young was known in the force as 'the brain', and she'd been one of Macallan's closest allies since she'd started in the old Lothian and Borders force.

'Okay, Felicity, your go, and give us some hope please.' Macallan smiled at the analyst.

'We've had a chance to have an initial look at the laptop and notes.'

Macallan interrupted. 'Before I forget – do we know where Nancy had been that night?' she asked, looking round the room.

Oliver came back in. 'Nothing yet, boss. But the CCTV team is on the case and trying to backtrack her movements. We have her at The Shore so we think she was in a pub there, and we've got a team doing the rounds. One publican has come forward and thinks she was in his place on the night. He's giving a statement at the moment but seems reliable. Sounds like she came in, waited on someone who never arrived and left. He remembers she seemed quite agitated.'

Macallan saw the picture fill in in her mind. So many parts were still missing, but she could see Nancy now – scared by something – and she could see the killer getting himself into place and waiting. She'd hunted down so many trained killers in Northern Ireland that she felt she knew them – saw how they lived, operated and how they could be caught. There was an arrogance about these men – and sometimes women – that could bring them down. A belief that the ability to inflict terrible aggression upon other human beings was always the answer. Investigators had to be as dedicated and driven as them and never give them a moment's peace until the moment of truth came and they were standing face to face.

Young carried on. 'The main line I'm taking with the research and analysis is, or will be, the notes, her phone and the laptop. Of course, first of all we've looked at Taylor himself. We have Maggie's statement, and although it doesn't tell us too much about the man, the intervention of Sandy Tait is interesting. Of course it may be nothing, but we have him in the Kangas case so we'll keep that in mind.'

Young never allowed conspiracy theories to lead her into a dark alley with no end.

'With the information about Nancy having a relationship with an army officer, and the possibility that she's a source for the story she was investigating, we've made initial contacts with the army for background information but found nothing yet. We've not told them too much at the moment for obvious reasons.'

Macallan frowned. 'Are they dragging their feet, Felicity? This is a serious incident after all.'

'Can't say yet but apparently they're sending an officer to see us tomorrow. Hopefully he or she will fill in some blanks.'

Macallan felt the first stirring of concern. Pieces of evidence were drifting among a flood of information, but already she felt there were other forces coming into play. Nothing connected, but somewhere in the circuits of her subconscious, her mind was straining for the links. They were there, and she knew it. *I'll find the truth,* she vowed and thought how fortunate she was to have this team. These were true allies, and she knew she would need them more than ever with this one.

Oliver took over again.

'There's nothing of particular interest in Taylor's flat – or rather no surprises. To say it was spartan would be an understatement. We should find DNA, and we've already picked up traces of cocaine on some of the surfaces, and empty whisky and beer bottles in the bin. So no problems for fingerprints either. Other than that, the neighbours couldn't tell us much apart from that he hardly ever spoke and was seen drunk a few times. We're making enquiries at some of the local boozers. A couple of neighbours also spoke of seeing him in pubs so we'll see if we can track that line down. There might be a drinking buddy somewhere, but given what we've heard, it's probably unlikely. Sounds like a loner.'

He handed back to Young, who had one more point to add.

'The notes are sometimes difficult to follow but seem to indicate what Jacquie told Grace. They were looking at a rogue army unit who operated during the Troubles, then in the Middle East, who seemed to carry out unsanctioned killings. From there, the information is that the men concerned left the forces at more or less the same time then moved into contract killing. So, a reasonable assumption is that Taylor was one of them. There are no names in the notes, just cyphers, but maybe Jacquie can clear that up for us. We're still working on it, and I'll send you updates as we're working, as I appreciate this is crucial.'

'Okay, it's a lot of pieces at the moment and we need to join up the dots as soon as. Right, Danny, what about Benny Green and Kangas?' There was a lot to deal with, but at least they had a strong suspect for the reporter's murder – that was a result as far as she was concerned.

Oliver gave his notes another look, pushing his glasses back up the bridge of his nose. Macallan suppressed a smile. He'd just started wearing glasses and still wasn't comfortable with the fact that he'd reached one of those unwelcome milestones in the ageing process.

'Nothing more on Kangas, although the Fins are still on the case. Unlikely we're going to get anything new for the moment as it looks likely he'll be in the pokey for quite some time. As you know, Edvin's been recalled to Helsinki, but they'll keep us informed if they pick up anything from their intercepts. We've also been talking to the travelling community locally to see if we could establish who the target was, but we're not getting anywhere. No doubt it came from some dispute over serious crime of some kind so it's unlikely the individual concerned is going to come forward. We've started on Benny Green and are making good progress – we've come up with new links to organised crime groups. I think we could bid to move him up the ladder and start a full operation, with surveillance and financial investigation. I know things are tight but I think it's worth it.'

He looked at Macallan, who turned to Tenant. 'If Danny gives me a proposal, I'll give it to you, Elaine.' She turned to Oliver again. 'As soon as, Danny – please?'

'You've got it – I'll have that on your desk this afternoon.'

He turned to a new page in his notes. 'We still have this issue of Sandy Tait. As far as we can establish, Kangas knew to ask for him, although it's unlikely they had a relationship beforehand. So it seems reasonable to suspect that when Kangas was prepped for this job, he was given Tait's name to use if things went wrong. Confirms what we knew about the man but tells us he's working in the big leagues now. Whatever he said to Kangas settled the boy down but we've still to work out what that means.'

Macallan tapped her pen on the desk, trying to make sure she was absorbing it all before speaking. 'Maggie's contacted the Garda, and I'm going over with her tomorrow to meet officers from the Crime and Security Branch. Agenda is a bit of a blank sheet but they seemed happy to meet. Apparently it was a bit of a struggle to start, but once Maggie got the right people, the walls came down. I've worked with them a lot, and they're no fools when it comes to the business.'

Macallan decided to wind the meeting up. 'Okay, let's get on it. We have Taylor in our sights and ample DNA. Might be coincidence, but we have Sandy Tait in both cases and multiple contract killers on our turf. In addition, our suspect is a Scot, and Danny has described the unresolved situation in Holland where there were Scots contract killers involved. We have the possibility of similar weapons. I'll keep saying it: this might all be coincidence, but we work the stories till we've proved there's something or nothing in it.

'Right, make sure we get Jacquie to sit down with Felicity and get us an analysis of these notes because we need them yesterday. Let's get to work.'

50

When Maggie Duncan had called the Garda to make arrangements for their arrival, she'd hit a few walls and been punted round all the wrong people. It turned out there had been yet another sophisticated gangland shooting, with two victims dead, so the major crime team were busy enough. Finally, she managed to speak to a DI June Garvey, who still had traces of a faint Glasgow accent – it turned out she'd moved to Dublin as a teenager and had never left. The only reason she was free to speak was because she was on leave for a couple of days but had called into the office to pick up her sports bag. She exchanged pleasantries with Duncan before explaining that they were up to their eyes but was interested in any call from her birth country.

'We're expecting a tit-for-tat situation so all the team are out on the road or on surveillance. Anyway, always nice to hear from someone from the old country. What can I do for you?'

Duncan gave her a brief outline of what they had – it was all a bit vague, she said, but if Handyside was in Dublin, he was top drawer and still wanted for multiple crimes, including murder and kidnapping. She half expected a knock-back but something had sparked in Garvey's mind.

'Look, I know we've picked up intelligence that the organised crime teams here have contracted work out, and a couple of the killings we've had have been pretty clean and professional. Our boys are hard but can be a bit crude, if you know what I mean. A bit like the Glasgow wars.'

'Would you be able to have a meet – here or Dublin?' Duncan asked. 'If we came over, it would be me and my super – Grace Macallan. She's ex-PSNI and served in the Branch.'

'Absolutely! God, I know Grace. I worked in CT for a while and attended a couple of meetings she was at. Impressive woman, with some track record. Let me speak to my boss when I can find him. I have a feeling I'll be recalled anyway with all this going on.'

Duncan was surprised when she received a callback just a couple of hours later. Garvey's boss was happy to meet and would take anything that might help get a result with their own unsolved murders. The only proviso was that the Scots go to Dublin for the meeting. Duncan had the flights booked before the day was out; Macallan had decided that they'd go to the meeting and come back the same day.

'The Guards like a wee drink after these things, Maggie, but we can't spare the hours,' she'd said. 'Maybe another time if we get a result.'

51

Macallan and Duncan were on the eight o'clock flight the next morning, and they both felt relieved just to be away for the day. Duncan had never been to Dublin and she was sorry she wouldn't have time to explore.

'Great place, Maggie, if you like your pubs traditional,' Macallan told her. 'As long as you stay away from the tourist traps like Temple Bar. Dubliners avoid it and leave it to the Brit stag parties. Tell you what, if we get a result, I'll make sure we get a night out here.' Macallan was buoyed by the break from the office and the endless run of cases she'd been handling.

'So, you remember June Garvey?' Duncan asked.

'Sure do. We ran a joint op on a PIRA dissident team that were running firearms between Dublin and the North for particular jobs. They were trying to bring down the peace process so it was high-priority stuff at the time. June was lucky to survive it – she took a bullet in the shoulder when they made the arrests. Lucky for her, it missed anything important and went straight through. She took the boy out even though she was injured! That girl has balls of steel, Maggie, and sound as a pound. It'll be good to see her.'

Macallan had plenty of experience with Dublin; during the Troubles, there had been constant traffic with PIRA targets, and the relationship with the Guards hadn't always been easy. They were tough operators, but politics often got in the way of the forces both sides of the border.

The detective who picked them up was Dublin through and through and never stopped talking all the way back to the Garda Crime and Security Branch at Phoenix Park. Macallan knew the Branch well – and the considerable clout they had in relation to terrorism and serious and organised crime. They were also responsible for liaising with other agencies such as Interpol and Europol.

When they arrived at the depot, Garvey met them at the door. Duncan was impressed with her as soon as they met and saw immediately what Macallan meant. Garvey was tall and leggy, with an easy smile, her long brown hair tied back in a ponytail. There was nothing fussy about her appearance, which was all natural – not a trace of make-up.

'Great to meet you again, Grace. Seems a long time since we ran that joint op. It was a good one though.'

Macallan shook her hand warmly and Duncan could see the respect between the two women.

'The boss is going to sit in,' Garvey told them, 'and one of our senior analysts if that's okay. Don't know if you know my boss – Paddy Toher?'

'Don't think so, June, although the name's familiar.'

'Good guy, a bit dour but the best. Earned his promotions the hard way. Front-line detective and totally on top of the job. Doesn't suffer fools gladly, but underneath the hard exterior there's a heart of gold. He just doesn't like to show it. So, it looks like I'll be responsible for the coffee.'

She laughed easily and Duncan relaxed. It was always unpredictable what the reception would be at this kind of meeting. Sometimes it was just a disaster and there was no chemistry, but this one had started well. Macallan knew how this team worked – it was what she'd been brought up on in Belfast. Hard, dangerous work where you relied completely on your team because they could mean the difference between life or death.

They were shown into a bright meeting room and Garvey introduced their analyst. Toher hadn't arrived yet.

'He's on a call and will just be a few minutes. It's the usual problem – the executive is in a sweat about the publicity round the latest double murder. You've a lot of people to pacify with these things, but then you'll know that, Grace.'

'Tell me about it. It's the bit I hate about the job.'

The door opened and Paddy Toher walked in. For some reason Macallan had imagined a big man, a tough Irishman that embodied all the usual clichés, and at first she thought he was another analyst. He was of average height and had a buzz cut, the hair a heavy mix of grey and black. It was a style that seemed to be in fashion just now, but Macallan suspected that was just coincidence – following trends wouldn't be high on his priority list.

He looked like he hadn't shaved in a couple of days and was dressed casually. He was a good-looking man, with a pale complexion – though Macallan wasn't sure if that was in his genes or just from the exhaustion she knew came with this kind of position – and she noticed Garvey giving him a look that said more than *here's the boss*.

Toher offered the merest of smiles but shook hands warmly as he greeted them, and Macallan recognised the wonderful soft tones of a Donegal accent. She knew it well, as Jack had family in that wild north-west corner of the island.

'Sorry I'm late, folks, but the phones are burning with our latest case. These boys just keep escalating the tit-for-tat thing and don't seem to get negotiation.' He sat down and put his notepad on the table in front of him. 'We got coffee or tea or anything to drink?'

'On its way, sir.'

Garvey's words came out slightly breathier, and Macallan hid a smile. *You can never hide it completely,* she thought, but she couldn't blame the woman. Toher was one of those characters who seemed to fill the room with his presence, and with no effort or vanity on his part.

They did the introductions plus small talk, and it turned out that although they didn't know each other personally, Toher and Macallan had worked with some of the same people.

'We thought it was all going to be roses at the end of the Troubles,' Toher said, 'but now we have the organised-crime problem, and we still can't take our eye off the ball with terrorism. Then there's a lot of boys and girls out there who want to keep the fight in the North going. Lot of stuff going on up on the border. Now what can we do for you?'

Macallan made her presentation. It was thin, she admitted, but even if they couldn't devote resources at least they would have the information should something else develop.

'Apart from the call from Ireland, we have this lawyer Sandy Tait taking care of both Taylor and Kangas. Again, might be coincidence, but my guess is not.'

'Lawyers, can't live with them and can't live without them… bastards!' Toher's comment lightened the mood in the room. He'd hardly moved a muscle as Macallan had made her presentation so his levity came as a relief.

'This man Handyside sounds like the real deal, Grace, but there's still nothing to suggest he's living here. There could be any amount of reasons he was here at that particular time.' He rolled his pen between his fingers, considering what he'd heard. 'Listen, I'd be lying to you if I said we could put resources on this right away.'

Immediately, Macallan's initial optimism dampened.

'However, I know June has told you we have a few cases where we think the hits were contracted out because they were different – clean, professional. It makes sense because all these boys know each other, so it's difficult to get to people without being spotted.' He paused again as if coming to a decision.

'I'll be honest with you, we have sources in the gangs that have been embedded for a long time, and one in particular is really starting to feed us top-quality intelligence.'

Macallan didn't ask but wondered if they had an undercover officer in place. It was against protocol to ask, and he would be right to blank her if she did. What he'd said was enough.

'Let's have a break,' he said. 'I need to see if I need to take any calls – so let's meet here again in half an hour and we can give you a broad rundown on what we're dealing with here.'

He stood up and turned to Macallan. 'Grace, can I have five minutes with you?'

52

When they were in Toher's office, he looked at the papers on his desk, sighed and ignored them. He asked her if she wanted anything to drink and she opted for water.

'More than a couple of coffees and I'll be stuck to the ceiling,' Macallan said and settled down, wondering what was coming next.

'Yes, gone are the days where a detective's refreshment came in a nice dark bottle regardless of the time of day.'

He rubbed the back of his neck and she noted the dark shadows under his eyes. He was tired and could probably have done without the meeting and greeting, but Garvey had been spot on – this was a good man who would go the extra mile.

'Well, they might have gone for some detectives, but not this one.' He pulled a nice bottle of Irish malt out of the drawer, a couple of small spirit glasses hanging on two fingertips. She grinned, and although she didn't like drinking early in the day, there was no way she would refuse the gesture.

'Well, it would be a shame to have you drinking on your own.' She smiled and reached for the small measure he'd poured.

'I'm not a huge drinker, Grace – although it might not look like it – but we had a bit of a result last night on a long-term technical operation and, to tell the truth, I've been awake for a couple of days so I'm having this, finishing the meet with you and then going home to sleep for a bit. By the way, are you staying tonight? We could grab a bite.'

She explained they had to go back. 'I'm the same, Paddy. The murder of the journalist is in the early days and the press are all over it, so we need to be back as soon as we're finished here. Maybe another time if we can find linkage here.'

She tipped back the sensible measure he'd poured and felt heat warm the back of her throat. He did the same then put the bottle away.

'So the story is that we have a UC in place. I know your background so you appreciate that this goes no further and I shouldn't have told you anyway.'

'Of course, but I did wonder.' Macallan was all ears now – this conversation was going to be interesting.

'Okay. He's been in place for a long time now, and if they uncovered him it would be a long, hard death. He's just reported confirmation that the team he's with have contracted out to ex-British military. We don't know much more than that, but it's done through a contact only the top gangster here knows and meets.'

'Who's the top man?' Macallan pulled out her notebook.

'A guy called Mike Regan. Born and bred in South Armagh but came to Dublin as a young man to make his fortune, and he did that alright. Hard man. We treat him as a target in two ways. He's the head of an organised crime group, but he's also supported the paramilitaries and still does. You might remember his brother Conlan was killed in Armagh; it was a big stink for the Brits, and it was blamed on an undercover team. It was denied of course, but the Republicans believed it was a death squad.'

Macallan remembered the case, although she hadn't been involved. Those in SB circles believed it had been the army as well, though that wasn't the official line, of course.

'So he's high-profile target,' Toher continued. 'He's in a turf war with two other family-run businesses, but he's getting on top. It's run for years this thing, and we're throwing everything at it now.'

He sipped some water and carried on. 'We've had reports that there was a meet recently and there's maybe a bit of a step forward. We knew from an intercept that he was leaving after taking a call on a clean phone. The car he used was beaconed and we tracked him to Glasnevin cemetery. Do you know it – big tourist attraction?'

'Yes, I've been there a couple of times on breaks to Dublin. Amazing place – you can get lost in it.'

'Well from what we can tell, he met his contact there, and a few days later, one of the opposition was taken out. Very clean – two men on a motorbike were seen getting away, cool as you like. They'd hit him when he was sitting eating an ice lolly in the park, with one of his team each side. Shot from a treeline about a hundred metres away with a high-powered rifle. Witnesses remarked how calm the gunman was – he just packed up his gear and hopped back on the motorbike that was waiting for him. The trip to the park wasn't pre-planned so they must have been tracking the target. A good job from their point of view.'

'Interesting. Sounds like pros right enough.' Macallan pictured the scene in her mind: the villain slurping an ice lolly one minute, his brains all over his two chums the next. *Nice.*

'So, they rarely say anything worthwhile on the landline of course, but with a bit of luck we might pick something off an audio plant in his house. We have a surveillance team standing by at all times to cover him if he leaves but we'll wait till we get an indication before deploying them. If our guys on the streets get anywhere near him, they'd be spotted a mile off. There's a suggestion from our UC that Glasnevin has been used before so we've installed a camera in a couple of the towers there that covers a lot of the graveyard, though not all of it. So if they come back, it might give us a lead.'

They finished off their chat and headed back to the meeting room where they finalised their agreement. Duncan and Garvey would be the contact points for the exchange of intelligence and any requests from the analysts working on both sides of the Irish Sea.

Toher and Garvey saw them back out to the taxi, and it felt like they were leaving old friends. Macallan smiled when she noticed Duncan giving Toher the same look Garvey had earlier when they were saying their goodbyes.

Well well, Macallan thought, *she'll have to beat Garvey to the prize then*. Though Toher hadn't really returned the overlong looks from Garvey or Duncan so maybe he wasn't on the market.

Macallan felt like the pieces of the jigsaw were starting to click slowly into place. She wondered where it would all end, images of Glasnevin swirling in her mind. She'd been strongly affected by the place when she'd visited it, and it still haunted her – the Angels Plot most of all. Indeed, the thought of all those children packed into that tiny corner had almost overwhelmed her with grief. It was something she'd buried in her *linen cupboard*.

She'd recently had her first session with the clinical psychologist who'd used a linen-cupboard analogy to describe her mind. It was like an overflowing space filled with tangled material, and in her case filled beyond capacity – so full of unprocessed pain and demons that the mess spilled out at times.

They headed back to the airport with hardly a word spoken, Macallan still thinking about Glasnevin while Duncan fantasised about Toher.

53

Later that night, Macallan dropped onto her bed exhausted and decided she was too tired to shower. She rubbed her eyes and sent a text to Jack, saying how much she was looking forward to their trip. It sent a warm glow through her gut, and she realised how much she'd missed the intimacy of words and messages, never mind physical contact. She made up her mind that from this point on, no day would pass without her letting him know she cared. He was due back from Antrim with the children in a couple of days and she couldn't wait.

She fell asleep on top of the covers still half dressed.

Macallan was in the middle of a dense wet fog. She had one arm out in front of her, trying to feel her way ahead, and the other hung heavy at her side. She looked down to find a gun in her hand. She tried to drop it, her hand snapping open as if the metal was burning her flesh, but the weapon stayed where it was.

There was a grey shadow in the distance. It had human form; wanted to kill her and take her from Jack and the children.

The gun became heavier and heavier until she collapsed under its weight. She needed to lift her arm to fire the weapon – it was her only chance.

When she fell to the ground, she turned her face to the side and saw what was left of Dominic Grainger's head. His blue lips quivered.

'You did warn me, Grace, didn't you?'

She tried to move away but it was impossible.

'We're together now, Grace. Always!'

She turned away from the horror and looked up to see Pete Handyside towering above her; he was still in shadow, but it was him.

She tried to scream as he leaned over, but she could only watch as he drove a knife into her belly.

She sat bolt upright in the bed, but her terror passed quickly. *It's just a dream, Grace,* she thought and waited on the edge of the bed, practising the deep breathing her shrink had suggested. She concentrated on Jack and the children, and the panic passed quickly.

That's progress, girl, she thought and stripped off the rest of her clothes. She looked at the clock and realised she'd only been sleeping for a couple of hours.

'Thank God,' she muttered and lay back down, staring at the photo of Jack and the children that sat on her bedside table till her eyelids dropped. They were all that mattered.

54

Sam Taylor stretched and yawned, blinking at the light pouring in the window of his mobile home. It was late afternoon and he'd dozed off watching some daytime shite on the box. He couldn't even remember what it was about beyond being some kind of cooking programme – which was surprising given Taylor's lack of interest in home cuisine.

He'd slept off his latest hangover and optimistically searched the empty fridge for something to eat. Finding nothing, he cursed and burst open the bag of crisps that was all that remained of his food supplies. He looked at the empty bottles and realised his crisis of provisions was complete.

Shopping was a pain in the arse as he had to jump on a bus to get to the nearest supermarket, but after looking outside and seeing the weather was fair, he decided to walk despite the distance – it would help bring him back to life and give him an appetite, and he could then feel justified in getting back into the booze.

Taylor was in near total lockdown apart from food shopping. Staying dark took will, and isolating was a hard business, though it was a bit easier for Taylor, who'd never really had close friends and had no idea where the family who didn't care about him were.

He'd followed the news, and the positive for him was the description put out for the journalist's killing. His hair was now much shorter, and although he hated doing it, he shaved every day – his look was at complete odds with the one being circulated. He'd even dyed his hair a shade lighter. The only problem was the scar. He used heavy make-up, which helped, but he still didn't go outside without a baseball cap, and that more or less covered it. He felt safe for the minute and eventually the description would fade from the public's mind. All that seemed to be concerning the news was the advancing virus from China, but he had bigger problems than a bug to deal with so mostly ignored it.

He picked up the clean phone he used to contact Dolan and switched it on to see if he'd tried to get in touch – but there was nothing so he switched it off again.

55

Handyside was reading the latest news from Edinburgh on the progress being made by Macallan's team. There was nothing important – just a quote from Danny Oliver saying that they were following a number of leads and appealing to the public to be careful as they believed the man they sought was armed.

Handyside's phone buzzed – it was another message confirming there had been a trace in a mobile-home site near Edinburgh. He squeezed the bridge of his nose, feeling the beginnings of a headache, then called Dolan and passed the information to him.

'Fair enough. We're on it and will have a look after dark to see what'll work. We need to tie down exactly where he's parked his arse and confirm he's alone. Doubt he'd have company from what I know about him but it's better to be sure.'

'The police think he's armed so they've not found the weapon.' Handyside knew he didn't need to remind someone like Dolan of that but said it anyway.

'Normally he would dump the piece, but if he's gone dark then maybe he felt safer staying tooled up. We'll prepare for that. Speak later.'

If there was one thing Handyside could be sure of, it was that Dolan would prepare for all eventualities. Still, there was always something that could go wrong so it would be a tense waiting game till they were done.

Taylor headed for the supermarket. The weather was a shade warmer than usual and he felt sweat trickling down his back though he knew it was more a result of the booze than exertion. He understood from years of experience that if you could stand the pain then exercise was the best cure for a hangover.

Although the sun was warm enough, there was a cool breeze blowing in from the North Sea – the curse of the natives of Scotland's east coast. For Taylor though, it was medicine, and the cold air helped the process of cleaning up his head. He needed to, because he would hit the drink again later. *What the fuck else is there*? he thought. It helped divert his mind from the fact that Police Scotland and any number of professional killers were all looking to meet him – though with entirely different objectives.

56

While Taylor was away from the park, Dolan and Baker pulled up near the site entrance but still well away from it. Dolan lit up a cigarette, lowered his window and blew a line of smoke out into the fresh air.

'So, there it is, Ronnie. You're the new boy on this team so Sam doesn't know you, which might be handy. All we can be sure of is he's staying somewhere on the south-east quarter of the site. We've got our contact up here trying to find out who owns what to see if it takes us forward, but I doubt it will – can't see an old dog like him using his own name. We don't know if it's a rental or owned. See if there's somewhere we can set up an OP if needs be. I'll hang back for now in case he walks into me. There's a car park over there that should give me a distant view but close enough if you need a quick RV. Right, son, get on your toes.'

Baker was about to get out of the car but stopped and turned to Dolan. 'Look, boss, none of my business but you okay with this? Old mate an' all that?'

'You're spot on, son – none of your fucking business, and you don't question, but now you've asked, here's the truth, and you better get your head round this. You fuck up in this game and put the team at risk then it's time to get your life insurance in place. I get an order, I carry out that order. You're military, same as me. We do what we have to do. Right?'

Baker thought about it for a moment, shrugged and nodded. 'Fair enough; had to ask.' He opened the passenger door, slipped out and headed for the site.

Dolan grinned. He liked Baker – the lad was just a younger version of himself, apart from the fact he was a London boy. They'd had the same start in life, a shit family, and he'd dabbled in street crime before joining the Marines and finding the home he'd never had.

Dolan drove to the car park; it sat on a shallow hill and gave a decent view over to the site. It was as good as they would get and safe enough to avoid an accidental confrontation with Taylor.

He pulled on his cigarette and hoped the job could be done as soon as. Every hour that passed meant something unforeseen could compromise it. The police had to be looking for Taylor, and the man was no mug. He might be turning into a pisshead, but he'd still be a formidable warrior if it came to it.

Baker was carrying state-of-the-art comms, so Dolan tossed the cigarette end onto the tarmac and gave him a shout.

'I'm in and just having a walk about to get the feel of the place.' Baker was miked up and his earpiece fitted perfectly so there was almost nothing to see, and in the days of hands-free phones, the sight of a punter apparently talking to himself was nothing suspicious.

'There's a heavy wooded area on the south-east side so pretty sure we can get a great view from there. There's only one way in and out that I can see.'

'I see it from here – looks like it might be a good spot depending on where our boy is.'

Dolan reached for another smoke then reminded himself he was supposed to be cutting down. He paused for a moment then said, 'Fuck it,' and pulled another one out of the packet, breathing a sigh of relief. A concealed observation post meant they could stay safe enough, although dogs might be a problem if there were any nearby. It was progress though, and he decided one of them would go back in when it was dark. From what he could see, they could deploy from his position into the other side of the woods so there was no need to risk going through the car park.

'Okay, that's a result. Get back here as soon as you're comfortable.'

Fifteen minutes later, Baker climbed back into the car and took the cigarette Dolan offered.

'Looks sweet, boss. The tree and scrub is really thick so there's plenty cover. What next?'

'We go back to the hotel; you get a couple of hours' kip then gear up. We go in tonight when it's dark. We still need to get the kit from the boss's man up here, but I'll take care of that when you're getting some Zs. Okay with that?'

'Sure thing, but it means you get no sleep.'

'Fuck off, Ronnie.' He said it with a grin. 'We train for it – this is luxury compared to some of the shit we had to do back in the day. Right?'

'Abso-fucking-lutely, boss.'

Baker had taken over in the driver's seat and had just switched on the ignition when Dolan put his hand on the young man's forearm. 'Wait one. Is that him on the main road – just three o'clock from the entrance?'

Baker had no idea – he'd only seen photographs of Taylor and this man looked very different, though it was likely he'd changed his appearance. Dolan pulled out the small binos and focused on the distant figure.

'Nice change, Sam,' he muttered, keeping the glasses trained on him. 'It's him, sure of it. He's got a distinctive walk – a lazy way of moving, unlike a soldier. He's carrying a bag I'd guess is full of booze if I know old Sam.'

They watched him walk all the way into the park and right to the door of what must have been his place. It was a result and a half to tie him down so quickly, and Dolan felt the gods were with them.

'Bingo! Okay, let's get going. He won't spend much time on the street apart from gathering supplies so we should be okay.'

They headed back into the city centre, and Dolan left Baker before calling Handyside.

'We've spotted him and identified the exact hideout so we'll be working tonight. Can we pick up the kit?'

'Wait where you are and someone will call with a number shortly. They're ready anytime.'

In less than five minutes, Dolan got the call telling him to head to the Calton Cemetery, where someone would meet him in twenty minutes.

Dolan was there early and was by Political Martyrs' Monument when an ape who looked like he ate children for dinner lumbered towards him and nodded, then asked if he was impressed by the city.

Those were the key words.

Dolan told him the city was great but he didn't like the weather, and the ape handed over a canvas travel bag. The weight of it felt right to Dolan. The ape didn't say another word, just turned and lumbered off towards the gates on Waterloo Place.

Dolan headed back to his hotel and decided to have an hour on his back because there was plenty of time before it was dark and he needed to be sharp.

57

Taylor flicked through the channels for the umpteenth time and cursed the TV. It was all shite and he wished he had something apart from Freeview.

'Fuckin' rubbish,' he slurred, then finished the shot of whisky that was in the glass and followed it up with a long neck-full of beer. He tried to focus on the clock and saw it was eleven thirty. *Jesus Christ, it's still early an' I'm pissed,* he thought. He'd arsed most of his booze already but realised there wasn't enough left to see him into oblivion.

'Fuck it.' He heaved himself out of the chair, decided to ignore the bog and went to go piss outside. Taylor felt like a bit of violence and hoped some punter would wander past and pick a fight.

He placed one hand against the outside wall and sprayed the side of the home, sighing with relief as his swollen bladder emptied. It was another sign of age – gone were the days he could drink beer for hours with no argument from his body.

'That's our man outside, pissing against the side of the home. Looks a bit unsteady, so well done I'd say by the looks of him.'

Even though the comms were secure, Dolan left out names or exact details just in case and whispered, despite the fact he was about fifty yards from Taylor and there was some traffic noise from the busy dual carriageway near the site. Pissed or not, Dolan was taking no chance of spooking Taylor. When they made the hit, they wanted complete surprise, and drunk or not, Taylor would fight for his life if given the chance.

'Roger that. No question it's him?' Baker was in the car. It had been left to Dolan to take the first turn at the OP, as he was the one who could positively identify Taylor.

'No question it's him and I've got a good position here. Quiet otherwise so think we've been lucky. Not seen one dog, thank Christ!'

He stared back through the binos. There was decent street lighting so he had a good view. *How did you get into such a fucking mess, Sam*? he thought as he stared at his old comrade. But he knew the answer – in their game, the odd person just folded under the weight of what their life meant. Ageing was a bastard for everyone, but for someone in their trade it came early. Razor-sharp reflexes started to fade in the early forties, and although experience filled in for a while, it was only a temporary fix. Then you either had to stare into the mirror and thank God you had a partner who loved you or, like Taylor, say 'fuck it' and reach for the bottle or your drug of choice – or both.

'Settled down again so let's see what happens. If he's that pissed, he'll fall asleep, so we might get the job done tonight.'

Dolan clicked off and eased down in the hide, well concealed but right on the edge of the treeline. A passer-by would have to walk over him to know he was there, though he was in full camouflage gear and just behind the perimeter fence, making an encounter with a citizen highly unlikely.

'That would be a bonus,' Baker replied and meant it. If they got the job done in short time, the pay would be the same and he could take that holiday to Thailand he'd promised his new girlfriend. *If this virus doesn't fuck it up,* he thought.

'SOPs again, just in case. Doing the same here,' Dolan ordered.

Baker sighed. It was a pain in the arse, standard operating procedures – checking the kit again and again to make sure – but it was army discipline. Test your friend the weapon and then test it again. No soldier wanted to hear their weapon jam on the money shot, especially if the other guy was pointing his piece at you.

He ran through the drill. 'Kit's good.'

'Roger that. Radio silence for now.'

Dolan settled down again and felt the old wound in his right knee act up. *Bastard,* he thought and cursed the incident where rock shrapnel from an IED in Iraq had entered his right knee. Although the op had been successful, it had left him with bouts of pain that reminded him he was human.

For a moment, his discipline deserted him and his mind drifted off to the beautiful seaside flat on the Med he'd bought with his wife. They'd been careful over the years, and his wife's legacy from her father's death meant they were secure now, so Dolan was planning to put his ticket in.

The man he knew as Joe Stafford had taken it surprisingly well. He'd worried that it would go the other way, but in fact his boss had seemed supportive, telling him that family was everything.

Stafford confused him at times. Though he wasn't military, he was a serious guy, and Dolan was in no doubt that he would be a dangerous one to cross. But there were times he could be almost warm, especially where they discussed their private lives. Dolan didn't know who his wife was, but it was clear he had something special going on.

He snapped back to the job when a shadow passed across the mobile home's window a couple of times. There was no further movement, so Dolan relaxed again and willed Taylor to put the lights out and sleep. That would be the best outcome – Taylor comatose with the drink so they could put him out of his misery without pain or a struggle.

One hour later, the lights went out in the mobile home. Dolan was certain Taylor would fall asleep quickly and figured they shouldn't hang about. The best time to do a drunk man was soon after he succumbed; otherwise, he might be awake again in a couple of hours – that cruel joke that booze plays with heavy drinkers.

'I'm going to do a creep in so standby for instructions.'

Baker acknowledged the call and tossed his cigarette out of the car window, then opened a flask and slugged back some coffee, hoping this was it. His adrenalin had already started to pump, that familiar feeling of exhilaration before it all kicked off setting in. He'd been frightened enough in firefights, but the buzz after you walked out of it all in one piece was like nothing else.

Dolan took his time and stuck to his discipline, moving slowly along the ground at the treeline and stopping every few yards to check his surroundings. He remembered climbing over a field wall in pitch darkness during his early training then falling into a stinking water-filled culvert and nearly breaking his neck.

When he was opposite Taylor's mobile home, he scanned the area, but apart from the path lights, the other homes were nearly all in darkness. He called Baker.

'Make your way down here and stay in the trees till I give the signal of two clicks, then come to me.'

Baker acknowledged the instruction and moved towards Dolan.

58

A light drizzle had started to fall. Dolan wanted to stay in the shadows as he left the treeline, so he took a long route around and came up behind the structure. He slipped in the space below the home and waited again.

When he'd settled, he listened for any noise from above, placed the listening aid against the skin of the mobile home and concentrated on the sounds from inside. He breathed more easily when he picked up the clear rhythmic sound of snoring. A drunk man's snore, but it told him roughly at which end of the home Taylor was. That was a positive.

He slipped back out, skirted the circumference of the home, stopped again and waited to check his surroundings for threats. He had to hope that, in his pissed state, Taylor had left a door open.

He approached the side door, but it wouldn't move and he cursed. Getting inside was the ideal – anything else meant a hit where the public might be about.

He climbed up on the tight little porch area and tried the French doors; his heart rate thumped up a few beats a minute when the handle gave a slight click and opened. He closed it again and headed back to the treeline.

'Get here ASAP. There's access and the target asleep.'

The fact Taylor had left a door open was further proof of the man's decline, but Dolan was glad of it. Picking the lock would have been doable, but there was always the risk it could alert the target and give them time to tool up. An open door meant one less problem.

Baker had pulled on his rucksack and scuttled through the wooded area to join Dolan. They'd worked out different scenarios earlier and had one for entry through the French doors, so they prepared their silenced weapons then headed back the way Dolan had taken originally, a couple of metres apart.

When they came up behind the home, they both slipped underneath and came out just below the French doors. Dolan took up a position facing the site, and behind him Baker opened the door and stepped inside.

He stopped and let his breath steady, then tensed. There was no snoring now; Dolan had already worked that one out when they were crawling under the home. Baker didn't move a muscle, crouched in deep shade away from the patches illuminated by the site lighting.

After a minute, Dolan was satisfied that nothing was moving around the site and entered the home, stopping close to Baker and letting his eyes adjust to the light inside. When they had, he tapped Baker on the shoulder and pointed to the other end of the home.

Baker took a deep breath then they moved slowly and almost silently through the space, checking for obstacles, dodging the bottles and cans that littered the place. Baker was in the narrow corridor that led to the bedroom when a late-night resident drove past on his way home. They froze. Dolan felt a bead of sweat trickle down the back of his neck and heard Taylor stir. *Fuck it.*

'Fuck's sake.' Taylor unlocked his tongue from the roof of his mouth as his bladder sounded the alarm again. He pulled his legs over the bed then started to get up just as Baker came into the room with the firearm at straight arm and ready. Split seconds mean the difference between life and death, and neither Dolan nor Baker had realised that there might be two single beds rather than one double. Baker looked to the right-hand and unmade bed first, and that brief moment allowed all Taylor's fighting instincts to spark.

There was no more than a short distance between Taylor and Baker as he launched himself at the intruder, intending to crash into the bastard as hard as he could. Baker swung, ready to fire, but it was too late – Taylor hit him like a professional rugby player and it did the trick.

Baker crashed into the flimsy wall and they both went down as Taylor locked onto him, grabbing his gun wrist and looking for a way to take the initiative. They ended up side by side, grunting with the effort of staying alive and trying to kill their opponent. Dolan came to the door of the room and cursed at the tangle of arms and legs that were blocking his way. Taylor kept a hold of Baker's gun hand and drove the heel of his free one up under Baker's chin.

Although he missed the point of the chin, he struck near the ear, disabling Baker, who gasped from the shock of the blow as Taylor swung over on top of him, still keeping hold of Baker's gun hand.

'Hold it there, Sam.' Dolan had stepped to the side and had a clear line of fire now Taylor was on top.

Taylor froze, then looked round, squinting at the shape of the man with the familiar voice, but the hazy light from outside blurred his features.

'Get the fuck up, Ronnie.' Dolan's voice was steady – he was in control again.

Baker shoved Taylor off him and backed off to a position beside Dolan.

At that point, Taylor's voice recognition program clicked on. 'Billy, not you, surely.'

'It's me, Sam. Just another job. You fucked up, pal, but then you know that.'

Taylor got up slowly and sat on the side of the bed. He shook his head and suddenly felt okay with it all.

'Fuck it. I'm tired of this shite anyway. Glad it's y—'

Taylor didn't get the end of the word out as the first bullet slammed into his chest bone. He fell back on the bed then slipped slowly down onto the floor. Dolan put two in his head to be sure.

'Right, let's get this done.'

They'd decided earlier to torch the home and rigged the accelerant so it would take time for the fire to start. The job would be done, and there should be no trail back to the team. Hopefully there would be no evidence for the over-stretched police force to investigate, but if they did some-how manage to identify what was left of Taylor then they'd have the man who'd killed the journalist and they could put the killing down to some gangland feud. It would be easy enough to put rumours to friendly journalists so the police could chase a trail to nowhere.

They made sure it was quiet outside and that there were no frantic neighbours who'd been roused by the sound of the struggle in the mobile home. The lights were still out and everything was quiet, apart from the heavy rain that had taken over from the drizzle.

But there was always the law of unforeseen consequenc-es, and what they missed was that the noise had been enough to catch the attention of Taylor's neighbour, who hadn't been sleeping well since his recent cancer diagno-sis. He ignored it, but he was wide awake anyway, so he decided a hot drink and a few pages of his book would be a good shout.

He was at the sink filling the kettle when he looked across at Taylor's home and saw what looked like two figures disappearing into the trees. Suddenly he had something to take his mind off the chemo he was due later in the day. He wondered if it might be housebreakers – there had been a couple of homes screwed on the site by local junkies – so called Police Scotland to do his civic duty.

It was when the operator answered that he noticed the flicker of a fire in Taylor's home and he completely forgot his own problems.

Dolan was only a couple of minutes back on the road when a fire engine flew past them at speed with the blue light going. 'Fuck it.' Dolan gritted his teeth, hoping it was a coincidence and they were headed somewhere else.

'Can't be ours, can it, Billy?' Baker asked, looking round at him.

'Better fuckin' hope not, my friend, because your DNA is all over that bedroom.'

Dolan lit up a cigarette and thought again about the home he'd bought in Spain – it had never looked more inviting.

59

Macallan sat in Tenant's office and thought about the meetings she'd had there over the years, good and bad, and wondered where it would all eventually lead. The revolving door spun constantly at the executive level, with endless changes in the senior ranks. Although she'd had one promotion and a spell in counter corruption, Macallan had stayed more or less in the same arena of serious crime, and for all its problems, she knew she would never have survived if she'd been promoted beyond that. Every time you opened your mouth at those ranks, you had to restrain what you really wanted to say. It was more politics than reality, though someone had to do it.

Tenant was perfect for that job and what she'd trained for all her service – a safe pair of hands – but for all that, Macallan had grown to care about the woman who'd once seemed like her worst enemy. They'd both changed and compromised on their belief systems, and it had worked.

She turned when the door opened and Tenant came into the room, carrying an armful of paper.

'Sorry, Grace, the chief caught me cold this morning. On his high horse about a story in the papers that we don't care about – small-time drug-dealing. Jesus, it never ends.'

'Isn't that the truth?' she replied. 'We gave up on that stuff a long time ago. Had to – we just don't have the resources to keep that nonsense going.' Macallan got up at the same time and poured the tea waiting for them on Tenant's desk.

Tenant smiled and sat down, dumping the papers in her tray. 'That's why you'll never be Chief Constable – because you think our world revolves around truth. Right, enough of that – let's get to the real world.'

It was their morning briefing and Macallan filled Tenant in on the developments so far, and although there was nothing startling, progress was being made, and Macallan felt confident the Dublin meeting had been worthwhile.

'We've ramped up the operation against Benny Green; just waiting for the operational authorities to come through.'

Macallan stopped when Tenant's phone rang. The ACC's expression gradually morphed to serious, her eyes flicking a couple of times to make eye contact with Macallan, who realised whatever it was involved her.

Tenant put the phone down.

'Danny's coming along to the office to brief us on an incident last night. Details just came in from the division.'

Oliver came in only a couple of minutes later and refused the tea offered by the ACC.

'Go ahead, Danny, tell us. Good news or bad?' Tenant said, trying to lighten the mood.

'Just got this after you left the office, boss.'

Oliver filled in what details they had. 'We don't have a full picture but basically there was a report in the early hours from Damside Caravan Park. It's mostly mobile homes but there's capacity for some caravans. One of the residents reported in the early hours what he thought was a couple of housebreakers near a neighbour's place. He was on the call when he noticed the beginnings of a fire, and luckily the brigade was able to get there quick time with no traffic on the road. The fire had taken hold, but they were able to control it very quickly, although there is a fair bit of damage – including smoke damage.'

Oliver checked his notes for a moment. 'To get to the point, there was a body, and the bottom line is that it wasn't the fire that killed him. The pathologist who attended reckons it was the bullets.'

Macallan bit her lip and wondered where the punchline would take them.

'Another pro job, Danny?' she asked.

'Hard to say at the moment but looks like head shots and chest. The PM is arranged for later this morning and we'll get a clearer picture then. But significantly, the victim has a scar high up on the forehead.'

Macallan tried to remain steady. *Here it is,* she thought. *Another piece of the jigsaw*. Whoever killed him had tried to destroy the evidence, but sometimes bad luck just got you, no matter how good you were.

'So, we think it might be Sam Taylor?' Macallan kept her voice even, but there was tension in the room – it was always the same when a rock was pulled back and something unpleasant crawled into the light.

'Well, DNA will prove it, but there's more. They found a Makarov well concealed in the caravan so pretty sure it's our guy.'

Oliver waited and let the information settle before adding, 'The other thing is that Lesley has just called and they've confirmed that DNA found in Hunter's flat is down to Taylor.'

Macallan let her breathing even out – so the man who'd been cleaning up had been cleaned up himself. She wondered if the path to the truth was being hidden before they could get to it.

'You need to go to the PM, Danny. I'll come along too, and let's take Maggie with us.' She tapped a pen against her notebook and thought for a moment. 'I've got this army officer coming but not till later this afternoon, then we've a briefing with the team, *then* the senior officers. Make it for eleven – okay? For now, let's head out and have a look at the scene.' She glanced at Tenant. 'Is that okay with you?'

'Of course, Grace. Do you want me to sit in with the army officer in case there's a problem?'

Macallan agreed and left with Oliver to head out to the locus.

60

Oliver pulled the car in at the entrance to the site and flashed his warrant card at the young uniform covering the entrance. He logged in their names and let them through to a space set aside for parking. They walked to the taped-off area; a good audience of local residents hung around the barrier, taking the scene in from a distance.

They suited up and walked along a prepared route to the mobile home. It was damaged but not destroyed, and the acrid smell of residue from the fire bit the back of their throats as they stopped for a moment to get a feel for the surroundings.

Macallan stared at the treeline – she was an expert in covert operations and considered how a pro might have approached the job. *You'd lie in those trees for hours, wouldn't you*? She imagined the blurred outline of a man there in the dark – waiting, checking and checking again before making their move. She would get the search teams to comb the treeline, though she knew professionals would have left nothing behind.

They met the senior SOCO outside the mobile home. He was a good man, and Macallan had worked with him many times in the past. She trusted his assessment.

'We've done most of it and the body's away to the mortuary. You know that two men were seen heading towards the treeline, and we're guessing they had a vehicle somewhere nearby. There's significant fire damage, but the bedroom isn't too bad so you can come in and look.'

They moved carefully on a line of raised steps to protect the locus and squeezed into the bedroom. It was as if all colour had been removed, leaving only a series of blacks and greys.

'It's mostly smoke damage, but apart from that it's more or less intact. The seat of the fire was in the kitchen area. Looks like they rigged it so it would look like an electrical fire to start with. You can see where the body was, and we think there was a significant struggle.'

'Why?' Macallan asked.

The SOCO indicated a large concave section of damage on the wall near where the body had been found. 'Could be wrong but you can see the walls aren't strong. There was considerable force applied to that one, and we have some fibres caught in the depressed fractures. So, it could have been him falling pissed, but just maybe it was a struggle with one of the assailants. He doesn't have much in the way of a wardrobe so we'll check the fibres against what we've recovered.'

'Good work. What about the gun?'

'Yes, the guys found it concealed below a small cabinet next to the bed.' He indicated where it had been. 'It's away to the lab for examination, but it's a Makarov.'

'What about the car park up on the hill for the escape vehicle?'

The SOCO shook his head. 'Honestly it's a tip. Rubbish everywhere – a million fag ends and God knows how many used condoms.'

'Nice,' was all Macallan wanted to say about it. She thanked the SOCO as they stripped off their protective gear and headed for the car.

'Let's get some coffee before the PM, Danny.'

Macallan's mind was swirling. That it was Taylor that had been killed seemed certain, but why? The motive had to be to cut off a trail but to where? And they still had to make sense of what Jacquie Bell had to offer and see if it took them forward.

There was a maze taking form – a journalist killed, Tam Hunter dead, the killer of both dead, contract killers, Russian guns and the appearance of Pete Handyside. On top of that, Macallan knew someone was creating a firewall between her and the truth. Maybe they'd spend months chasing shadows. Professional killers were never easy to track down, and would Police Scotland let her spend a fortune chasing ghosts?

'No way,' Macallan muttered.

'Sorry, ma'am?' Oliver was driving.

'Just thinking there's no way the higher-ups will let us chase these guys for long.'

'Fair enough; kind of agree with you.'

They turned to each other for a moment and smiled.

61

Macallan, Oliver and Maggie Duncan walked into Edinburgh's mortuary – the bland almost insignificant brick pile where some of the city's darkest events would be examined. The pathologists were detectives in their own way, looking for answers in the indecently exposed bodies that entered their domain day after day. In most cases, it would be obvious why the star of the show had died. The pathologists would confirm the cause of death and add to the sum of scientific knowledge. Every so often, the police would bring them a victim and ask them to help solve their latest puzzle.

Oliver rubbed some vapour up under his nose and offered it to Macallan, who declined.

'Call me old-fashioned, Danny, but I was taught you have to smell it to get it. But fill your boots.'

Duncan was about to take some of the rub from Oliver but realised what Macallan was getting at. For all her time in the army, she'd little experience in the mortuary. She wasn't trying to ingratiate herself to her boss but saw what she meant and declined the offer.

Macallan felt the ever-present cool air and hum from the fridges that held the mortuary's current crop of guests. Her nose twitched at the faint odour. Hardy anything, but just there, reminding you – if it was needed – that although outside the walls, death might still be the great taboo, in here it was the main source of business. Bodies arrived night and day, and death waited for no one.

When the detectives walked into the working end of the building, Sam Taylor was ready and waiting for the gathering audience. Macallan never got used to the indignity of it all and prayed, when her time came, she would never face that audience naked and defenceless. Nothing was hidden under the glaring lights, inside or out, and the pathologists would dig, cut and probe till the victim gave them their answers. A SOCO and productions officer were already there and would make sure that any samples were labelled and recorded to maintain the integrity of the evidence chain.

The Procurator Fiscal had joined them. He was obviously uncomfortable and looked almost the same colour as the man on the slab. It was clear he would rather be somewhere else, and that was okay as far as Macallan was concerned.

'Hello, Grace. Never get used to this bloody place but has to be done I suppose. Funny thing is that, apart from the pathologists, none of us have a clue what's going on so they could tell us anything. How's things with you?' The Fiscal was a good man and had worked at the legal end of a few of Macallan's cases.

Although Macallan liked the man, she couldn't be bothered with small talk in the circumstances, so she kept her response short and just the right side of friendly to avoid offending him – she might need his help another day. They were joined by the forensic officers and the mortuary assistants who'd prepared Taylor for his final show.

Macallan rarely spent time looking at the victims before the pathologist got to work, but Taylor's whole body seemed to be a map of conflict. Although there was some damage from the heat of the fire, the brigade had arrived in time to recover him more or less in a complete state. Apart from the scar on his forehead, there were at least half a dozen marks that were clearly the result of old injuries and wounds inflicted God knows where. His body might have softened from his army days, but he was still impressive. Even in death, Taylor looked hard, right down to the para tattoo on his right arm.

As PMs went, there was nothing too surprising once he was opened up. The harsh lights shone into the depths of his abdomen as the pathologist confirmed the shot to the chest and recovered the bullet. When they examined what was left of the brain, they confirmed what they knew already: that the head shots had ended his life. Macallan was left in no doubt that they were dealing with trained people.

The only other points of interest were that there was significant damage to the nasal septum, mostly likely through drug use, and significant inflammation of the liver. A variety of specimens were taken from the body, but Macallan guessed that they probably wouldn't tell her anything surprising.

When the pathologist was finished, she left the tidy-up to the assistants, pulled off the gloves and washed her hands as she spoke.

'So, our boy liked a bit of nose candy, as well as a wee drink. Think the shots were from fairly short range, but your experts will work that out at the locus. We've all the samples we need and it's straightforward – the shots to the head killed him. I'll get the report done first thing.'

Macallan thanked the pathologist, said her goodbyes to the Fiscal and escaped the building with Oliver and Duncan, keen to get the cloying stink out of her nostrils.

'So just what we would expect, but the drink plus drugs are probably a factor in why it all went wrong for the guy. Doesn't take us far but let's think positive, and it's all part of the evidence when we put someone in court.'

'Where to?' Oliver wiped the residue of the vapour rub from under his nose.

'Back to the ranch. Need to see how we're getting on with what's coming in from Felicity.' She looked round at Duncan and smiled. 'What did you think of that, Maggie?'

'Last week I was chasing a flasher through Dalkeith town centre and now I'm watching a killer make his final appearance. A bit different, boss.'

Duncan had taken in every moment of the PM and wanted to learn as quickly as possible. She was in big company and wanted to show what she could do. After years of chasing an ambition she couldn't quite define, she felt she'd arrived exactly where she wanted to be. Her time in uniform had been about getting through the ranks, but that had dropped away like snow off a dyke. *This is what I want,* she thought and felt the rush of the hunt burn through her.

Oliver was on his own high of adrenalin from being back in the fray of major crime investigation.

Macallan saw it and was satisfied she had all the talent she needed around her to succeed. Her job was to use her own experience to make sure it was there for them when they needed it. It was hard, but she knew she had to delegate wherever possible and let them have their heads. That was how the best teams worked, and she knew among her faults was a tendency to try and do it all herself.

'We're good. All good, and we're getting closer all the time.'

She sank back in the seat and settled into her thoughts.

62

Felicity Young was waiting in Macallan's office when she got back from the mortuary with Oliver and Duncan. As she settled herself down, she was joined by Tenant.

Macallan explained she wanted to make sure everyone knew what the significance of Nancy Gilhooley's notes might be. She filled them in on the PM, but as there were no surprises, it was almost a routine report.

'The good news, if I can put it that way, is that the fire hadn't taken control – we would have lost a lot of evidence otherwise. Okay, where are we with the notes and Jacquie's statement, Felicity?' she asked.

'All done, and the notes and Jacquie's statement are all on the HOLMES system now.' It was no more that Macallan would expect from Young, who was the ultimate professional.

Macallan nodded back. 'Excellent, Felicity. That's fast work. The floor's yours – what can you tell us about Nancy's investigation?'

Young pulled the glasses off her nose and spoke carefully, trying not to lose any of the threads.

'Well, first of all, the main thrust of the research has been on Nancy's telephone and laptop, Jacquie's statement and the notes in the rucksack.' She paused and shoved the glasses back onto the bridge of her nose.

'As Jacquie had mentioned, I did get the impression that Nancy was a talented reporter – and thorough. According to Jacquie's statement – and what she told me in conversation – although Nancy was talented, she was headstrong at the same time. However, she went to Jacquie a few weeks ago and said she'd picked up a story from a contact in army intelligence about a rogue team who'd carried out unsanctioned killings of paramilitaries in Northern Ireland. It was a five-man team and three of them were Scots, so there was immediate interest. The full details of the allegations are all in Jacquie's statement, and if anyone hasn't read it yet, I'd suggest they do.

'We know now that this came from a relationship that had developed between Nancy and this female officer. It seems clear that she gave Nancy the lead on this story and Nancy followed it up. According to the notes, one of the original team in Northern Ireland was sick, had found God – though mainly through alcohol – and looked like he was ready to disclose his sins. She used codes for the names but I'm as sure as I can be that we're talking about Tam Hunter.'

Everyone's attention was fixed on Young.

'The officer had indicated to Nancy that when the peace process was in full swing, there was real concern in the military that a can of worms could be opened. Then later, there were similar concerns in the Middle East and Afghanistan. Later on, the team seem to have been… let's say *encouraged* to leave the military before the post-mortems started – on the Troubles in particular. The main allegation was that this undercover team carried out extra-judicial killings to take out active paramilitaries opposed to the peace process. The twist to this is that this team left the army but then appear to set themselves up as contract killers. It seems from the notes that army intel knew that, but as far as I can establish, they didn't share the information with the police.'

Young waited a moment for any observations then carried on. 'The notes indicate that the activities of the team had been directed by army intelligence in Northern Ireland and that they maintained unofficial contact with them after they left the army, despite the intelligence about contract killings.'

'Jesus.' Tenant rarely invoked Christ's name, but what was unfolding was a swamp, and Police Scotland had enough problems as it was without going to battle with the dark forces.

'So, the officer gave Nancy the name of the old soldier – Tam Hunter – who was living in the East End of Glasgow. There were concerns that he was coming apart and might talk to the wrong people. This is where Nancy seems to have made an approach to Hunter, who was indeed willing to talk. That must have been about the point that Nancy spoke to Jacquie. She'd realised just how deep this sewer was, and from there I think you know the rest of the story. The notes don't tell us much more than that but it's enough.

'As I mentioned, Nancy used a form of code, but I'm satisfied that we can work out who the players are and, most importantly, the intel officer, Hunter and so on.

'From what I've examined, Hunter confirmed in some detail that he'd been part of an undercover team in the army, working from Belfast, who carried out targeted killings of leading paramilitaries both in Northern Ireland, particularly the border area, and in the UK. He seems to have been a bit reluctant at first but was prepared to go on the record. I think, from the notes, we can identify who this unit has targeted and killed.

'Hunter said that when they left the army and set up as contract killers, he was already starting to come apart. They'd killed a number of people in a clean-up job, and he'd found out that two of the victims who'd died in a rigged car crash were a mother and child. That was it and he bailed out; told the rest of them it was health reasons, which was true. He wasn't fit for operations anymore. The important point is that the only one of his old team that he kept in touch with was someone he called Sam – the only one of the team who still kept his base in Scotland, somewhere near Edinburgh.'

'So probably Sam Taylor?' Macallan asked.

'Well, given what's happened, it has to be. They only met from time to time – drinking pals according to him.

'So, Nancy was speaking to Jacquie and they spoke to their boss at the paper. Of course, they considered speaking to the police, but they weren't there yet.'

'With the greatest respect, I think they were already there,' Tenant broke in. Her face had paled.

Macallan tried to change the tone, which had cooled at Tenant's words. 'Right, so what happened next?

'Well, the decision was that they'd do more research – open sources and so on. Nancy was told to have the next meet with Tam and then they'd reassess. It seems she went off-script though and kept digging, but when she went to the next meet, it wasn't just Tam that was there. Apparently, Hunter thought Sam would talk as well, but this man went crazy and she was really shaken. She couldn't get in contact with Hunter after that.

'To summarise, the notes are quite detailed. There are references to individuals killed in Northern Ireland and some research on contract killings they might have been involved with. We're working on the code but think we'll be able to work out most of it eventually.'

She paused and removed her glasses before carrying on. 'There is one interesting point, though it's possibly just one of those coincidences that we come across all the time.' She put the glasses back on. 'One of the killings seems to have been Conlan Regan in South Armagh. He just happens to have been the elder brother of Mike Regan, who is of course the main target for Paddy Toher in Dublin.'

Macallan remembered the Regan case, although she hadn't been involved herself. She didn't know what to make of it, but all they could do was leave it in the file marked *coincidence* for the time being.

'There's decisions to be made before we go any further, but we can't mention the Regan thing to Paddy Toher at this stage,' Macallan said. 'Might mean nothing and it's too sensitive to share at this stage. Maggie, you were army intel at one time. What do you think?'

Duncan had been following the briefing closely. She'd faced so much and yet she felt raw in the company she was in. She paused and looked at Macallan, who smiled and nodded, which seemed to calm her.

'Well it's common knowledge that there were no clean hands in that conflict, so I can't say I'd be surprised if there was a unit working undercover. There are still ongoing investigations into all sorts of activities over there, not excluding what the army did on certain occasions. Investigations would be hard going, but it's getting to the right people. No doubt, Nancy's story sounds plausible.'

Macallan nodded. 'Given your experience, I think we'll give you the job of finding Nancy's source.'

Young came in again. 'I've mentioned Nancy's phone and laptop. We've made good progress, and through the examination of her email and phone, we've a number that seems to crop up and coincide with some emails. The other party is never named or identifies themselves in the messages. That on its own is unusual enough. Sometimes the language is quite intimate, but other times it's clear they're using coded language that would seem to fit who we're looking for. Of course, as a reporter, she had other sources, but the intimate nature makes it likely this is who we're looking for. The messages crop up regularly up to her death.'

'So we have a phone number?' Macallan hoped this meant contacting the source might be straightforward, though she knew that wasn't usually the case with intelligence officers.

Young sipped some water and took her glasses off again.

'Jacquie Bell mentioned in her statement that Nancy had told her that she'd met the intelligence officer at a conference in Edinburgh run by our very own Police Scotland. So I've been in touch with the department that organised that conference and discovered the army sent two delegates – one male and one female – so we have a name. It turns out that she's also liaised with Police Scotland on a number of occasions on counterterrorist issues and jobs.'

'Hallelujah!' Macallan slapped the desktop. Another piece of the road map had fallen into place. 'We hardly ever get these kinds of breaks. Good work, Felicity. I know you're not a drinker, but I'll get Mick a large one at our next meet.'

Young gave one of her rare smiles. She was perfect company when she was away from the job but almost robotic when she was delving into a mass of intelligence that needed to be processed in the system. 'Her name is Ruth Conway – Captain Ruth Conway – and she should be contactable. She seems to be the whistle-blower, and I think we can presume this is going to finish her career, but that's not the issue just now. We can see that an unknown number called a couple of hours before Nancy was killed – turns out it's a phone box in Leith, which could be relevant as we still have no idea why she was out with the notes on her. We also saw that she tried to call Jacquie but couldn't get an answer.'

Macallan looked round the room and nodded. 'Okay, let's get to work. I'll talk to the ACC now and come back with whatever the plan is. Thank you.'

The team filed out of the room, leaving Tenant and Macallan alone.

'Well, there's a story and a half, Grace.'

'Sure is. So, what we have is almost certainly Nancy's killer identified and dead. Because he tried to take the notes, it's likely that was the motive. We don't know who or why he was killed but it was probably a clean-up job to sever links elsewhere. Catching pros at this level is rarely successful, and much of the investigation won't even be in Scotland. We have military intelligence with their grubby hands somewhere in the mix, which could be another major investigation, but it's all part of the same bag of worms.' She paused to let her words settle.

'What's first then?' the ACC asked. 'I know you have the Kangas thing hanging, but it's unlikely we'll get much further just now, and we're relying on our friends in Dublin if there is something linking to Pete Handyside.'

'What do you think, Elaine? Full backing for this?'

'It's going to be a huge strain on resources, but we can't avoid it I guess. Give me a page on what you'll need, plus likely risks, and I'll square it with the chief.'

'Right, I've got this army boy next. You want to sit in?'

'No, I think it'll make my head even more painful than it is. Why not get Maggie Duncan in with you? She seems the business.'

Macallan had already thought of that and was pleased they were on the same page.

When Tenant left, she called Duncan in and told her what was planned. Duncan was delighted but tried and failed not to show it.

63

Paddy Toher looked up wearily from his notes when June Garvey knocked and walked in.

'June, sit yourself down and grab some of that coffee there.' He smiled – he was glad of the interruption from writing a note to his chief, explaining why he was spending another small fortune on the gang wars.

'Stay at the rank you're at,' he told her. 'You really don't want to deal with the shit you inherit in this chair. So, what's the word? You sounded hyper when you called.'

Garvey looked pleased with herself – she was in the company of a man she wanted, though she wondered if he'd ever make a move. It was frustrating, but she convinced herself it would come if she was just patient.

Toher had caught the signals she was giving out but hadn't made up his mind how to react. He was still coming to terms with a messy divorce and that was enough to deal with, so he'd decided that a new relationship could wait – he didn't want to walk into another emotional mess.

Garvey began her briefing, breaking him from his thoughts.

'We've had our agent on and he's picked up there's another meeting coming up, but he's not been told where.

He's driving Mike Regan to the appointment. He'll be left in the car wherever it is and can tell us then. If it's Glasnevin then maybe it's the man who organises the contract jobs.'

'Sounds like a good one. Are the surveillance team ready to go?' Toher felt a surge of energy – he needed a break to get the executive off his back, even if it would only be temporary.

Garvey confirmed the team were ready – she was going out with them as operational commander and they would deploy as soon as they had a location. There was no other option: the UC hadn't been told where he was picking up Regan or what car he was to use, and trying to follow them conventionally was too much of a gamble with someone as streetwise as Regan, who might have spotters watching. Regan also wasn't averse to strip-searching his team without warning, meaning the UC wouldn't place a beacon their own person unless the circumstances were extreme.

'Well, let's hope it's Glasnevin again. The CCTV's all rigged up there and working, right?'

'Yes, the tech boys have it up and running. It's pretty well covered. Not the whole place, but fingers crossed.'

Garvey felt a tremor in her stomach – this could be a major breakthrough, but their UC was in a precarious place and they couldn't gamble with his life.

'Okay, we wait. I'll be in the ops room. You take care out there – just remember Regan is an animal, and I don't want to have to tell anyone that someone they love spent the last hours of their life being tortured by that bastard.'

Garvey left to kit up for the job.

64

As Garvey was testing her equipment, the UC smoked another cigarette, trying to quell the tremors in his gut. He could usually control them, but every so often reality seemed to pour over him, and the tightrope he walked looked decidedly thin. It had been a long, hard job infiltrating the gang, and he'd been undercover so long he struggled at times to remember what his life had been like before he took on the role. He was one of the best – and had to be to take on this particular job.

There had been reluctance by the executive to actually take such a risk, but the gang wars had reached such a pitch the decision was made before there were more bodies to deal with. The public were pissed off with the conflict, and the press had been giving the Garda permanent bellyache over the mounting body count.

He was in his flat and wished he could drink some coffee, but he was stretched enough – a caffeine overload would just give him the shakes. Regan had taken a liking to him, and driving the top man around took him as deep as they'd get in the organisation.

The phone startled him, and he took a couple of slow, deep breaths before he answered.

'Go to the shop at Croke Park. There's a Beamer parked outside, keys under the offside front wheel. Pick me up at the house. Okay?' Regan never expected questions. If the man said jump, it was just a case of how high.

'Got it, Mr Regan. On my way.'

Regan had an ego and a half and liked the paid staff to call him mister or boss.

The UC called his handler and passed on the information. The system kept a firewall between the UC and the operational team on the ground. The information was passed immediately to Garvey, who decided they would head out but stay well back because it could be a trap – Regan testing the UC.

There was no time to beacon the car, but the UC decided to take the risk and use a small beacon on himself. His hands trembled as he fitted the tiny device in his jacket. It was less reliable than some kit and risky, but he decided it was worth the chance.

The UC got out of the taxi near the imposing structure of Croke Park stadium. His headache was passing; he'd swallowed a couple of tablets to ease the pain. The job was getting to him, and he hoped they could get a result soon and pull him out.

There was another problem in that he'd become involved with Regan's niece, which was a complete no-no. His handler would have pulled him straight out if she'd known. But he couldn't help it – it was some human relief from the constant strain of living a lie – some warmth in a cold existence – and he liked her a lot. Regan would have kicked the life out of him if he knew. He was protective of his family, who he considered some kind of criminal royalty, and didn't like the paid staff mixing with them.

The UC shook his head and tried to clear his mind for the job in hand. There was never a moment he could relax – one mistake, one unscripted moment that might expose him would mean certain death. *Get a fucking grip, boy,* he thought and squared his shoulders as he got back into his role.

He dipped down and found the keys, then, once inside the car, he called the dedicated number for his handler. Even if his phone was checked, this number would go to the female handler, who would pass for a girlfriend. He gave her the make, model, colour and number of the car.

'I'll come along Clonliffe Road and then turn left onto Drumcondra Road so you can get me there. He wants picked up at his place so that hasn't changed. I'm wearing my beacon and switching on now so let me know when you've confirmed the signal.'

Only a couple of weeks earlier, Regan had made the whole team strip before one of his men checked through their clothes, but this beacon was tiny and concealed in the fabric of his jacket so would probably survive most searches.

'That's it working. So take care and no risks.'

He drove the car carefully, remaining below the speed limit. Regan insisted on that – there was no need to attract a pull from some eager young recruit trying to make a name for themselves.

When he pulled up outside the expensive pile that was the boss's home, he switched off the engine and waited. A few minutes later, Regan appeared at the door with his wife, who waved to the UC. He waved back and smiled. It never ceased to amaze him how ordinary she seemed, and yet she had to know at least some of what her man did to keep them in such style. He'd been in the house a couple of times; she would make him tea, fussing over him like he was her favourite nephew.

When Regan got in the car, he seemed to be in a good mood for a change and was still talking on his phone. When he finished the call, he looked round to the UC. 'You look pale, son. You okay? Not been on the sauce I hope? I like my boys in the right condition, especially if they're driving.'

'No, I'm fine, Mr Regan, just had a bit of a headache this morning but it's cleared up. Where to?'

The question was unnerving – there was always the fear that such queries were a precursor to exposure, but Regan seemed relaxed – it was no more than small talk.

'Glasnevin. Find a spot near the main gates and wait there.'

On the way, Regan talked about his favourite subject, Manchester United, and the trials of the club since the departure of Sir Alex Ferguson. 'Costs me a fuckin' fortune for my season ticket and travelling back and forward just to watch that shite!'

When they pulled up near Glasnevin, Regan lit up a cigarette.

'Right, wait here. I hopefully won't be too long. Then I've got a wee treat for you. I'm going to see my wee bit on the side and she has a couple of friends over. You can take your pick. What do you think? Am I a good fuckin' boss or what?'

The UC tensed – there was no way out of this one. All the team regarded *a bit on the side* as the norm, and he could hardly use his relationship with Regan's niece as an excuse.

'Sure thing, boss – sounds like a plan.'

When Regan left the car, the UC cursed, knowing he wouldn't report this one back, although he was supposed to disclose everything. *With my luck I'll get a dose of the clap,* he thought and lit up a smoke. He phoned through to his handler and told her Regan was on his way into the cemetery.

65

Regan stopped for a moment at the Necrology Wall, raised to commemorate all those who had died in the revolution, including the Easter Rising. He hated what the Brits had done in Ireland, and although he'd never been in the paramilitaries himself, his brother Conlan had been a high-profile PIRA commander. It was believed he'd been murdered in South Armagh, although his body had never been found.

A couple of witnesses had seen a team getting into a vehicle near his farm at the time he'd disappeared – all dressed in camouflaged combat gear. The authorities denied it, but he was convinced some undercover team had been responsible. He grunted at the names of the dead Brits on the stone. The decision to include them was a controversial one, and the memorial had been vandalised more than once.

'Bastards,' he murmured and spat at the part commemorating the British dead.

He turned and headed along the path towards the Botanic Gardens entrance, where he was to meet the man he knew as Joe Stafford.

*

'That's the target on the move – just walking past the Angels Plot.' Garvey breathed a sigh of relief that they were within range of the CCTV and there was no need for the surveillance team to move too close. The CCTV team were experts and kept a running commentary on Regan and what he was doing. When he reached the gate, he stopped and browsed among the graves there.

'That's an unknown male joining the target and they're walking slowly back in the direction of the Angels Plot. We've got a good view of him so wait one for a description and photo on its way.'

Garvey's pad lit up with a picture of the two men. 'Bingo,' she said with relief, then murmured, 'Now we just need to find out who you are, boy.' There was a lot to do before they could pat each other on the back.

'Get a team ready in the Botanics in case the unknown male exits that way,' Garvey instructed her squad. 'Regan is no longer the main target; we know who he is, but this other target may be crucial. Repeat: the unknown male is now target one and we let Regan run after this meet. The priority is to identify this man. Description to follow and picture on its way to the rest of the plot.'

Regan offered a smoke to Handyside, who declined the offer.

'I try to keep the filthy habit to a few a day, Mike. Still run a bit, so I try to hold it to a minimum, but I gave up trying to stop years ago. When the going gets tough, there's nothing quite like a smoke to ease the pressure.'

Handyside had built up a good relationship with Regan, and although the Dubliner was a violent bastard of the first order, he was good at what he did and took his business seriously. As importantly, he was security conscious and constantly checked for problems, which suited Handyside. So many gangsters thought they were invisible and fireproof till they ended up doing fifteen years.

Regan sucked in a lungful and nodded in agreement.

'True, Joe, but I'm not much of a drinker so I allow myself ten a day. Too much but could be worse. I'm in the gym every day so still in decent shape.' He paused for thought. 'Christ knows you've got to be in this game. Never know who the fuck is trying to put one in your head or your back. Speaking of, this thing in Dublin is out of hand so I want to discuss an idea with you.'

'Go ahead. That's why I've flown here this morning. We aim to please.'

Regan told him that the tit for tat killing had solved nothing for any of the gangs – it had just brought constant hassle from the Guards, and all their businesses were suffering.

Handyside agreed, but it wasn't in his interest to involve himself in the politics of the war. The other gangs didn't know a man called Joe Stafford existed – Regan had been put in touch with him through the Russians, who'd supplied him with a regular supply of trafficked women.

'There are two other gangs in this fight and it's time to finish this thing. I want a double hit, Joe. It has to be the top men, taken out near enough at the same time. Can it be done?'

Handyside thought for a moment. 'It's a tough call but anything can be done if the investment is right. We'd need a full team on this, but it'll cost, and to be honest, if we did it then we'd leave Dublin up to you after that. We'd take no further part in what was going on till things had settled – if ever again.'

'But it could be done? These guys are no fools.'

'Get me the usual details of the men you want taken out. We'll need a bit of time for surveillance and planning, then we'll okay it with you before it happens. One thing though: you tell no one else what's happening. Total security or we're out of here.' Handyside stopped and turned to face Regan. 'We clear?'

Regan wasn't afraid of much, and yet this man could reach a nerve as if he'd cut through his flesh with a scalpel. He pulled on his cigarette. The plan was ambitious, but he was tired of this never-ending war. It needed a bold move and this was it.

'Clear. What do you think?'

'Honestly, I think you're right; if it was me, I would have taken all the top men out long ago. Make them bleed, make their families bleed – dominate them. You've been playing like teams going for a draw. So, I agree.' He said it without emotion – he had been asked for an opinion and he'd given it.

If it had been anyone else, Regan would have probably kicked off at the implied criticism of weakness, but this was not anyone else. Someone who was best pals with the Russians and could command professional ex-soldiers had to be given respect. He was almost jealous – this man was everything he could never be. Regan might be a crime prince in Dublin, but he knew he lacked the business acumen and strategic thinking to operate on the world stage.

'It's funny, Joe, but I hardly know a thing about you. I don't know where you live or much else apart from that north-east accent. I used to worry about it, but after the jobs you've done for me, I know you're not the law playing a game.'

Handyside gave a rare smile. 'There's one thing I'm not and that's the law, Mike. I keep myself safe, and that's how it works for me.'

Regan nodded and put out his hand, and Handyside took it. It was the first time Regan had offered this gesture.

He was a powerful beast and was surprised that the man's grip was equal to his own, but what threw him was that the Englishman clearly had much more in reserve.

He never wanted his team to find out who he was dealing with – that he was paying ex-Brit soldiers to carry out his business. Most of them hated the Brits, and some had connections to the paramilitaries. All his life, he too had expressed his hatred of the forces he believed had killed his brother and, as he saw it, had ruined Ireland. However, they were what he needed for the job. He had some hard men on his side, but they lacked the training and professional skill required to finish the war.

'Okay, Joe, I'll get the details run off for you today. Call me when you're ready.'

Handyside headed towards the Botanics as Regan turned, walking slowly back past the Angels Plot, where he could smoke again and think for a bit before returning to the car.

As Regan approached the main gate, he stopped again beside the grave of Michael Collins, once more mulling over the fact that he was using a team of Brits to kill his opponents, despite his lifelong hatred of the bastards.

He couldn't have known – and neither could Handyside – and the team he'd hired were the same men responsible for his brother's death.

66

'That's Regan and the new target separated. Regan heading back towards the Angels Plot and the new target towards the Botanics. Instructions?'

Garvey straightened up in her car as the message came over the air, her heart rate moving up ten beats a minute. 'Let Regan run – we take the new target wherever he's going. No risks. If there's any hint of a compromise, we hang back.'

Garvey ran through a series of instructions, placing the footmen and cars in positions all around the area so that Handyside could be picked up and followed wherever he went next.

Regan stopped outside a café and flicked his cigarette away, staring back towards the Angels Plot and the ground that, according to family legend, contained two tiny bodies borne by his aunt and grandmother. *Fucking life,* he thought, the weight of responsibility bending his shoulders. The atmosphere round that sad ground never ceased to make him pause and wonder why he was where he was in life.

'Fuck it,' he growled, and the words broke the dark spell of the place. The game was in play and there was no going back now. He headed back towards the cemetery entrance and cheered himself up with the thought of the hooker he was about to meet and enjoy.

As Regan thought about life and death, Handyside turned through the gates into the Botanic Gardens and decided he had plenty time before he caught the flight back to London. He decided to walk around the beautiful gardens – it would give him time to think through Regan's proposal.

'That's the target on walkabout in the gardens on his own, and I have the eyeball,' the footman confirmed.

'Give him plenty of room,' Garvey replied. 'We have the exits covered. We only want to know if there's a meet of any kind – the priority is intelligence gathering.'

She didn't want to take any risks when it wasn't necessary.

Handyside called Billy Dolan, who was at home in Malahide; he'd based himself in Ireland since meeting his wife, who was a Galway girl. Apart from Dolan, the team were well split up in various parts of the UK, which made security less of a problem, as they only came together for the jobs. He told Dolan where he was and that he wasn't flying back till the evening.

'Get something to eat there – I'll jump in the car now and be with you as soon as.'

Dolan was keen to get on with the job – if this was a big one, he'd take it then hand in his ticket and get out, before his luck turned and he ended up in prison or dead.

Garvey decided to put a male and female in the café, acting as a couple, though it would mean they could only do that job and would then have to leave the plot, in case they were recognised. Five minutes after Handyside sat down, the two surveillance officers took a table well away from him, but with a good view of what he did. They signalled that they were in place and that he was alone.

Garvey waited, starting to get anxious when there was no movement. If she could just identify this man, the day would be a success. She wanted to do it for herself and for Toher, who deserved a break from the constant pressure of his job. He'd broken his back trying to keep a lid on the wars, and no one could have done more.

She called Toher and filled him in on the developments. He sounded positive and asked if they need anything else out on the plot.

'We're fine here. Anything from the CCTV boys?' she asked.

'They think they might get something from lip-reading, and the long-range listening device is in place, but it depends. There was some traffic and wind noise so not sure what the tech boys will get once they've cleaned it up. The way they were positioned wasn't ideal but never mind.'

A call came in from the surveillance team in the restaurant that their target had been joined by another male and gave a full description.

Garvey fretted because splitting the team to follow two targets was a big no-no.

She came back to Toher. 'What do you think? I don't want to split the team, but now we have two unknowns, so this might be a break identifying this other man as well.'

Toher told her that he'd get another team to them as soon as possible. 'We've spent a fortune, and the executive want to hang me anyway, so what's another few thousand euros going to matter.'

Handyside told Dolan what Regan had proposed and waited for a reaction. Dolan thought about it and shrugged.

'Well it's coordinating the two jobs and trying to time it close together. That might throw up problems, but leave it with me. I'll get the boys organised and see what we can come up with from the recces and research,' he replied, then asked, 'No fallout so far from the Edinburgh job?'

'Doesn't seem to be any problems so far – my contact up there is probing his police contacts for any news.'

Handyside didn't mention Macallan as he knew Dolan would research her and maybe put two and two together. He was a big target who'd escaped, and there was more than enough about that on open sources.

They agreed what they needed from Regan and that there would be daily contact till they were ready to go.

'Look, when this one's done, I'm out,' Dolan said. 'It's time.' He waited for Handyside's reaction.

'I told you, Billy – do what's best. This business is hard, and most of us end up dead or inside, so you're making the right decision. We're careful, but you never know what attention these Dublin cowboys are attracting from the law. I'll not stand in your way or try and make you reconsider.'

They finished and carried out the usual fieldcraft. 'I'll leave first,' Handyside said; Dolan would wait five minutes before doing the same. 'Let me know if anyone leaves after me. Better safe than sorry.'

Dolan sat with his back to the wall, so he had a decent view of the packed restaurant. He watched Handyside move off into the gardens while pretending to read his paper.

After no more than a minute, he noticed a couple vacate their seats and head outside as well. Dolan left his table and went out behind them, walking quickly to close the distance.

'To the footmen: clear the air – target two is closing quickly behind you. Be aware.'

The backup surveillance officer was some distance away, waiting to take over from the couple with the eyeball, but could see what was happening behind them.

There was a moment when the two officers heard the call and couldn't tell what was coming at them from behind. It could be an attack if they'd been compromised, and while they waited for a command from Garvey, the male officer froze for a mere moment and turned his head. It was an instinctive but human reaction to a threat in one's blind spot, but it was a wrong move and contrary to all his training. He cursed when Dolan grinned at him and lifted his hand in a friendly gesture as he overtook them.

'Lovely day.' He walked past like just another punter in a hurry.

The male surveillance officer cursed at his momentary lapse and hoped there was no damage, but his gut told him there was.

He called it into Garvey.

'Right, the two off you get away from the plot and we'll continue the surveillance.'

When Dolan was well ahead of them, he called Handyside.

'Don't know for sure but I think the law might be around. A couple left right behind you, and I went as near as I could – the guy looked a bit spooked when I closed up behind him, and when I passed, I noticed he was wearing an earpiece. Could have been a hearing aid, but he was only in his thirties. What do you think?'

Handyside didn't panic – they could be wrong, but it was likely Regan had some attention. He was the top dog in the Dublin crime world so it would be naive to think otherwise. The important thing was that if there was a tail, they had to lose it as quickly as possible.

'Lose them and anti-surveillance till you're sure. I'll contact you later, but let's just be careful.'

Dolan started to jog, and although his car was close enough, he headed for Drumcondra Road and jumped on the first city-bound bus, knowing he could lose a follow in the bustling city centre. It took an hour in Grafton Street, entering shops and exiting through the back doors, before he was sure he was clear. He always carried a change of dress, hat and glasses in his rucksack, and donning them had no doubt helped.

Garvey called a complete loss on Dolan.

Handyside had used the Botanics to cover his way out, walking into a residential area full of some of the most expensive bricks and mortar in Dublin. He'd stepped calmly up to the front door of a six-bedroom pile and found the only person at home was the cleaner. He'd then worked his way in with the cover that he was a police detective.

The police team moved to start covering his exit, thinking they'd discovered another criminal contact within the house, but while they were still thinking about it, Handyside was out the back door, leaving the cleaner open jawed and wondering what had just happened. He exited through a gate at the rear garden and into a lane that took him clear within a couple of minutes.

The police didn't work it out till a few hours later, when he still hadn't exited. They'd suspected it might be his home – then the intelligence checks came back with the information that the house belonged to a well-known local politician. They were left hanging until they accepted that the timing meant the target could have brassed it and got out through the back before they'd managed to cover all the exits. It happened.

Handyside had done exactly the same as Dolan and had spent another hour making sure he was clean. When he was certain he was okay, he jumped in a taxi and headed for the airport. He was calm and knew it could have been something or nothing, but as far as he was concerned, he would only work with Regan remotely in future – if at all. The job they'd agreed would have fallout so maybe it was time for a break in the relationship.

He called Dolan. 'You okay?'

'I'm good – if there was anything, it's gone. Hard to know if it was a tail or not but it's certainly possible. It happens when you deal with these boys too often. The cops have to be on their case so we might end up infected.'

'True, so we'll do this job and then sever the relationship. I think.'

Garvey had called in to Toher and broke the news. 'We lost both of them. They might have been spooked in the Botanics as they went into complete anti-surveillance mode. You know what it's like – almost impossible to track them if there's no technical assistance.' She was down and felt she'd failed him.

'It's fine, June. Don't beat yourself up – been there and done that. Remember that Mike Regan isn't retiring and we have the UC right up his arse. We've descriptions and photos of these visitors so it goes on. You get back here and we'll debrief then get some rest.'

Garvey felt reassured. That's what Toher could do and why the team always went the extra mile for him. The two new targets were obviously the real deal, and she hoped she'd get another crack at them.

67

Major Roger Bowman, the army intelligence officer, was exactly what Macallan had expected – she'd had enough experience during her time in Northern Ireland. He was confident and walked in as if he owned the room, and she knew he would have done his homework on her. Tenant and Duncan had joined them. He'd opened up quickly, confirming that he'd worked in Northern Ireland, and threw out a few names of high-ranking police officers he'd come across to impress her – or so he hoped. But it was all tedious ice-breaking as far as she was concerned – a way of feeling out who seemed to be controlling the conversation.

Macallan played it easy and let him have his head. Tenant did her usual thing and promised full cooperation like the good ACC she was, but the meeting wasn't about being nice to each other and they knew it. Macallan had agreed that they would be completely open with him, and there was no point in anything else. Everyone in the room knew that could never be absolute – it was just another part of the diplomacy. The crucial question was what would the army give them?

When she introduced Duncan, she saw it threw him for a moment – he clearly hadn't expected a DS to be in the room. When she told him Duncan was ex-RMP and had worked in intelligence, his smile was forced, but he was well trained and carried on as if it was all friends together.

Macallan carried out the presentation on what they had, but Bowman never made a note. She guessed he was recording some way or other and was okay with that but thought, *You might have declared it, you bastard.* She left nothing out apart from the army intel source, and when she finished, she asked Tenant and Duncan if they wanted to add anything. Duncan nodded.

'As you've heard, I arrested Taylor originally and saw him up close and personal, as they say.'

Macallan nodded in appreciation at her new DS – Duncan's initial apprehension was gone and the Mighty Atom, as she was known, was emerging.

'Sam Taylor is, or was, the real deal but damaged. Seen enough of them before, and I've no doubt he's been in some hot zones in the past. The puzzle was the lawyer. Sandy Tait and Taylor don't go together – they're from different worlds. So this relationship comes from some wider arrangement.'

Macallan had skipped over that part – as they'd arranged before the meeting, Duncan was to come in and almost confirm that something was going on in the dark.

'So, what we need to know is…' Macallan paused for effect. 'Everything!' She did her very best friendly smile as he was about to speak, then cut him off.

'When I say everything, I mean everything. This is the murder of a young reporter who was looking into extra-judicial killings in Northern Ireland and elsewhere by a group mostly made up of Scots. They left the army nearly all at the same time and I wonder why? Then there's an allegation that this group went on into the area of contract killings. Now Sam Taylor and Tam Hunter are both dead. So we have a pile of mysteries, and the question is: where do we go from here?' She looked at Tenant to see if she had a comment to make as the senior officer in the room.

'That's it exactly, and Superintendent Macallan is in overall charge, but I'm here to tell you that there is full backing from the executive for a thorough investigation into what has taken place on our ground.'

Bowman shifted uncomfortably in his seat before he answered. They all knew he would have a clear remit on what he could or couldn't tell the police, and the ball was in his court.

'You mentioned that the information came from a source. One question I should ask is: who is the source and are they connected to the military in some way?'

He knew what the answer would be but as it was in his script, he asked anyway.

Macallan was ready for the question and decided that was the moment to show him who they were dealing with.

'I'm surprised you've asked that question, because of course you should know as an intel officer that it's a hanging offence to disclose a source or agent.' At the back of her mind she felt a twitch of guilt, remembering what she'd done to bring about the death of Dominic Grainger. It was only a moment, her secret and burden.

'I can't reveal the source at the moment.' She said it again for emphasis.

Bowman relaxed – this was probably good news.

'So, it could just be someone with a conspiracy theory. There are plenty of those still going on in Northern Ireland and in the army – we investigate fully and rarely come up with evidence against our men and women.' He smiled like he'd just won a small victory.

But Macallan was ready with her next play.

'Well if it's just a conspiracy theory that killed Nancy Gilhooley, Tam Hunter and Sam Taylor them I'm in the wrong job.' She let that one hang.

He was about to try and answer when she got in before him again.

Duncan barely suppressed her smile – every time she was with her, she saw more evidence that the stories about Macallan's grit were true. Bowman, on the other hand, tightened his lips and decided he didn't like Macallan, who seemed far too smart for a plod.

She carried on. 'So, can you provide us with information on where Taylor served in Northern Ireland and who was in his team, given that we're still looking for his killer? Secondly, why did they all leave at the same time? It will help us enormously if you can confirm and corroborate what we've seen in Nancy's notes and what we've learned from her colleagues in the newspaper.'

Bowman decided that he was being outmanoeuvred – there were too many questions he couldn't answer. The police investigation was going to be a pain in the arse that the army didn't need, given the problems still going on in Northern Ireland. 'Do you mind if I make a call to my HQ? And will I get to see these notes?' He knew the army might end up in a corner over the killings and there was too much at stake to get it wrong.

'There's an empty office nearby – you can use that. We'll get some fresh caffeine in us and see you back here. As for the notes, not yet as we're still analysing them.'

Macallan was pleased to see that he was on the back foot. She took no pleasure in the games being played but knew from her experience in Belfast that if she let them, they would give her nothing – or nothing dressed up as something. She didn't hate them for it – she knew they were doing what they thought they had to, but so did she.

When he was away, she turned to Tenant and asked her what she thought.

'Well, I think he certainly got the message, Grace which is why we're here I guess.'

Macallan asked the same question of Duncan.

'I think he'll be completely rewriting the script. It all depends on round two. They'll be desperate to trace the leak, and secondly, they'll want any investigation into historical cases in Northern Ireland to die at birth. As you know, the enquiries have been going on for years and are still tying the government in knots. The thought of more soldiers being brought to court to face what the army knew perfectly well was going on at the time is bottom of their wish list.'

Macallan nodded – so much hung on what the army was prepared to give them.

'Okay, let's see what round two brings.'

Her phone interrupted her train of thought. It was Paddy Toher, who told her they'd had some success on a meeting they'd covered with Regan.

'Our UC was in place, and as it turned out, it was Glasnevin again.'

Macallan felt her breath catch just for a moment. Glasnevin – a place so full of ghosts – was becoming the epicentre of what she was facing. She didn't know why but sensed it as Toher carried on.

'We had significant technical in the place and managed to CCTV an unidentified male who met Regan. When they split up, he met another unidentified male, but we have a good description. Problem was, they might have been spooked – they carried out a masterclass in anti-surveillance and lost our teams.'

It was strange because Macallan almost felt encouraged by that news. *So, these boys are good, whoever they are*, she thought. It seemed to tie into everything she sensed but couldn't prove yet.

'It happens,' she told him. 'And as we all know, it rarely stops what they're doing. At that level, they treat it as part of the job to outthink us.'

'Right, Grace. Listen, when we get tidied up, we'll send you over some of the images. We've also got some poor-quality talk from long-range listening – the tech lads are working on it at the moment. Don't think we'll get conversation but hopefully bits of the chat. All helps anyway.'

'Thanks, Paddy. I'm with army intel at the moment, trying to squeeze cooperation out of them. Hopefully we'll get back over to see you soon.'

'Good luck with those boys – they're not the best at sharing. Just let us know when you're coming over and we'll try and get a night here so we can show you the delights of Dublin pubs, though we'd better do it quick. This bloody virus is starting to start terrible rumours of shutdowns. What a world.'

'I'll probably bring Maggie Duncan again and our senior analyst.'

There was a slight pause as Macallan thought about the news that was dominating the media now about the new virus. She'd almost ignored it to start with, thinking it was another scare story that would fizzle out with time. Now, it was heading across Europe like a dark wave and was becoming real. She thought of Jack and the children – human and fragile. She shook her head briefly, aching for them, then cleared her thoughts and concentrated on the details of the UMs the Dublin team had encountered.

When the call finished, she turned to Tenant and Duncan and explained what Toher had told her. Whoever these new UMs were, they might not be of any value to Macallan, but her gut told her otherwise. She saw the outline of a man – he had no face, but they could see each other across the void.

Bowman came back into the room and seemed slightly warmer – his initial overconfidence was gone.

'I need to talk to you alone, Superintendent – national security issue.' He left it at that.

'The ACC stays and that's not up for discussion. Maggie, would you mind?'

Duncan kept her face straight but was pleased because she knew the request meant the army was at least going to take a step towards them. She nodded and left the office.

'I've spoken to my people about this, and we need to be frank with you,' Bowman began. 'Firstly, we will do what we can – within the bounds of the obvious national security issues – to help with the murder of Nancy Gilhooley. Having said that, you seem certain that it was Sam Taylor, so we can agree that the crime is solved. Yes?'

Macallan nodded. 'It's solved, and probably Tam Hunter is solved, but the problem is… who killed Sam? We have a duty to investigate his murder despite what he did. Agreed?'

The army officer's face tightened again. 'Agreed,' he said through gritted teeth before carrying on. 'With regard to Sam Taylor, we will acknowledge that he worked on covert operations in Northern Ireland and subsequently there were discipline issues that led to his unit all leaving the army at more or less the same time.'

'What were the issues? And were they disciplined for something – or charged perhaps?' Macallan kept her tone even.

'I'm not allowed to discuss this, but the issues were fully investigated and no serious criminal conduct was uncovered, apart from minor procedural problems.' Bowman sat back – there was little else he'd been approved to share.

'Can we get their details so we can interview them? After all, they might be able to help us in relation to Taylor's death. It seemed like a professional killer or killers.'

'Well that seems to suggest that the fact they were in the army makes them contract killers. Surely that's not what you're suggesting, Superintendent?' He used her rank like an insult.

'Sam Taylor and Tam Hunter were part of that unit so it's a valid line of investigation. We're not here to investigate the sins committed in Northern Ireland, but we have almost no details of Taylor – who he was for instance. As far as we can gather, he grew up in care and what family do exist don't give a toss. All we have is the army, and we can't progress the investigation unless you give us something to work on. The fact that Nancy Gilhooley was investigating an army unit involved in extra-judicial killings in Northern Ireland that retired to kill for money is going to be a matter of public knowledge. Her newspaper apparently knows all this, and do you think they'll keep it a secret?'

She watched for a response, but he held still.

Tenant stepped in to make sure he saw no fracture in the police position. 'We can't make progress if you don't help us. That will be a matter of great concern to Police Scotland and, in fact, the Scottish government.' Tenant leaned forward and made sure he got the point. 'Even where there's national security involved, we have systems to protect information, and you know that.'

Bowman knew he was getting nowhere. 'Let me go and look at what we have and I'll send you a report in the morning detailing what we know, but as I say, they left the army years ago, so what we have now might be limited.'

He looked like he just wanted to go so Macallan decided to throw her last shot. 'Has military intelligence been in touch with them since they left the service?'

He paused just too long before denying it – Macallan saw the truth in the moment but decided to leave it there. She knew if the intelligence services had contracted out to them, the evidence would be buried in a place where no one could find it.

'We'll wait on your report, but make no mistake – we will investigate this. We have three murders all connected and it's not going to go away.'

Macallan stood up and offered her hand; Bowman took it as if it was contaminated and left the office.

'What do you think, Grace?' Tenant asked with a grin.

'I think we've just started to lift a stone and God knows what's under it.'

68

Macallan called Duncan back into the office and they ran over what had happened but decided to wait for the army's reaction. Oliver came in and told them that Toher had called again – he wanted a video conference on a secure system.

'That's good, Danny – let's do it.' Macallan sensed the request from Toher meant something positive.

When they'd all assembled, the link was made to Toher. Garvey was there too and gave them a rundown on the operation up until the point they'd tracked Regan to Glasnevin. It was at that point they cut to the CCTV images.

The quality wasn't the best but it was good enough. The camera panned slowly, and they all watched Regan take his time, stopping at the commemorative wall. Macallan thought how many times she'd halted at that same spot, wondering at the tragedy and eventual glory of the Rising.

Garvey continued to comment on the small details, and for all the world, it was like watching another tourist taking in the ghosts that haunted those grounds. The images took Macallan back to the many hours she'd spent across her career watching men and women who didn't know her eyes were on them.

'If you watch now, you'll see this other contact come into view,' Garvey said calmly.

The room in Edinburgh was quiet, and they all strained as the camera picked up the contact coming into view. For a moment, they watched and processed the details – then Macallan sat forward in her chair. She waited, trying to discount what her eyes were telling her. 'Jesus Christ.'

'What is it, Grace?' Tenant asked, alarmed at the change in Macallan's expression.

It's him – heavier and he's changed his appearance, but it's him, she thought.

'It's Handyside. Pete Handyside.'

'Are you sure?'

The commentary from Dublin had stopped when they'd heard Macallan's comment. After a pause, Toher cut in.

'Do you want to study this a bit further, Grace? We need to be sure.'

'I'm sure, Paddy. Never thought I'd see him again, and believe me, you have enough problems without this man coming into your game.'

Toher waited for a moment before speaking, absorbing the realisation that he now had more headaches to add to the heap he owned already. He played the rest of the recording and Macallan's team watched transfixed, as if Handyside had risen from the dead – another ghost among so many others.

'The sound recordings weren't up to much,' Toher said, 'and we just got snatches but enough to think they're planning something else. If this man is connected to contract killings then maybe we have more problems on the way.'

Toher sounded calm enough but Macallan knew he must have been cursing this latest development. 'I'm going to a meeting with the team now, so what about calling me in an hour? I think you said there are still a stack of warrants for this man?'

Macallan agreed and sat back in her chair, trying to process what she was facing. The man she thought might be Handyside had cropped up on the Kangas investigation, and now he was definitely involved in the Dublin gang wars. So, he was the link – possibly the organiser of the contract jobs.

'Jesus,' she murmured again, trying to calm her racing thoughts – she knew everyone in the room was looking to her for the next move.

She decided to push ahead while they waited for the information from the army. She needed progress on the efforts to trace the army intel source, and she worried that if Handyside had been spooked in Dublin, he might go dark again. If that happened, it was unlikely she'd ever get another shot at him.

That's not going to happen, she thought. She was determined she'd find him and look into his eyes when she arrested him.

Though even as she thought that, she knew somewhere in the back of her mind that Handyside would never allow himself to be taken. For a man like him, prison would be a living hell – the constrained life and separation from his family would kill him if someone else didn't get to him first.

69

As Macallan and Young were discussing the latest developments, Handyside called Regan on a safe line and skipped the niceties.

'Look, we had a possible follow away from the meet. I met one of my team after it and we don't know what they have.'

'Okay, my friend.' Regan seemed unfazed but had already decided to do another security check. 'Listen, I get attention all the time, and the main thing is that I'm always at a distance when work takes place. So, I wouldn't worry too much. I take it you lost them?'

Handyside felt anger rise in his chest, which was unusual, as he rarely let his emotions come into decision-making. *You're missing a great big fucking point, my friend,* he thought.

'But I do worry. The difference is they know all about you and what you look like. I'm careful not to be identified, so it is a problem, and you better take this seriously or our relationship is over here and now. Understood?'

In any other circumstance, that level of disrespect would have meant Regan reducing someone's face to a pulp, but this man had an almost hypnotic effect on him. Regan occupied a city where he understood his friends and enemies equally because they had all been born in the same gene pool. He'd always believed he was a kingpin in the criminal world, premier league – until he'd met this man. Now he knew he was only top of the second division.

'I get it and I'll do a clean-up just in case, but I told you, I spend my life cleaning and I've even put a couple of boys in the ground who it turned out did fuck all, but I never took risks if I wasn't sure. Are you still going to do the job?' He tried to sound like the man's equal, but he was on the back foot and couldn't change that.

'We'll do the job alright but the price has doubled because the risk has increased, and I want it in advance. Okay?' Once again it was a statement, not the opening gambit in a negation.

Regan had to control his natural instinct to kick off over the cost but held back, knowing the outcome would probably still be worth it in the end.

'Okay, I'll get all that to you—'

Handyside interrupted him. 'I want it delivered by hand. No emails. When it's ready, send one of your boys with it. I'll tell you where the meet is. We'll use the agreed codes for where and when, and make sure you use your bent sources in the Garda to see what's happening.'

'I don't have anyone in the unit that's looking at us, but people near them might pick up something.'

Handyside finished the call and phoned his wife as he looked out over the Thames from his office. He told her to meet him in the West End and that he'd booked a meal. She was surprised as he was a complete home bird and wondered what had prompted it.

'Well, it's just to remind you that I love you, lass.' He meant it, but deep down he was concerned about where all this would end. She wanted him to retire one day, but he knew the chances of that were slim.

He walked out of his office and headed to the nearest coffee bar. They charged a fortune, but the product was good and the window seats let him people-watch safely.

As he sipped the coffee, he watched the endless progression of office workers stream by and thought that he might be seeing each one for the first and last time in his life. *Is that it, a few seconds in view and then it's all gone*? he thought.

His wife's face drifted into his imagination, and he wondered what the future held for them. He rubbed his temples with the tips of his forefingers, agonising about what might happen now she was involved. He could cut and run again, but how could the children cope with taking on new identities?

His thoughts turned to Macallan – out there somewhere, hunting for him. She was as driven as he was, and if he made any mistakes, she'd find them. He hoped the fact that his latest operation was in Dublin would restrict her reach, but he doubted it. Taylor had been taken care of on her patch, but there might be a loose end somewhere. It was in the lap of the gods, but he had to play the game to the end. What else was he without it?

70

Macallan had pondered the best way to get a hold of Captain Ruth Conway. She couldn't ask the army because that might set off the alarm bells, and she had to get to her first. She was sure they'd already be trying to track down who Gilhooley's source was. But she had no idea where the woman was – there was no information from the conference she'd attended, and all contact had been through the formal lines Police Scotland had with the armed services, though it did look like she was based somewhere in Scotland and had been involved in a number of joint operations with the police. She was highly regarded by the police officers who'd worked with her and described as a real professional. Macallan decided there was no other way than to try the number Felicity Young had come up with.

She stared at the window for a moment before making the call. Jack and the children were back in Edinburgh, and all her worries about their relationship had disappeared. Most importantly, they were both working at it, and the previous night had been special. By some miracle, the children had gone to sleep without hours of stories, and it had been as if they were discovering each other all over again.

'Well, whatever the shrink is doing seems to be working,' he'd told her. 'I'm proud of you – it's brave to admit you need help. So how often will you see her?'

'Every week. And she recommends lots of physical activity,' she'd replied, grinning as she watched the words slowly work their way through the wine he'd drunk before hitting the mark.

She loved when Jack was just a little bit under the influence. He laughed easily and became almost boyish. He'd turned slowly and grinned back. 'Ah right!' Then he'd leaned over and kissed her.

Macallan grinned and snapped back to the real world, then dialled the number she hoped would take her to Ruth Conway. It rang three times before it was answered.

'Captain Conway.' The accent was Scottish and sounded fairly local.

Macallan identified herself and first of all wanted to make sure Conway could actually speak freely. 'We have an operation running you might be able to help us with, but it's Saturday so just wanted to check I'm not bothering you at home.'

'Not at all – it's my day off anyway. What can I do for you?'

There was tension in the voice, and Macallan was sure Conway must have wondered if and when this call would come.

'Listen, please don't put the phone down till you hear what I have to say. I'm the SIO on the investigation into the death of Nancy Gilhooley. We know you were close to her.'

Macallan paused, needing to know what Conway's reaction would be.

'Okay, I wondered how long it would take. I'm sorry, I should have been in touch with you but—'

Macallan heard her sob on the other end of the line before she spoke again.

'I've fucked up – Jesus. Look, I'm not day off – I reported sick. Couldn't face what all this might mean… Sorry, what really matters is Nancy, not what happens to me.'

'Can I call you Ruth?' Macallan understood what Conway must have been going through. She'd lost her lover and had disclosed information that would probably end her career if the truth came out. She wouldn't judge Conway with the sins she carried herself.

'Look, there's no question we need to speak to you, and although we've had contact with the army, we haven't named you. It's going to come out though, and you must know that.'

Macallan knew there was no point in pretending – all she wanted was to get Conway's story before the army prepared a script for her.

In the end, it was easier than Macallan had imagined, and as it turned out, Conway lived in Queensferry so distance wasn't a problem.

'Okay, I can come to you, or you can come in here. I'm based in Leith Police Station. Whatever suits, but we need to do this as soon as.'

Macallan heard Conway blow her nose, and when she spoke, she sounded beaten.

'I'll get dressed now and be with you in a couple of hours. Is that okay?'

Macallan agreed, relieved.

71

When Conway was shown into Macallan's office, she stood up and shook the young officer's hand. She was an attractive woman with short blonde hair and grey-blue eyes. She managed a smile, and Macallan thought she was probably an easy person to like. Conway refused coffee but asked for some water.

'To be honest, I've been drinking more than normal so I'm a bit dry. Just the pressure of it all.'

'Been there, done that, Ruth. Comes with the territory we occupy.'

Duncan joined them and took notes. Macallan thought her army background would come in handy for the interview, and it did – after the introductions, it turned out that they knew some of the same people in the service.

Conway didn't put up any fight – it was clear that she just wanted to unload it all.

'I know it was wrong, that I didn't come forward right away, and I'm going to have to pay for that. I was with Nancy not long before she died. She told me about meeting Sam Taylor and I was beginning to panic. I wish I'd never mentioned anything about the team in Northern Ireland.' A tear trickled down her face and she reached for the paper hankies in her bag.

'Take your time, Ruth.' Macallan knew she would have to take it slowly – the woman opposite was battling with more guilt than she could handle.

'Why did you disclose this to Nancy in the first place?'

'I'll tell you what I know – that's all I can do. To be honest, the issues in Northern Ireland and then the Middle East really troubled me.' She paused and blew her nose. 'My parents are from Downpatrick and Catholic, so when I saw the intel reports on some of the unauthorised actions in the border war, I found it hard to deal with. The army knew full well what these men had done and were up to, and we were letting it go – or rather burying it. There was a suspicion that the intelligence services may have actually used them for work abroad after they'd left the service. Tell the truth, I think I would have managed to live with it, but when I met Nancy and it turned out she was a reporter, well… it just came out. If I could turn the clock back, I'd have kept my mouth shut.' She stopped and paused for a drink.

Macallan had tried to say as little as possible that might seem judgmental – it was obvious that Conway needed to unload and required little prompting. Now that she'd gone this far, Macallan relaxed. The first hurdle had been crossed – now it was only a matter of extracting every detail that might help bring closure to the investigation.

'Ruth, do you have the names of the army team who were operating in Northern Ireland?'

'I don't know them all but enough. Tam Hunter was the first name I gave Nancy because there was intelligence reporting that he was a broken man, and I felt that if anyone would speak to her, it would be him. The reporting suggested that when he was on the piss, he'd been mouthing off about Northern Ireland. I guess he was probably a classic PSTD case, but the army wouldn't have suggested help back then. There was real concern within the military about what he might say.'

Macallan asked if she need a break. but Conway declined and said she wanted it done.

'I left Nancy to it. She assured me she would take it carefully and get support from her paper. Anyway, the next thing, Nancy is pushing for more from me, and I wondered then if I'd done the wrong thing. So I gave her the names of the two other Scots in the team. I had no idea where Sam Taylor was, but I knew he visited Hunter from time to time. The leader of the team, both in Northern Ireland and afterwards, was a real hard nut called Billy Dolan... another Scot and a Highland boy originally. He lives a few miles outside Dublin. The two Englishmen in the original team were out of the picture. One died in a road accident in France and the other has been ill for years with cancer.'

'So, were they operating shoot to kill in Northern Ireland?' Macallan asked. She knew from her time there that there had always been suggestions this was happening.

'Yes, no doubt about it, and here's the thing – and I didn't tell Nancy this. We know they do work for the Dublin mobs and Mike Regan. Ironic or what? Mike Regan's brother disappeared from his farm in South Armagh and witnesses saw what looked like an undercover army team leaving the scene. This was denied by the army, but we knew they were targeting Regan. So, Mike Regan – a man who supports the Republican cause – is paying the men who probably killed his brother to kill other Irishmen. You couldn't make it up.'

Macallan sat back and absorbed what Conway had said. 'Jesus, that takes the cake.' She tapped the desk with her pen. 'Maggie, is there anything you want to say or ask?'

Duncan hesitated; she wasn't sure if she should say what was on her mind but took her chance.

'All of this raises a big question. There have been umpteen enquiries, public enquiries, Stalker and so on... Was any of this passed to investigators or police? Because of not, this is dynamite – but you must know that?'

Conway shook her head at the obvious point as Macallan came in.

'I was coming to the same question, so let's address it now because it will release a shitstorm when it comes out.'

'Of course.' Conway suddenly seemed weary with the strain of the revelations. 'I went into the intelligence world all bright-eyed then realised I was just another worker justifying their existence by the ever-present *Big Picture*.'

'Where is this information being held? I've got Major Roger Bowman coming back to me. We've spoken to him already and found him a bit slippery.'

Conway shook her head wearily. 'He's a climber – and yes, definitely slippery. Watch him because if he can outflank you, he will. Follows orders, and someone further up the line will be pulling the strings.'

Macallan felt Conway had gone far enough for the time being and that it was better to keep her fresh. Duncan took a few more details then Macallan told her to go home and rest – they'd speak to her again after they'd seen Bowman.

72

Macallan was surprised how quickly Major Bowman was back in touch. He wanted to meet in person again and was in Edinburgh twenty-four hours later. When he arrived at her office, he'd completely dropped his defensive attitude – now he was all smiles.

If the army cooperated, it would take them a long way towards getting a result for the investigation. Even if they played dirty, she had Conway's information, but there were so many sensitive issues that there would be obstacles all the way – and it would be near impossible if the army called in political favours. She'd seen it all before in Ulster and knew it benefited no one in the end. She also knew that as much as Tenant was on her side, the executive would not want her investigation to grow arms and legs.

They had all the evidence they needed that Sam Taylor had killed Gilhooley and Hunter, but some people were already writing it off as score-settling by criminal elements. *Who cared if the bastards killed each other*? was the line from some quarters.

Macallan had even been called in to see the chief, who was concerned that they might be dipping their toes into matters that were the responsibility of the PSNI and the Guards south of the Irish border – and that was before you considered the military skeletons that might rise from the dead. But the chief surprised Macallan by supporting what she was doing – he just wanted regular updates in case it did become a swamp or trampled on Whitehall toes.

'Go to it, Grace,' he'd said, 'but we need fallout like a hole in the head because I seem to spend my life putting out fires. I used to think this was the dream job and now I'm sure it'll kill me.' He'd grinned and, before she'd left, had a dig at her. 'I hear you stole one of our brightest uniform stars – Maggie Duncan. She was destined for dizzy heights and now you're going to corrupt her in the evils ways of detectives.'

'I promise to look after her, sir.' Macallan had closed the door to his office feeling reassured yet knowing she would have to work fast.

Now, Bowman sat down, and this time he produced a file which he put on the table in front of him. Macallan took that gesture as a positive sign but remembered what Conway had said about the soldier. Elaine Tenant joined them, but he seemed relaxed considering he was outnumbered.

'I've discussed this with my colleagues and we want to cooperate with you as much as possible. However, you also have to understand that if this source you have is army, we will try and find out who it is. In addition, there will be consequences for that person... serious consequences. Regardless of the issues, it's a serious breach of regulations and, of course, the Official Secrets Act.'

Macallan decided not to get into a bun fight and accepted that, from the military point of view, he was right. But she still had to protect Conway's identity for the time being – otherwise, she was sure they would put her out of reach.

Macallan looked at Bowman and smiled, but she'd already decided to stretch the truth for the time being.

'Look, Major, cards on the table. We've spoken to the source now and have obtained significant information, with serious allegations from that source, some of it directed at the army. I'm duty-bound to make sure I have all of these allegations to hand, so I intend interviewing the source again as soon as I'm finished with you.'

She saw Bowman's face tighten at the words *serious allegations* and *army*. He looked like he was going to speak then changed his mind so Macallan carried on.

'In the spirit of cooperation, we'll disclose the source to you later today. I'm also going to tell you what the allegations are regarding the army.'

And she did. Bowman remained still, trying not to give away any non-verbals to the detective, but there was no doubt he was taking in every word.

'Now, one of the problems is that these investigations have moved beyond the Scottish borders and we have to work out how we do this. We're going to need a lot of support to bring it all to a conclusion. We have support from other forces and now we need to know what you can do.'

She watched Bowman hesitate as he considered a range of options and no doubt the parameters of the script he'd been given. His next words surprised her, and she wondered if he was lying.

'I really appreciate your candid summation of what you have. These allegations will cause us pain, no doubt about it, but then you know that. I think the position we take is that the investigations into the Troubles won't go away, and we need to put a lid on it. This team that Taylor served in was known as C Troop 5. To be frank, they went rogue at some point and so were not working under legal authority. We didn't know that at the time, and it was only after tours in Iraq and Afghanistan that it was decided that they were operating outside their orders. So we believe it's better to bring this sad matter to a head.'

Bowman paused then carried on. 'At the end of the day, Taylor and Hunter are dead now, another one died two years ago and number four has been terminally ill for two years with non-Hodgkin's lymphoma. He's near death now as far as we know. So that leaves just one of the original team who may be of interest to you, and he was in fact the squad's leader. A very highly regarded soldier in his time. His name is Billy Dolan, but I'm guessing you have his name from Nancy's notes. Is that correct?'

Macallan nodded. 'We have his name.'

'I'll give you his address. He lives in the Irish Republic – Malahide, not far from Dublin.'

'Do you have a photograph of him?'

'Yes – full description, scars and all that.'

'Did the army use them after they left the service?' Macallan fired the loaded question without dressing it up or disguising it and didn't expect the truth.

'Not that I'm aware of.'

The answer was what she'd expected – plausible deniability. Other players in the army might know, but Bowman could perhaps be telling the truth or be confident that there was no evidence to show that he did know.

'You tell me what you need from me and you'll have it today. I'll stay in Edinburgh till you've finished with your source, and we can meet again to say where we go next. I'll leave you to it for the time being – just call my mobile when you're ready.' He shoved the file he was carrying towards Macallan, and they shook hands before he left.

Tenant had said very little, but when Bowman left the office, she raised her eyebrows. 'What about that then, Grace?'

'I think the army know that they can't stop this becoming public because just too many people know now, never mind Jacquie's paper. There are three dead bodies here, and they can't be swept under the table, so I think our soldier boys will play ball but won't miss a chance to shift the blame. To be honest, the best result for them would be someone taking out Billy Dolan because the trail back to what happened in Northern Ireland would be cold.'

'You left out Pete Handyside.' Tenant knew it had been intentional.

Macallan grinned. 'Wanted to keep that one up my sleeve, and anyway, Pete Handyside is mine. Okay, let's get Ruth Conway again and secure her evidence.'

73

Dolan peered through the binos and saw his target Sean O'Reilly standing just inside the French windows of his home in Castleknock, a few kilometres west of Dublin city centre. This was a top-end executive property and, if anything, proved that for O'Reilly crime really had paid. He was the head of one of the two teams that had been at war with Regan's gang for years.

It had all started after an incident in a pub between O'Reilly's daughter and one of Regan's nephews – a constant disappointment to the family and a pisshead of epic proportions. Until then, there had been peace between the gangs, who'd all been doing well during a boom period for organised crime.

There was no motive for what had happened, other than the fact that Regan's nephew was an arsehole. He'd walked up behind O'Reilly's daughter and groped her in front of enough witnesses to convict him a dozen times. There was no history between them; they'd never exchanged a word – his drink-addled and pocket-sized brain had just convinced him it was a great idea then wondered why no one else thought it was funny.

Although the girl was pocket-sized in build, she was from fighting Irish stock, and as he'd stood sneering in her face, she'd driven her knee right into his balls then watched him collapse in a heap on the deck. To compound her little victory, her friends had all poured their drinks over him before the bouncers moved in to finish the job. The pub was owned by a friend of O'Reilly's, so the bouncers had known exactly what they needed to do and had given him some serious digs before throwing him onto the pavement outside, where he'd then been subjected to late-night drinkers stepping round him and enjoying his predicament.

His humiliation had been complete when one of the witnesses decided to empty his bladder over him, and that's when the need for revenge had started to ferment within him. When he'd finally got off the deck, he'd moved into the shadows and waited.

When the girl and her friends had left an hour later, he'd stepped out in front of her and slashed her face from forehead to jawbone, then compounded the sin by spitting on her and telling her that her father was a paedophile. He'd bolted from the scene before the doorman from the pub could get to him again, but there were more than enough witnesses who knew him. There was absolutely no evidence for the claim that O'Reilly was a paedophile, but it didn't matter – the opening salvos of the war had been fired.

Regan had been furious with his nephew when he'd heard and told him he'd kill him himself if there was one more fuck- up. He'd let him live but beaten him mercilessly because he'd known that the incident would cost blood and treasure before it was resolved.

He'd tried reaching out to O'Reilly, who'd said they could talk and find a way to sort it. But it was a tactical lie, and O'Reilly had only been buying time to take his own revenge. Regan had thought there would be a way to resolve it because business came first so he'd grabbed what appeared to be an olive branch with both hands. He had been wrong though, and would never forget the lesson that no one was worth trusting – even though he should have known it already.

There were three main gangs in Dublin and two of them, including O'Reilly's, were connected through a blood relationship. So they'd combined forces against the much bigger organisation headed by Regan, and twelve hours after the call for peace, Regan's pisshead nephew had been found in his bath with a large hole where his left eye should have been and a good part of his brain in the water beside him.

Regan hadn't wanted conflict and knew the fault lay with his family, but it was a matter of face and his brother had wanted blood for his son. Thus began a tide of tit-for-tat killings, some of them quite brazen, and if there had ever been a chance to reign it back, that was long gone now. The Garda Síochána had struggled to contain the subsequent conflict and no one had been able to deliver a knockout blow to finish the struggle. But that was about to change.

74

Dolan and Baker had carefully tracked O'Reilly for a few days. The man was cautious and rarely left his substantial home and grounds. It made sense – according to their intelligence, he was expecting an attempt on his life, and had become almost fixated about his own security.

But Dolan knew that was the wrong decision because it actually gave them an opportunity. They would know exactly where he would be most of the time, and the substantial grounds around his home would give them cover at night if they wanted to make the hit there.

O'Reilly had a couple of dogs but kept them in the house at night, which was another mistake. He would let them out in the grounds for twenty minutes at exactly the same time every night before taking them back inside. Around ten each evening, a couple of his heavies would walk round the house, and then, regular as clockwork, one of them would do the rounds every hour after that. The timing was always the same so Dolan and Baker retreated well before the dogs' leisure time. It played right into their hands. They'd created a perfect hide, and even if the heavies stood beside them, they still wouldn't be discovered.

Dolan had decided that they'd snipe O'Reilly. He spent most nights with a drink in his hand and would often stand at the French windows, smoking, illuminated by the internal lights – an almost perfect target.

The other gang leader, Tony Collins, had been tracked by the rest of Dolan's team. They'd discovered that he visited the same two sex workers every Thursday and spent most of the evening there. There was a problem with his two bodyguards, who sat outside in the car all the time he was there, but it could be overcome. They took regular breaks and left the car one up while one of them went for food or comfort breaks, so that job looked doable as well. The omens were good for the double hit.

Dolan had often wondered, over the course of the jobs he'd done, how targets who were under constant threat could make so many mistakes. But he knew the answer – human beings were easily bored with routine and discipline, so their guard always dropped at some point. Constant vigilance became too much to bear and they expected the paid staff to cover them.

Dolan was pleased with the preparations they'd made, and he firmly believed they could coordinate the hits. When he was sure, he called Handyside and told him where they were with the job.

'I think we can go ahead. We just need another couple of days to make sure everything is right. It's the old army thing of getting the preparation right. I want to have a meet and brief with the rest of the team, and if that's all good, we go on Thursday when both the targets are in place.'

Dolan sounded confident and that was all Handyside needed.

'Go for it, and let me know as soon as it's done. I'll be in the city you're in but will stay well away and let you do your job. Hopefully I'll see you after we're all cleaned up.

I've got a bonus for you so you can retire and grow fat, my friend.'

Handyside put down the phone. The call had been all positive and yet he felt chilled even though the room was warm. He shivered and wondered where Grace Macallan was. There were few opponents who got to him, and the others who had were in the ground – where he'd put them. But Macallan had that same effect, and he wondered why. All the others had been men, and before he'd met her, he would never have imagined that a woman could take him on. He'd always associated women with warmth or home thanks to Jeannie, but he saw Macallan as a predator. She might not know it, but she was one – one of those creatures who thrived on the chase. It made her dangerous to him – even more so given that he'd escaped her after their last encounter.

This time, she would want to even the score.

75

The UC lay back on the gym bench in his flat and pushed the weights till his arms burned with the effort. He was drinking too much but kept hard with the weights – he knew he had to stay as fit as possible for what might come. The threat of exposure hung over every minute of his life – a constant strain. Most of the time he was the man in his UC legend, and would forget who he'd been before he'd volunteered for this life. It was the brief spells in between when he would struggle to control the fear. Being afraid came with the territory though; it helped keep him focused on the hazards. UCs who relaxed wound up uncovered, and in some cases that had cost them their lives – or their sanity.

Regan had called earlier before he was even out of bed and he'd struggled to cover his hangover. He'd crossed another line when Regan had insisted he use a sex worker while he'd taken care of his own impulses. The UC was sure it would never come to light, but between his discreet affair with Regan's niece and this, he was now walking a dangerous line. He wanted out but knew that things were coming to a head, and he was the only listening device available to the Guards, as Regan constantly changed cars to avoid such a problem and had his home swept regularly for bugs. There was no doubt in the UC's mind that something was brewing and Regan couldn't quite contain it. There was nothing clear, but when he was on the phone in the car, and in casual conversation with the UC, he'd become just a little bit cocky. There had been a subtle change in mood that suggested things were on the move. He wouldn't come out with it, but it was there.

The UC had met with his handler the previous day after Regan had told him he wouldn't need him. 'Fill your boots, son, and have a day off,' he'd said. 'It'll soon be party time, and I think we'll celebrate with the girls again. How does that sound?'

Now, the UC squeezed his eyes shut at the thought of having to perform with the hooker again. He'd struggled the last time, and if Regan got wind of one of his boys failing to rise to the occasion, he'd be in trouble. Regan would probably come to absolutely the wrong conclusion and presume he was gay, and that would be a sacking offence – the bastard hated the gay community as much as he did the police.

He'd met his handler well outside the city and reported what he felt.

'Don't have anything exact, but he was high as a kite after that meeting as Glasnevin... as if he'd just won the lottery. And ever since there's been these small signals that something is coming, and I get the feeling it's close, though I've not heard anything from the other boys about being on standby for a job. They've been told to stay low in fact. That's all there is, but I guess I'll be picking him up tomorrow so I'll be in touch if there's anything else.'

As always, the meeting had been short, but before they wrapped up, the handler had checked on the UC's well-being.

'I'm good – no particular problems and keeping myself clean. I work out every day, and I'm being a good little boy.'

The lie had been easy and necessary, but the handler hadn't quite been convinced – they had razor-sharp radar when it came to the men and women stationed on the wrong side of no man's land.

'Listen, you've been under too long on this and I'm concerned. I'd be happier if you told me you had a problem or two. I've been there – I know what it's like. If it's all sweetness and light then there's something wrong. Tell me again you're okay.' The handler was a hard-arsed veteran and had given the UC serious eye contact.

'I'm fine for fuck's sake – I know what I'm doing. We're close on this and I want to see it done.' He'd struggled to hold it together but got away with it. The handler had nodded and left the UC, who'd decided to buy another coffee and enjoy just being out of Dublin and away from the job for a few hours.

76

When he picked up Regan the next day, the gangster was all good nature so the UC decided to push the boat a bit further.

'You seem like you've just scored for Ireland in the World Cup, Mr Regan?'

Regan stared at the back of the UC's head and grinned. 'You have it right there, son. Listen, I've said to the rest of the boys to just stay low for the next few days. I'll still need you, but maybe not as much as usual, so just relax and enjoy the down time. We'll look up the girls later in the week when we have something to celebrate.'

'Something to celebrate, Mr Regan, that sounds interesting.' The UC played it low-key – he knew that was how Regan liked it.

Regan didn't answer immediately and it unnerved the UC.

'Listen, son, you're a good lad and I like you, but you've just asked two questions and that's two more than you've ever asked before, so it's two more than fuckin' necessary. You get my drift?'

The UC tried to keep it together. 'I'm sorry, Mr Regan; didn't mean to pry. I'll keep me gob shut.'

Regan laughed quietly – he loved it when he could frighten the crap out of one of the staff with a few choice words and confirm how much control he had over them.

'That's alright, son. You're forgiven. By the way, I heard that wee pro just fuckin' loves you and can't wait for the next round.'

'Good with me – she's a right bitta fluff. Jesus, I've still got the scratches.'

He heard Regan laugh again just before his phone rang.

The call was from Pete Handyside – the man he knew as Joe Stafford – who'd said he wouldn't phone, so Regan thought there must be a problem.

'Didn't expect to hear from you. You got all the details?' Regan's face had straightened – he didn't want any issues at this stage of the game.

The other man kept his tone even. 'No problem, my friend. Your man brought all the details we needed – everything is in place and we're ready to go.'

'Fuckin' great – so Thursday this week – we do them both?' Regan could hardly contain himself.

'Well, it's on for Thursday but you forgot something. You need to make the first payment. That's how it works. No down payment, we pull out and we don't come back for the job. It's sloppy.'

Regan ground his teeth as he listened. Once again, he couldn't work out how the man on the other end always seemed to have control. In that moment, he wished he could press his thumbs into his eyes and squeeze till they popped. He was angry but didn't let it show – there was far too much riding on what the Brits could do.

'It's my man that handles the money side of things; he's a fuckin' gimp and has caused me a couple of problems recently. Swear to God I'll swing for him one of these days. It'll be paid today. So definitely Thursday?'

'All going well. I'll be in Dublin too. I have business there but nothing to do with this. I want to say goodbye to someone who works for me.'

'Okay, see you then?'

'No, that would be foolish, and there's no need for a meet. I'll just be doing what any good businessman does. I don't want to be anywhere near your little war. The job will be done and then we're out of it.'

Regan felt the rage choke in his throat – this man was talking to him like he was a fuckin' dingwop. He'd treated the man like a friend, and this response was like being whacked across the face. He ended the call and put the phone back in his pocket, wishing he could hurt someone.

'Fuckin' Geordie – fuckin' Brits. I hate them all… bastards.' He stared out of the window and tried to calm himself.

'Sorry, Mr Regan. Where to now?' In his rage, Regan had almost forgotten he wasn't alone in the car.

He remembered that there was a local bookie who'd been slow to pay back an extortionate loan. Normally, it would be left to some of his apes to sort the man out but needs must, and Regan definitely needed to sort someone out. He gave the address, and half an hour later they were in the guy's living room, knocking his teeth in. Regan had damaged one of his knuckles on the man's face, but he thought there was more to do.

'Go on, son – fill your boots.' Regan grinned and nodded towards the man tied to the chair – his nose broken and a couple of teeth gone.

'Think he's had enough, Mr Regan.' The UC felt trapped and knew he was now a long way over the line.

'I'll fuckin' decide when he's had enough – now box the head off him, will you?' Regan was high on violence, and the UC knew he was as likely to turn on him for refusing an order as he was to keep punishing the bookie.

*

Later the same evening, the UC bathed his swollen hand. He'd already swallowed enough whiskey to topple a horse, but he felt no effect. He decided he'd call in and finish the rest of the booze after that.

When he contacted his handler, he left nothing out about the conversation in the car. Thursday was the day, he'd mentioned 'we do them both' and Regan had said the word 'Geordie'.

The handler seemed pleased and agreed to call back the next day once the information had been passed on to the operational team.

'With a bit of luck, we'll pull you out soon; I'll make arrangements to get you out safely. Now make sure you play it safe from here.'

The UC put the phone down and sobbed like a child before filling the glass to the rim and drinking the Irish malt in one go.

77

Macallan was in her office with Oliver and Young. They were discussing next moves and the latest information and forensics from the various crime scenes. The forensics from the mobile home had thrown up another piece of evidence that would be a valuable part of a chain if they ever got someone to court. The SOCOs had already identified a large dent in the soft wall of the bedroom area as possibly from a struggle between Taylor and the attackers. Now, they'd confirmed that the fibres, a few hairs and minute spots of blood found in that particular spot were not Taylor's. They appeared to have lodged in fissures from the impact, but they didn't suggest a serious injury as all the other blood spatters were from Taylor himself.

Macallan scratched her chin and considered – it wasn't a direct breakthrough but still a valuable step along the way if they could match it to a DNA profile. They were checking against the national database and keeping their fingers crossed.

'Okay, this might be promising evidence, but if it's negative for DNA, it's another question we can put to the good major. The army keep some DNA profiles from men and women who've served in conflict areas so if they end up missing or dead, they can be identified.'

Macallan's phone broke the moment – she was going to ignore it till she saw it was Toher.

'Paddy, good to hear from you. How's it going over there?'

'We might have a bit of a break, Grace. We've learned from our main source that something significant might be happening on Thursday. We don't know exactly what, but Regan referred to a Geordie when he came off a call that seemed to be connected to whatever this is. The other thing is that it does sound like they might hit two targets. He seemed annoyed at whatever this caller had said, so make of that what you will.'

'What's your guess?' she asked.

'Well, if this is your man Handyside and he's the contact for contract killing then maybe it's another hit. Trouble is, we don't know who the target is. Now, the good news is that we've located Dolan's home address from the info you got to us. We've set up surveillance there but no sign of him so far, although we've seen his partner – or at least we presume his partner – coming and going. We spotted her on the balcony so sure she's resident there. He's not been at home the last couple of nights, but we'll stick with it and hope he turns up. From the army photograph you sent over, we're convinced he was one of the men we saw in Glasnevin – and the man who seemed to clock our surveillance officers.'

Macallan sat back in her chair and tried to steady her breathing. *It's close now,* she thought – she was drawing ever closer to Handyside.

'Listen, Paddy, there's almost nothing that can take us much further forward here. If it's okay with you, what about I come across with a few of my team? We wouldn't get in the road but could set up a short-term office to support you with intelligence and analysis. Handyside must be part of it, and I'm sure we can help.' She closed her eyes for a moment, hoping Toher wouldn't see it as guests he didn't need in the face of another round of violence on Dublin's streets.

'Exactly what I was thinking, Grace, and if this is an opportunity then I'll take all the help I can get. I've got executive officers who keep asking me when I'm retiring. Not very reassuring when I've still got six years to go.' Toher laughed heartily at his own joke.

'Great, I'll get that organised today. I need to speak to the army intelligence officer again too. Some loose ends to tie up before we leave, but expect us midday tomorrow. I'll bring our senior analyst and Maggie Duncan.'

Toher seemed genuinely pleased.

'We have time to get everything in place, but we need a bit of luck and Dolan to come home for a bit. So, time to say my prayers and ask the good Lord to forgive my sins and back me on this one.'

They finished the call, and Macallan saw the others in the room had heard enough to know that the pace of the investigation had picked up and that they were now on the move. Macallan called Duncan into the room and told them all exactly what had been said.

'Right, let's finish up what we want to do today; we'll head off to Dublin tomorrow. Danny, I want you to hold the reins here. I'll see Major Bowman this afternoon; Ruth Conway will be here as well so that might be a bit difficult. Maggie, I'd like you to sit in again. Danny, where are we with Sandy Tait and Benny Green?'

Oliver flipped open his notepad.

'As of this morning we're struggling to get a thing on Tait, and let's face it, he's not going to admit anything without evidence. Benny Green is a bit more promising. We've uncovered some good stuff from the financial investigation and think we can get solid evidence on trafficking women once we hit a few premises and pop-up brothels.'

'Are we ready to go on that?' Macallan asked.

'Yes, the surveillance and investigation teams have really done the business so we can go anytime. Still plenty to find out but would be a good time to get him lifted and show him that he's not fireproof after all. Think he's one of those characters who've had little or no attention for years so he's come to believe that it'll never happen.'

Macallan nodded. 'Right, work away, and let's make it provisional for Thursday to crash into his life.'

When Macallan was on her own, she called Jack and explained the situation. 'Think that weekend away might be on its way, big man.'

'Sounds good to me, Grace. I'll order those new jammies!'

She put the phone down and stretched her back, which seemed to be inventing new forms of knots. Dominic Grainger flashed through her mind but only for a moment, and she put the thought away, determined to do this one right. Grainger would remain an aberration, one that she would never forget, and she accepted that she deserved the burden of guilt. She reminded herself constantly that he would have fallen at some stage, as if that would absolve her from the crime, but it never would; the truth was that, like most people, she'd thought she was the true voice of justice, and she'd been wrong.

Noble cause – she said the words to herself time and time again. She'd fallen into the same trap as her friend Mick Harkins; he'd tried to make his own version of the law and it had almost killed him. But Jack was a lawyer – and a good one – and he constantly reminded her that she was human and the law always had to be more than the interpretation of one individual.

She'd come to accept through bitter experience that five minutes after even the great detectives retired, the job just moved on as if they'd never existed. And within a few years, the younger men and women who'd revered them as legends had gone as well, and with them any evidence of their place in the storybook, their memories like those rows of neglected graves in cemeteries – just names on stone that a passer-by would notice for a moment and forget just as quickly.

She sighed and flicked her mind back to Handyside. She almost admired him, which always troubled her because it didn't make a lot of sense. There was something in his sense of purpose – that he could lead a good family life yet take the only road that had been open to him as a young man.

She went through to the main office and went round the detectives and civilian staff, just to make sure they were okay – and, more importantly, to ensure they knew she cared. She was determined she wouldn't knowingly let any of them make the same mistakes she had.

78

When Macallan was satisfied the team were okay, she headed back into her office and closed the door. She looked at the clock and realised she had an hour before Major Bowman arrived; half an hour after that, Conway would come to her office.

She decided to attempt some of her sandwich before something else occupied her time and was on the second bite when Young knocked at the door, apologising when she saw her friend was trying to eat. Macallan wrapped up what was left of the cheese and tomato special and decided that not eating the damp excuse for nutrition was probably a good thing.

'Just to let you know that we're pretty happy with the cyphers Nancy used in her notes. I'm as sure as I can be from the last note that she had a call from Conway and went to a meeting a few days before the murder. We have two statements from staff members in the pub on The Shore now that indicate Nancy was there with another woman, so we can be pretty sure that's Conway.

'There's something else though – there's a similar statement from the pub staff confirming that they knew Nancy as a regular and she'd been there a couple of nights before and met a man who answers Taylor's description. We can only guess what was said, but the staff say she looked anxious. That's probably as far as we can take that, but it would fit the pattern of behaviour. Then, to round it off, she had a call from a clean phone on the night of her death and went to the pub, but whoever she was meeting never turned up.'

Macallan tapped the desk with her pen. It made sense. 'So, he was setting a trap. He wouldn't know where she lived so had the first meet, appeared to play ball then followed her home. Then, the night of the hit, rather than sitting at the bottom of her stair, hoping she appeared, he set up a late meet then didn't turn up, pretty sure she'd head back to the house, where he had good cover for the kill.'

'There's a bit more, Grace, that confirms the story about Dolan.' Young took her glasses off and used them as a prop. Macallan forgot about her coffee, sat back and let the analyst do her thing.

'From what we've got from Conway, the army, open sources and, most importantly, Nancy's notes from Tam Hunter, we've confirmed this coincidence – or paradox – which is quite off the scale. We're sure now that Mike Regan's brother was active in the paramilitaries in Northern Ireland and was killed in South Armagh by an undercover army unit. That unit seems to be C Troop 5.'

Macallan nodded – it was turning from intelligence to possible evidence so there was progress. She wondered who would actually use it or bring it to court, but that was probably a decision for the PSNI down the line.

'Another question to put to Major Bowman. You couldn't make it up, Felicity.'

'I'll leave you to the remains of the sannie,' Young said. She seemed pleased with the development. 'By the way, Mick says you're meeting him tonight. Be gentle with him,' she added with a smile. She never worried about Harkins' friendship with Macallan – she knew it gave them something they both needed but found hard to enjoy with other people.

'More like he needs to be gentle with me. Anyway, we've got the flight in the morning – though it's not till late morning so I'll survive. We don't want to arrive in Dublin too early when Paddy and his team are so involved. He'll have all the morning briefings to take care of and making sure the pieces are right in place for what they're doing. It's vital we don't get in the way.'

After Young left, Macallan made fresh coffee and sat lost in thought about what she'd just been told. More pieces of the jigsaw were falling into place, and now there was the outline of a picture. It was a game of chess now, with the players making their moves for the final battle. Toher had been right – they would need some luck, and it was ever thus, but the same rules applied to Regan, Handyside and whoever else was involved. She reminded herself that, at the end of the day, Nancy Gilhooley had been robbed of her life – that was no board game and she still deserved justice. She *needed* justice, and if Handyside was out there, he needed to lose to balance the scales.

79

Macallan managed to eat a few more bites of her sandwich as she called Harkins to confirm their meet. Bowman then arrived a little earlier than expected, so she looked in disgust at what was left of the sandwich and tossed it in the bin as if it had offended her.

Bowman looked much more relaxed than he had at their first meeting, and when he sat down, he pulled another file out of his briefcase, laying it on his side of the desk opposite Macallan. She called Duncan into the office to take notes and break in if there was anything Macallan should have asked when it came to army intelligence. Macallan's very nature meant that she normally had an idea what her next move would be, but she accepted that for this meeting, it would just be a case of throwing the dice and seeing what the numbers said.

Bowman made some small talk but gave up when he recognised the look in Macallan's eyes that said *let's just get the fuck on with it*.

'We've had another look at any information that might help you and there's a bit more on the backgrounds of C Troop 5.'

Macallan stiffened at the words *a little bit more,* as if she'd half expected this, and cut in before he started the next sentence.

'You do understand that at some stage we're going to pass what we have to the PSNI for them to consider any action. All I want to make clear is that I will leave nothing out. I also want to remind you that Nancy's newspaper have a significant part of the story, and there are now a number of their staff who know what that is. Are we clear, Major?'

Bowman nodded but gave nothing away. He seemed completely unruffled by the intervention, and Macallan guessed he'd expected it – he probably had a new brief from his masters.

'Superintendent, let me be clear as well. I'm here with a brief to assist you in any way we can. I've brought this file that our team have put a lot of work into. So please, let's agree that we will both cooperate fully. After all, I have to be sure that you're being open with me and disclosing all information. I'm not sure that's the case, but we'll see.'

The atmosphere in the office had turned cooler by several degrees, but they were both professionals and it had been a score draw, so they settled back to what was, in reality, a negotiation.

'Okay, we're going to hand over the source of Nancy's story and our information. I think that should prove our good faith.' Macallan waited as Bowman's eyes narrowed at her words.

'So she's helped you?'

Macallan was in no mood for any more shadow-boxing. 'Of course she has, and it was my duty to make sure she did. She's a vital witness in what is now more than one murder, and I had to be confident I have all I can from her.'

Macallan sighed and took a moment, remembering that the man opposite her was just doing what the army expected of him. She'd had to accept that same old shit over the years but was tired of the everlasting competition between large government establishments – fighting not for the common good but their organisation's own sometimes narrow interests.

'Look, this source— No, wait a minute, let's give her a name – Captain Ruth Conway. You know her?'

Bowman sat back and considered. 'Yes, I do and I'm disappointed that it's her. She had a fine career and would have gone further. However, I'm grateful that this one is on the table now. There's no point in denying that she faces a difficult time, and her career is more than likely over.'

He seemed to have calmed, and the tension of the initial skirmishes had disappeared. They'd reached the point where it was time to get on with things and represent their teams as best they could, though accepting, at the same time, that there would have to be some give but probably not full disclosure by either of them.

'Well, you'll learn that there was a human element to this – Nancy and Ruth were involved with each other and the disclosure came later. She strikes me as a decent human being and, to be fair, I think what she knew about C Troop 5 and what came later genuinely disturbed her. It happens.'

Bowman nodded and pushed the file towards Macallan. 'There's what else we've come up with. Look, before there's any contact with the PSNI, I think we should let our higher ranks discuss the implications.' He waited for Macallan's response.

'That's something they can decide, but it's not for this meeting.'

She opened the thin file and scanned through it. There didn't seem to be much more than fleshing out what they knew already. She closed it as if it was unpleasant to the touch and returned her attention to Bowman. 'Right, can I ask you a few questions before Ruth arrives – on the record?'

'Of course.' He seemed unsure and waited.

'Were C Troop 5 acting under orders in Northern Ireland and Iraq?'

'They were acting under orders of course, but legal orders. However, we now have suspicions that they may have been involved in actions they were never sanctioned for. Of course, it makes it difficult that some of them are beyond reach for us and the only one left that might clear up these matters is Billy Dolan. Given what you've told us about him, it seems unlikely that he'll cooperate. Of course, there is no physical evidence of any potential crimes in Northern Ireland, Iraq or Afghanistan.'

There it is again, she thought, *plausible deniability.* She knew it was a card that would be played time and time again before the investigation was over.

'So there were no suspicions before Afghanistan that they were operating outside the rules of engagement?' Macallan looked towards Duncan, who raised one finger above her notepad. She wanted to ask a question. Macallan nodded the okay.

'There was a lot of speculation that Conlan Regan, who was believed to have been killed in South Armagh, was the result of action by an undercover army team. Witnesses saw camouflaged men in the area at the time. The army must have looked into this – what was the result?'

Duncan had been primed by Macallan to ask this question beforehand. Given that she was ex-army intelligence, Macallan believed it might make Bowman think they had more than they did.

'Many of the paramilitaries used camouflaged gear, so that means nothing on its own. We had no evidence this was the case, and we believe Regan was killed by Loyalists.'

'Major Bowman, I worked in Northern Ireland, as you know, and the chances a Loyalist team carried out that job in South Armagh at that time is a hard one to accept.'

'We'll never know.' Bowman sat back as if that was the end of it.

'Well, let me tell you that we believe that there is a strong possibility C Troop 5 was there at the time and that the army knew that. Ruth Conway believes that and has seen intelligence that suggests so too. So we now have the almost bizarre situation that Dolan and his team may have killed Conlan Regan and are now working as contract killers for his brother Mike. Full circle so to speak.'

Bowman saw exactly where the situation was heading. 'Interesting and complicated for you.' He left it at that.

'Well, it's just a bit complicated for you as well, my friend! Ruth is due here anytime, so let me just tell you that things are on the move in Dublin, and we believe that Dolan is involved. We don't know what's planned but believe that Dolan and his associates may be involved.'

Macallan sat back and nodded to Duncan, who came in again.

'We have forensics material from the locus of Sam Taylor's murder. We have DNA that may have come from one of his killers. We've checked the national database with no success, but I know the army keeps some records of DNA from soldiers operating in conflict zones. Will you check this profile against your records?'

'I'll check the legal restrictions and get back to you, but obviously we want to help.'

Macallan decided that they'd sparred enough – the messages from both sides had been delivered, and things were on the move elsewhere.

When Ruth Conway came into the office, it became a completely formal procedure; Bowman was polite and did it all by the book. Conway agreed that she would leave the office with him and travel to an army camp near Edinburgh.

Before they left, Conway shook Macallan's hand. She looked broken.

'I hope I've helped, and sorry again for not coming forward at the start. I'm happy to help if you need me again.'

Macallan nodded and watched the two leave, wondering what the future would hold now for the talented young woman. She was headed for a journey through a meat grinder, but there was nothing Macallan could do about that. Her mind turned instead to Dublin and what might take place there over the next few days. So much rested on that.

80

Macallan was still thinking about Dublin when the phone broke her train of thought. It was Garvey, and her message lifted the detective.

'Billy Dolan came back to his flat and is still there, so we have a full surveillance team on it. His car is parked well away from the house so we might get a chance to put a tracker on it, and there's some serious technical work going on to identify his phone from his location.'

'That's good news, June. Let me know if there are any developments overnight. Don't worry about disturbing me – I just appreciate your cooperation.'

'Well, at the end of the day it might be your man's team that's going to carry out whatever the action is on Thursday. Let's hope we all get a result on this one. See you tomorrow, Grace.'

Macallan put the phone away, confident that, as far as possible, everything was in place. She had an appointment with her clinical psychologist arranged a little later and there was no reason not to keep it. She'd felt so much more confident after that first appointment and it *was* making a difference – now it just seemed something that she would do routinely.

The initial appointment had been no more than an hour, and the doctor was so laid back she was nearly on the floor, but Macallan had taken to her immediately. What surprised her was how quickly she had started to disclose her problems – she'd been convinced that she'd struggle to speak honestly, and yet it had all poured out in a stream. It had shocked her for a moment, until she'd realised that she wanted to do this more than anything. From there, all her concerns had evaporated. She knew she had to do the work for Jack and the children more than anyone else – although, as her doctor kept reminding her, it was for her as well.

When the appointment was over, Macallan packed her things for the Dublin trip and remembered that she was supposed to meet Mick Harkins. She never usually let her friend down, and a few weeks earlier she would have gone without thinking, but Jack was at home and he was the priority. She felt her chest tighten at the thought of letting Mick down, but from her therapy, she already understood that her permanent guilt and inability to say no was a problem she needed to confront.

She lifted the phone as if it was infected and held it to her ear. When her friend answered, she almost stumbled over the words but explained that she was off to Dublin in the morning and the job was at a critical stage.

'I'm sorry, Mick, but tell you what, when it's wrapped up, we'll do it right. I'll buy the first three rounds. Hang on – I do that anyway.'

'Aye, right, Grace. No worries. I've got a good documentary on tonight anyway. Don't worry – the job comes first. Always does, but you better not let me down for the next one so get it done. Be good to hear what you're up to. You're taking Felicity with you so I'll get a free pass to go out on the lash anyway.'

Macallan called Jack and suggested they cook the steaks she'd bought then follow them up with a bit of TV. He sounded pleased and relaxed. She was enjoying finding him again, and it seemed he was of the same mind.

'I'll pick the wine and get it opened,' he said with that old undertone of intimacy that made her grin.

As Macallan headed for home, Handyside held his wife in his arms and didn't want to let her go. He was troubled and wondered if he should have pulled the plug on the Dublin job. Regan had been right that even if there was police attention in Glasnevin, that was just part of the world they lived in and would never change. Yet, he felt uneasy and couldn't put his finger on why.

Kangas had been arrested in Edinburgh, and then there was the whole mess created by Sam Taylor, but it was the consequences of those problems that really gnawed at his bones. Macallan was in play because of them, and it was as if he could feel her close. There was no evidence for it, but when he stared out of his window, he wondered if somewhere out there she was staring back. It was illogical, but he couldn't shake the feeling.

His wife pushed him to arm's length but didn't speak – the look in her eyes said it all. She was worried and knew he was troubled, but also that there was no point discussing it because he'd just tell her everything was alright.

'I have to go to Dublin on Thursday, lass, and should be there for a couple of nights. When I get back, we'll plan some holidays. What do you think?'

She didn't answer; she just pulled him in close again and closed her eyes, trying to contain her tears.

81

Garvey had joined up with the surveillance operation and fretted at the lack of movement on Dolan. She worried that this was a red herring and it might be that they'd taken their eye off Mike Regan, whose team might be planning something else. Dolan had been seen going back into the flat earlier in the day, and neither he nor his partner had appeared again.

'What does it mean?' she said without thinking.

The officer beside her in the car looked round. 'Sorry?' He knew this was always the worst part of surveillance – sometimes waiting for days for the target to move, with the constant worry that they were just wasting time.

'Sorry, speaking to myself again. I hate this bit – never get used to it.'

The older detective smiled – it was the same conversation that tended to take place time and time again on these operations. He was a twenty-five-year detective so had seen it all before and snapped off a piece of dark chocolate from the bar he carried – his drug of choice in the long hours of inactivity.

'Seems to me this fella is the real deal. Ex-para, fought all over the world and now contracting. Or to put it another way, a murdering bastard. Plus, he lives in Malahide, and it takes serious money to set up home here. I couldn't afford a garage in this place, never mind what he's got, so he's guilty of something.' He was a deadpan expert.

Garvey sniggered. 'Okay, Sherlock, that'll do for me. Gimme a bit of that chocolate bar. You're getting fat anyway – been sitting in these cars for too many years.'

The radio burst into life and Garvey felt the surge of adrenalin focus her back into her command role.

'That's a sighting of the target walking in the general direction of the car. He's carrying a holdall. Full description on the way to all units.'

There was silence as the eyeball monitored Dolan. Being away from the house didn't mean he was on the move, and anyway, the units were all ready to take him on if he started driving.

Less than a minute later, a full description of Dolan and what he was wearing had been sent separately to each unit. A photograph followed the description.

Garvey confirmed that the chopper was in the air and was told it was nearly in position to monitor Dolan's car. She tried to relax her shoulders but so much depended on her to make the right calls on whatever came next.

'That's the target deposited a bag in the target vehicle and he's headed back towards the target address.'

'It's fine, June. He's going to move shortly. No doubt about it. Bet he's going back to kiss the wife.' The old detective broke off another piece of chocolate and seemed so relaxed he might fall asleep. Garvey hoped he was right and they would soon see some movement.

'That's the target back at the target address. They've kissed and he's turned back again towards the target vehicle.'

The driver wrapped up the chocolate. 'I'm so clever at times it frightens me.' He straightened himself and got ready for what came next.

'Okay, smart-arse. You win again.' Garvey smiled, glad she had someone with his experience along. Her only worry was that Dolan's car was in too exposed an area, meaning they hadn't been able to get near it to plant a beacon – there was always a risk they could lose him if he went into serious anti-surveillance mode, but they had the chopper and three motorbikes on the job, and time after time, the bikes would recover a target that seemed lost.

As it turned out, the darkness was starting to come down, but Dolan drove carefully – he obviously didn't want to attract attention. He did some anti-surveillance, but Toher had deployed almost double the resources they would normally have and this gave Garvey lots of options.

'Driving carefully tonight, June. That means he's up to something. Trust me.' Garvey's driver was completely focused on the job – he was one of the best surveillance officers in the business and a driver with tungsten nerves.

Garvey called Toher and filled him in on what they were doing. He was in his office and told her he'd stay there for the duration – there was too much riding on this job. 'I'm spending a fortune on this one, June, and when the exec get the bill, they're going to skin me if we don't get a result. No pressure – right?'

'We'll do our best, sir.' Garvey knew he'd be sweating blood and wasn't that far off herself. 'We seem to be heading in the general direction of Castleknock. Might change but that would be interesting if that's where he's headed.'

'Jesus! Trouble is, we just don't know where he's going till he's there, and we have to go with the intelligence that Thursday is the day for whatever the fuck this is.'

It was unusual to hear Toher swear, and Garvey saw it as a little sign that her boss was human, although he did a great job of always looking in control.

'It's a hard one – if we go too early, we might end up with nothing; but it would be Sod's Law if an attack took place before Thursday and we ended up watching the killer do his work.'

'No worries, June. There's a firearms team close to you, and those boys and girls won't hesitate if it comes to it.'

Garvey put the phone back in her pocket and looked round at her driver. 'You got your lucky rabbit's foot?'

'Don't need one.' He quoted the old Irish saying. 'When God created the Irish... he didn't do another thing but sit down and smile.' He nodded sagely as if that was all that was required.

'And your point is?'

'Your man here is a Brit. So that's all the incentive we need.'

Garvey sighed, wishing she could be that confident.

When Dolan parked up in a quiet area on the outskirts of Castleknock, Garvey was confident that Sean O'Reilly must in fact be the target. She'd made a good move and had deployed two units ahead of the surveillance convoy and Dolan to find and take up positions to cover O'Reilly's home and control Dolan if he went near the house. Garvey had been on previous surveillance operations on O'Reilly and knew there was ample woodland cover round his home. It was too late to put someone in there though – they might collide with Dolan, and the chaos that could cause would be humiliating.

Dolan parked then walked almost a mile to O'Reilly's home, carrying the holdall. The eyeball eventually reported that he'd disappeared at a secluded spot next to the eight-foot wall surrounding O'Reilly's grounds. It was on the edge of the wooded space that covered most of the area at the back of his home. They decided he had to have gone over the wall.

Garvey made sure the firearms team were as close as possible without alarming the locals.

It was a gamble but she then called in the technical team to beacon Dolan's car and breathed a sigh of relief when that went down without a hitch.

Garvey felt her breathing tighten; she was worried that this might in fact be an attack rather than groundwork by Dolan. She said a little prayer when the eyeball reported that five minutes after he'd entered the woods, another man had exited at almost the same spot. They had a description, and another team had followed him to a car, which had left and was being followed back towards the city. Garvey blessed Toher because normally they would have struggled to assign enough troops to do this. She called him.

'Thank God it looks like they're prepping a job, right enough. One in and one out at O'Reilly's, and thank God you gave us the extra troops.' Garvey's back was sticky with sweat, but her worries had eased – what they'd seen fitted a pattern of behaviour they could understand.

'These boys are pros, June, so they'll prepare properly. We need to identify where he is in there and get our own coverts in as well at some point. There's still a lot we don't know so let's get everything we can. Grace Macallan seems to be on the money, so we go with this all the way. I guess he'll settle down there for a few hours so I'll see you in the morning. I'm here, so make sure you keep in touch, and good work. Hopefully the other team will ID this other boy and we'll have something to tell Grace in the morning.'

In the wooded area, Dolan had changed into his night gear and settled down with his eyes on the house. He'd spotted O'Reilly a couple of times – it looked like the man didn't sleep much. As they'd already seen, every so often he'd stand at the back of the house and smoke. *Perfect,* Dolan thought.

82

Garvey checked her watch again – it was almost one thirty in the morning. There had been nothing to report, and as far as they knew, Dolan was still somewhere in the wooded area. The surveillance team at the front of O'Reilly's home had reported that, as far as they could see, all the lights were off and he'd been spotted drawing the curtains in an upstairs room. It looked like he'd settled down for the night.

About twenty minutes later, Dolan was seen carefully exiting the woods and heading back to his car. Garvey gave the order to let him run well ahead and monitor him with the beacon. It was too much of a risk to go near him at that time of night because he'd surely spot a follow. She decided to stay in Castleknock and supervise locating where Dolan had positioned himself. It was a gamble, and she hoped he'd head straight home for the night.

She waited for the call that he was heading generally on the way back to Malahide before setting up pickets round the area so that if an associate of Dolan turned up unexpectedly, they would have time to withdraw. Two of the remaining team were experts in covert hides, and she sent them into the wooded area when she felt it was safe, but the waiting put her nerves on edge again – it was always the same peaks and troughs of emotion on these jobs. She'd noticed the first signs of grey hair the previous morning and wondered how many years major crime investigation took off a detective's life span.

The call came in that they'd located the spot where Dolan and his associate had been watching the house. It gave a perfect view of the back of O'Reilly's home and so could be used to monitor him. The problem for Garvey – and ultimately Toher – was if they thought this was a threat to life, regardless of O'Reilly's track record, what did they do? For the moment, she didn't need to worry because Dolan was away, and she presumed neither he nor his associate wouldn't be back till it was dark again.

'Can we get our own hide in place so we can cover what they're doing?' Garvey asked.

There was a delay but the answer came back that there were good spots available to monitor Dolan if he came back. It was risky but an option. She called Toher, who couldn't have been sleeping because he answered the phone on the first ring, and ran the idea past him, letting him know too that Dolan had just arrived home in Malahide.

'It's a good idea,' he replied, 'but we need to get the boys in place as soon as. It takes time.'

'I've got two trained men on the plot here, but they don't have gear and they've had a hard day already, so can you call out a team and get them here as soon as possible? They might need to stay in the hide for a full day or more.'

'I'll get it done right now.'

Garvey stretched her legs, hoping she could get a few hours' sleep before Macallan arrived. She would have to be at the meeting and then probably back out on the plot for the night.

Fifteen minutes later, Toher called her back and confirmed that a covert team were on their way with all the equipment needed for an extended hide.

'Right, you wait there till they're in. I've arranged a support team to be there and relieve you. You need to get some rest – we've a busy few days coming up.'

Garvey felt relieved – she'd done all she could, and for the moment, there didn't seem to be any serious issues with the surveillance – in fact, it had gone like clockwork. That didn't seem right because there was always a problem of some kind, but she accepted the gift.

'Right, I think we might actually get some sleep tonight.'

The old detective nodded back at her, giving her a thumbs-up at the same time. 'I don't need sleep. Sleep's for wimps.'

The relief team arrived an hour later, and the two officers were settled in the hide forty-five minutes after that.

On her way home, Garvey received a call that the other surveillance team had followed Dolan's associate back to a central Dublin hotel, where he had settled down in the bar. They had a photograph of him and were continuing the surveillance. She called Toher again, and he arranged a relief team to cover the hotel and Ronnie Baker – who'd booked in under an alias.

83

Garvey headed back to her flat in Dublin and fell asleep on top of her bed fully clothed.

About the same time she closed her eyes, Dolan had given up on sleep and risen quietly, trying not to disturb his wife. He made some coffee and sat on his balcony, smoking one cigarette after another. The goal of retirement was so close now he could almost touch it. That's what worried him. The thought of losing it all at the last moment scared him, and fear wasn't something he did very often. He had that Presbyterian gene that made him worry that everything would go wrong at the last call, but this was only one job after risking his life more times than he could remember. He wanted the flat in Spain so much – to have nothing to worry about but which restaurant to visit with his wife – and the man he'd known as Joe Stafford had called and said he'd see him after the job, before he headed off for the Med, so it was real – it *was* the last one and definitely no dream.

He thought about the old team and those days during the Troubles and what they'd done. They'd started off believing that what they were fighting for was righteous and the men they'd killed deserved nothing better. It was strange the way they never noticed what they were morphing into – if they'd ever been innocent human beings, it was long ago now. His wife had no idea what he was, and he never wanted her to find out.

He shook his head, thinking about the job to come. What would Joe Stafford think if he knew that he'd killed the brother of the man they were working for in Dublin? More than that, what would Mike Regan think if he knew?

He heard his wife's footsteps behind him before she kissed the top of his head.

'Come to bed, love. I'm cold without you.'

He took her hand and realised that at least there was one good thing in his life to hang on to.

'Just thinking about Spain. Can't wait.'

He stood up and they headed back to bed, but he knew there was no chance of a restful sleep till this was all settled.

84

Grace Macallan felt her knuckles tighten on the armrest. She'd accepted a long time ago that she'd never get used to flying, no matter what she told herself about it being the safest form of travel. She did it, but it stressed her from the time she got to the airport till she was safely back on the ground.

They swept in low over the Irish Sea towards the runway as she watched the ground take identifiable shape, and when the rubber hit the ground, it was almost a textbook landing. She'd hardly spoken during the flight, concentrating on any noises or movements that might spell the end, and sighed as the plane slowed, the tension in her shoulders easing.

She turned to Young and smiled weakly. 'Thank God that's over. I'll never get used to it. Worse today with an early flight when I couldn't sink a G&T for some courage.'

'It never bothers me,' Young replied, 'but Mick's like you – he has to get plastered before I can get him on a plane. In fact, I don't think we'll fly again because it's too much of a trial – plus, the last time, I thought he was going to punch a guy who was mouthing off about Nicola Sturgeon.'

Macallan had to laugh because Young sounded so serious and she could just imagine Harkins, who was a big fan of the First Minister, losing it when he was already stressed about flying.

A Garda detective was waiting for them and took Macallan, Young and Duncan straight to Toher's office. He shook their hands warmly, explained that Garvey was on her way and that his senior analyst Ciara Kelly would join them for the meeting.

'June's been up half the night and just grabbed a couple of hours' sleep, so if you'll forgive me, we'll have some coffee and wait for her. Been a very interesting night, and I think we're moving towards some sort of action on Thursday. Will you be staying here?' Toher seemed genuinely pleased that they were there, and Macallan wanted to give him any support they could.

'I'll stay here for the duration unless something comes up back in Edinburgh before then. We have something planned for Thursday back there ourselves, but it's in hand and supports what you're doing here.'

Macallan took her seat and felt a tremor in her gut, knowing that maybe, just maybe, they were closing in on Handyside. It wasn't Toher's priority, but for her it was unfinished business – though she wouldn't make that too obvious. Making it so personal wasn't professional, and although her team knew it, she didn't want Toher to see it.

She was finishing her coffee when Garvey walked in. Her hair was tied back and she looked tired, but that came with the territory, and Macallan had been there often enough herself. It was what bound these detectives together like a blood relationship.

They took their seats when Ciara Kelly arrived, whereupon introductions were made cordially and with the minimum of fuss. Toher opened the meeting, and despite the fact Macallan knew he must be under tremendous pressure for a result, he was cool enough. He outlined the latest developments and intelligence but avoided what had happened the previous night – he wanted to leave that to Garvey. When he'd covered all that was required, he nodded to her.

'We had to work hard on Dolan, but he moved eventually, and the long and short of it is that we took him to Castleknock, where we realised he was relieving an unknown associate who was in a hide covering the home address of Sean O'Reilly.'

Kelly had prepared folders and handed them to the Scottish officers. Garvey carried on once they'd opened them.

'O'Reilly's CV is on the first page, and you'll see he's head of one of the two rival teams who've been at war with Mike Regan's gang for years. A hard man and a smart operator.

'So, Dolan went into the hide then the unknown associate left, and one of our teams followed him to a city centre hotel. The security manager in the hotel is an old Garda officer so we have a photo from their security system. We should get DNA from his room first chance, and of course the details he gave are false so no surprise there.'

She looked towards Toher. 'Have we had any luck identifying this man yet, sir?'

He shook his head. 'Nothing so far.'

'We might be able to help there,' Macallan said. 'There's a good chance that this man is ex-army so we can run the photo, maybe the DNA, past Major Bowman, who I've been dealing with on the Scottish cases. If you agree, we'll do this as soon as you like.'

Toher agreed, thanked Macallan and told her she could do it right away before Garvey carried on.

'Dolan then settled down, and we managed to get a technical device on his car when he was in there. In the early hours of the morning, O'Reilly settled down for the night and Dolan withdrew. He headed home and is still there. We've set up our own hide, with CROPS officers in the area covering their hide. So we're all set up and expect them back when the darkness comes down. That's it for now.' She sat back and reached for a drink.

Macallan smiled at the fact they'd the nerve to put their own hide in. That took balls.

'Excellent – sounds like great work, June.'

Garvey grinned, enjoying Macallan's genuine warmth.

Toher filled in a few more details, then turned to Kelly and asked her if she wanted to add anything at that time. She was a diminutive woman in her mid-thirties with fiery copper hair, tied back off her face. She had an earnest look, and Macallan thought she saw traces of Young in her expression. She always found that the top analysts tended to be serious about their job – it was what made them a vital part of the intelligence machine needed to take on the premier-league gangs. It was an everlasting cat-and-mouse game, and Macallan had just read a report that organised crime teams were trying to recruit exactly the same people to ensure an equality of arms with law enforcement.

When Kelly spoke, she seemed confident, without any pretence, and Macallan recognised her accent as mid Ulster.

'I've put together a package of information and intelligence that covers the main issues we've faced and where we are now. Mr Toher has arranged that Felicity and I spend time together after this meeting to run through our analysis and work on both sides to make sure we're working in tandem. At the moment – and despite what June's team monitored last night – I have reservations.'

Macallan almost expected this line and saw Young nod, as if the analysts were already joined at the hip. Kelly tapped the end of her pen on the table as if she was a teacher delivering an important lesson.

'We know that an outside team of professional contractors have been brought in, clearly to carry out some significant mission – possibly on two targets, and of course we know about O'Reilly, but who is the other one? Our problem is that this implies a threat to life on Reilly, but we just don't know.

'The other problem is that we have no interception of Dolan's communications with anyone, so we have no idea of plans, and what worries me is that – according to what we know from our Edinburgh colleagues – the two men we've seen are part of something bigger. My question is: who are they talking to here and where are the other contractors working in Dublin at the moment? I think we need an urgent effort to identify what the planning is here. What we have looks good on the surface, but there are so many things that could throw us.'

Kelly sat back in her chair. The mood in the room had changed. The analyst had been right in every sense, and even Toher, the eternal optimist, seemed subdued by the weight of the potential problems she'd raised. It only lasted for moments, because he knew he was in charge of the mood, and it was his job to make everyone believe they were on the right track.

Macallan knew exactly what he was thinking – and what she would have said in the circumstances.

Toher smiled. 'Right, we need more coffee – especially looking at June's eyes.'

That broke the mood for a few minutes, then they returned to work over the problems. Toher had taken a phone call during the break and seemed energised by whatever he'd been told.

'Right, Ciara is perfectly correct. We have this problem of a threat to life, so let's do our duty and warn O'Reilly that there's an unspecified threat. We've done it often enough before, and there's no reason to think he'll take one bit of notice. In fact, his answer will likely be…'

He turned to Garvey, who grinned and chimed in. 'It's always the same. Fuck off!'

'That's exactly right, June. But we do it and we're covered. There's no reason to think Dolan or whoever is working his strings will know, so we carry on.

'In the meantime, I had a call from our technical people. Obviously, Dolan and his associate must be in contact, and we guess because they're using a hide it will be via text. Our people have identified the number of a phone used in the area of his home in Malahide and near the hide in Castleknock. And of course, it follows that we've identified what seems to be the associate's phone in Castleknock and the area of the hotel where he's staying. The timing seems to work perfectly.'

He nodded across the table at Macallan. 'We waiting for authority to intercept Dolan's phone and to do a technical operation on the associate's room in the hotel. I think we're in the game. But the quicker we get this associate identified, the better, so let's break here. We've set it up so Felicity and Ciara can work together, and there's an office next door that we can use as a joint base for now. That sound okay, Grace?'

'Absolutely.' She turned to Duncan. 'Maggie, will you get on to Major Bowman and see if we can identify the associate as a matter of urgency.'

The mood had changed again and they got to work.

85

Dolan woke with a start, remembered where he was and looked at his watch. He felt like shit and knew the years were taking their toll.

He heard his wife in the kitchen, and the smell of fresh coffee meant there was no chance of falling asleep again. He swung his legs over the bed, stretched down and tried to touch his toes, but his sciatic nerve was playing up again. He groaned as he straightened and rolled his shoulders.

His wife came in the room, fully dressed and with a cup in her hand. He lay back on the pillow and they talked about Spain. She was like a girl ready to go on her first foreign holiday.

'The estate agent called first thing, Billy, and we've had an offer for this place already.' She told him the amount and his eyes widened in surprise. It was much more than they'd hoped for and his anxiety calmed – this was a sign that everything was going to be okay.

He told his wife he was going to shower then head out for a walk to clear his head.

At the same time he was drying himself, the authority to intercept his phone came through to the Guards. The technicians locked onto his number and the monitoring was immediately up and running.

Half an hour later, he strolled along the marina, lost in thought. They'd been lucky and happy living on the Irish coast; it was a good place to be, but Spain would be a complete break from his past where he could leave everything behind, grow fat and pretend he was just another well-off escapee from the UK, which he'd come to dislike intensely. Living in Ireland and marrying into an Irish family meant his views on their history and grievances had changed. It clashed with all he'd ever believed, and his greatest fear was that his wife might find out what his past had involved.

He sat down on a bench overlooking anchored yachts and lit up a smoke, heaving in a lungful and holding it before releasing it back into the air. He felt almost human again when the phone rang – it was Baker checking in.

Even before they started their conversation, the Monitoring Unit of the Crime and Security Section were recording them.

Baker sounded annoyingly perky, but then he was twenty years younger and still hadn't been through the soldier's version of a mid-life crisis.

'Everything okay, boss. What time do you want me in tonight?'

'As soon as it's dark. I'll relieve you a bit earlier. Can't fuckin' sleep right anyway till this is done.' Dolan flicked his cigarette onto the pavement. A passing senior citizen was about to give him some words until Dolan gave him the eyes. The old man realised he was on a loser and looked straight ahead.

'Make sure your kit is ready. It's still Thursday for the job, but you never know when we might have to move.' Dolan kept his words to a minimum.

Baker had one more question. 'Is it going to plan with the other target?'

Dolan felt a surge of anger. This was always the problem with bringing youth into the game – that info was need-to-know, and Baker just didn't need to know.

'Listen, son, I've told you before: you worry about our target and the other team can take care of theirs. That's how it works. Now shut the fuck up.'

He cut the call and felt it again, that sinking feeling that it could all go wrong. On these jobs, they had to get every detail right and then hope Sod's Law wouldn't trample all over the course. He shook his head and decided to go back to the flat, put his arms round his wife and pretend they were in Spain.

86

Within ten minutes, the contents of the conversation had been relayed to Toher, who was already with Macallan, the two analysts and Duncan. Garvey had gone to get another couple of hours' rest before she headed back out with her surveillance team. Duncan had some information from Major Bowman and she spoke first.

'Army intelligence have confirmed through their links with naval intelligence that the unknown associate is Ronnie Baker, ex-British Forces as we thought and was in fact a Royal Marine, so goes without saying – highly trained and served with distinction in the Middle East and Afghanistan. He left the service a year ago, and as far as we know he was off the radar until now. We've asked for a DNA profile, but we just have to wait and see if that's forthcoming. So, we have a good description plus a history – basically another very capable individual. We've been given his CV, associates and places he frequents. That's it for now.'

'That's good work.' Toher seemed pleased and went on to disclose what had been picked up on the intercept between Dolan and Baker then gave both analysts a moment to make notes. Young was going to speak first then remembered where she was. She turned to Kelly and let her have her say.

'There has been a lack of information on key points, but I think now with the assists we have in place, the blank spaces are filling in. What we know from what we've learned and hypothesised is that Dolan is the team's most experienced man, was the senior rank in the army and very likely the link man to Handyside. What Baker said suggests that Dolan will be in touch with whoever is in this other team. So, we still have today and tomorrow before Thursday. We continue the analysis and hopefully the intercept will lead us to the other team.' Kelly seemed much more positive than she had been previously.

Toher scratched his chin and gave a wry smile.

'Christ, I've got half the force's detectives on this job and this means I might need to ask for more. The top brass are going to love this one. Anyway, that's my job.' He looked towards Young for her thoughts, and she flipped her glasses off before she spoke.

'I agree entirely with Ciara, and of course the next question is: now we've confirmed there is another target, who is the other team and who are they watching? This may be an even more ambitious move than we thought. We know they're targeting O'Reilly, and now it appears that there are two contract teams in action for whatever Thursday holds. We also know there are two main gangs at war with Regan, so a reasonable hypothesis would be that the other target is Tony Collins, the head of the other gang. A double strike on the top men would be a bold move, and why not? The war has got none of them anywhere so why not escalate to try and de-escalate?'

Toher asked Macallan if she had any thoughts.

'I agree. Whatever this operation is, they're in serious preparation mode so it's unlikely they'll risk being caught with weapons at the moment. We might get an indication from the surveillance. Dolan's asked the associate to check his kit. They were specialist troops and will be fanatics about making sure their weapons are checked and ready to go – or standard operating procedures as they would call them. The associate doesn't go into the hide till tonight so he might check in today. Or the weapons might be concealed near the hide. Might be an idea to get your CROPS team to do a creep and see if they're there.'

Toher nodded in agreement. 'I'll get them onto that as soon as we're finished here.'

Kelly came in again. 'We have to remember that although Dolan seems to be planning their strike at O'Reilly's home, our intel confirms Collins lives in a high-quality flat in the city centre. There's significant security round that complex – high fence, underground parking and security men. So, it could be that the plan is quite different there if indeed it is Collins.'

Toher rubbed his chin again and thought for a moment. 'Okay, it's steady as we go. We have time, the surveillance operation and now the intercept has to give us something. The main thing is not to spook them.' He turned to Macallan. 'What about Handyside, Grace? Presumably he'll not be near this?'

Macallan shook her head. 'He seems to be a facilitator, and although a violent man, this is specialist work. Even if we get this wrapped up, we might not get him. We know he made a call from Dublin in the Kangas case, and he's identified in the Glasnevin meet, but that doesn't mean he lives here. My feeling is if he did, you'd have come across him. It's that kind of city.' She looked at Toher for confirmation.

'Totally agree. Dublin is a village, and a man like that would have come up on our radar. He's a smart operator, and my guess is he's in one of the big cities in England or Europe. What were you thinking?'

'We need a trigger,' Macallan replied. 'As you know, it's a well-tried strategy during an operation to make a move, for example through the press, to try and force a reaction from the target. My proposal, if you agree, is to publish the photo you have of Handyside from the series in Glasnevin. Regardless of what happens here, he might be nowhere near the job and we lose sight of him again. There are still outstanding warrants for his arrest for serious crimes in England and Scotland, and we can dress it up in vague language that we're looking for him for other serious crimes. We publish it here and in the UK.'

Macallan let the proposal settle and waited. She knew it might not go down well, and Regan might end up spooked if the Thursday operation never happened.

'Let me think about this,' Toher said finally. 'I'd need to discuss it with the top brass. However, for me it makes sense. Handyside seems to be up to his eyes and has probably organised outstanding murders here in Dublin, so we have an interest in putting him away. Okay, let's do what we have to do and hope the god of detectives is kind to us.'

Toher closed his notebook and headed for the door.

87

Dolan had gone back to the flat and, after eating a late breakfast with his wife, decided to take a walk back along the waterfront with her.

'Not many chances to enjoy it now, Billy.'

His wife was like a little child at Christmas, and the innocence of it all soothed him – as if he'd never inhabited that dark alternative existence where his main purpose was to dispose of people he didn't even know. Sometimes the closest he came to them was a little picture in his crosshairs before he pulled the trigger and watched them fold into death.

They were about to leave when his phone buzzed – it was one of the team watching Tony Collins. He mouthed the word *work* at her, stepped onto the balcony and closed the French windows.

'How's it going?' Dolan didn't want chapter and verse – he just wanted to hear everything was on track.

'All good and no problems. Going to plan, and hopefully he'll keep his appointment with the girls on Thursday.'

The man was a rock-solid ex-para. Although they hadn't served together in the army, he'd been in the team for years, and Dolan trusted him as a reliable pro who did exactly what the job required. His type of soldier.

'Okay. Call tomorrow same time.'

Dolan put the phone away and smiled at his wife when he joined her again. 'Thank God I'll soon be retired and there'll be no more of these work calls.' He took her hand and they headed out into the sunshine.

Ciara Kelly was about to give a presentation to Macallan and Young on the key factors and intelligence on the years-long Dublin gang wars when Toher walked in.

'Sorry to interrupt – well actually I'm not, but it's nice to be nice.' He grinned to show it was in jest, and Macallan marvelled again that he was always ready with a bit of banter or just a touch of grim humour. She wondered if it was an Irish thing – a people who had suffered more than most always knew the past was worse than the present.

'Just wanted to let you know that we have the okay from our side to release the photos of Handyside. But the main news is a call from Dolan to another unknown.'

Toher explained the contents of the call, then helped himself to the biscuits and fresh tea in their office while the analysts scribbled notes.

Macallan noticed he was barely suppressing the need to gorge on the snack rather than nibble it politely. *The curse of detectives,* she thought – constantly eating on the run. It always took its toll. She wondered what condition she would have been in by now if it wasn't for her settled life with Jack. Probably doing the same thing in Edinburgh.

For a moment she ached for the children and Jack, and without thinking, she reached into her pocket to touch the photo of them she carried everywhere now. Just that touch seemed to prove they were real.

'So, we know from the current intelligence, previous surveillance and an informant that Collins has a thing for two sex workers he visits on a regular basis – normally a Thursday – and now we have this mention of "the girls" and "Thursday". What do you think, Grace?'

'Well these guys constantly break their own rules of changing their routine all the time to avoid attempts on their lives. Most of them become like the rest of us and return to being creatures of habit, and that seems to be the case here.'

She turned to Kelly. 'I think you said that the intelligence is that O'Reilly rarely leaves the house when he's not working.'

Kelly agreed. 'Yes, and that seems to make sense with what we've seen. Why would Dolan go in at night and spend so much time watching him doing nothing? That has to be where they plan to make their move. The rest of the day, they leave him alone so his home seems to be part of their plan. Of course, they may have been watching him during the day before we were onto him, but we have to go on what we're seeing now.'

'It's a perfect spot for a snipe, Paddy – that would be my guess,' Macallan said, turning back to Toher. She let go of the photo in her pocket and focused again. She had plenty experience of snipe jobs in the north.

He nodded. 'Just my thoughts.'

His phone started to move across the desk as if it had a life of its own. He picked it up, nodded and locked eyes with Macallan, and she saw that whatever he was being told meant another piece of the jigsaw was falling into place.

He put the phone back down and closed his eyes for a moment, as if he was making a quick plea or thanks to his god.

'The CROPS team have located a concealment about fifteen feet west of the hide. Obviously they can't just dig it up, and there's always the possibility that there could be a booby trap or something that could place them in danger. We can't discount explosives. Jesus! We need to get other specialists in there without alarming the whole town.'

'Roadworks or an accident,' Young said instantly.

'What?' Toher left the question in the air, but he was already running through options as Kelly developed the idea.

'A staged accident or roadworks would cause a bit of commotion – we could control who passes the entry point and let the specialists get in and out. O'Reilly does go out during the day, but in any case, that road and entry point is well away from the house itself and shouldn't cause alarm.'

'Right, it's going to be a headache organising this in the window of time we have, but the targets are under control of the surveillance teams. Thing is, who do we need to send in?' Toher was thinking aloud.

He turned to Macallan. 'Grace, this kind of scenario must have been common enough when you were in Northern Ireland?'

Macallan knew he was as capable as she was but was doing the right thing and making sure he missed nothing.

'Well, you're absolutely right to be careful. We had experience of situations like this going badly wrong. There could be explosives, but more likely a firearm and *most* likely a rifle for a snipe. Anyway, you need a bomb disposal team to check it, and have your technical people on stand-by, because if there is a gun, it will have to be taken out and worked on to make it incapable of firing without the targets knowing. Then you have to get it all back in place as if it's never been disturbed. These ex-army specialists we're dealing with may have put in little traps almost invisible to the eye to tell them if there's been disturbance on the concealment. That's their tradecraft, and by the sounds of it, Dolan is a serious customer so we have to presume these issues.' She grinned. 'No one said it would be easy, Paddy.'

Toher nodded as he realised he would now have to draw in even more resources. But if it was all too much, he didn't show it.

'And no one said it would be this bloody hard,' he replied, 'but I like the roadworks idea because with my luck, if we stage an accident, one of our boys will go too far and put a Guard in hospital.'

The task was massive; they all knew it, but the pressure seemed to lift them – if they could make it work, they would be stepping ahead of the other side for the first time in the game.

'Well, the first job we need to take off the table is warning these lads that their life is in danger,' Toher said. 'It's not certain Collins is the second target but a reasonable assumption. They'll just tell us to fuck off, but it's our duty, and let's hope we keep them alive so we can lock them up another time. That's the thing – those boys don't deserve it and the world wouldn't be any worse off without them, but such is life.'

He stretched his back to ease off the aching muscles and knots of tension that were becoming a permanent feature.

'The good news is I'll take care of it. Shouldn't take us long. I'll need a second witness, so I'll take one of my sergeants who has no connection with the case. I've got a flyer attached to my office and being groomed for high office. He's being kept away from any chance of damage so I'll take him to meet two angry men for probably the only time in his career. It'll stand him in good stead when he heads the force in a few years.'

There was no venom in his remarks – just the healthy disdain working detectives had for the men and women swaddled in cotton wool in case they were damaged or developed flaws on their way to the stars.

88

Toher briefed his DS on the way to O'Reilly's home. He could barely suppress a grin at the young officer's obvious distress but decided not to enjoy it too much.

'Listen, all you have to do is be there and let me do all the talking.' He knew that was quite obvious. 'They'll both give us dog's abuse, but let it slide off you. It's just gangster talk, and I've taken on those lads for a lot of years now so it's a bit of a game that we always play. Just noise. Good experience for you and a wee change from sitting behind your desk, no doubt.'

The young man had turned a shade paler since they'd left the office. 'Yes, sir, glad I can help.'

The flyer didn't really look like he meant it.

That was all he said, just grateful that Toher was fully equipped for this kind of thing. He'd decided a long time ago that, as far as possible, he'd stay away from this kind of nonsense, but it would be a story he could embellish and grow for his own legend, such as it was.

They parked up a short walk from Collins' flat, which was a stone's throw from St Stephen's Green, where buying property took serious money and meant that you'd absolutely arrived. The famous and popular green had been one of the focal points in the Easter Rising, where the rebels had made the tragic mistake of trying to occupy open ground. Now it was a favourite spot for tourists and Dubliners alike, close to the main shopping area in Grafton Street and replete with cafés, bars and restaurants. Today, the sun was shining and there was real warmth in the air.

'I remember when this fella didn't have trousers with an arse in them. He's done well the boy, and sometimes I have to admire these lads. Wonder what they would have done in another life with a bit if steering? No chance though – his father was an eejit who couldn't tie his laces.'

Toher was speaking to himself as much as the flyer walking nervously beside him; he couldn't find the words for a reply so he stayed quiet.

Toher had called Collins before he left the office. There was no point in wasting their time if he wasn't home, and they didn't need to keep this visit secret.

When the door opened, Toher recognised the minder who answered as an ex-boxer who'd done alright but never quite well enough. He was a short-arse but looked as broad as he was long, and his face bore the evidence of a few fights too many.

'Mr Collins is expecting you.'

'I'm right glad about that or I would have wasted an awful lot of time. We're busy men – criminals to put away, son.'

Toher couldn't resist the opportunity to wind up the opposition, although his companion thought it was unprofessional and planned to mention it to his backers in the executive.

The minder just looked confused for a moment as the damaged circuits in his brain tried to analyse the words. He couldn't quite work out how to respond, so he just opened the door wide enough for the Garda officers to squeeze past him and grinned at the young officer, sensing his nerves.

Collins was standing in front of the lounge window; his lawyer was sitting drinking what looked like whiskey by an ornate fireplace. The place reeked of money but had a strange blend of quality furniture and pieces mixed with overpriced tat that clashed against the senses like a nuclear hangover.

'Nice, Tony, very nice indeed,' Toher lied, and it worked – Collins looked really pleased.

'Shows you what hard work can do, Paddy. We're much of an age, you and I. You were a fuckin' smart-arse an' thought I was a spanner when we were kids. There's the truth. Now look at us. Where do you live? Oh hold on a minute, I know that – in fact, I'm sure I've got your address somewhere. Always meant to drop you a Christmas card.'

If Collins hoped to wind up Toher, he failed miserably – the detective just let him speak and waited for him to stop. His expression never changed – he just gave the gangster complete and unbroken eye contact.

'Is that you finished then, Tony? I'd like to get on with it, as I was just saying to your butler.' He turned and nodded to the little minder, who looked like he'd just been poked in the eye and was ready to trade blows.

The young flyer sensed the hostility in the room heat up like a sauna and impersonated a statue, hoping that everyone in the room would realise he had no aggression for anyone.

'As I was saying, I'm here to deliver a message – and of course offer you any assistance from the Garda Síochána if required. The thing is, we've received credible intelligence that there may be a threat to the life of someone in your organisation and our analysis is that there is a strong possibility that it's you. Now, I know we've been down this road before, and I guess I know the answer, but I'm duty-bound to tell you this.'

The lawyer put his drink on the table and decided to speak, given the fortune he was charging Collins for the privilege.

'Is my client in any sort of trouble, Superintendent?'

Toher knew the lawyer only too well and despised him – the man had made it his business to defend the worst of the Dublin gangsters and had come to enjoy their company too much. Toher wanted to press his face to the man's ear and whisper that he'd built up a dossier on him and was almost ready to put him on a long holiday beside his friends in Mountjoy.

'He's in no trouble from us.' Toher paused for effect before speaking again. 'Well, not at the moment. Never say never and all that shite.'

That pushed Collins' buttons too far – the gangster took two steps towards Toher, who never moved a muscle, as if he was watching the antics of a child.

'One of these fuckin' days I'll wipe that smile off yer gob, Toher. Maybe I should do it now. How would ye like that?'

The minder was almost bobbing on his feet beside Toher, as if he was getting ready to return to the ring. The problem was that as much as Collins wanted to tear the detective's eyes out, everyone in the room knew that Toher had been a boxer himself – a prize-winning middleweight.

The detective grinned at his little victory – the wind-up had worked perfectly, a masterclass in taking the piss. He deserved it given the problems the gangsters caused him every day.

'I think you should leave, Superintendent, and I shall be reporting your behaviour as a complaint,' the lawyer sneered.

'Right, well, I think we're done, gentlemen, so I'll wish you goodbye, and no doubt we'll meet again.'

He glanced towards the young officer, who looked like rigor mortis had set in. 'Let's go.'

They left the house, and when they stepped outside, Toher looked at the sky, breathed in deeply and smiled broadly.

'I love this job. You know that? There's just moments when it all makes sense.'

He strode off, and the young officer scrambled after him. He had no idea what Toher meant.

89

'O'Reilly never even let us over the threshold. We gave him the warning; he slammed the door in our faces after telling us to "fuck off and die!" So that was a result and we've carried out our duty of care. My God, what we have to do in this caring, sharing world!' Toher shook his head ruefully, but it was all water off a duck's back.

Garvey was in the office for the briefing but getting ready to go out to Castleknock for the next round of the operation. She was rigging up her covert radio and almost down to her bra, which seemed to alarm the analysts, but for Duncan, Macallan and Toher, dressing and undressing wherever they happened to be was just part of being a surveillance officer. The men and women in these teams spent endless days in cars, hides and observation posts together so modesty tended to be put away during the operations. What it did do was tie them together in a way that most people – apart from the armed services – found hard to understand.

'How was your partner for the day, boss?' Garvey asked, barely suppressing her look of amusement – she knew the young flyer well.

'I think we could say that he found it a moving experience; I noticed he disappeared right into the gents when we got back here. Let's leave it at that, but I'm sure it'll stand him in good stead when he gets his backside on the big chair.'

Toher looked invigorated; he was already feeling the buzz of leading the various teams into a potentially tricky and very hard few days.

'Are you happy with the plan out there, June? We got everything that we need?'

Garvey pulled on her jacket and picked up her holdall, which held all the other paraphernalia and food required for a long session out on the road.

'I'm good. We've gone for the accident idea after all because trying to rig it as roadworks would have meant involving the local authority, which might have caused a compromise. We've got three old bangers on the way so there'll be a controlled accident shortly. When that's done, we close off part of the road, traffic department boys and girls control the flow of cars passing through, and bomb disposal and firearms officers go in and check the hide. Dolan and Baker are still at home and in the hotel, so we have them under control. We'll be able to spot anyone approaching the site, and apparently O'Reilly is away from the house with his minder now anyway. We're on his tail so covered there.'

'Good work,' Toher replied. 'Get yourself out there and make sure you're all safe. We're going to do this, so any problems, let me take the strain. I'll be here and available.'

She nodded and headed for the door, knowing that he would be as good as his word – though it didn't change the fact that so many decisions had to be made in real time. If it became critical, and there was time, he would take the decisions that might need his authority, but if not, the pressure would fall on her.

Macallan felt a pang of envy, wishing she was going out

with the team, but she was in another country and it wasn't her role. She knew Toher and Duncan were probably thinking the same thing.

On top of that, she had the same feeling she'd had so many times before, as if all their roads were converging, carrying the main players towards a drama that would end up in terrible failure for some of them – though hopefully it wouldn't be Paddy Toher or his team. The gangsters, the police and the countless other characters involved would all be affected by what the next few days brought into play.

Then there was the almost opaque shape that seemed to lurk in the back of her imagination, as if he was inside her like a disease. Pete Handyside.

Where the hell is he? she wondered, but she was certain he would be watching and waiting somewhere in the margins.

Does he think about me? Macallan had asked herself that question so many times and knew that it made no sense. It bordered on a fatal attraction, this thing between them, and she needed to purge the dark shadow he cast in her mind. It was unfinished business but couldn't remain that way for either of them.

She had clearance from the Crown Office to go ahead and issue a press release that they were seeking Handyside, using the Garda pictures of him. They weren't top quality but enough to identify him and put pressure on him, wherever he was. As an added touch, they'd decided that Macallan would do her press release in Dublin and make it clear where she was. She calculated that it would heap further pressure on Handyside, given how much he loved his family and what it would mean to have his life disrupted again. He would have to go very dark to escape her this time.

90

At the same time Macallan was lost in her thoughts, Handyside's phone buzzed. It was Regan.

'I didn't expect to hear from you just yet.' Handyside kept his voice level and gave nothing away.

'It's just to make sure the money has been paid. I'm sorry about that – the idiot responsible has been sorted.' What Regan actually meant was that the guy who dealt with his finances was nursing a broken jaw and taking his food through a straw.

'Yes, it's done and met your lad this morning so we're good.' Handyside didn't want a long conversation but decided not to show it given the man on the other end had just paid him a small fortune. 'Everything okay your end? Anything from your sources inside the Guards?'

'I've told you I have people in place and in the top office but not inside the teams looking at us, so all I really get is who's who,' Regan replied. 'Apparently there's some Jock law over here visiting the main man in that team. They were logged at reception so I've got that info.'

Handyside stopped what he was doing and felt his throat tighten, because he already knew the answer to his next question. He tried not to give his feelings away to Regan, but he almost wished he could squeeze the man's throat to speed up that answer.

'What were their names? I have connections up there.'

'Hang on.' He heard Regan raking for something and muttering, 'Where the fuck did I put it?'

Handyside lit up a smoke.

'Here you are. There's a Sergeant M. Duncan – female; an F. Young – female; and a superintendent Grace Macallan. That's it. Can't imagine they're anything to do with us.'

Handyside's skin turned cold, and an image of his wife came into his mind. He struggled to control his voice, but he didn't want Regan to know about his past any more than anyone else, because he knew full well, he'd be worth betraying if it came to it.

She has to be here because of me, he thought. It would be too much of a coincidence for it to be anything else.

Why, Grace, why are you here?

Handyside felt as if the edges of his existence were closing in on him and the day he'd worried about so often was approaching. It was fate, just the randomness of life coming his way. He didn't fear for himself because he knew what his fate would be, but he worried for his wife and children. Jeannie loved him – he'd never doubted that – and she would survive. She was made of the same tough material as him, formed on the banks of the Tyne.

He looked out of the window, dreaming he was somewhere else, but he knew that was wishful thinking. He was where he was, and he would do everything in his power to stay safe and carry on.

He wondered if the gamble to come back into the business had always been doomed, but this was what he was, and Macallan was what she was. He wondered if in another life they might have actually had something in common – maybe even been friends. A life where he'd never had to kill, never had to make the decisions that only a few could stomach.

'I agree,' he told Regan. 'And we're on track.'

There was nothing else he could do – pulling out of the job would kill his team's reputation for getting things done.

'I'm coming to Dublin tomorrow so I'll not be far away when the job is done – but like I said, there's no need for a meet.'

On the other end of the phone, Regan bristled. There was an undercurrent of disdain in the other man's voice; just the faintest hint, but he could hear it. *I'm just shit on his fucking shoes* – the thought burned in his brain, and he squeezed the armrest in the back of the car.

'Sometimes you don't show a lot of respect, Joe.' He imagined his thumbs pushing into the bastard's eyes and feeling them pop like ripe fruit.

'Don't use names – you know the drill.'

It was another slap in the face and Regan decided to end the call. They were too close to the big day to ruin it now.

'Okay, let's leave it there and hope it all goes well.'

Regan hung up and cursed. 'Swear to God I'll rip the fucker's face off if this doesn't work out.' Regan was shaking with rage and needed a release.

'What was that, boss?' The UC asked, glancing in the rear-view mirror.

'What's up, son, is I'm going to kill some fucker shortly. Some people don't know how to show respect. That's what's up. You concentrate on the driving or you'll be next.'

The UC swallowed and did as he was told.

When the UC dropped Regan off later in the day, he called his handler and relayed what he'd picked up.

'He's raging at this guy Joe who he seems to be involved in some way. Thursday was mentioned again and I've got to stay with him all day. He wants to be seen out and about around the city. If it all goes down, what's the plan to get me out?'

'Don't worry about it. We'll be close to you, and as soon as it's happening, you'll get the signal to walk away into the sunset and we'll have that bastard. Make sure everything is clean in the flat.'

'There's almost nothing there, and it'll be sterile before I go – trust me.'

91

The accident had been set up perfectly and Garvey breathed a sigh of relief – it actually looked genuine. She watched it on the monitor in the command vehicle rigged up as the communication centre for the operation. There was no need for her to be nearby for the time being. Everyone who needed to be there was in place, and the bomb disposal and firearms technicians were already on the job. She'd received the first report that they were satisfied there was no trace of explosives, and a rifle had been extracted and was being worked on to disable the firing mechanism. She was in contact with Toher, who was in his office with Macallan and Duncan. Felicity Young was still working with her counterpart on their respective lines of intelligence and evidence where there might be crossovers.

Toher was happy with the way everything was going, but his gut still churned, because the risk of unforeseen consequences was always there and it was rare that nothing went wrong.

He turned to Macallan. 'So far so good, Grace. Anything from your end?'

She nodded. 'I've just talked it over at exec level back in Edinburgh and we've agreed – with Crown Office blessing

– that we'll put out a press release on Thursday morning. The line will be that we're anxious to trace Handyside, who we believe is involved in serious criminal activity in Scotland and elsewhere, and it will be released to all the major media outlets in the UK and over here. We'll say he may have operated in Ireland at some point and leave it as vague as that.

'We'll put out one of the images we have from the Glasnevin surveillance – it's been worked on so that the background won't be identifiable – alongside an older one, so a photo of him as he was and as he is now. We need this trigger to put pressure on him, and it will. He loves his family and he'll be settled somewhere no doubt. I've told you he's an incredibly complex man who'll kill without a moment's hesitation, yet the perfect family man in other ways. With a bit of luck, this will put him on the back foot. God knows what he'll do next, but we need to make a move.

'The next bit of good news is that Major Bowman provided more information... I think! We sent him the DNA profile from the murder at the caravan park and they're pretty sure it's down to Ronnie Baker, but the testing isn't finished. So we may have hard evidence that could convict him for the murder. The military have supplied more photos and background. We're sure anyway he's the man June's team have identified as working with Dolan on the Castleknock job. If you agree then we'll leave that be and hopefully you'll round him up at the end of all this.

'It's a lot to think about, but Maggie and Felicity are going back in the morning to support our teams in Edinburgh. We'll lift Sandy Tait and Benny Green then see what we can do with them. We'll coordinate that to take place on Thursday too, but the problem still is we don't know exactly when your job will take place.'

Macallan felt that Edinburgh was well organised and she could afford to stay in Dublin where the main action would take place.

Toher nodded – he seemed pleased with what the Scots had planned.

'Ciara believes our job should take place in the evening to give some cover of darkness. I agree. That would also tie in with when Collins usually visits the two sex workers, who work from a flat in a fairly quiet street just off Golden Lane. We reckon it would be a perfect spot for a hit. The contractors could do the job and be lost in the crowds two minutes from the scene.'

Macallan flicked through her notes. 'I should have mentioned that it looks like my team have turned up enough evidence to get Green for money laundering plus trafficking in Edinburgh so he's going nowhere, and we hope he might turn. Sandy Tait, on the other hand, will make a lot of noise, and we'll probably do no more than give him a fright, but at least it'll tell him we know the score, and then I guess he'll make a complaint. You know the rest.' She smiled grimly – it was a story they all knew so well. Tait would act out perfectly as the wronged victim of the overbearing plods who'd trampled all over his human rights.

'What about you, Grace?' Toher looked at the photos Duncan had put on the table – there was no doubt that the man in the photograph was Dolan's partner at Castleknock.

'I'm staying here if it's okay with you? At least one of the suspects for the Sam Taylor murder is here in Dublin, and I can't imagine Handyside is anywhere near Scotland so I'll stay to see if we can get a lead once you make the arrests.'

'I like the positivity in "once you make the arrests".' Toher grinned and tried to suppress the feeling that everything was moving the way they wanted. He knew that was dangerous and there had to be a problem eventually. *But where is it waiting for us*? he thought.

Macallan knew it as well but left the concern unsaid. There was no need.

'You'll get them,' she told Toher, 'and anyway, I want to be here for the piss-up when it happens. Long time since I had a hangover in Dublin.'

Toher turned to Duncan, who'd kept quiet – still getting used to the world of organised crime. 'What about you, Maggie? Any thoughts?'

'To be honest, I'm surprised the army have come across with support. I was convinced they'd try to bury this one, but I suppose it's gone too far, though if this was UK soil, I think they'd take a different approach. My only thought is that as an ex-soldier myself, I can't see Dolan going quietly. When your team make the arrests, Dolan particularly won't go without a fight. He's come a long way, and spending the rest of his life in prison is not an option for a man like that. Every job he does, he'll plan for that eventuality, so even if the rifle is disabled, he'll have a number of concealed weapons. I guess you know this already, but you did ask.' Duncan worried she had perhaps gone too far and stated the blindingly obvious.

'You know something, Maggie, you're absolutely right.' Toher leaned back in his chair and nodded. 'I've been thinking all day this is going too well and when's the cock-up going to appear? It doesn't do to forget and I needed reminding. We have hard men in this city, but these boys are hard *and* trained for all the tricks of the trade. Thank you.'

It was one of his great gifts – that he could make any rank feel like the most important person in the room, and Macallan admired it, suppressing a smile as she watched the touch of pink flush Duncan's neck. If Toher asked the sergeant to jump out of the third-floor window, she wouldn't even stop to ask why.

Toher's phone buzzed and he nodded, hardly saying a word, as he took the call – it was obvious it was Garvey giving him an update. When he put the phone back on the desk, he scribbled a brief note before looking up again.

‘That was June. The rifle has been disabled and replaced in the hide. The technicians have been withdrawn, the mock accident has been cleared and the road is open again. So, my friends, we’re good to go. One more day and we can see where all this leads. I’ll arrange for a car to take Maggie and Felicity to the airport in the morning, then let’s get something to eat before I die of starvation. We’ve done all we can so far and let’s hope the gods are with us. If this job fails, my head will be on a spike outside HQ, but never mind, eh?’

92

Toher took the Edinburgh team to a small Italian restaurant near his office, and although the food was excellent, they all resisted the wine, knowing that there was too much at stake in the following days to risk being at less than their best. There would be plenty time for celebrating if the dice fell their way.

When they were drinking their coffee, Toher received another call from Garvey – there was no sign of Dolan or Baker making a move that would suggest that they were heading back to Castleknock. Dolan was at home and Baker was necking beers in the hotel.

'Keep me posted, June, but let's not get stressed if there's no movement. Remember, they've obviously done their homework; everything is in place so maybe they don't need another night out there. I'll head back to the office, and if there's nothing by midnight, you get some rest and leave a small team in place to monitor in case there is sudden movement.'

Toher drank the last of his coffee and looked at Macallan. 'June's getting surveillance jitters because our boys aren't moving. Apparently, Dolan is tucked up at home and Baker is drinking beer and chatting up a young lady in the hotel bar.'

'Surveillance.' Macallan held up her coffee cup in a toast. 'It takes years off our lives trying to predict a target's next move. Mind you, I miss it – there's days when I'm in management meetings I'd give my right hand to be where it really matters.'

Toher raised his own glass. 'Amen to that.'

93

An hour later, Macallan was back in her hotel and on the phone to Jack.

'How's the bairns, big man? And by the way I miss you.'

'They're good. Excited about staying with Elaine soon. Speaking of, I've a friend who has a lovely place near St Andrews and it's ours if we want. Nice there, plus we can hop across to Anstruther and get fish and chips.'

'Fish and chips – my God you know how to treat a lady but sounds like a deal to me… This thing should be over one way or another in the next couple of days. We'll have the bad boys in the bag or it'll be a giant car crash and nothing in between.'

'Nothing new there then,' he said wryly. 'Anyway, get some rest and be careful. We need you here soon.'

Macallan put the phone down and pulled the bedcovers up, a smile on her face. It was like falling in love with Jack all over again. She was so glad she'd finally sought help so she could find her way back to him.

She was asleep in minutes.

As Macallan lay peacefully in her bed, Dolan kissed his wife then turned out the lights, knowing that, as always, she would be asleep almost as soon as her head hit the pillow – the result of an easy conscience.

Waiting till her breathing had slowed, he eased himself out of bed, padded through to the living area then stepped out onto the balcony and lit up a smoke, promising himself he'd stop as soon as they were on their way to Spain.

As he blew a line of smoke into the cool sea breeze, he lifted his left hand and frowned again as he stared at the slight tremor there. It scared him. Dolan had been through a thousand dramas in his time, but this job gnawed at his gut.

They had done too much work for the Dublin gangsters. Normally, it was a one-shot job and they were out, but for some reason they'd become part of the never-ending blood feud in the Republic's capital. He wondered what unknown force had drawn him to work for the brother of the man he'd killed in South Armagh.

Something's wrong with this fucking job, he thought. It felt as if the gods of war had brought him to his final battlefield.

He shivered and drew heavily on the cigarette. The tobacco was strong – just how he liked it. He knew the weed would catch up with him if he didn't stop, but it had been his only luxury through so many operations. Even thinking about stopping reminded him that time was passing. When he'd been in his prime, they would go to war and then, when it was over, they'd drink, smoke and fuck their heads up with whatever was available and it never made a difference. Now the hangovers lasted for days.

'The target is sitting on his balcony smoking. Doesn't look like he's going anywhere tonight.' The surveillance officer operating the long-range camera passed the information back to Garvey, who relayed it to Toher.

'Let me check with the team covering the hotel,' Toher replied, 'and if it's all quiet there, you get yourself off and home.'

Toher checked with the team covering Baker, but it appeared that he'd taken the woman he'd met back to his room. At the same time, he received a message that the comms team had established that the call Dolan had made to an unknown associate had been picked up in an area near Tony Collins' flat. The phone was clean, but it probably confirmed that Collins was the other target for Thursday's operation. They were discretely searching the area to see if they could spot whoever was on Collins. *No chance you'll sleep, Paddy boy,* he thought but there was plenty of time for a break when it was over.

He felt weary – the years of trying to control Dublin's gang warfare were taking their toll. He was seriously considering a move away and had already completed an application for a job in Interpol HQ in Lyon.

Toher was satisfied that putting a team on Collins had been the right move, although they'd have to be careful not to run across whoever intended killing him. It had happened before, and he felt his nerves stretch at the thought. He called Garvey back and stood her down for the night – he would stay in the office himself, just in case.

94

Across the city, Pete Handyside sat in his hotel room with the lights off and watched the bustling street below. It was full of mostly young people enjoying themselves as if there was no tomorrow. He'd ordered a drink from the bar, and he sipped the peppery malt. It mixed well with the tobacco smoke and felt soothing and indulgent. He needed it, and the pulse in his forehead that had thumped to the beat of a headache for hours started to ease off. He knew what would be would be, and whether Macallan was in Dublin by chance or something else, if she was on his tail again, he'd soon find out.

He wondered if she was in her hotel room. Regan's source in the Guards had told him what hotel she was staying in, and he'd been tempted to go there, but that was an unnecessary risk – although he'd imagined meeting her in the bar and talking like old friends… or lovers. But then maybe she was still in a Garda office planning his downfall.

He was the most practical of men, and although some would describe him as a cruel and violent person, he had never killed or hurt anyone for pleasure. To stay alive in his business meant acting first – and acting without mercy where it was required. He felt regret watching the youth of today laugh, unconcerned with the sins of the world. He'd never had that luxury, never had the space to operate as most people do.

Handyside despised most of the men and women who were in his business – so often they enforced conflict and violence when it wasn't necessary. He admired people like Macallan – they chose their corner then fought with everything they had. Was that really so different from him?

Handyside called his wife and told her that he loved her before returning to the window, struck with an odd, sudden fear that he might never see her again.

The day ahead should have been the calm before the storm, and it was to a certain extent, but there were other forces at play, making their own plans for what might take place in the heart of Dublin.

95

Macallan, Duncan and Young joined Toher in his office first thing. He was making a bad job of shaving with an electric razor and looked tired, but he deserved to be and still managed a grin as he pointed to the tray loaded with coffee and pastries.

'This is no time to worry about the waistlines so get stuck in while I go and try to shower some life back into myself. The car will arrive in an hour to take Felicity and Maggie back to the airport. Be back in ten.'

He headed for the door with a towel over his shoulder and was back by the time they'd poured the coffee and checked their emails, wearing a clean shirt and looking much more awake. The talk was light – he told them there was nothing to report on Dolan or Baker from the overnight watch and they hadn't identified anyone watching Collins' flat.

'It's just too busy for a hit there so I'm sure it'll be the sex workers' place.' He swallowed some coffee. 'Anyway, as it stands, we have everything covered as far as possible. Something will come out of the blue no doubt, but we'll handle it come the time. When are you making the press announcement, Grace?'

'Three o'clock tomorrow. It's going to be clear that I'm being filmed in Dublin but there'll be no explanation as to why I'm here. The press office is going to push it hard, so we just need a bit of luck, someone to recognise him maybe, and that will push him to make a move he hopefully hadn't bargained for.'

'Okay,' said Toher. 'Let's toast coffee to locking some people up tomorrow.'

96

As Young and Duncan were on their way to the airport, Macallan worked on her press briefing and Toher tried to take care of some paperwork but dozed off in his office chair. At the same time, a meeting was taking place in an office in the MOD in Whitehall. Major Bowman took a seat at the table with three other intelligence officers all senior to him in rank.

The man chairing the meeting was a colonel, a veteran of decades in the intelligence world, and what occupied him and the other officers in the room was the sins of the past rising out of some shithole in Northern Ireland – making them account for what had happened in the dirty wars fought against PIRA, Saddam, al-Qaeda and ISIS. He didn't need to look at his notes before he spoke. He was that kind of man – he knew exactly where they were heading with this problem, and he was fucked if anyone was going to disagree, as unlikely as that was.

'I've read your report, and it's comprehensive enough but doesn't tell us what the answer is. Let me summarise, because we need to move on this if your information is correct.'

He drew himself up, and such was the fear factor in the room that the other three men there barely moved in case he found fault with them. They all knew he was in a blazing mood because government ministers were pouring fire on his ulcer over historical abuse cases in several theatres of operation. He looked like he wanted to shout the words and barely contained himself with his summation.

'C Troop 5 carried out a number of unauthorised operations in Northern Ireland and Iraq, with allegations that extra-judicial killings took place. Is that part correct and were those killings unauthorised, Major Bowman?'

Bowman squirmed in his seat because he was aware the colonel already knew the answer to the question and Bowman had no choice but to tell the truth – even though the colonel would despise him for it.

'The thing is, sir… as you can see in the report, there are serious questions about the brief and rules of engagement that C Troop 5 had when they were deployed. I'm afraid they may have understood that they could terminate certain targets for the greater good that was the peace process in Northern Ireland.'

'So, they were operating beyond any law and those bastards that are making waves now are telling the truth? Is this what you're telling me? Thank God I was working in the States when all this happened.'

The other men in the room said nothing in reply, but they all knew that even in the States, he would have known exactly what was happening. He was making sure that he could put distance between himself and the crime if the shit hit the very large fan that was beginning to spin out of control.

'I think the problem is that we should have got rid of them then, but our solution was to take them out of Northern Ireland and deploy them in the Middle East, where basically the same thing happened again and there are secret intelligence reports of killings involving men, woman and children who were unarmed.'

'Who the fuck is responsible then? If – let's be blunt, gentlemen – there were ever arrests or trials, who is in the dock? That is not in your report, Major.'

Everyone in the room stared at Bowman as if he had some magic wand that would make it all disappear.

'My calculation is that dozens of our people were, or should I say could be viewed as, actually complicit – art and part as they say in Scotland – or at least guilty of failing to report serious crimes, including murder.'

The colonel stood up, walked to the window and stared outside with his hands clasped behind his back. It seemed like an age before he turned again, but he'd calmed down, ready to move forward. Being a ruthless bastard of the first order, when he needed to act, he would do so without hesitation.

'Right, so you believe these plods and particularly what's her name, Inspector Macallum, are about to rake up some of these long-dead corpses. Correct?'

'Correct, sir, and it's Superintendent Macallan. Very experienced and ex-RUC and PSNI SB. No fool, I can assure you – I was impressed with her.'

As soon as he said it, Bowman knew he'd made a mistake.

'Well, Major, why don't you go and marry the woman if she's so fucking impressive!'

He was a physically imposing man over a head taller than the others in the room and his stare could melt tungsten. He gave Bowman full eye contact as the other two officers in the room thanked their gods that they were only there for show and weren't Major Bowman.

After time seemed to have stood still for an age, the colonel sat down and leaned back in his chair.

'Right, listen to me, and this does not go beyond this room or in any notes. This meeting did not take place and neither did the decisions we, and I repeat we, *are* going to make. The rest of the original C Troop 5 are dead or gaga apart from this ex-para Billy Dolan. It's ironic, a monumental coincidence and to our advantage that he allegedly killed this gangster Regan's brother. You're sure Regan doesn't know this, Major?'

'I can't see how he would. He wasn't in PIRA himself but supported the cause and believes that a British UC team were responsible, but of course there's never been any proof.'

The colonel grinned for the first time, but there was no warmth in the expression – just a predator seeing its prey from a distance.

'We don't want to be anywhere near what needs to happen so let's get Mike Regan to clean up for us. You're sure about your sources in all this?'

'Yes, sir, I've been liaising closely with Police Scotland so we know exactly what's going on with Macallan's operation both in Dublin and Edinburgh, and we know from our own intel where Dolan is.'

'Good work there, Major, so here's the plan. I believe your family are from Northern Ireland and you spent your early years there. Correct?'

'That's right, sir, from the border area near Newcastle.'

'I believe you worked there for a while. Correct?'

'I did, sir.'

Bowman felt the spotlight had raked back onto him, but all he could do was play the game.

Half an hour later, Bowman left the room, feeling like he'd just survived a near-death experience and hoping he could someday fuck up the Colonel's life – perhaps when he was retired and drinking himself to death in his club. The man was an arrogant bastard, and Bowman made sure he had copious evidence of what had taken place so that if the shit ever came his way, he was well armed.

He headed for a washroom well away from the meeting place and undid the recording device he'd been wearing. It would be put away safely, just in case. In the age of never-ending disclosure, the past was always far too close to the present and could easily come back and bite you on the arse.

He splashed his face with cold water and decided to have some coffee before he made the call to Mike Regan.

97

Mike Regan was bench-pressing 120 kilos on a barbell when his phone rang. It was the UC telling him he was waiting outside. He heaved the weights back onto the stand and sat up slowly, enjoying the burn in his arms. He'd always been proud of his sheer physical strength. Men in his line of work had to be ready for threats that could appear in a breath and take your life in that same moment. He'd boxed as a younger man, and part of the Regans' DNA came from the Irish travelling community so fighting with his fists came with the territory. He was hard but knew that there was always someone just that bit harder, so he never underestimated his opponents – even where he seemed to have an advantage.

He'd meant to switch the phone off before his session as it was one of the few chances he could be on his own with nothing in his head but the physical exertion – usually he would train till his legs and arms shook.

'No fuckin' pain, no fuckin' point' was his guiding principle, and he enjoyed throwing the motto at the slackers in the gym who all knew him and didn't tend to argue.

He showered quickly and put on fresh clothes, greeting the UC warmly as he got in the car.

'Good day to be alive, son. We have a few calls to make then maybe we'll go and see those wee girls again, eh? You fancy that as a bit of a bonus?'

He was interrupted by his phone going off in his pocket.

The number didn't identify the caller, but he took it anyway. His world was full of people who didn't like disclosing their numbers.

'Mike Regan?'

He frowned; he didn't recognise the voice, which was from the north, maybe around the border. This phone was mainly for family and non-criminal activities, so it was odd to hear from someone he didn't know. He presumed, quite rightly, that the Guards would be monitoring it like his house phone, so he answered cautiously. 'Who wants to know?'

'I want you to get a clean phone and call the number I'm about to give you in fifteen minutes. That's it.' The caller reeled off a number, which Regan entered into one of the clean phones in the car, then hung up without another word.

Regan stared down at the silent phone, enraged. He wanted to smash it, to ignore the call, but how could he? The bastard had asked for a clean phone so he clearly had something important to say.

Agitated as he was, he managed to wait the full fifteen minutes before calling the number he'd been given.

'Talk.' He would restrict his words till he could work out what this was about.

'I'm the person who knows the truth about your brother Conlan. Never mind how I know what I'm about to tell you, but we still fight for the cause and we've found out something from a bent Branch man.'

'I'm still listening.' Regan hated not being in control – even for a phone call – but he listened.

'You use a team of Brit contractors, am I right?'

'You think I'm fuckin' stupid or something. Don't know what the fuck you're talking about, boy, but I'm listening.'

Regan wanted to reach out and kill whoever was on the other end of the phone.

'One of the team you're using is called Billy Dolan, ex-para who did a lot of our boys during the fight. I'm calling to tell you he's the murdering bastard who killed your Conlan and got rid of the body. Now he's working for you. It's a fucking disgrace and on your head, boy.'

'Billy Dolan – never heard of the man. Tell me what the fuck you're about or I'll put the phone down. If you've called just to wind me up, you've done it, you bastard. What do you mean he's working for me?'

'I want to share something with you, Michael, then you can do what you will. See, we know you use these Brit contractors. Correct?'

'I don't know what you're talking about, but I'm still listening. If this is some kind of set-up, I'll fuckin' find you and cut your eyes out.'

'That's all fine, but clean your house, Michael. The Branch man has it all, and you can please yourself, but we're telling you because Conlan was a good man, a hero for the Irish cause. As far as we're concerned, you're just a common criminal, but you helped us with money and arms, and we don't forget these things, so we're returning the favour. Dolan stabbed your brother to death like a pig. Do what you will, but this is a stain on you if you let this go.'

Regan ground his teeth as the caller told him exactly where Dolan lived and who his wife was. Then the call ended without a further word.

Regan stared at the phone in his hand as if it was contaminated, but he wasn't quite sure what to do with it. The words collided in his head, and he couldn't find a way to put his thoughts in order. He growled like a dog and punched the back of the front passenger seat till it gave way.

*

The UC pulled into the side of the road, alarmed, and considered bolting. His flight instincts were telling him to run. He barely managed to control himself and gripped the wheel as if his life depended on it.

'You okay there, Mr Regan?' he asked, swearing to himself that he was out of this tomorrow no matter what happened. He couldn't take another day driving Regan about, never knowing if the next minute might be the one he was discovered, the man in the back of the car primed to put a bullet in his head.

Regan took a few deep breaths, as if he'd run a hundred-metre sprint. 'Am I alright, son? Now there's a question.' His voice had calmed as quickly as he'd erupted. 'The world is full of snakes. Can't trust a fuckin' soul, can I?'

The UC gripped the wheel even tighter, knowing if he let it go, he would shake as if he had the DTs. Was this about him?

'I want you to drive me to Portmarnock Beach. You stay in the car – I need to take a walk and make a few calls.'

The UC calmed – whatever was up was someone else's problem.

They were only a fifteen-minute drive away and Regan never said another word.

When he pulled up in the car park and Regan had disappeared towards the sands on the northside of Dublin, the UC fumbled for a smoke, but before he could light it up, he had to push the driver's door open and throw up at the side of the car. He wiped his mouth, then took a few deep breaths to try and steady himself – his heart felt like it was trying to escape his ribcage.

He managed to light a smoke and took a few heavy drags before getting back in the car and calling his handler to pass on what he'd heard.

'The other thing is I'm out of it tomorrow. I can't do another day.'

The handler assured him that was agreed – no matter what happened with the operation, he would be withdrawn.

Within a few minutes, the handler was passing the information on to Paddy Toher, who was with Macallan at the time. Toher paled as he listened to what was being said – he looked like he'd been struck in the gut. He thanked the handler and shook his head, trying to make sense of it.

Macallan remained expressionless as he relayed what he'd been told, but her mind was racing. Of all the things they'd thought might come up, this scenario wasn't one of them.

Just then, the monitoring unit contacted Toher and told him about the initial call to Regan, asking him to switch to a clean phone. That was all they had apart from the fact the voice on the other end had a border accent – maybe Armagh or South Down.

'I don't get it, Grace. Why does someone discuss Dolan with Regan right now, the day before the job? He's gone off his head so whatever he's been told must be big.'

'It has to be about Regan's brother – someone must have told him it was Dolan's unit that killed Conlan.' She paused and pulled at her chin. 'I think the question is: who would do this and why? Let's pass it to the analysts then we can set up a video conference and see what their thoughts are.'

Macallan always expected the unexpected, and although she hadn't bargained for this development, there was something chewing away in her subconscious. It was her own question to Toher. *Who and why*? Billy Dolan was a hardened soldier who would be difficult to break, but he was a walking time bomb for a lot of people, given his past.

She took a deep breath and put it aside for now – she still had a press conference to plan.

98

As Regan walked along the beach he'd enjoyed since he was a child, he tried to make sense of the call he'd received. If it was a set-up of some kind, it made no sense, because he couldn't see how he could lose from it. If it was the Guards at some game then it meant they knew about his use of the contractors, but then was that such a surprise? The police always knew a lot – the trick was making sure they never knew enough. It could even be genuine dissidents in the North – Conlan Regan had been a bit of a legend with the boys in his day, and the New IRA were certainly still giving the PSNI problems, so the fight was still on.

He muttered as he walked, the rage rising and falling in his soul as the loss of his brother came back to mind. The truth was he'd always felt he lived in the shadow of his only sibling, who'd been dedicated to a united Ireland and had fought for what he believed in. Mike Regan had chosen crime as his future, though he'd often wished he could have had the martyr's death and the glory that went with it. He knew few people would mourn his own passing and that squeezed his heart almost every day of his life. Whatever was going on, Regan had loved his only brother, who'd looked after him when his mother had been widowed at an early age and all they'd had was each other.

He called Joe Stafford. 'We need to talk. Where are you? This can't be done on the phone.'

Handyside knew from the tone of Regan's voice that something was seriously wrong – at least in the mind of the Dublin man. Normally there was a kind of deference when they talked, but this time he sensed anger, although he couldn't be sure why. It was dangerous, but he thought not discovering what this was about posed more risk, so Handyside suggested they meet at his hotel, and Regan agreed without argument.

He guessed that if this anger was somehow about him, Regan was unlikely to try and kill him in a hotel bar with CCTV all over the place. He wouldn't discount it though – some of the tit-for-tat killings in the gang wars had been brazen beyond belief.

As Handyside waited, he sipped a soda water and flicked through the pages of the daily paper but took in nothing from the stories as he tried to predict what Regan's problem was. The bar was quiet and he'd taken a corner seat almost out of sight of anyone else in the place so they could talk without being overheard, but he decided he might need some extra form of security with so many forces in play at the same time and called Dolan.

'You okay?' Handyside said softly, trying to comfort the soldier he placed so much faith in. He paused before continuing. 'Always the same before one of these things.'

'I'm fine, just watching the world go by on my balcony. Taking it easy and everything is in place. All good for tomorrow.' Dolan sounded glad the man had called.

'I need something from you. Can you set it up for me as soon as? I'll send you a safe email rather than this. Are you ready?'

'I'll be online in one minute.'

Dolan grabbed his laptop and fired it up, fully alert. They had a secure system for comms that was as safe from the law as it could be.

He sat back on the balcony and drummed his fingers on the edge of the laptop as he waited for the email to arrive. When he read it, he felt the tremor in his hand again and stared at the words, trying to make sense of what could have changed.

> Don't read too much into this but I need a piece with a suppressor and full ammo. It's just for security as I don't trust these local boys. Told them we're withdrawing after the job and don't want them to pull any surprises. It doesn't affect you. Can you do it?

Dolan tried to imagine what could be behind it, but he stopped himself because it could be a thousand variations or even the truth. But whatever it was added to his feeling that there was just something out of sync with the job. He almost thought about throwing his hand in and heading straight to Spain and the rest of his life, but that wasn't really an option. He could be found, and, in any case, last-minute worries were just part of the job. He'd never doubted that his boss could use a firearm if required, and he had every right to be careful – Dolan wouldn't have liked to deal with the Dublin men without a bit of protection either.

He tapped out a message and pressed send. Dolan had backup firearms stored in a number of places and sent details of an address in Ballymun. All his boss needed to do was go to what was the front counter of a shop and the kit would be waiting for him.

Dolan then called the contact in Ballymun, told him what he needed and the keywords the man who'd pick it up would use.

Handyside replied with a brief message saying he'd see Dolan after the job.

The contents of the phone call were passed to Toher immediately, and he turned to Macallan as soon as he put the phone down.

'There were traces of a Geordie accent. That's all we know. They must have some encrypted email system, but we have no idea what that is. So, if it is your man, we don't know what it is he wants.'

Macallan knew the call could mean everything and nothing, though going over to the encrypted system meant it had to be important. But she knew there was no point in dwelling on it without more information – it was logged if anything else came up.

99

Handyside thought again about Macallan as he waited and wondered how close she might be now to finding him – if part of him might even want her to. He loved his wife and had never betrayed her with another woman, but the detective stirred something in him that he thought it best not to examine too closely.

When Regan arrived in the bar, his face was dark with suppressed anger, and Handyside could see he would have to be careful handling the man. He wished he had Dolan's firearm already, but it was what it was and he would let it all play out. But he stayed on his feet and kept enough distance between them so he could act if something went wrong.

'Rest yourself, Mike, and let me order you a drink.'

He was surprised and relieved when Regan slumped in a seat looking exhausted, but the anger was still simmering not far below the surface. Handyside thought quite rightly that whatever the problem was, Regan couldn't work it out, and that gave him an advantage.

He carried the Irish whiskeys from the bar to the quiet corner and checked again that nobody was looking or listening in. He handed the double to Regan, who swallowed half of it without waiting for a toast. Handyside had a smaller measure but avoided drinking it.

'Right, Mike, tell me what's got you so upset.'

Regan looked across the table, his eyes burning. It was hard to tell what he was thinking.

'Who the fuck is Billy Dolan?'

Handyside tried not to show too much of a reaction, but it was impossible to hide the tiny non-verbals that Regan would pick up. He knew there was no point in lying because the man opposite knew or had been told something, and he needed to know what that was.

'First of all, I need to know why you're asking? My business runs on confidentiality.'

'Because I've been told that he works for you.' Regan sat forward and the colour in his face deepened. 'And furthermore, I've been paying the fucker's wages through you.'

'He works for me, so why does it matter? He's good at what he does – killing people.' Handyside decided to sip the whisky after all because the conversation was knife-edge tense and every word could mean someone was going to die. He just knew it.

'Billy Dolan was a para and Billy fuckin' Dolan killed my brother Conlan. The bastards didn't even leave his body for us to bury – he's still lying in a bog somewhere on the border. That's who Billy Dolan is.' He paused and swallowed the rest of the drink. 'Did you know about this, Joe? I really hope not.'

The question threw Handyside for a moment, but he realised that however this information had come to Regan, it had to be possible, although it had never crossed his mind. Dolan should have disclosed the connection though, because in the vermin-infested world they lived in, what kept Handyside alive was knowing more than everyone else. Dolan had let him down, and although he could understand why, it had given rise to a situation that might run out of control very quickly.

'Listen, Mike, the one thing you must understand about me is that I'm a good businessman and I deliver to my clients. They can trust me to get the job done… correct?'

The delivery of the statement pushed Regan back enough for Handyside to take control again.

'Yes, of course, you've never let us down so far, but this is something else. You have to understand this, Joe. This is about honour.'

It would have been easy to sneer at a man like Regan using the word honour to describe his own actions, but the situation was too serious to raise the temperature.

'Where did you get this info from and why at this time? Doesn't the timing strike you as odd?'

Handyside watched Regan ease back and hold out his glass for another drink. Handyside stood up and waved at the barman for a refill.

'I got a call from some boy in the north. No name but fights for the cause. He says they've turned an ex-Branch man and they got it from him. No mention of your name – just that they know this boy Dolan has done work here for me.'

Handyside thought about it for a minute but knew it really needed more time to absorb than he had to pacify the man opposite. There were endless possibilities on what was at play, but he needed to be positive – the last thing he needed was Regan thinking he knew because that would be taken as an insult requiring retribution.

'Listen, Mike, this needs to be thought through. It could be genuine or it could be someone playing a game. Either way, don't react till we know… right?' He tried to convey that he meant business. 'Let me look into this, and if it's true then we can come an agreement on what happens next. Thing is, he's central to taking out O'Reilly, and if he's out, the whole job is off. Do *you* understand?'

Regan's face had set – he understood enough to know it made sense, but that couldn't be the end of it.

'Okay, my friend, but you better be straight up with me, and if that bastard did do my brother in then I want him. That's non-negotiable. Do you understand? Because no matter what, I have his name and where he lives. I will find him, and if not, I'll take one of his family.' He held out his hand.

Handyside's great strength was that when an action had to be taken, he never hesitated, and apart from his family, everyone was dispensable. Yet, for the first time since his teenage years, he felt a gnawing doubt, because in so many ways Dolan reminded him of himself. They'd both been born with no advantages, yet had something inside them that meant anonymity and the quiet life were never going to be their lot. They'd chosen hard roads that very few men could have taken, and in their own way they'd succeeded. He knew he had to speak to Dolan before he made a decision, but first, he needed to calm the situation with Regan. He reached across the table and took the other man's hand.

'Leave it with me, Mike, and we'll sort this. First, let's drink to a good job tomorrow.' They clinked glasses, each aware that the game had started and they were playing for the highest stakes possible.

What neither of them knew was that the game was being acted out on a far broader canvas with more players than either of them knew. All their moves were converging into what would be the chaos of the next twenty-four hours.

100

When Regan left, Handyside called Dolan before they moved to the secure email system, where Handyside advised the ex-soldier he needed to see him right away. Dolan agreed and suggested the other man come to his flat. His wife had gone out with friends for a farewell dinner and wasn't expected back till late.

'This is a very nice place, Billy. You'll miss it.'

Handyside pulled off his jacket and took a seat as Dolan offered a drink. 'Not for me thanks. Had a couple already tonight and tomorrow's a big day.'

Dolan was concerned but not alarmed by the visit – he presumed it was some last-minute glitch as there was always something to straighten out.

Handyside got straight to the point. 'Don't ask me where I got this information, but I wanted to check with you that it's correct. It doesn't affect the job, but I need to understand. I know you worked in Northern Ireland during the Troubles and they were tough times.' He paused and looked directly at Dolan before carrying on. 'I've never asked you about it and didn't expect you to tell me too much anyway, but did you kill Conlan Regan?'

Dolan could lie and cheat with the best of them, but the question caught him off guard – his reaction told Handyside everything he needed to know, so there was no point denying it. 'How the fuck did you find that one out? The only people that knew were military intelligence, and even then, it was only need-to-know. You could count them on one hand.'

'It doesn't matter. There are always people trading information – you know that as well as I do – and that includes military intelligence. Apart from that, some of your old mates turned to the bottle or their brains just scrambled, so I guess like all of these things, there are actually a lot of people who knew about it. It really doesn't matter, and what it means is we – or should I say *I* – can't risk doing business with these Dublin cowboys again. I'd more or less made up my mind to let them get on with it anyway – the bastards will probably just keep killing each other till there's no one left to murder – but I need to know these things, Billy.'

'You sure there isn't a problem here?' Dolan asked. 'We've planned this Spain thing for years and I don't want it to go to rat shit. It's a big payday, but I can live without it.' He paused, then said, 'Has this got anything to do with you needing a weapon?'

'No, that's just for insurance. You haven't met Mike Regan – the man's a nutjob, and I'm going to make sure he understands we do no more business with him. Look, just leave it at that, and this thing remains between us.'

When Dolan locked the door behind Handyside, he felt a ripple of nerves run along his back and pondered again who this man he worked for actually was. Not for the first time, he wondered if he was connected to the intelligence services because they'd carried out jobs that seemed to him to be in the UK's interest rather than straightforward contract killings. Whatever it was, he'd always hoped that the truth about Conlan Regan's killing would stay buried in the bog with him, but Northern Ireland's Troubles kept rising from the dead.

101

Handyside left the block of flats but the OP covering Dolan's place only saw a man wearing glasses and a newsboy hat entering then leaving the main door. There were other visitors at the same time, and it wasn't possible to say what flats they were visiting or leaving, so Handyside was logged as an unidentified male alongside a description of his build and clothing.

When Handyside was in his taxi on the way back to Dublin, he thought through what he'd been told, but he kept coming back to Dolan's view that only military intelligence should have known who'd killed Conlan. There were other possibilities – he knew that a lot of ex-soldiers could run off at the mouth when they'd had a few, and there was every chance one of Dolan's unit had leaked it somewhere, but he wondered how that linked to the call Regan said he'd received. If it was MI5, why would they want to pass a death sentence on Dolan? He was struggling to keep up with all the possibilities. And this was on top of Macallan being in the city – he still had to work that one out. She was in charge of the Edinburgh murders so what did Dublin have to do with anything?

Dolan had assured him they'd left a clean job, but it was always possible the police had found evidence. Committing serious crime now came with endless risks, and he had to factor in that Dolan and Baker may have been identified, so that was another decision he'd have to face. First and foremost, he had to consider his own life and those of his wife and children. If Dolan was the common factor – first by not disclosing what had happened in South Armagh then by leaving evidence for Macallan – then he knew the only way to clean the trail to himself was to kill Dolan or let Regan do it for him. He shook his head and cleared it for the time being. He needed more time to see what the runes told him.

102

The following morning, Handyside rose from his bed as most of the country was still asleep. He hadn't slept and hadn't expected to. There was too much to think about, but he didn't lie worrying and spinning the same ideas round his head as most do under stress. He simply used the quiet of the night to run and rerun different scenarios through his head to prepare for what lay ahead. He was fortunate that losing a night's sleep meant nothing to him. There was a paradox there, because when he wasn't involved in the culmination of a job, he slept like a baby, as if there was nothing on his conscious, and truthfully there wasn't. He believed that he was guilty of nothing other than being himself. He knew that it had confused people who'd known him – or thought they did.

He worked out with press-ups and stretches as far as he could in the hotel room before showering and taking an early breakfast. Then he travelled by taxi to Ballymun and picked up the weapon without a hitch.

The man who handed it over stared at him for a few seconds as if he was cross-checking whatever he'd been told, then nodded and handed it over. Handyside stuffed it into a rucksack and made his way back to the hotel.

He called Regan on a clean phone, told him he had answers and asked if he wanted to meet.

'Of course I want to meet. I was beginning to think you were going to let me down.'

Regan had become more aggressive in his speech since the revelation about Dolan, and Handyside knew that showing the Dublin man his jugular would be like an invitation to dinner. He had to remind him he was a force to be respected and, more importantly, feared.

'Mike, you need to listen to yourself. I'm not one of your Dublin cowboys. I treat you with respect, and I expect the same back. You want to end this job today, I can pull the plug now and you can all go on with your little gang war – and I tell you this: you'll never find Billy Dolan if I decide to cover him. Remember I work with the Russians, and if you want them stepping in and taking over your business then it can be arranged. Are we clear?' Handyside had never raised his voice and didn't need to.

'I hear you, Joe. I just want justice. Where do you want to meet?' Handyside's words had held Regan off for the time being.

'Our usual place – twenty minutes.'

The UC was waiting for Regan, who told him to head to Glasnevin. He knew anything that happened that day would be important, but there was no way to get in touch with his handler before they got there. Ideally, he would have planted an audio device in the car, but Regan was so surveillance conscious that he swapped cars constantly for that very reason. However, he was wearing a device that would give the surveillance team their position so they could stay well back and not risk discovery – he'd decided it was a necessary risk given how important today was.

Regan was unusually quiet and hardly spoke a word during the journey. The UC saw enough in the rear-view mirror to know the man was troubled, but it was the big day so it could be no more than the pressure of waiting on a result.

When they arrived, Regan said no more than, 'Wait,' and left the car. The UC called his handler and informed her he had no idea who Regan was meeting.

'It's okay. We have your position. We don't have the CCTV there anymore, but we'll cover all the exits. We shouldn't lose him, so we'll let this one run. It could be something quite routine, like visiting his old mother again. Wee bit of a chat before the big event.'

The UC had one concern above all else. 'Everything set for me getting out tonight or today or whenever this thing happens?'

'When you see the agreed signal, just walk away and don't look back, okay?'

The UC agreed and felt a great wave of exhaustion run through his body. He'd been brought up a long way from Dublin on the west coast and wanted to be there so much it hurt. He hadn't spoken to his family for months, and he ached for them.

103

Regan picked at the faded flowers he'd placed on his mother's grave the last time he'd visited and cursed at the state of them. The shadow that grew on the headstone made him turn.

'Never heard a sound there, Joe. You wearing brothel creepers?'

Handyside smiled and offered his hand. Regan took it, and the other man pulled him up in the friendliest of gestures.

'You must have been fond of that lady, Mike. I'm the same, although my father was a bastard of a man and God knows what she did to deserve him.' His tone was easy, intimate, and Regan couldn't help but reciprocate.

'Same here. What would we do without our poor old mothers?'

They walked side by side. An early mist was clearing, and they felt the heat of the sun warm them as they remained quiet for a few moments, almost like family there to honour their ancestors' ghosts.

It was Handyside who finally broke the silence.

'Billy Dolan killed your brother. I didn't know this till he told me. That was a mistake on his part, and it's put us all at risk because now you know and there has to be a resolution. The question is: what do we do?'

They stopped and faced each other before Regan spoke. 'I appreciate this, Joe. The question for me is where do you stand?'

'To tell the truth, I'm still not sure if the timing of this is coincidental or something else, and chances are we'll never find out. The other thing is this Grace Macallan, who's here as we speak, was Special Branch, so I wonder if there's a connection somewhere?'

'She was Branch was she? Fuckin' bitch!' He spat on the ground beside them. 'Maybe I should pay her a visit as well. Must be a connection.'

Handyside had decided that he needed to do a lot of cleaning, and he couldn't risk doing it himself. He preferred others to shoulder the risk. He knew full well that whatever Macallan was up to, others in her team could act on the same information, but it didn't matter – it had always been personal with her.

'Listen, I'm going to give you the details I have for Dolan, but it's in your own interests to let him do the job. After that, you can do as you like.'

'You're a good man,' Regan told him. 'I should never have doubted you.'

He held out his hand again, and Handyside pulled him a little closer as they gripped each other once more.

'You might not see me again after this, Mike. I have other business apart from here and, as I said, I think we've been involved enough in your affairs.'

He told Regan what the plan was and where Dolan and Baker would make the kill, and that they were all his after that.

Then they parted. Handyside pulled on the newsboy hat and glasses then made his way through Griffith Park, heading for the ever-chaotic Drumcondra Road, where he spent the next hour making sure he had no tail.

When he was sure he was clean, he headed back to the hotel where he would rest up for a few hours after calling home. He felt uneasy – there was so much at play and he could only see a small part of it. That meant miscalculations were possible, and he had to factor that in.

He couldn't know just how right he was – in the end, almost everyone had miscalculated, and only one of the players involved had a clear plan and exit strategy.

104

Across the city, Macallan called Oliver, who was running the coordinated operations in Edinburgh.

'I'm just going in to make the press announcement shortly. How's it going there?'

Oliver was glad to hear Macallan and was buoyed up by the action on the ground in Edinburgh.

'All good, boss, and we got a great start last night. We hit a couple of saunas – turns out three of the women there were trafficked and they're all talking. Looks like we can tie them nicely to Benny Green, and the financial investigation team have hard evidence of him money laundering, plus a string of financial crimes. He can sit and say nothing with his lawyer when we lift him, but he's toast already. We're kicking off the main operations at two so we should have some news for you before things start happening in Dublin.'

'Don't suppose we'll get anywhere with Sandy Tait, but make sure the whole city knows he's been lifted. Jacquie Bell is going to lay that one on thick.' Macallan detested bent lawyers more than the men and women they defended.

'Been saving the good news till last, boss. The financial team have also identified Sandy Tait as part and parcel of

Green's money laundering schemes, so he can sit and say nothing as well if he likes, but it won't do him a bit of good. Maggie is going to bring him in. I think she's just the person to spoil his day – she's doing a great job here and in her element.'

Macallan punched the air and mouthed *yes* so that Oliver wouldn't see she was human.

'Just get someone for our murderers over there, boss, and I'd say we're on for a giant piss-up.'

Macallan felt like someone had just shot happy juice straight into her veins. She was in the perfect mood for the news conference but took a minute to get the smile off her face and focus back on the main business. There was a hard day ahead, and it could still all go terribly wrong. In investigations like this, the evidence trails were like gossamer billowing in the wind – the connecting threads were so delicate they could be easily broken, leaving behind only spectators to what might have been.

She took a deep breath, straightened the sleeves of her blouse and walked into the press briefing room to pull the trigger on Handyside.

105

Safely back in his room, Handyside breathed a sigh of relief as he checked the weapon over; it was in excellent condition and had been cleaned, though that didn't surprise him – Dolan would only accept the best. He stashed it in the room safe for the time being, then decided to take it easy, watch the news and relax.

He dozed for an hour, but even that short snatch of sleep refreshed him. He splashed his face with cold water then made a coffee before lying back on the bed and reaching for the TV remote control, the steaming cup beside him on the bedside table.

There was nothing that interested him too much, though he shook his head at a clip that showed the President of the United States lying through his teeth again. *Nothing new there,* he thought and persevered with the news.

The main story was the spread of Covid. It had now hit Europe hard and was being classed as a pandemic. Was it only a matter of time until this new invisible enemy washed over the UK and his family? He shuddered and started to flick through the free newspaper he'd picked up in the foyer instead.

The TV was still on, but the newscast was a blur of words he'd stopped interpreting until the name *Handyside* crashed into his mind – as if he'd been struck by a clenched fist. He snapped his head back and saw Macallan delivering a news conference. Handyside swung his legs off the bed and stood up, his eyes fixed on the detective as he started to process what was being said.

She spoke very deliberately, without any unnecessary detail, the strapline across the bottom of the screen telling the viewing public she was in Dublin. She told the audience they were looking for a dangerous criminal – Peter Handyside – who was believed to be operating somewhere in the British Isles and Ireland and was actively organising and committing serious crimes, including murder. There were warrants in place for his arrest, and the public should be vigilant but not approach him.

A photograph of Handyside as he had looked previously and a blurred version of how he looked now were released and it was left at that. No questions were allowed, but Handyside knew the media outlets would have substantial information on him from his days in Tyneside.

It had been brief, to the point and Handyside felt his gut squeeze with the tension of the moment.

He sat back on the bed, stunned, rerunning her words through his mind. At least he knew for sure now that Macallan was after him, and regardless of what exactly had put her on to him, she was close now. It was hard to be positive, but at least the photograph from Glasnevin was grainy – he doubted someone would pick him out easily. Whatever was going on, there was no turning back.

One problem was what would happen if Dolan or Regan saw the news and how would they interpret it. They were the only people in Dublin apart from Macallan who could definitely identify him. He guessed the fact Joe Stafford was a fictional character wouldn't be that surprising to them, but it left him horribly exposed, because if either of them were arrested, the knowledge they possessed gave them a powerful bargaining tool – they knew so much of what he'd been up to since those original arrest warrants had been issued.

Handyside took the gun out of the safe and checked it twice to make absolutely sure it was ready for action. When he was done, he called his wife. He talked as if nothing had happened, but it was remarkable what so many years together could do – Jeannie Handyside knew instantly that something was wrong.

'It's nothing, pet, just sometimes I think we should retire somewhere warm by the sea. I'm getting old – have you seen the grey hair on me now?'

His attempt to reassure her didn't work; she knew him well enough to be sure it wasn't the colour of his hair that troubled him. 'Take care and hurry home,' she told him.

When he pushed the end button, something happened that took him by complete surprise. He squeezed his eyes closed to cling on to the tears, took a deep breath, then released the emotion that had come from a place locked away since childhood.

Leaning over the sink, he stared into the mirror at the evidence that he was human zig-zagging down his cheeks then splashed more cold water on his face to hide it.

'What have I done?' he asked his reflection, then held a towel against his face until the raw emotion had passed.

Lying back down on the bed, he wondered what a court and jury would make of him and was sure the tabloids would paint him as a monster. A man who'd ordered young, trafficked women to be thrown overboard into the sea rather than risk discovery by the police.

What if there is a God? he thought, and for a moment he was afraid. He wasn't used to dealing with such inflamed emotion.

He stared at the ceiling and calmed himself. *What's new*? he asked himself and the answer was nothing. His game meant ever-present danger and threats that appeared out of the shadows like predatory animals intent on ending his brief life. But he would survive – he always did.

106

When he was in his car, Regan called two of his best and toughest men for the job he intended taking on personally with Dolan. He got back to his home, leaned forward and put his hand on the UC's shoulder.

'You've got the rest of the day off, son, so fuck off and enjoy it. Find yourself a wee lassie to play with.'

The order threw the UC for a moment, then came an overwhelming sense of relief, but he needed to at least try and find out what had changed.

'Thought you needed me for the day, Mr Regan?' He left it at that as he realised he was about to walk away from his worst fears much more easily than he'd anticipated.

'No worries, son. There's a job to do, but it's for the big boys, and you deserve a day off. Off you go now and leave the car here. Here's some money for a taxi and a wee drink.'

Regan pushed the wad of notes over his shoulder and the UC stuffed them in his pocket.

When he was well out of sight of Regan, he started to run, then sprint till he was exhausted and bent over, heaving in breaths at the side of the road. He turned his face to the sky as fat spots of rain pelted his face. It felt wonderful.

When he sensed his heart steadying, he called his handler and told her what had happened.

'From what I heard on his calls, he's got two of his hardest boys to meet him, and from past experience that means someone is going to get hurt.'

The handler was relieved for the UC, but it threw up a problem for the surveillance operation. The UC driving Regan meant they could follow him safely, but now they had no idea what car he would use so the only option was conventional surveillance or real eyes on the target, with all the risks that entailed. Regan was ultra-surveillance conscious, and with two extra gorillas, it was going to be tough.

The handler called Toher, who then broke the news to Macallan in the operation centre they'd opened up.

'There's always the chance we could lose him,' Toher said, rubbing his neck. 'It looks like they're going after someone or why would he bring out the muscle?'

'Maybe he's just getting extra protection in case there's a reaction to whatever happens tonight. God knows – we just have to throw the dice and see where they roll now.'

They knew it was going to be a long night, but the game was in play so all they could do was wait.

107

'Well I'll be fucked.' Regan sat forward in his chair and put the tray of food on the side table next to him, grabbing the remote and pressing rewind.

'What's that, Mr Regan?' one of the two muscle men eating in the kitchen asked him.

'Shut the fuck up and eat your bananas. Let me hear this.'

It's that Branch bitch again, he thought as he watched Macallan deliver her piece to the press. When the picture was put up, he sat back straight-faced before a slow grin spread over his face. 'So, Joe Stafford doesn't even exist. There you go.'

'What was that, Mr Regan?' the muscleman asked again.

'I thought I told you to shut the fuck up. Are the bananas finished?'

Regan reached for his laptop and typed in the name 'Peter Handyside' like a shark seeing an approaching meal for the first time. *So, you lied about who you are. Have you lied about Dolan*? he wondered. 'Better not have or I'll gut you,' he whispered.

It was as if he'd been given new power over Handyside, but he wasn't quite sure how he'd use it.

By the time he closed the lid on the laptop, he conceded that if Handyside had been on the run, it made sense that he'd build a new life and identity, so maybe it wasn't so bad. He guessed he would do the same thing in the circumstances.

Then he considered whether it would affect the job that night. Probably not – if there was a problem, they would have been rounded up already. Either way, he didn't think it could hurt him. If they wiped out the opposition then it was all good, and if they took off without doing the job, it should still be okay for him.

'Fuck it. I'll still gut that Brit bastard if I get my hands on him,' he whispered, but just loud enough for the minder to get it wrong again.

'Did you want something, Mr Regan?'

Regan stood up, pressed the *off* button on the remote then whacked the minder about the head with it until he drew blood. The minder was a monster of a man and could have taken Regan in a fair fight, but Regan paid the wages and, in their game, the main man was allowed to beat up the staff whenever he felt like it. When he was done, it was as if they'd just played a child's game where it was all pretend and nothing had really happened – though the minder was bleeding all over the carpet, which seemed to annoy Regan again.

'Look what you've done now! I'm taking that out of your wages. That's a brand-new carpet and top quality. Now get cleaned up – we've work to do.'

He turned to the other stone-faced gangster who'd simply taken what had happened as just another day in the office. 'Get the guns and check them over. Don't want the bastard jamming when a bullet should be going into a man's head now, do we?'

108

Across the city, the UC headed back to his flat for the last time, feeling the weight drop from his shoulders – but not completely. As far as he could see, he was in the clear. All he needed to do was disappear – whatever happened in Dublin didn't matter now for him. Job done and he'd survived.

The problem was that he'd made a terrible mistake, and he knew it. The relationship with Regan's niece was real, and he agonised over how to deal with it. He knew the sensible thing was to just go, but it was possible that it would come out later, and the shit would hit the fan anyway.

The conduct of UCs was already under the microscope, the red tops full of stories about them sleeping with the enemy, and although it was enough to keep him awake at night, it was the least of his worries. When their heads were together on the pillow on those nights they'd spent in his flat, what he'd told her about his feelings towards her were true.

Unsure whether to contact her, he looked at his phone several times on the way back to his flat, where all he had to do was pack a few things, clean and wait to be picked up by a specialist Garda team.

He packed up his sparse belongings and scrubbed the place from top to bottom, the stench of bleach burning his nostrils by the time he'd finished. The whole time, the competing areas of his brain argued about the right decision.

The UC packed up all the cleaning materials and stuffed them in a bin bag so he could dump them once he was clear of the place, opened the door to leave then stopped for too long, his eyes drawn to the bed where he'd made so many promises. He shut his eyes, said, 'Fuck,' then turned back into the flat and called her.

'I need to see you right away. I mean right away… here at the flat.'

Regan's niece had a day off from the job she loved – which had nothing to do with the family business. She hated what Mike Regan stood for but accepted they were the same blood and that, given their background, they were almost destined for some kind of trouble, whether it was crime or fighting the Brits north of the border. That was the only thing they agreed on – she believed in the cause of a united Ireland with a passion, like her father Conlan, who was still a hero for her.

When she arrived at the flat, her smile was wide – she'd started to believe that they really could have a whole life together. She recognised that he was a smart man and knew he could do much better than driving her uncle around.

At their last meeting, he'd told her that he was going to be with Regan all day and they wouldn't be able to meet, so she took his unexpected call as a sign that he was finally ready to talk about them going public. She threw her arms round him and then the stink of bleach hit the back of her nose.

'For the love of God, what have you been doing?' She withdrew her arms and looked round the flat, trying to work out why his personal stuff was gone and two stuffed holdalls lay just inside the door.

He told her to sit down. She bit her lip because she saw the look of guilt on his face and she didn't have to be Sherlock Holmes to realise that whatever she might have thought and hoped for, it wasn't going to happen this day.

'I'm frightened,' She said, and meant it. 'What's going on? Is it another woman?'

It was all she could think to say though she knew in her gut it wasn't that.

'I have to leave and I'm not coming back. It's complicated, but I couldn't leave without saying goodbye or asking you something.'

'Well ask, for God's sake, because this is not what I expected to find today.'

He sat down, held her hand and struggled to find the words because he knew he could put her at risk as well as himself. He told her that he had to go, that he was in danger and he would be in touch when he'd worked things out. For a moment he hesitated before promising he loved her.

She became angry, then cried, then fell quiet. She was deep in thought, and he let her be till she spoke again.

'I'm going,' she said. 'I don't know what this is and you won't tell me, so you go on with your life, but if you can't trust me then just don't bother getting in touch.'

She threw her jacket over her shoulder and left without a word. He wished he hadn't called her but knew that not calling would have been worse. The future was a big unknown, and whatever happened, there would be a price on his head if Regan was ever arrested and he had to give evidence.

He closed the door behind him, and half an hour later, a team of plain-clothes officers picked him up. He was gone as if he'd never existed – though of course the man who'd driven and listened to Mike Regan for so long never had.

109

Handyside was trying to figure out his next move when his phone rang – it was his wife. He felt his heart beat a little faster; he'd already accepted that whatever happened, life was going to change – it would have to. As soon as he heard her sob before she spoke, Handyside saw these changes were already moving in a direction he probably couldn't control anymore.

'I've seen the news, Peter. What are we going to do?'

For all that had happened to them in the past, he'd never heard so much fear in her voice. Even when they had to close down their lives and run to the Balkans to escape Police Scotland, she'd been calm and known exactly what was required.

'I've seen it, Jeannie. I'm sorry. This time it might be more difficult, but you know that, lass.'

'What do you want us to do?'

She sounded broken because she knew there was a truth that they could predict with some certainty, and that was that she might not see him again, except perhaps in the confines of a prison visiting room. But Jeannie Handyside understood her man – he would never choose prison and would only end up there by misfortune.

'Has anyone said anything yet?' He couldn't think of something else to say and there was no way to avoid the truth.

'Those stuck-up buggers two doors along passed me a few minutes ago and couldn't look at me. They usually pretend to be civil. Guess they must have seen it. I don't know, maybe I'm imagining it.'

Handyside was about to answer when he heard a crash on the other end of the line and his wife screaming. Then the words *armed police* shook him to his core – the sounds hammered his brain and almost closed his throat.

'Jeannie, Jeannie,' he almost pleaded down the line, even though he knew she couldn't answer.

He looked at the phone as if it had assaulted him, then listened and imagined what was happening. His family was the only thing in his life that made sense and now his wife was probably on the floor with a gun pointed at her. She would be helpless, and it was all because of him. He waited and a man's voice came on the phone.

'This is Inspector Nelson, Metropolitan Police. Who am I speaking to?'

'You're speaking to the man you want. She's done nothing wrong. Believe me.'

'Apart from meeting you perhaps, and we'll be the judge of what she's done. You need to come in, but you must know that. We'll find you wherever you are.'

'Don't you worry – you'll find me when I want you to find me,' Handyside fired back with a lashing of venom. He put the phone down, shoved his face in his hands and was afraid in a way he'd never experienced before.

Half an hour later, Macallan took the call in Toher's office and the Met inspector gave her a rundown on what had happened in the normally sedate suburb of Hampton. Handyside's neighbours had called after the news release, and from there the operation had moved quickly – the Met were now on it with all the resources they could muster. When Macallan had explained what was involved, they'd seen a headline case and wanted in on it.

'What about the wife?' Macallan asked.

'She's a tough one, and her lawyer was on our doorstep as soon as we got back to the station. Doesn't sound like we'll get much from her.'

'I don't expect you will – as far as we know, she's always been kept well away from the business. But we've done this as a trigger, so the longer you can hold her, the better, and there are charges we can use against her to slow the process. We'll send one of our team from Edinburgh to act as the liaison officer.'

Macallan thanked the Met inspector, put the phone down and called Oliver to explain what had happened. She was finding it hard to contain the buzz she felt now that the operations were in progress. The parts were all coming together, the jigsaw in her mind finally given form.

'We'll send Pam Fitzgerald – she's switched on and will do a good job for us in the Smoke.'

'How's it going with your operations, Danny?' Macallan squeezed her eyes closed for a moment – would it be good news, bad news or no news?

'Not bad, boss. The operation is well under way. Benny Green's places are being hit as we speak, and some are already done. Maggie brought him in, and apparently when he found out we were about to take all his money and might put him in a cell with someone of doubtful morals, he cracked like an egg. He wants to shop everyone, including his granny, but more importantly Sandy Tait for money laundering.'

Macallan grinned and mouthed *ya beauty*.

'Have you got Tait?'

'Can't find him, boss. He seems to have gone to ground, but the money-laundering case is looking solid. Can't see him talking though – he'll always see a way of beating it – but we've picked up more girls who've been trafficked and are willing to make statements against him as well as Green – they're accusing Tait of rape.'

'Good work,' Macallan told him. 'Remember and get something from Green on the comms with Handyside.'

'We've touched on it already – he says he only knew Handyside as a voice on the phone and they were introduced through Sandy Tait, who is obviously his man up here, hence turning up for Kangas and Sam Taylor. He was paid for any services through Tait, and I think we should be able to prove that through the financial investigation.'

Macallan said her goodbyes then put the phone down and told Toher the good news.

110

When the surveillance operation lost Regan, there was no indication where he might be headed, and while the team waited on instructions, Macallan and Toher discussed what he might do.

'We're stretched to the limit with resources, Grace, and can't send a new team to cover every possibility. I've been told I have to see this through with what I've got, and to be fair, I've drafted in a small army of specialists for something that might never happen.'

Toher was having doubts, and Macallan could see the strain on his face. She had her own feelings but knew she was on safer ground than the Dublin man, who she'd grown to like and admire in a short space of time. The pressure she felt was to a large extent self-inflicted, because events in Edinburgh and what they had already achieved meant that, on a public level, they would be able to claim success in their investigation into the three murders in Scotland. The added bonus was that it looked like Benny Green was going to be the gift that kept on giving and that included handing them Sandy Tait's arse on a plate.

But for all that, Pete Handyside gnawed at her. He was the biggest prize she'd ever lost, and it bothered her for reasons she could never quite work out or accept.

'The game's on, Paddy – we just need to see where the cards land now. It's always the same, and every time I'm in this position, even as a confirmed atheist, I say a little prayer for the Lord to grant me a bit of luck.'

'Amen to that,' Toher replied with a grin.

111

As the two senior detectives sat in the operation centre, Regan crouched in the back of the van chain-smoking, trying to steady the thought that, somehow, he was being fucked about – though he couldn't work out why, or who by, although he imagined a few suspects.

He'd done something rare and had a drink when a job was on, but all it had done was heat up the growing paranoia infesting his brain. He'd visited a safe pub off the city centre and drank doubles as his two men – sitting at the bar beside him – tried to hide their alarm. They'd seen the wrong side of him often enough, but with a drink he was a gold-plated arsehole whose decision-making process went AWOL.

They'd been joined by a third hard nut who was driving the van and waited outside. Regan had already torn up the guidebook on common sense, deciding that the only way he could prove he had honour was to kill Dolan and do it now, regardless of the job he was paying for.

He was still at the bar when he took the call from his niece, who managed to drive his paranoia to DEFCON 1.

She was distraught and could barely get the words out as she sobbed out her story. Questions he had no answers for flew at him like mosquitoes – all about the man she loved and who she'd thought had loved her right back.

What trouble is he in?

What have you got him into?

Why is he gone and where?

It came at him like gunfire, but he had no answers – only questions of his own. In normal times, Regan would have been furious that someone from a lower caste had dared to associate with his niece, who he genuinely cared for. She was the only living link to Conlan, and although he knew what she thought of his business, he'd sworn he would protect her for his brother's sake and memory.

'I have no idea, and I swear on your father's memory that's the truth.' He didn't dare show anger towards her because losing her completely would have added to his sense of failure. He became calm as the possible implications of the call swirled in his brain.

'Leave it with me and I'll see what it's about. Maybe the boy just had family problems he needed to take care of.'

He put the phone down and stared at his reflection in the mirror behind the bar before throwing the drink down his throat and grinding his teeth. He believed now there was a conspiracy, but the question remained in his mind: *Who the fuck is behind all this*?

Half an hour later, one of his team kicked in the door to the flat the UC had called home till earlier that day, Regan walking in behind him. It looked like it had never been lived in, and the smell of bleach raised an alarm in Regan's mind.

'Why the fuck would a young, single fella like him scrub down a hole like this? There's not a fuckin' mark on the place.'

The men he employed were certainly not going to open their mouths and answer him because Regan just wanted an excuse to lash out at something – anyone who made themselves a target.

He ran through the options but the problem was that they could all be right. It might be that the boy was pissed off with work, or his niece, or there was some trouble he'd got into that he knew Regan would blow a gasket over. Then there was the last one: that the boy had been turned by the Garda or, worse still, was an agent.

At that thought, he broke, and the rage made him drip saliva from the edges of his stretched lips. He picked up a chair and threw it through a window. This drew the attention of the elderly woman next door, who came out onto the landing.

'What the feck is going on here? I'll get the Guards tae ye.'

Before they left the building, he slapped the old lady about the face and left her groaning on the stair at her front door.

112

Regan ordered the driver to head to Malahide and told his team what needed to be done.

'You lift him, hood him and we take him to the warehouse where I can have a bit of peace to work on him.'

The order hung in the air until one of his team worked up the courage to ask the obvious question.

'Fair enough, boss, but we don't know what this fella looks like. How do we pick him out? If he's an ex-para, he's not going to thank us for the visit.'

Regan decided he'd hurt the man later for asking the right question.

'Because while you fucking morons were reading your comics, a couple of the boys with brains have been out there scouting. They've seen him on his balcony. We got a bit of luck – the boy went out to his car and put something in the boot. So if I give you a description and his car, will that do? They're watching his front door so that's five of you. Will that do or do you want me to get reinforcements?'

The man who'd asked the question knew that, at some point, he'd take a serious digging for opening his mouth; the other two were just glad he'd asked and not them.

They drove slowly into Malahide and parked up well away from Dolan's flat. Regan called the two men who were already there and asked them if there was any sign of their target.

'He's still there, boss. He put something else in the car, and we've seen him a couple of times at the window.'

They were reporting exactly the same information that the police crew manning the long-range camera were doing, even though they were unaware of each other.

Regan gave his crew their final orders then told the two men already there to come to the van for a break – two of the hard men with him would take over in a car near Dolan's home. They'd picked up another vehicle in Dublin – Regan took that and moved away but remained in distant sight of the area. The rest of his crew took the van to another position, meaning that no matter what route Dolan took when he exited, they could grab him.

Regan switched off the engine, lit up a smoke and felt a dull headache from the effects of the booze start to beat at the back of his head. At the same time, he felt a tingle of anticipation as he imagined what he would do to Dolan when he had him where no one but his own witnesses could hear the screams.

113

The team manning the OP looked again at the car and van parking up at almost the same time, though some distance away from each other. It shouldn't have aroused their interest, but after a few minutes they put down their brews, studied what they were seeing, then one of them got on the radio to Garvey, who was well away from the area. The OP reported the car and the van stationary but no one leaving the vehicles.

'Get a footman to do a walk past to see what's going on,' Garvey ordered. It might be nothing, but it was best to check.

The footman was on his way seconds later, and it took him just three minutes to get to the area. He walked casually past the vehicles, smoking, as if he was just another punter on his way home from the boozer. When he was clear, he reported back to Garvey. His radio was concealed in his clothing so he didn't need to use his hands for anything and could just talk as he walked – in the digital age, that wouldn't alarm anyone.

'Van and car both two up, boss, and they're heavies by the look of it.'

'What the fuck?' was all Garvey could whisper to herself when the OP called a standby – Dolan was leaving the flat. And it was at that point that all hell broke out on the streets of Malahide.

The next message was the OP again. 'Dolan out out out of the target address and beware – two males away from the white van and closing fast in behind him.'

Garvey realised what was happening and told everyone to clear the air.

'To the firearms team – close in now. Looks like the target is going to be attacked or abducted.'

The firearms team were already on the move towards Dolan's home and ready to act, but unknowns arriving on the scene meant there was a terrible risk of confusion in identifying who was a target.

'Hold your guys back, June,' the firearms leader cautioned as he jogged towards the scene. 'We need clear targets.'

Garvey tried her best not to let panic show in her voice because she knew it was highly infectious. Her job was to produce a steady response because everyone on the plot would have heard the calls and realised that the whole thing was about to turn into the equivalent of cage fighting with no rules.

'To all units, move to positions where you can block all roads and exits to prevent the targets escaping.'

She hoped to God that whoever the unknowns were, they'd stick their hands up in the air, or Malahide was about to get its own version of Gunfight at the OK Corral. Garvey nodded to her driver and he moved off slowly in the direction of Dolan's front door.

'What do you think, June?' The driver didn't seem the least bit fazed by the news that they were about to enter a world of pain.

'I think we're going to need a few Elastoplasts before the night's done.'

She picked up the phone, called Toher and gave him a quick update.

'I'm getting it over the waves,' he told her. 'For God's sake be careful there.'

It was just then they heard a call from the footman who'd redeployed where he could give a distant commentary on what was happening. Toher heard him speak and then the sound of gunfire in the background. He tried to speak to Garvey but the line had gone dead.

Dolan was about halfway to his car when his instincts kicked in. He couldn't say what it was exactly – it was as if the atmosphere and temperature had changed in the same way it did just before rainfall; the birds in the sky felt it, but few men did. Trained soldiers like Dolan though unconsciously scanned the environment every moment of their day – they had to.

He'd felt easy enough when he'd left the flat after kissing his wife goodbye, but he picked up the slight changes in the cool air like any good predator – and when he heard a car door close not quietly enough behind him, he moved immediately to defence mode.

He walked a few more steps, because he could tell there was still distance between his back and whoever was coming at him. His rucksack was across both shoulders, but he wanted freedom of movement and slung it off his shoulders. As he did so, he pulled his firearm from under his jacket with his free hand. His attacker wouldn't have seen it, so he took five more steps to steady himself then tossed the rucksack over a low wall next to him, knowing that would be the signal to the men behind him that he was aware and ready to act.

A moment before he spun round, he saw the doors of a van ahead of him open and two beasts exit. They were further away; the priority was at his back and closing.

He blinked twice to clear his vision, whispered, 'Fuck,' then noticed that they were slow, which gave him an edge. There was enough distance to engage, although they were raising their own firearms into position.

Dolan fired first – the first man who was slightly ahead of his partner stalled, staggering for a moment before falling face first. The other attacker screamed something incomprehensible and managed to fire off a shot that screamed past Dolan's ear – close enough for him to feel the air move. Most men would have crumbled, but he'd had enough near misses in his life to know that what mattered was he'd survived, and now it was his turn.

He fired again from a standing position. An almost imperceptible trip meant the bullet that should have entered the man's breastbone took him nearer the left shoulder, and although it didn't kill him, it put him out of the game for a moment as he dropped to his knees. He was still dangerous with a gun in his hand but Dolan knew he had bigger problems approaching behind him.

He spun again and moved sideways to use the cover of a parked car. The two attackers knew what they were facing, having seen what had happened to the other two, and were approaching him slowly, either side of the line of parked cars. Dolan took three deep breaths and steadied himself again – although outnumbered, he was better than the opposition; he just had to prove it.

Regan heard the gunfire and cursed because he'd hoped the job would be done quietly, but now the local citizens would be calling the cavalry. *Fuckin' eejits,* he thought and promised himself he'd hurt them one at a time when this was all finished.

It was just then that his head snapped to the left and a car with a man and woman inside moved past him at walking speed with the lights off. He knew in that instant they were Guards and slipped lower in the seat.

'What the fuck?' If Regan had been paranoid before now, he was in meltdown – the only way the Guards could be there was if some other devious plan was in place. He thumped the steering wheel till his hand ached with pain and vowed he'd kill someone that night and more than Billy Dolan.

Dolan knew the power of the mind in close combat and unless the two men creeping towards him had also served in the military, even if they were the toughest gangsters in Dublin, they wouldn't know what he knew.

'Are you two fucking idiots allowed out in the dark without your mothers?'

Dolan grinned, revelling in that familiar rush of elation that made him feel more alive than anything else he'd done in life. He knew that his instincts had been right and this job was cursed – that there was unlikely to be a good outcome – but he was fucked if he was going out without a flourish.

For a moment that counted, he looked up towards the balcony of his flat and saw his wife before the high he was on crashed as suddenly as it had come.

Those moments in combat counted, and that decision would cost him, because one of the men closing on him was ex-army and knew exactly what he was doing. He was close enough to lie flat on the tarmac, and under the three cars between them, he saw Dolan's hips and legs.

It was enough – he fired off two shots. One missed, but he knew the other had hit the mark when he saw his target jolt with the impact. He stood up, preserving his ammo till he could check what state Dolan was in and cursing under his breath. Regan wanted the bastard alive, and wounding or killing the man would come at a price.

Dolan felt like a car had slammed into the lower part of his back and knew, even as he gasped in reaction to the shock, that his fighting days were over. He also knew that he'd misjudged the other guy – who *had* known what he was doing after all. He was alive but helpless, the right side of his face resting on the pavement. All he could do was stare back towards his own flat. He could still see his wife who, like the other locals, was peering down into the street, wondering what the hell was going on. He gave a great sigh and felt the darkness come down.

The two men walked slowly and carefully along the edges of the cars to where Dolan lay unconscious, because a wounded man could still pull a trigger – as so many dead men could testify.

The man who'd shot Dolan felt his phone go off. Knowing it would be Regan, he stopped, signalled to the other man to do the same and they halted either side of a car.

'Get the fuck out of there – the Guards are here.'

The phone went dead, and he looked round at the same time he heard the sound of several sets of boots hitting the tarmac. Then the police warnings followed and black-clad figures seemed to appear all round them, pointing too much firepower to take on. Both men knew if they fired a shot, they were dead, and they didn't want that.

They looked at each other for a moment and nodded before dropping their weapons. As they stuck their hands in the air, they sank to their knees, cursing Regan, whose decision-making was going to cost them the best part of what was left of their lives in prison.

Garvey stayed well back and called it in to Toher and Macallan, who jointly felt as if they were cooking up ulcers with the stress of listening to events they had little control over now. They were like football managers who'd sent their team onto the field but put their hearts under strain trying to play every ball in their mind.

Regan slipped quietly out of Malahide then cursed and thumped the steering wheel, as if it might make a difference. His face was drawn tight, the need to ease the rage in his chest overwhelming, and twice he almost ran cars off the road on the way back into Dublin.

He stopped in Drumcondra Road and lit a cigarette, trying to calm himself before making his next move. The lights of a bar across the road caught his eye, so he left the car and ordered a double before he phoned Handyside.

114

Handyside picked up the phone and waited without a greeting because he knew pleasantries weren't on the menu.

'So, Peter... I hope you don't mind me calling you Peter, do you?'

Regan was back in his car and said it quietly, although the anger in his voice couldn't be disguised. He'd phoned a bent Guard to see what the damage was and bared his teeth when he was told the score was one dead, one badly wounded and two arrested. Dolan was seriously injured but alive.

'Of course not, Mike. Why would I?' Handyside had no intention of being drawn into a shouting match and decided he'd let the other man go wherever he wanted.

'That's nice of you. See, the only problem isn't with your fucking name. The problem is that four of my best men are either dead, wounded or arrested all because of your man Dolan. And, worse than that, the Garda Síochána were waiting for us. Imagine that! Now tell me how in the name of God were the Guards waiting for us because I'm at a loss? I don't think I could be blamed for thinking there's something underhand going on. What do *you* think? I mean you're a man facing life so it would be in your interest to help those boys.'

Handyside struggled to make sense of what made no sense, but only for a moment. He quickly worked out that Regan had acted on instinct and tried to take Dolan even before the job on O'Reilly was done, so it was reasonable to presume that the Dublin gangster had lost it.

He squeezed his eyes shut, trying to steady himself for what was coming – he needed every word to count against a man who would undoubtedly try to kill him if they were in the same room. The pillars of Handyside's world were collapsing all around him, but he knew panic would help no one, and his wife was still his first priority.

'What's happened to Billy?'

'Well, I suppose the good news for you is he's alive, but just, which is bad news for me. Does that help?'

'What do you want? And what have you done?'

'What have I done?' It was at that point that Regan's temper broke.

'I decided to do the right fucking thing and kill that Brit bastard. The Guards were there and ambushed my boys so I've decided that I'm being played for a fucking fool and you're all in this together. The Guards will come for me, but I swear to God I'll hunt you and take your eyes out, then I'll find whatever slut you live with and I'll cut her so she never looks in a mirror again. If you have children, I'll find them as well, and just leave that to your imagination. As for that Special Branch slut Macallan, she has to be part of it. I'll do her and the fucking lot of you. You hear me?' Regan screamed the last sentence as Handyside put down the phone – any further conversation was pointless.

He stared at his hands and saw he was shaking.

He tried to clear his mind and assess where he was in the game. Dolan was out of action, and he felt an almost physical pain that the man had seen his dream only one day away and now he was facing God knows what. He felt an urge to call Dolan's wife but knew it would do nothing.

His own wife was in custody and helpless for the time being. Worst of all, he had no contacts he could lean on to help in this particular situation. He'd already had a brief text from Sandy Tait telling him what had happened in Edinburgh and that Police Scotland were looking for him.

Handyside leaned forward with his palms on his face and saw his fate play out before his eyes.

After a few moments, he sat back, remembering that Ronnie Baker was out there and, in all probability, still on the job. He sighed – there was nothing he could do. They did the jobs two up so that if something went wrong with one man, there was cover. It happened – accidents, sudden illness and all forms of Sod's Law.

Handyside went to his hotel bar, ordered a treble of the most expensive Scottish malt they could deliver then sat down and tried to work out his next move. There were only a few options, and they were all bad, but he'd have to pick one of them.

He tried hard to ignore the one he knew he'd have to take.

115

The Guards had set up an OP opposite the flat that Tony Collins visited every Thursday evening for his date with two of the most uninhibited sex workers in Dublin. It was his drug of choice, and he just couldn't get enough, despite knowing how often such habits had been the cause of death for men like him.

Bertie Walsh led the surveillance operation on his tail and had seen him leaving his home right on time, but it was a call from the OP that set the game alight.

'The two women previously identified as the occupants are leaving the premises carrying bags.'

The call didn't register as a problem initially, but Walsh contacted the OP to confirm the part about the bags, which had flicked an amber warning in his mind. The OP confirmed the call and in mid conversation called a further alert that two men carrying rucksacks had entered the same flat. There was a pause as everyone on the plot tried to analyse the situation – it had *sudden and unexpected change of plan* plastered all over it.

Walsh called Toher, who was still with Macallan in the control room. He knew as soon as he heard the intel that it was one of those turns of events that can infect every best-laid plan.

'These men will be referred to now as targets one and two. I want descriptions, and did you get photos?' Toher barked down the phone.

'Photos obtained. Not great given the light and distance, but the pictures are on the way.'

Toher looked across the desk at Macallan. 'Never fails. Jesus!'

What happened next caught Macallan off guard: Toher froze, his face set.

'I can't do it, Grace. I just can't do it.'

He started to shake as if he had hypothermia, and although Macallan hadn't seen it coming, she knew exactly what had happened, because she had been close to the same thing before in her career. She cursed herself, realising that she'd taken an easy route, indulging herself by staying in Dublin and observing because in a way she was in a no-lose situation. But that had put Toher under even more pressure than he was in already, and now she was watching a good man break – though she was the only person who saw it, and she knew he was more than this moment.

Macallan walked round the table, kneeled down before him and gently pulled his hands away from his face, where they'd been trying to hide the tears no detective was allowed.

'Look at me, Paddy.'

He didn't react, but the second time she said it, there was something in her voice that couldn't be ignored.

'I know what this is. I'm sorry. I've sat here like a fucking tourist watching you burn. You're okay. Give yourself a minute and we'll do this together. I'm with you.'

The photos came through at the same time; they meant nothing to Macallan, but it didn't matter for the moment.

'Listen, these guys have probably come to kill Collins in the flat, but we already saw that as a possibility. It's perfect, and I'm sure all they had to do was threaten the girls or offer them an envelope full of money. You're on top of this. All you can do is what I would have to do if it was Edinburgh or Glasgow. You have no choice but to get the firearms team in and a negotiator to take these guys out with their hands up. We've just seen their plan and it's not rocket science. You have this under control, Paddy I promise you, so just get on the radio and make it happen. The teams out there need you.'

Macallan sat back, feeling almost embarrassed at her lack of action, and wished she was back in Edinburgh, spoiling someone's night instead.

'Give me your hand.' She took Toher's hand and meant it.

Toher looked up and sniffed like a child, thanking his god that he was in the right company at the right time, and saw in Macallan's face that she'd been exactly where he was in that moment. He took a lungful of air and shook his head. The moment had passed, and he nodded towards the woman who he'd only known a short time, yet possessed a secret he hoped she'd keep to the grave.

He got back to work.

'To the firearms team, make the area secure and arrest the two men, but if negotiations are required, I'll be there shortly.' Toher was a force negotiator and one of the best.

'Do you want to join me on the ground, Grace?' He smiled as he felt the rush of confidence that reminded him that he knew exactly what was required – that he was the man to give the orders, and if it cost the lives of the new targets then so be it.

'Is the Pope a Catholic?' She grinned at seeing the man behind the mask find his way again, but before they could get to a car, events overtook them. The call came in from the surveillance team that Collins was only minutes away from the flat.

The firearms team leader had looked at the schematics of the building and realised that it was made for an aggressive entry. There was no time to wait on further orders, and he ordered in extra uniformed officers to clear the area. Fortunately for the police, although the area was in the city centre, it was in a quiet lane off a main thoroughfare where they could control the movement of people quite easily. It was a main-door flat too, which was one less headache, and the priority was to move any neighbours out of harm's way. There was risk in so much activity near the targets, but they had was no choice.

116

The two men who'd entered the flat were confident with the plan and couldn't wait to take out Collins then get the hell out of Dublin. They were professionals, both ex-military and knew that preparation was vital. The older of the two was pissed off because he'd tried to call Dolan and hadn't been able to reach him. It was a pain in the arse, but problems were always possible and they just to deal with them. That was what they'd been trained for – to adapt to any situation.

He was setting up the screens on the windows where they could watch for their target's arrival when he saw a Guard firearms officer run across his vision. There wasn't a single other soul around, and he felt his gut squeeze in alarm.

Collins was smoking a cigarette in the back of the car; his bodyguard for the night was driving. He couldn't wipe the grin from his face thinking about what he was about to do with the two girls whose combined age didn't come close to his.

He saw the blue light ahead and behind at the same time, his grin dropping – ahead and behind meant something he probably wouldn't like. He swore under his breath because there was a Glock stashed in the boot and it wouldn't take much of a search to find it – plus it would have his prints and DNA all over it.

He waited on the uniforms to swagger up to the car and give him some of the usual abuse reserved for these occasions but sat up when he saw it was detectives heading his way. He wondered for a moment if it was a set-up – if these were men who'd put a couple of bullets in his head. The Glock was in the boot and there was no time to get it before they got him.

He drew deeply on the cigarette, his whole body stiffening at what was coming. *I've been a fuckin' arse,* he thought as he realised all the warnings he'd had about his Thursday night hobby becoming common knowledge had come true – and it was all his fault.

A few minutes later, he was in the back of an unmarked van, and despite the Glock found in his car, it looked like a result when the Guard detective told him that there was a reception committee waiting for him in the flat. A couple of years in a Dublin prison was something he could survive, and he'd decided in those moments that life really was sweet.

'What the fuck do we do now, Alan?' The younger of the two men in the flat looked round at the other gangster and waited for him to think of a way out from what looked like a trap. They'd already spotted a police sniper taking up position on the roof opposite, and there was no doubt they were the meat in the sandwich.

The old soldier sat down in a corner seat and seemed to study the array of sex toys ready for use next to the bed. 'Well, I think Tony Collins was about to get well and truly fucked, just like us. Have a look at the back.'

He lit up a smoke and leaned his head on the seat as if deep in thought, before the other man came back into the room and shook his head.

'They're behind as well. No way out unless we try taking them on. Full bhuna.'

The older man snapped to full attention and shook his head as if he was in conversation with a child.

'This isn't a western, son. Those boys out there aren't going to shoot blanks, and if they see one of our guns, they'll put enough metal in us to sink a battleship.'

He pulled a hip flask out of his rucksack. 'This was supposed to be for after the job, but I don't think they serve this brand inside.'

He walked through to the kitchen – which looked like a Petri dish for all known diseases – found a couple of glasses, ran them under the tap for a minute then filled them with the contents of the flask. He stepped back into the room, handed the drink to the other man and smiled.

'Here's to absent friends.' He whacked the drink back in one go and squeezed his eyes closed, feeling the burn on his throat. 'Jesus, that's good stuff.'

It was at that moment that the front of the house was lit up like a Christmas tree and they heard a warning and instructions come through a loudspeaker.

The older man paused for a minute, grinned again and said, 'Fuck it. You wait here, son; I'll go and negotiate.'

It had dawned on him that at his age, he would die in prison, and he might never taste that expensive booze again.

He walked out of the door with a grin on his face and started to fire, although he couldn't see a thing with the light in his face. He dropped like a stone when the first two bullets thumped into his chest – exactly the way he'd wanted it.

The younger man dropped what was left of the drink and lowered himself onto the ground for a few minutes, and when the police finally called for him to walk out with his hands up, he did exactly what he was told. There was a chance he could still have a bit of a life after prison.

117

Toher was back in the game and the news that one arrest had been made and one target had chosen to end his life was good with him. No civilians had been hurt, and there was the bonus that Collins had been found in possession of a gun that should put him away for a few years.

'Not bad so far,' he told Macallan. 'The dead ones so far are all gangsters.'

'Any sign of Regan?' she asked – she knew the events of the night were far from finished.

'Nothing so far, but he'll turn up, and through these associates, we'll tie him up for a long stretch inside. Maybe he'll try and take one of our boys but God help him if he does.'

'I'm heading back first thing in the morning,' she told him. 'Unless Handyside turns up, I want to go back to Edinburgh and sit over the table from Sandy Tait. He'll say nothing, but I want to see his face when I charge him.'

Toher looked disappointed for a moment, but he saw it made sense and nodded. 'Of course. We've still got a lot to do.'

His phone went off – it was the surveillance operation at O'Reilly's, advising that Baker had arrived at the locus and had moved into the wooded area.

Toher thumped the table. 'He's there, Grace – now we just need this one to fall into place.'

Macallan smiled and hoped that the Guards executive would give Toher a break once the dust had settled on the operation. He'd spent far too long trying to fight with one hand tied behind his back. He was getting a result at last, but at what cost to himself? She knew better than anyone that there would still be criticism because men had died at the hands of the police on Dublin's streets. But Toher wasn't seeing that yet, and she wasn't going to remind him when what he needed to do was just get over the line.

118

Baker swore quietly again and crawled towards the hide. Dolan was the lead man on the team, but he hadn't turned up and wasn't answering his phone.

At first, he'd worried that Dolan had been taken out by someone, but he'd checked as far as he could and couldn't see any evidence that he was being followed. And if it had been the law then *surely,* he thought, they would already have taken him out, so perhaps Dolan had just fucked off. He reassured himself that this was why they had two-man teams – so if there was a problem the job could still go ahead. It was big money at stake, and he had a gambling habit to feed, so he said, 'Fuck it,' and carried on.

When he got to the hide, everything was in place, so he picked up the rifle and moved into the firing position. As he readied the firearm, he could see O'Reilly in the distance, moving about behind the French windows of his house.

Baker popped a wad of gum into his mouth and chewed like a horse to ease the slight tension he felt. He'd been a model soldier; his training had taken over now and he was operating by the manual.

He turned onto his back for a couple of minutes, breathing deep and slow, savouring the sweetness of the gum as it sat trapped between jaw and cheek till the breathing exercise was over. He counted to 120, snapped his eyes open then turned onto his belly and positioned the money shot. He took his time making the final adjustments and grinned as O'Reilly stepped out into his garden, smoking a cigar.

'Enjoy it,' Baker whispered as he centred O'Reilly's head in the crosshairs. He imagined that moment when the shell would tear through bone and brain, a small cloud erupting where his head had been.

He squeezed the trigger and blinked when nothing happened. 'What the fuck?'

The rifle had been rigged so that when he pulled the trigger, it would send a signal to the firearms team leader, who would then give the word to go.

Baker was an experienced soldier, but as dark camouflaged figures rose like ghosts out of the undergrowth, he was disorientated for a moment – and a moment was all the police team needed.

Baker worked it out and ground his teeth, trying to figure out who was responsible. Then he decided that being found pointing a sniper's rifle at the head of a Dublin citizen was going to put him away for a long time, so he went for it.

He got up and launched himself at what seemed like a dark space between the trees not fully covered by the men aiming guns at him. He guessed they wouldn't shoot if he clearly didn't have a gun in his hand, and he was partly right.

He got about fifty yards when the police dog who'd caught up with him remarkably quickly hit the back of his left leg like an RPG. By the time the handler and chasing firearms officers decided it was safe, the dog had given him a significant chewing, and Baker was glad he was being arrested.

Toher punched the air at the news of Baker's relatively easy arrest and then sat down as if someone had taken the plug out. He was crashing after the initial highs – the many deaths, injuries and arrests meant there was now a shitload of work to do to get it all together and prepare for court.

'I'll get you something to drink, Paddy. Think you'll need it.' Macallan felt slightly deflated herself, convinced that Handyside was gone.

'Can't you stay another day, Grace? Have that drink?'

There was something more behind Toher's words and it surprised Macallan, but only for a moment. 'I need to get back and clear up my mess in Edinburgh.' She stirred her coffee and looked up again. 'Apart from that, when we get this put to bed, I've a husband I've promised to take away for a weekend without the kids.'

She watched his face fall just for a moment then he nodded and smiled ruefully. 'Lucky man.'

'Lucky me,' she corrected him.

119

Regan was certain that a lot of the Guards would be tied up with the mayhem in the city, and he'd found out from his bent officer exactly what had been going on. Whatever the details, when the police got him, he knew he was facing serious time, and there was no doubt he only knew part of it – it seemed the bastards had been up his arse this whole time.

He could barely contain his rage – in the space of hours he'd gone from being on the verge of destroying his rivals to witnessing the collapse of everything he'd built. Someone had to pay; someone always had to pay. Dolan was under police guard, and he had no idea where Handyside was, so that left one person he decided must be involved in his imagined conspiracy.

Handyside ran over his options again and again, but there was no happy ending. If his wife had been safe there might have been a chance, but even that wouldn't really work. The children had been young enough when he'd gone on the run the last time, but now they were older, had lives and were happy.

He thought again about Regan and what he would do if he could locate him. A man like that wouldn't be satisfied with Handyside's life alone, and though his threat to Jeannie and the children might be just angry words, he couldn't take that chance. He had to find him, and as he sat and analysed the problem, he could only see a one-way street.

If he had an advantage, it was that Regan was a creature he completely understood so any action the Dublin man would take would be direct and obvious.

He finished his drink and readied himself to head to the hotel Macallan was staying in. He needed a slice of luck and his predictions to be on the money, but he had no plan B for the time being. He put on dark, easy-fitting clothes, hat and glasses; checked his gun and silencer; then examined his room but realised he didn't need to take anything else. Before he left, he turned back, opened his laptop and stared at the photo of Jeannie and the children he'd saved there, trying to suppress the emotion that threatened to choke him.

Two hours later, Handyside wondered whether he'd completely misjudged Regan as he sat in the city centre hotel where Macallan was staying. She was still booked in, and he'd called and asked to be put through to her room, but she wasn't there. It made sense – she'd likely be involved in the police actions that night.

It was nearly midnight and there were only a few die-hard drinkers in the bar. He had a perfect angle to watch the front doors, some distance away, without being seen himself.

He was starting to rethink what he might do when he saw Regan walk in and head to the reception desk. He watched the gangster talk to the man behind the desk, and the look on the concierge's face told him all he needed to know. Men like Regan had all sorts of people in their pockets, and hotel staff were always useful – not least for details of their guests' bank cards and other personal information.

He saw the concierge hand something to Regan then look round nervously. Regan turned and headed for the lifts. Handyside had to move quickly, but he'd measured the distance to the lifts and knew what he needed to do.

Regan was facing the doors of the lift, which was stopped on the second floor and would be down in moments. Handyside came up soundlessly behind him, and Regan knew nothing till he felt the wrong end of the gun pushed against his lower back. No one could see what was happening unless they were up against them.

'Don't get brave, Mike, because the first one will take out your kidney.'

Regan stiffened, accepting that Handyside wouldn't hesitate. He knew they were both in a bad place and killing someone, even in a hotel foyer, couldn't make their problems much worse.

The lift doors opened and a woman who seemed half-drunk exited; she didn't even give them a look as she headed for the bar.

When they got in the lift, Regan cursed through clenched teeth. 'I swear to God I'll fucking kill you.'

'Right, take the key card for Macallan's room and we can have a talk in there.'

120

Macallan was exhausted. It was 1.30 a.m. when she decided to head back to the hotel to get a few hours' sleep before travelling back to Edinburgh. She ached with the strain of the last few days and just wanted to be back with Jack and feel his arms around her.

She pushed opened the door to her room and pulled off her coat as she stepped into the offset area where the bed was. She wondered if she could be bothered to remove the rest of her clothes.

That was when she stopped as if she'd walked into a wall.

'Sit down, Grace. You look tired, but then no wonder.'

Handyside sat well into a corner, and he'd placed a chair where she could be well away from him on the other side of the room. He wasn't going to underestimate her.

Macallan felt her skin go cold and struggled to control her fear. She thought about the children and wondered if she'd see them again, then imagined her cold, white body on a mortuary slab.

'What do you want?' She saw the gun and silencer in his hand and felt her throat squeeze.

'I want to talk to you. It's been a long time, and I must admit I never thought I'd see you again.' He'd taken a miniature from the fridge and poured himself a drink. 'Do you want one?'

She ignored the question. 'Are you going to kill me?'

'Let's come to that later. I want to ask you how you got onto me. I'm sure you've worked out this has cost me everything, and your friends in the Met have Jeannie.'

Macallan stared at the gun, but at least for the moment, it seemed he just wanted to talk. She looked discreetly around the room, trying to work out whether she could get to him before he put a bullet in her. But he was too smart for that, as well as being a physically powerful man, so she settled back in the chair.

In normal circumstances, answering that sort of question would have meant a serious breach of the rules on intelligence gathering. But this wasn't a normal situation, and her life could depend on the answers she gave. It occurred to her that what he'd said was true – he had lost everything – so she would play along. 'You could say it was bad luck. We were involved in a job with the Finns, and on one of their phone intercepts, they heard a voice they couldn't identify arrange a gun for a job in Scotland. I was in the room when it was played and recognised your voice. All we knew was that the call had been made in Dublin, so that's how we ended up here.'

'So it was the Kangas job and not the reporter?' Handyside couldn't hide his surprise that Sod's Law had stepped in and ruined his life.

'That's right, and it developed from there. And… now we have evidence against Ronnie Baker for Sam Taylor's death. DNA!' She waited and let him digest the implications.

He sighed and shook his head when it all fell into place.

'Jesus, so it sounds like you have Ronnie?' he said then stared into the distance, as if he was trying to see something far away.

'We have Baker.' She paused, but he didn't speak so she carried on. 'Pete, if you're going to kill me, let me call my husband. Please?'

A tear escaped the corner of her eye, but the fear had gone. She was sad and thought it was a cruel way for it all to end – in a hotel room so far from home.

Is this what it was all for? she wondered and rubbed the back of her hand across the trail left by the tear. She decided she wouldn't give him the gift of seeing her fear and straightened in her seat.

'I want you to lift the phone, but not to call your husband,' Handyside replied. 'That would just upset him, and you know I'm a big family man. I want you to call whoever you've been working with in the Guards and tell them where you are and who you're with.'

Macallan's eyes widened in surprise, but she called Toher and explained what was happening. As she spoke, she watched Handyside savour the drink in his hand as if it was just a nightcap before bed at the end of a very ordinary day.

'Stay calm, Grace. We'll get you out of there,' he told her, though they both knew that was for Handyside to decide and not the Guards.

When she put the phone down, she waited and watched as Handyside lit up a cigarette.

'I know there's a rule against it in here, but sure they'll forgive this one. Can I ask you a favour, Grace?'

'You're holding a gun. You know I'll agree to anything.'

'That's true, but I think it's in you to do this. In any case, Mike Regan came here to kill you tonight but I didn't, so surely you can at least think about it. Jeannie has no part in the business. She has no idea about where money is, laundering or anything to do with what I do. If she can get a break, please give her it.'

In that moment, Macallan realised that he truly didn't intend killing her and wondered what the reference to

Regan meant. They both turned their attention to the windows as multiple blue lights pulsed across them, signifying the arrival of the police.

'Draw the curtains,' he said. 'I don't want a sniper taking potshots at me in here.'

Once she'd done so, he stood up, drained the last of the drink and headed for the door. He stopped there and turned round. 'Don't follow me,' he told her. 'Stay in this room and think about what I've asked. I love my family. They're not me.'

Then he turned and left the room, the door closing behind him.

Macallan sank to her knees and started to hyperventilate, bile rising in her throat. She got to her feet and staggered into the bathroom – then gasped in shock at the sight of Mike Regan's body stretched out in the bath. The top of his head was a pulped mess, and his lips were stretched in a horrific grin.

Macallan threw up all over the floor then leaned on the door pillar when she heard the dull thump of gunfire coming from somewhere in the hotel. The lights started to swirl in her eyes as she tried to regain control.

She had no idea of time passing till she heard the police coming along the passageway, telling everyone to stay where they were. The footsteps stopped outside her room, and her name was called out. Her legs were liquid, but she managed to open the door and could have kissed the armed officer she found standing on the other side.

'You okay?'

'I'm okay. What about Handyside?'

'We had no choice. He discharged his weapon so we took him out.'

Paddy Toher arrived seconds later and put his arms round her. 'Come on, Grace. You're safe now.'

'I don't understand it. Mike Regan's in there. He came to kill me and Handyside stopped him. It makes no sense.'

121

Macallan sat across the table from Sandy Tait, who'd walked into the station with his lawyer. He had been all arrogance to start with, and she'd enjoyed watching the show because he obviously hadn't fully understood what they had on him. Now she decided the best strategy was to just be businesslike and watch the effects unfold.

When she presented the evidence that trafficked women provided by Benny Green had made statements that they'd been raped by him, his face became expressionless. Like the skilled lawyer he was, he held on to his emotions – but only just.

Macallan knew she was on solid ground so she just ran through the script, going on to explain the extent of the evidence they'd gathered on the money laundering. He kept repeating 'no comment', but the colour slowly dropped from his face and a slight tic developed at his left eye – it was as if someone had pulled the plug out of an overinflated ball.

When she went on to explain that Green was doing everything he could to send him down the swanny, Tait finally broke, and Macallan struggled not to gloat as the scourge of the police ignored his lawyer's pleas and threatened her with everything he could think of. She just sat quietly waiting until he ran out of steam.

Tait eventually sat back in his seat, chest heaving as if he'd just finished a sprint. Macallan gave him another moment then made sure she locked eye contact.

'Anything else?'

She didn't wait for a reply and charged him with a number of offences that would make sure he'd remain locked until he appeared at court.

Tait never said another word and was like a frightened child when they showed him the cell that would be his home for the night.

When she was finished with Tait, Macallan felt a great weight lift off her shoulders, and although there was a lot of follow-up work to do, they were on the home straight now. For all intents and purposes, the murders were solved and Ronnie Baker was going nowhere for his crimes in Ireland, never mind what they had on him for the murder of Sam Taylor.

Tenant was expecting her for a prearranged meeting, and she headed for her office with Tait's file still under her arm.

When she went into her friend's office, Tenant's face lit up as she gestured to the seat opposite her.

'How's it all going, Grace? Mr Tait charged?'

'All done. He nearly collapsed when he realised what we have on him.'

Macallan suddenly felt weary but knew this was par for the course as things started to wind down.

They discussed what Tenant needed to know to brief the executive and make arrangements for a major press conference – the media were breaking the doors down for a story that had become national news.

'Have you heard anything from the army?' Tenant asked.

'Not a thing from Major Bowman – can't get a hold of him. The line is that he's been deployed on a sensitive mission, and they can't disclose where he is or put us in touch with him. It's the way of these things, and we can live without it. No doubt all part of their own internal politics. It's not going to make much difference anyway, because the press are up and running with the C Troop 5 story and the extra-judicial killings in Northern Ireland.'

'Their problem, not ours,' Tenant replied. 'Now, more importantly, when are you and Jack going to take that break away and let us look after the kids?'

Macallan grinned wearily – that was the line she'd been waiting for.

'Whenever you're ready, Elaine. I'm knackered, and the way things are developing with this virus, we'd better get it done now.'

'Right, Superintendent, get it booked up and be on your way. There are rumours coming down the line from the Scottish Government about lockdowns, so go now, girl.'

Macallan spent the next couple of days wrapping up what she could, although the follow-up work would take weeks, and briefing Oliver on how to steer the ship while she was away with Jack.

After the press conference the following day, she sat quietly in her office and ran through everything to make sure there were no loose ends before she went. Before she left the office, she called Mick Harkins and arranged to meet him when she came back from her break. Going out on the lash would be okay then because they were winding an operation down rather than up – unless some horror cropped up, which was always a possibility.

Macallan put the lights out in her office, looked round as if it was her last time then headed to see her doctor.

122

'How's it been, Grace? I got your message that you were busy last week. I saw the reports on the telly so that sounds like an understatement. That must have been awful, so tell me how you are?'

The doctor had become like a friend to Macallan in a very short space of time, and it had surprised her. She'd spent a lifetime struggling to share but had been able to trust the clinical psychologist from their first meeting. It was particularly surprising as the doctor was a younger woman, and Macallan tended to gravitate to friends who were a good deal older that her.

'It's amazing that even with what happened in Dublin I'm fine, although I'm shattered; I feel really alive and I'm looking forward. Isn't that strange?'

The doctor nodded. 'That's good. And what about Jack?'

Macallan settled in and told her about Jack, and how excited they both were about their upcoming break and just being together. Therapy had become an almost natural part of her routine, and, most importantly, it was working.

She'd never felt more confident about the future.

EPILOGUE

A storm erupted over the allegations about C Troop 5, and the PSNI opened up a new investigation into the allegations of state collusion on the extra-judicial killings in Northern Ireland, the UK mainland and the Middle East. Jacquie Bell sank her teeth into it like a dog with a bone and dedicated the follow-up story to her friend Nancy Gilhooley.

Ruth Conway was allowed to leave the army quietly and agreed to help the PSNI with the investigation. The army had threatened her with criminal charges, but she'd stood her ground, and with the help of Jacquie Bell's reporting, they backed off and left her alone. They'd leaked fake stories about her character, but that just made her more determined to tell her story.

Macallan did all she could for Jeannie Handyside, and in the end, she faced only relatively minor charges. She eventually disappeared from view and moved to France to try to make a life without the man she'd loved since she was no more than a child.

When the chaos of the events in Dublin had settled, the gangs were quiet for a while before hostilities were renewed

– the only thing that had changed was that there were a few new characters at the top.

Paddy Toher took some flak for the number of deaths that had occurred during the operation and was moved to a role in administration. He didn't object, became involved with June Garvey and had never been happier in his life.

The Russians had followed the events in Dublin with interest and decided that there might be a good opportunity to do business in Ireland. It would mean controlling the local crime organisations, but they decided they would look seriously at the proposition.

And then the pandemic swept across the UK and Irish borders, a multitude of new opportunities arising from the fires of this new chaotic world – and the worst types of criminal ready to take advantage.

GLOSSARY OF TERMS AND SLANG

ANPR	Automatic Number Plate Recognition
Bairn	Scots for children. Similar to Nordic
Bam	nutter
Bawbag	scrotum
Bizzies	the police
BKA	*Bundeskriminalamt* – federal investigation police agency in Germany
Branch	Special Branch
Brothel creepers	thick-soled shoes
Box the head off	Irish term
Charlie	cocaine
Cherry berries	colloquial name for the paratroopers, referencing their red berets
CHIS	covert human intelligence source
Conventional surveillance	surveillance without the use of technology

Crap hats	colloquial or derogatory name for the Royal Marines
CROPS	Covert Rural Observation Post
C Troop 5	fictional title of Dolan's army team
Comms	communications
Coupon	face
Developed vetting	highest level of security clearance
Dingwop	Dublin slang – an idiot
Double tap	two shots fired quickly and close together on target
DTs	delirium tremens – confusion caused by withdrawal from alcohol
DV	developed vetting
Europol	European police agency based in The Hague, Netherlands
Extra-judicial killing	killing by government authorities without judicial process
Facility	a phone intercept or wiretap
FIB	Force Intelligence Bureau of the armed services
Garda Síochána	national police service of the Republic of Ireland
Galoot	a clumsy or stupid person
Gimp	common Irish term for a fool
Gom	fool
GTF	get to fuck
Going dark	cutting communications
Heid-nipper	Scots slang for a puzzle or dilemma
Hawala banking	honour system of banking and money transfer
HOLMES	Home Office Large Major Enquiry System
INLA	Irish National Liberation Army
Jakey	a down-and-out

Legend	cover story used by an undercover officer
Locus	Scots legal term for the scene of the crime
Makarov	Soviet semi-automatic pistol
Mams	mammary
Monkey	derogatory military slang for military police
MP	military police
MIT	major investigation team
Ned	Scots slang – non-educated delinquent
New IRA	dissident Irish Republican paramilitary organisation
Newsboy hat	popular cap style based on 1920s newspaper boy fashion
Numpty	Scottish urban term for someone who's not that sharp
OP	observation post
Paras	the Parachute Regiment
Peelers	Slang for police in Northern Ireland
Plot	surveillance operation
Pokey	prison
PIRA	Provisional Irish Republican Army
PSNI	Police Service of Northern Ireland
Radge	Scots slang – nutter
Rammy	street fight
Recce	reconnaissance
RPG	rocket-propelled grenade
RUC	Royal Ulster Constabulary – forerunner of the Police Service of Northern Ireland
RV	rendezvous – meeting point
Shottie	Scots slang for keeping watch
SIO	senior investigating officer
SIB	special investigation branch

SOP	standard operating procedures
Source	source of information and can be human or technical
Spanner	Irish slang for someone who makes mistakes – an idiot
Swanny	colloquial phrase – completely lost or wasted
Sweaty	rhyming slang for sweaty sock – Jock
Tie-up jobs	robbery – home invasion where the victims are violently restrained
Third eye	where criminals may be watching the watchers
Trigger	strategy used to draw a response from a suspect e.g. a press release
UM	unidentified male
Wait one	surveillance slang – wait one minute
Weegie	someone from Glasgow

ACKNOWLEDGEMENTS

This book is dedicated to my grandson Angus, born in Dublin at the start of this pandemic. Hopefully he'll remember nothing about it.

Huge thanks to my editor Laura, who is a wonderful guide through the process of turning my rough manuscript into something readable. Her support and patience through all of Grace's trials has been wonderful.

Thanks to everyone who encouraged me to give Grace another case – I had thought of letting the poor woman have a rest after what she's been through. It was great using Dublin for some of the scenes and of course the remarkable Glasnevin cemetery, which gave rise to the title and cover picture.

Printed in Great Britain
by Amazon

68594339R00277